BREAKING POINT

Also by Olivier Norek in English translation

The Lost and the Damned
Turf Wars

OLIVIER NOREK

BREAKING POINT

Translated from the French by
Nick Caistor

MACLEHOSE PRESS
QUERCUS · LONDON

First published in the French language as *Surtensions*
by Editions Michel Lafon, Paris, 2016

First published in Great Britain in 2022 by

MacLehose Press
An imprint of Quercus Editions Ltd
Carmelite House
50 Victoria Embankment
London EC4Y 0DZ

An Hachette UK company

A CIP catalogue record for this book is available
from the British Library.

ISBN (HB) 978 0 85705 970 3
ISBN (TPB) 978 0 85705 969 7
ISBN (Ebook) 978 0 85705 971 0

10 9 8 7 6 5 4 3 2 1

Designed and typeset in Garamond by CC Book Production
Printed and bound in Great Britain by Clays Ltd, Elcograf S.p.A.

To Chloé, Marianne and Xavier,
who have it all to build.

CONTENTS

Prologue 9

PART ONE – Between Four Walls 11

PART TWO – The Ransom 63

PART THREE – Home Invasion 173

PART FOUR – Butterfly Effect 211

PART FIVE – Out of Control 337

Epilogue 395

PROLOGUE

The shrink pushed the glass ashtray away from her. Although the blinds were three-quarters down, a shaft of sunlight penetrated the room, picking out the smoke curling upwards.

"Would you care to tell me how it all began?"

With a flick of his wrist, the man stubbed out his cigarette.

"It's a story that has several beginnings," he said.

The shrink was rolling a pen nervously between her fingers. It was plain she was intimidated by the man facing her.

"You do know why you're here, don't you?"

"Because I killed two people. Are you worried it'll become a habit?"

"You only killed one, and that was in self-defence. As for the second death . . ."

The man didn't let her finish. He snapped:

"A member of my team is dead. It was my responsibility. It amounts to the same thing."

Searching in his breast pocket, he took out a crumpled packet of cigarettes. The pen spun round in the shrink's fingers.

"Few people have experienced what you had to face. No-one would dare judge you. I simply want us to go back to the beginning."

"From the murder or the prison escape?"

"A bit before that."

"So from the kidnapping of the boy?"

"That's a good place to start. And please, leave nothing out."

The man shrugged and lit another cigarette.

"I really don't see the point; I've already made my decision."

"I insist. Besides, as you know, in such circumstances this conversation of ours is obligatory."

He blew out a long mouthful of smoke, then reluctantly began:

"My name is Coste. Victor Coste. I'm a capitaine with Seine-Saint-Denis Police Judiciaire."

PART ONE

BETWEEN FOUR WALLS

*"You're all alone in here. And if one day you think
you've made a friend . . . don't trust him"*

SCALPEL

I

Three months earlier
Marveil Prison
B Wing – New arrivals' cells

Madly in love. Almost totally reliant on her. Suffocating. She needed air. And the further she backed away, the more he fell into a morbid depression. Too many pills, his nerves shredded.

One evening, suitcases in the hall, she said goodbye. He refused to accept it, blocked her way out. She told him about the other man, and something snapped in his brain. He attacked, punching her in the face. The shock made her lose her balance and she crouched on the floor, terrified by this first ever display of violence. Her nose was pouring blood. He looked at her lips, thinking another man had kissed her there, and pounced on her, hitting her again and again with both fists, sending her head rocking from side to side. Like an artist slashing his canvas in a fury.

In their report, the police stated that the victim's face was completely staved in. The paramedics tried unsuccessfully to save her left eye.

Following his arrest, he had seen a psychiatrist and been given some pills to keep him calm. But nothing now for more than twenty hours. Nothing since appearing before the magistrate, who decided he should remain in custody.

He had gone from the holding cell at the court to the cage of the police van, and from the van to the one-man cells at Marveil Prison reserved for new arrivals for their first few nights.

Before the wood and metal door clanged shut behind him, he asked the guard:

"How is she?"

The guard was half his age, but wanted to play the grown-up.

"Step back so I can close the door."

"Will you be coming back? I can't be left without my meds."

"Tomorrow you're seeing the chief officer for your evaluation. You can make an official request to visit the shrink, and if everything goes well you'll have your pills within a fortnight. Especially if you behave, if you take a step back and let me close the door."

"O.K., but what about tonight?"

The guard dropped his hand to the tear gas canister on his belt, and the detainee took a step back.

"O.K., O.K. Can I at least have a cigarette and a light? I haven't had a smoke for three days."

"You're not the only one. Let me finish my round and I'll come back."

Marveil Prison
C.T.T.V. – 11.30 p.m.

On the control monitors, the cells of new arrivals all displayed the same scene. Every new detainee was sitting on his bunk, staring into space as he tried to come to terms with his situation. Above all, to accept it. Hope prolongs time, frays the nerves. Resignation allows you to be at peace. Accepting the sentence is the only way to make it bearable. But this can take time.

In cell No. 6, the prisoner stood up. In the control room,

the two night-duty officers were taking it in turns to heat their meals in the microwave. The prisoner wrapped himself in his sheets and blanket and sat in the centre of his cell. One of the guard's meals was rotating in the microwave, reheating the previous evening's gratin. A first wisp of smoke rose from the sheets and the blanket's synthetic fibres. The microwave pinged: the food was ready. The guard picked up his Tupperware, opened it without much enthusiasm, and, seeing that the small table had already been occupied by his colleague's plate and magazines, went over to the chair in front of the screens. He put down his cutlery, unfolded his napkin, looked up. He shouted:

"Fire! Oh fuck, Number 6 has set himself alight!"

The flames leaped up so high that the C.C.T.V. cut out, leaving only a blank screen.

The two guards ran out to join their colleague doing the rounds, who had been alerted by their cries. He had already begun to unroll the fire hose, so the three of them started to pull it towards Cell No. 6. The one at the far end of the corridor, of course.

"Pull, for fuck's sake! Pull!"

The man shouting, plainly the one in charge, barked an order at the younger man.

"Demarco! Open the cell, we'll flood it! Get a move on!"

They rushed past Cell No. 3, came to the end of the hose, pulled harder and undid a knot, gained a metre, got past No. 5 and came to an abrupt halt, the hose stretched to its limit, exactly fifty centimetres from the door to No. 6. Impossible to train it on the blaze, to send so much as a drop of water in that direction. Demarco stood paralysed in the doorway, staring at the intense fireball surrounded by flames so high by now they were licking at the walls and ceiling. The sheets and blanket were melting, combining with the prisoner's skin in a fusion of cloth, plastic and flesh. And there was a ghastly smell of grilled meat.

"The hose is too short!"

"Impossible! Pull, for fuck's sake! Shit, Demarco, give us a hand!"

But even if the three men had had the strength of six, it would have made no difference. The hosepipe had been a metre short since it was installed, and had never been inspected.

One of the guards ran for an extinguisher. Skin and flesh had already been consumed, leaving the fat to burn and give off a choking black smoke. After howling for what seemed like an eternity, the prisoner had fallen silent.

With two extinguishers emptied on him, the white chemical foam turned his charred body into a snowman.

The guard in charge called it a "barbecue". He said it wasn't the first he'd seen, but he wanted to give the new guy, the one doing the rounds, some comfort.

"There was nothing we could do, right? Do you hear me, Demarco?"

Demarco didn't reply, and it was more than likely he hadn't even heard these words of encouragement. He only seemed to wake up when he caught his colleague's next remark.

"We're going to have to inform the Rotunda so they beef up searches on new arrivals. How did he manage to set himself alight?"

Hearing this, Demarco's stomach churned. He slid his hand down to his trousers pocket. Empty. The older guard saw the new recruit's face go from shocked white to sickly green.

"You should never have seen this on your first week, Demarco. I'm really sorry. I'll ask them to give you a day off."

Demarco nodded and went off to the toilets, letting the others think he was going to throw up. On his own in front of the mirror, he searched desperately in his jacket pockets. Empty as well. He almost passed out, had to brace himself against the wall.

The chief officer woke the prison governor up in the middle of the night, in his charming Marveil home. The lights went on from room to room as he strode through, telephone to his ear. His subordinate continued his report.

"Given the way the new guard looked, I bet he was the one who left his lighter with the prisoner."

"Are you sure?"

"I searched the prisoner when he came in. He had nothing on him."

In his kitchen, the governor poured himself a glass of cold water. He waved reassuringly at his wife, who was leaning on the door jamb, encouraging her to go back to bed.

"O.K. Give him a few days off. If he comes to see you with feelings of remorse, send him to me. Let's make sure the blame is laid elsewhere: the prison isn't responsible for people who die here."

2

The town of Marveil houses the largest prison complex in Europe. Like an undesirable neighbour, an evil twin. The two cover exactly the same area: a hundred and forty hectares. If you take a map of Marveil and fold it in two, the town and the prison fit exactly over one another, as symmetrical as a Rorschach test.

To make matters worse, prisons are known only by the name of the place where they are based. So, if you say you live in Fresnes or Fleury-Mérogis, people immediately think you're a killer or a rapist. Marveil is no exception to the rule.

A prison the size of a town, where the mayor is the prison governor, the police are the prison guards, and the inhabitants are all criminals.

Five hundred metres from the town centre where families do their weekly shopping are the first rolls of barbed wire topping the flaking walls of this brutalist concrete monster, hailed as "a model for the French penal system" when it was opened in 1970.

Nowadays it's no more than a violent jungle the guards watch over from a safe distance. They don't dare enter the cells or the exercise yard. An environment where the toughest jailbird becomes as vulnerable as a soap bubble.

And it's in this mad dog kennel that Nunzio Mosconi, known as Nano, has found himself. Twenty-two years old, attractive enough, not exactly well-built, but above all not well-prepared. He carried out a successful raid on a jeweller's, but was then stupid enough to go around wearing a registered luxury watch. The mistake of a greenhorn, a novice.

Bad karma, Nano.

Alex was waiting patiently outside the main prison gate. She stamped her third cigarette out on the ground. All around her, other women as well as entire families were waiting to visit, in a vast car park surrounded by fields. No-one was there to receive them, but a loudspeaker over the door spat out a list of names. Hearing her own called, Alex headed for reception, carrying a small black sports bag. Behind the bulletproof glass, the guards' blank stares. Prisoners themselves.

"I've come to see Nunzio Mosconi."

"And you are?"

"Alex Mosconi. His sister."

Her name checked on the visitors' list. A bell, the sound of a door being unlocked. To the right of the huge main entrance, a smaller door had opened. Alex went through a metal detector, then an X-ray tunnel, clutching the sports bag, hoping its contents would bring her brother some comfort. She was directed to the Rotunda, the prison's nerve centre.

From the Rotunda, the prison wings branch out like a five-pointed star. Each wing is separated from its neighbour by an exercise yard. They are designed to hold a maximum of eight hundred prisoners, making four thousand in total, but a clever usage of space (which some might call simply cramming the cells even fuller) has allowed Marveil to exceed its maximum capacity by a thousand inmates.

Alex was escorted together with the other visitors towards a staircase and passageway leading to the visiting room. Every corridor, every cell is identical, so that once you are inside Marveil there are no distinguishing features. You could be anywhere in the prison. You're nowhere.

Alex swapped her national I.D. card for a visitor's permit and was given a cubicle number. Her bag was opened and searched. Clean clothes, magazines, a pack of cards. By now she knew almost by heart the list of personal effects prisoners were permitted.

The corridor door opened; another identity check, another metal detector. Three days earlier, a guard had had the sharpened end of a toothbrush stabbed into his throat. His carotid artery severed. Saved *in extremis* by the prison medics. Blood all over the white tiles. Authorities in a panic, prison staff on edge. Ever since, checks had been redoubled inside and outside the prison.

Alex looked at the number she'd been given and headed for Cubicle No. 8. Transparent plexiglass screen, no chance of any privacy. Nano was waiting for her, head down. When the door to the cubicle opened, he looked up. Alex froze.

"Shit . . . who did that to you?"

Apart from the difference in gender and her being eight years older, Alex had exactly the same features as her brother. The same angelic face, pale green eyes, and a long, slender profile.

"Say something, Nano."

He sniffed, and his dislocated nose sent an electric shock to the back of his brain. The stabbing pains from his swollen right eye and his aching ribs merged into one.

"You don't want to know. Besides, there's nothing you can do. Did you see the lawyer?"

Alex looked him up and down. Her kid brother was refusing to face reality.

"I'm sorry, Nano. There's no more lawyer. Apart from a reduced sentence, I don't know what else we can hope for."

This was what hurt her the most: making him see reason when all he wanted was hope.

"You know I'd take your place if I could," she said somewhat inconsequentially.

Nano replied, his voice choking:

"You have to get me out of here, Alex. I'm dead meat. If they don't kill me, I'll end up doing myself in."

Behind them, a guard in ranger boots, uniform and blue short-sleeved shirt came and checked their cubicle through the perspex. He dawdled, staring at Alex's thighs, then calmly ogled her legs. Out in the street, she would have kneed him in the groin as a warning. In prison, she gritted her teeth and did nothing.

"Nano! Tell me who left you like this!"

"My cellmate."

"The bastard. Are you serious? The lawyer assured me new arrivals had a cell of their own."

"Yeah, that's what I thought too. But they put me straight into the main wing. It seems there was a fire in the new arrivals' cells last week. They're still scraping the walls clean."

"Can't you speak to the screws about it?"

"They couldn't give a fuck. They wouldn't even spit on me if *I* was on fire."

Looking around cautiously to make sure nobody was watching, Alex plunged her hand into her bra and took out a S.I.M. card. The metal detectors were so badly tuned that if you were ingenious and bold enough you could smuggle anything into Marveil.

"The sort you asked for. Do you think you can get hold of a mobile?"

Nano put the card into his mouth and pushed it between his gums and cheek with his tongue.

"It's not for me. It's for Machine."

"Machine?"

"That's my cellmate's nickname. We all lose our real names in here. Everyone gets re-baptised."

"And you? What do they call you?"

"Smart Guy. Because I speak properly."

A loud bell rang insistently, marking the end of their visiting slot. Nano seized his sister's hand.

"Alex, can you do something for me?"

"Anything you want," she said firmly.

The other visitors were already standing up, and since they were the only human distraction all week, all the prisoners were curious to see who had come to visit who. Out of envy or mockery. Nano lowered his eyes, because what he was about to ask was embarrassing for them both.

"Before you go . . . kiss me on the mouth, will you? In front of the others."

At first, Alex didn't follow. Then she realised her brother wanted to show he was a heterosexual in a place where any weakness is exploited.

She stood up, and as she leaned across the table between them allowed her T-shirt to ride up and reveal her hips. She hugged her brother and gave him a long, tender kiss. Long enough for everyone to get a good view. The guards, normally so quick to prevent any physical contact, gave them a few more seconds. The other prisoners took in her golden skin and curves, storing them up for nightfall.

Alex left Cubicle No. 8 and, before following her escort out, turned back to Nano and shouted:

"I love you, baby!"

3

C Wing – Cell 342
Machine (murder) and Smart Guy (armed robbery)

The guard's heavy bunch of keys clanked as he opened the cell door. Nano was alone again with his cellmate. The door slammed behind him, and the lock turned with a sharp metallic sound that was as doom-laden as a judge's sentence.

Narrow walls covered in posters of cars or full-frontal nudes, a filthy floor, two flea-ridden bunks, a flickering portable T.V. on 24/7, a wooden table singed by gas burners, toilet area screened off by a curtain. The smell of sweat, piss, heat and dirt. A barred window. No air.

In the centre of the regulation nine square metres, an imposing black guy was counting out loud as he did press-ups. He stopped at 230 and got to his feet covered in sweat, two damp patches under his arms, veins still standing out on his forehead. His nickname was apt.

"Well, Doe Eyes, did you see your fancy man?"

Nano sat on his bunk and laid the bag his sister had brought next to him.

"It was my girlfriend."

"You don't have a girlfriend, Doe Eyes. You're queer."

Nano would definitely have preferred Smart Guy, the nickname he had invented for his sister. But his soft eyes, his youth and his delicate features counted against him, and made him a victim. He accepted the insult without reacting. It wasn't the first.

"Have you got my S.I.M. and my pack of cards?"

Nano opened his bag and started rummaging for them, but Machine snatched it from him, emptied everything on to the cell floor, and picked up the pack of cards. Nano stuck his fingers into his mouth and handed him the S.I.M. card. He'd done what his cellmate had asked, so maybe he would be left alone for the afternoon. But it had been a long while since Machine had last had any visitors, and he was feeling frustrated. A frustration he knew of only one way to relieve.

"Come here. I didn't hurt you, did I?"

Nano stood up. Once, in a reckless moment of rebellion, he had refused to comply, but by now he knew that wasn't a good idea. Machine lay down on his bunk.

"Go gently, kid."

Nano kneeled down, closed his eyes, and took hold of Machine's penis. He began to repeat to himself, like a prayer: "Twenty-first day of remand. Maybe the twenty-second will be better."

4

C Wing exercise yard
AKA: The Jungle
One hour. 300 inmates, one guard in watchtower

The twenty-second day. Nano had slipped into a corner between a reinforced concrete wall and the barbed-wire fence. He was in the midst of one of his favourite daydreams. Dreaming he was invisible. Invisible among a pack of wolves.

Another of his daydreams took him back to his Corsican childhood, when he could run, eyes closed, along the beach without fear of colliding with an inmate or getting the barbed wire in his throat.

Running with his eyes closed. Invisible. Free.

Several hundred inmates were scattered around the yard. Some playing games, others smoking joints or exchanging the latest gossip. Boasting of their exploits or selecting their next target. Sizing the others up, judging them, challenging them. Several hundred inmates, every one of them a threat.

In the north-west corner, a watchtower twenty metres high. Inside its glass cabin, a guard was watching the comings and goings down below through a pair of binoculars. To prevent prisoners climbing up it, the watchtower wasn't built directly on the ground, but on a plinth. This meant that below the cabin there was a blind spot it was better not to find yourself in.

In Marveil, the future didn't extend beyond the following day. This prospect had reduced Nano to despair. Shortness of breath, tunnel vision, lump in the throat. The symptoms of a panic attack, precisely where it was best not to have one. He knew he wasn't going to be able to stand this much longer. No-one, least of all him, was made to endure such a hell. Another inmate came and leaned back against the fence a metre from him.

"Take a deep breath."

Nano focused on him for the first time. His body tensed: another person meant potential danger. He studied the newcomer: about forty, dull skin, shaven head, jaw set in a hard line, impenetrable dark look. The stranger went on:

"Take a deep breath. If they see you blubbing, they'll make you suffer for it."

Nano came out of himself.

"I wasn't going to cry."

"So much the better. What are you doing here?"

"Armed robbery."

"I couldn't give a fuck about that. Unless you're a grass or a paedo, nobody gives a shit about why you're in here. I'm asking what you're doing so near the Ring?"

Seeing Nano's puzzled face, the stranger realised he would have to explain a few things to him.

"Shit, how long have you been inside? You ought to know all this stuff. The area under the watchtower is called the Ring, and you don't want to spend much time here. Come on, walk with me."

Nano knew that every expression of sympathy, every small act of kindness or piece of advice, had its cost. He didn't want to get into debt. Jerking Machine off twice a day was bad enough.

"I'm fine. I'll stay where I am. I didn't ask for anything, and I've nothing to give you."

26

"Take it easy, kid. You're not my style . . ."

The man's attention was drawn to the far side of the yard. Worried, he repeated his advice.

". . . but believe me, you need to get away from here."

Twenty metres from them a stocky man, a kind of Aryan skinhead covered in tattoos, was sitting on a patch of tired-looking grass. He was casually rolling himself a joint. A group of six young prisoners came up to him, pretending to be talking among themselves. Tall and thin, all of them in tracksuits, sniggering as they walked, they looked like hyenas, constantly glancing around as if expecting an attack from any direction. In fact, they were the ones preparing the assault. No sooner had they walked past the tattooed man than they turned on their heels, caught him by surprise, lifted him up and carried him over to the Ring. Trussed like a game bird, he kicked out and struggled, but in vain. Loud whistling all over the yard. Not from the guards, but from prisoners alerting others to the fun about to start. Someone was going to get a beating, and none of them wanted to miss it.

In the opposite corner, Machine was playing poker with some other inmates. He looked over in the direction all the noise was coming from. A punishment in the Ring. He had doled out many more than he'd received, and they had long ceased to interest him. He turned back to the game.

A dense crowd gathered under the watchtower, preventing Nano from seeing what was going on. Cries of pain mixed with joyous shouts of encouragement. In less than thirty seconds, the sixty or so spectators dispersed, leaving the victim's inert body on the ground. His face was a bloody mess, and his left arm was twisted at an impossible angle. Two of the hyenas were delegated to grab him by the legs and drag him out of the Ring, leaving him visible to the guard in the watchtower.

The sun glinted on his binoculars as he saw the body, and the loudspeaker crackled:

"To the gate."

The hyenas dragged the body across the yard, leaving a bloodstained trail in their wake. They dropped him at the entry gate, which opened cautiously. The arms of several guards appeared; they took hold of the still unconscious prisoner, pulled him out of the yard, and the gate swung closed again. Officially, nothing had happened, and calm returned to the yard. Taken aback, Nano addressed the stranger.

"Shit, they could have killed him. How can there be no surveillance at all over there?"

"In the Ring? It's somewhere to let off steam, to get rid of tension. If they didn't do that here, they'd be fighting in their cells, the corridors or the canteen, and that scares the shit out of the guards. So they let them have this Ring where they can settle their arguments. The closer you are to it, the more you risk getting drawn in, and no offence, but you're not exactly built for it."

There was a big red patch beneath the watchtower. Nano now realised the yard was probably even more dangerous than his cell. Even with that louse Machine. He held out his hand.

"Thanks, pal. I'm Nunzio. Well, Nano."

"I know, Doe Eyes. I'm Gabriel. In here, Scalpel."

"Why?"

"They say I slit a woman's throat."

"And is it true?"

Scalpel burst out laughing.

"Obviously."

The bell rang to signal the end of exercise. Nano took advantage of his guardian angel to ask him for something.

"I'm having a hard time in my cell. Do you think you could help me? I can get some money to you if you want."

All smiles, Scalpel patted him twice on the back.

"You're all alone in here. And if one day you think you've made a friend . . . don't trust him."

5

C Wing – Cell 342
Machine (murder) and Doe Eyes (armed robbery)

Machine entered the cell, fists clenched, obviously furious. When the door clanged shut behind him, he punched the wall twice as hard as he could. Nano shrank back on his mattress. Machine walked over to his bunk, slipped his hand under the pillow and took out a joint. He went back to the door, banged on it, and shouted in a deep voice:

"Guard, hey, guard!"

An eye darkened the spyhole.

"Hey guard, give me a light."

"What happened to yours?"

"I lost it at poker."

The sound of a key, then a lock, and the door opened. The guard held out his lighter and lit Machine's joint. He took two deep drags. The guard disappeared in the sweet-smelling cloud and the door closed again.

Cannabis. Another way to get some peace. Many prisoners find themselves in Marveil on drugs-related charges. Ironic then that their use is tolerated inside the prison.

Before Machine could get it into his head to take it out on him, Nano tried to show some sympathy.

"Sorry about your lighter."

Machine drew on his joint like a vacuum cleaner, making the tip glow bright red.

"I also lost your pack of cards. You'll have to get me another one."

"I'll ask my girlfriend."

"You can also ask for some photos of her naked. Don't mind sharing, do you?"

Nano imagined Machine's head being pounded against the wall.

"No, of course not."

C Wing – Cell 321
Scalpel (homicide) and Chef (poisoning)

Scalpel was finishing shaving while his cellmate, a seventy-year-old Turk with a spicy odour, was putting the final touches to a food heater made from a tin can and two bits of wire.

One razor a month. The blunt blade nicked Scalpel's throat. He stuck a scrap of toilet paper on it to stem the drops of blood.

"Do you know Machine?"

Chef was busy with his contraption and didn't even bother to look up. He'd been given twelve years for poisoning, and over the past few had become the prison's quartermaster. If anyone needed toilet supplies, decent food or fags, Chef could get them for you.

"Yeah. He's one of the Saint-Ouen gang of blacks. Not an easy customer, and not very bright. A dangerous combination."

Scalpel wiped away what was left of the shaving cream and stroked his skin. After a pause, Chef continued:

"Are you asking because of the kid? I saw you talking to him in the yard."

"Do you think we could do something?"

"Whoa there, you know the first rule: protect yourself. I sell

31

these animals food, that's why they leave me alone. And also because I'm going to croak in here. They respect that. And you, since they've heard you chopped off your wife's head, they're scared you'll do it to them."

"I slit her throat, I didn't behead her. And she wasn't my wife. I still have a wife. I hardly knew the other one. And besides, I didn't do it."

Exasperated, the Turk raised his eyes to the heavens.

"What are you saying? I had a hard enough time creating your legend. I even came up with your nickname. Do yourself a favour, Gabriel, forget that kid."

Scalpel checked the time, picked up his towel, and stood in front of the door.

"Aren't you coming to the beach, Chef?"

"No, I have to finish this heater for 323."

Together with ten other inmates, Scalpel followed the guard to the showers. Machine and Nano were first in line. Mould on the floor, broken, jagged floor tiles, the walls deeply imbedded with stains from every fluid the human body can produce, rats and ticks, guaranteed mycosis. Each of the prisoners stood under a rusty showerhead from which dribbled a thin stream of water.

"You have ten minutes," the guard shouted before leaving the room without any surveillance.

Machine and Nano lined up next to Scalpel. Machine stared at him for several seconds. Scalpel wasn't going to let this challenge go unnoticed.

"Stop staring at me like that. I might fall for you. And you know what happens to the people I love."

Machine smiled, revealing two broken teeth. He knew the reputation of this man with shaven head and a dark, almost blank look in his eyes. He glanced round, then turned his attention back to Gabriel.

"I think you're clean enough now, Scalpel. You need to give us a bit of privacy."

No sooner had he said this than three young punks sauntered into the shower room. It quickly emptied of other prisoners. Nano kept his head down, while Gabriel weighed up the new-comers. If he roughed one of them up, maybe the others would back off. Machine was astonished he was still there.

"Are you sure about this, Scalpel? Do you really not hear what I'm saying?"

Gabriel remembered the first words Chef had said to him: "If there's one thing there's no shortage of here, it's trouble. You can be sure you'll have plenty of your own, so don't go looking for other people's, you're bound to regret it."

He exchanged looks with Nano. The youngster's slumped body spoke volumes. He had given in: he had become a victim. Gabriel reluctantly took his shower gel and towel and left. To Nano's surprise, Machine did the same. For a brief moment, the youngster thought this meant he might win some respite. Picking up his things, he prepared to follow his cellmate, but Machine grasped him by the shoulder.

"No. You stay here."

Nano looked anxiously at the three other inmates busily undressing. He said politely:

"But I've finished."

"I know. But I lost you at poker as well."

6

A few metres from the door to the shower room, Demarco was counting the prisoners for a third time. He'd already done it twice, and there was still one missing. Demarco had been working in the prison for less than a month, replacing Chabert, who had apparently had his carotid severed by a toothbrush that had been scraped against the floor until it was as sharp as a knife. He had been quick to identify the most dangerous spots: the exercise yard, the showers and the canteen. Rebaptised by the cons as the Jungle, the Beach and the Restaurant.

The prison at Marveil had been through three distinct eras. From 1970 to 1990, it had kept to the recommended ratio of guards to prisoners. This allowed internal supervision that helped facilitate communal life among the most dangerous elements in society. In the nineties overcrowding began, together with budget cuts. With one guard for every hundred prisoners, trouble was inevitable. This meant the guards began the second great period of Marveil's existence: the era of repression. Violent, sometimes unjust, constant and authorised. Out of fear, self-protection and, as things drifted, occasionally for pleasure. This descent into violence, when permitted by the authorities, is known as the Lucifer Effect. In 1971, scientists and psychologists in the United States carried out an experiment at Stanford

University, and the results proved that if you're allowed to, you end up punishing others.

Then after the year 2000, with even more prisoners, staff even more hard-pressed, and horrific abuse a daily occurrence, the third and last Marveil era had begun. The era of secrecy and abandonment. The guards' only concern was to get home in one piece, and so they let the inmates insult and fight one another, trade goods, take drugs and fuck as they wished. The only moral limits were suicide and murder.

Demarco was slowly coming to recognise the chasm between what the job had promised and the reality. Like the difference between the photo on the sleeve of a frozen meal and the disgusting brown sludge it really contains. All he wanted was to go home at night to his wife and kid, but at this moment there was no getting away from it: he had counted twice, and there was still one prisoner missing. No. 4657: Nunzio Mosconi.

Demarco opened the door to the showers. In a corner he saw an inert body onto which a last few drops of water were dripping. Blood was coming from his mouth and the inside of his thighs. He went in, checked the prisoner's diaphragm was still rising and falling, and that he was still breathing. Panicking, Demarco pressed the alarm – even though his superiors had strongly advised against it. In less than twenty seconds, two other guards came running. They looked disgruntled.

"Is somebody dead?"

"No, but he's been badly beaten," Demarco said.

The second guard blew his top.

"Shit! What have you been told? Now they all know something's going on. The alarm's for when someone's dead. Otherwise it's like Viagra for these cunts."

The other one added:

"You little cock-teaser! You've turned them on. Now you can be the one to calm them down tonight."

"We'll lead your group back to their cells. You take your pretty boy to the hospital wing."

They went on their way, their dressing-down leaving Demarco with the impression that he was the one responsible for everything. That he himself had beaten and raped No. 4657.

7

Nano had dived deep into the sea, turned on his back, and was now gazing up at the sun from beneath the water as it shimmered on the waves. The silence was hypnotic. A breaker crashed over him in a million bubbles, a cloud of foam in a watery heaven. He pushed up from the sandy bottom, and as his head emerged above water and he began to swim towards the shore, with every stroke he could hear the sounds of the breeze and the Mediterranean. Soon he felt the fine sand caking his ankles as he strode up the beach. The sun on his shoulders was like a comforting caress. The taste of salt on his tongue. Behind the pine woods, Cargèse, a peaceful coastal village, his parents' home. Panting and with water still streaming from his body, he sat on a rock beside his sister. The fact that she had five watches on each wrist didn't seem at all odd to him. After all, she could do as she pleased.

"When I was a kid, you used to tell me there was treasure buried in the sea here. An old pirates' tale."

"There is, but you don't know where to look, 4657."

"I've dived here so often that if there'd been a single gold doubloon I would have found it and given it you."

"The treasure exists. You need to open your eyes, 4657."

Nano's feet left the sand. His whole body rose into the air, and the sea suddenly withdrew twenty metres, just like before a tsunami.

"Hey, 4657! Open your eyes! How are you feeling?"

The doctor turned to the nurse.

"He's in a bad way. He'd better spend the night here."

Nano closed his eyes and fell back on to the Corsican sand.

C Wing
Hospital unit

The medical staff were well aware that spending the night in the prison hospital had to be an exception, otherwise everybody would be clamouring to enter, and the facility would soon be overrun. So there was no question of Nano spending another hour in the warm. The nurse nudged his bed with a hip, gently enough not to wake him with a start. Nano had to undergo two seconds of torture before his brain kicked in.

Two seconds every morning since he'd been in prison. Two seconds when he could imagine he was anywhere. In Corsica or Paris, in a hotel room or in a strange woman's bed. Then his mind stirred and his eyes began to recognise where he was, as if he were being sentenced all over again: Marveil Prison.

"Wake up: Martineau wants to talk to you."

"Who?"

"Martineau. The chief officer. About yesterday evening."

Nano sat up in bed. As he did so, pain clouded his eyes, and the base of his spine clenched. The nurse saw his reaction.

"It's torn. Not badly enough to be sewn up, but you need to rest it."

Nano looked at him disdainfully.

"Yeah, I promise to try not to get raped anymore."

8

C Wing
Rotunda – guards' quarters

Demarco entered the chief officer's room. Martineau was giving a guard from another floor a hard time. Demarco walked over to a corner and let them get on with it.

"Did he request a visit or didn't he?" Martineau wanted to know.

"Yeah, but he always asks for ten things every day."

"You know visits are the one thing you mustn't screw up. If you take that from them, they'll make you pay."

The guard being grilled tried to wriggle out of it.

"Does it have to be me who goes? Can't we get one of the new guys to do it?" he said, looking over at Demarco.

"You made him miss his girlfriend's visit. Because of you he smeared his whole body with shit. It wouldn't look good to send someone else. So get the fire hose and clean him up."

Grim-faced, the guard got to his feet and made for the door. Demarco took his place in the chair, and couldn't help commenting:

"Doesn't it ever stop in here?"

Martineau looked him up and down. It had taken him two hundred and ten stitches, most of them on his hands and arms, to become the unflappable chief officer he now was. He knew that a fortnight earlier, Demarco had witnessed a "barbecue". Now, a gang rape. He wondered how long it would take this youngster to crack. Because everyone cracked in the end.

"I've got close to five thousand wild animals who have twenty-four hours a day to think up what they're going to try next. So no, it never stops. Wipe that gormless look off your face and show the prisoner in."

Now Demarco was standing behind Martineau, who was comfortably seated in his upholstered armchair, both of them facing Nano. The chief officer, with his wispy moustache and monk's tonsure, was speaking:

"So what was that nonsense in the showers yesterday?"

Nano tried to stay calm.

"You're asking me that?"

"Why didn't you call the guard supervising the showers?"

"Are you joking? There's never any guard."

"That's what you say. It's obligatory, it's in the rules. So yesterday, there was a guard."

Nano soon realised the only point of this interview was to help the prison administration to cover itself in case there were any consequences.

"Well, do you want to make an official complaint and go back to your cell?"

"No, I want to make an official complaint and be moved somewhere on my own. If I go back to my cell after making a complaint, I won't last a night."

The chief officer settled on his throne. He clasped his hands in front of him.

"Mosconi, isn't it? Listen, Mosconi, either you consider that what took place yesterday was unacceptable and you make a complaint, or you agree with me in saying that these things happen, and that a more appropriate attitude might have helped you avoid this kind of problem."

Nano leaped out of his chair, only to be pushed back down again by a third guard he had not noticed until then. This immediately reopened the wound inside. The pain brought tears to his eyes.

"A more appropriate attitude? Are you out of your mind? You mean I was asking for it?"

"If you don't agree, please don't hesitate to give me a list of your aggressors. I'll listen to what they have to say, as I'm doing with you now, and we'll see where it all leads."

Martineau pushed a ballpoint pen and spiral notebook in his direction, and waited. Nano glanced at Demarco, who so far had not said a word. The young guard was studiously trying to avoid exchanging looks with prisoner 4657. Nano sighed and pushed away the notepad.

"No, that's fine, thank you."

Martineau turned to his subordinate and dismissed the Mosconi case in a sentence.

"Perfect. Demarco, get him to see the shrink, then back to his cell."

Smug behind his moustache, the chief officer must have been telling himself he had dealt with the situation impeccably. If there are no waves, the boat doesn't rock.

A considerable number of the inmates of Marveil are there for sexual offences. The fact that these are covered up, even tolerated, inside the prison is yet another small irony.

9

C Wing
Psychiatrist's office

The doctor had considerately placed a small cushion on Nano's chair. Nano might have been touched by this gesture, but instead found he was horrified that the shrink was prepared for prisoners who found it hard to sit down. He dismissed the thought and went on the attack:

"If I've been told to see a shrink, it's because they're aware I'm the victim of something, isn't it?"

The psychiatrist, well into his sixties and with a bureaucratic paunch to go with it, rubbed his eyes behind thick glasses. Nano could read his indifference and fatigue as clearly as if they were tattooed on his forehead.

"Mosconi, is that right? O.K., I'll keep this short, Mosconi. If you think I have the slightest chance of resolving your problems, you're making a big, big mistake. I treat addicts, depressives, would-be suicides and every other psychiatric patient in exactly the same way – with anti-depressants and methadone. In here, I'm nothing more than a dealer."

"So your gig as a shrink is in your spare time?"

"You're being funny? That's a good sign. My dear friend, I haven't practised psychotherapy since I don't know when. In here, there's nothing but inequality and extreme violence, so therapy is useless. And besides, most inmates are convinced they're worthless. They've been told that so often it's not surprising the re-offending rate is so high. Sixty per cent – that's terrible, isn't it? Have you heard of the Pygmalion Effect and the work of Doctor Charisse L. Nixon?"

Nano paid scant attention to what the doctor was saying or to his final question, but what little he took in saw whatever remaining hopes he had evaporate.

"Tell me why I'm here then, doctor."

The psychiatrist opened the folder in front of him. Although there were only two sheets of paper inside, he shuffled them endlessly.

"Sexual acts in the showers, no complaint lodged. I suppose I'm meant to discuss your homosexuality with you, and the problems it can cause in a closed, exclusively male environment."

Despite his predicament, Nano couldn't stifle a guffaw.

"You've got to be joking! I'm not queer: I was raped! It's just that the guy with the little moustache refuses to give me protection if I name names."

"Martineau, he's called. And don't make fun of his moustache, he's very sensitive about it."

Sensitivity was one of those feelings that no longer had any place in Nano's life, along with vexation, bitterness or feeling offended, melancholy, or indignant. They were the emotional states of a free man.

"I couldn't give a fuck if he's sensitive. I want you to tell me how I can avoid going back to those shitholes. There must be a disciplinary wing where I can be kept, mustn't there?"

The psychiatrist seemed to consider this question seriously, and replied with disheartening world-weariness.

"Of course, but for that you would have to commit a serious offence, such as attacking a guard."

"Is that what you're recommending?"

"Of course not. That would only extend your sentence a few months. But if you're homosexual, you could get a segregated cell."

"Excuse me? I can't be segregated to save my skin, but I can if I'm queer?"

"Or a paedophile or a transsexual – or an ex-policeman. You choose. In fact, any serious deviational behaviour that would put you at risk from others. We have to take it into account."

Nano buried his head in his hands, not sure whether to laugh or cry. The shrink continued as nonchalantly as if he had a summer job in a restaurant and was taking an order.

"So, what will it be?"

Nano hesitated for a second.

"Write that I'm queer."

"Do you want some anti-depressants?"

"What are they like?"

"They work."

"O.K."

10

Alex Mosconi had been waiting for more than an hour on a bench in the Rotunda. She had seen the group of visitors being led to the visiting room, but hadn't heard her name called. She wasn't so much impatient as anxious. She saw the guard with the roving eyes heading towards her.

"You're here for Nunzio Mosconi, aren't you?"

She nodded.

"It's not going to be possible today. He's been segregated."

"Segregated? What kind of bullshit is that? What's happened to him?"

"They didn't tell me," the guard said feebly.

"For how long?"

"They didn't tell me that either."

For a split second Alex felt an urge to kill him, but she soon regained her composure.

"So what do I do?"

"Go home and make another visitor request."

Leaving her no time to protest, the guard signalled for Alex to get up and follow him. Her mind was so busy trying to work out why her brother had ended up segregated she didn't even notice where they were going.

From a walkway on the floor above, Demarco had seen her leaving and instantly noticed the family resemblance with

No. 4657. He was well aware of the reasons why her visit had been cancelled. When she moved out of his line of sight, the guilt stuck to him like a shower curtain.

Escorted from the prison, Alex found herself in a deserted car park. She took out her mobile and hastily dialled a number she had known by heart for years. Somewhere in the eighth arrondissement of Paris, the telephone of a firm of lawyers began to ring.

At the third ring, Maître Tiretto picked up. Ebony desk, impeccable suit, perfect haircut, well-groomed forty-something – the kind of man Barbie would go for. On the wall behind him, a huge painting with blobs of colour splashed on the canvas like the morning after a paint-drinking session. Modern art ugly enough to be priceless.

"Good morning, Mademoiselle Mosconi. How are you?"

"Hi there, Tiretto. Not good. I'm not good. Nano's been segregated and I've no idea why."

"Didn't you tell me he was a little the worse for wear last week? Perhaps he defended himself this time?"

"Nano? You know him. It's not his style."

"Well, it's not the disciplinary cells, only segregation. Maybe it's better for him."

"With no window and no personal belongings? And an even smaller cell? It took him six months to start getting used to Paris. You have to tell me what's happened. Why they've put him there. I can't leave him like that."

"I've got several clients in Marveil. I can check, but that's going to take time, and a wad of notes."

Alex clenched her fists. Her voice went up a notch.

"Tiretto, if it's money you're after, my family's already given you a shedful. Far too much. So get me the info I need or I'll stuff your balls down your throat."

46

The lawyer tried to calm her down, but she had already hung up. He sat there cradling the receiver. Alex Mosconi was from one of those Corsican families that lawyers love. Always on the lookout for the next heist, always with a cousin or brother to get out of a scrape. Doing business with the Mosconis and pleading on their behalf had built him his swimming pool in Nice and secured his swanky Audi TT. He couldn't ignore the phone call.

11

First night
Segregation cell No. 2
Nunzio Mosconi

Nano had gone from nine square metres to four. He wasn't complaining. The segregation wing consisted of twenty individual cells, and he'd been given Number Two. First came the door, the same as all the other cells. Behind it, a security scanner that took up one square metre, then steel bars, and finally the inmate. Inside the cell, a cement bench, a table welded to the floor, a washbasin and a Turkish toilet. On the walls, hundreds of messages, not all of them coherent, written in ash, blood or shit. On the ceiling, a neon tube covered with wire mesh cast a harsh white light like the kind you get in hospitals, as though at any moment a medic in a white coat was about to come in, scalpel in hand.

For the first hour, Nano rejoiced in the silence, relieved of the weight of fear and threats. The second hour seemed strange. Tense, he began to pace round. The hours that followed gave him the impression his cell was shrinking; he found it increasingly difficult to breathe. Before the night was out, he came to understand why some prisoners couldn't hack it.

In the centre of the far wall, one of the messages written in clumsy letters leaped out at him: "You are your only enemy."

At around nine in the evening, he heard a strange noise: a loud thud against the wall, followed by a howl. A few seconds later, the same sound, louder this time. Then silence once more. Nano closed his eyes: he was lying on his beach in Corsica. But it was no good, even in his dreams he couldn't escape reality. The sand stuck to him like tar, the sea smelt of petrol. His sister was no more than a vague silhouette in the distance. The night would be a torment.

Segregation cell No. 13
Antoine Doucey

The inmate had made the request twelve days earlier. What can seem simple on the outside becomes an administrative obstacle course between these four walls. Even a request to see a dentist. It wasn't the twelve days that were a problem. But Doucey could count every second of the twelve nights, when the toothache flared up. On the scale of bearable pain, toothache was at the suicide end. The sort that makes you think death would be a release. So for twelve long nights Doucey curled up on his bunk and refused his meal, because every mouthful sent ten thousand volts juddering to his brain. He spent the whole time in tears, hand cradling the right side of his face, as swollen as if he was concealing a golf ball in his cheek. Nights he spent dreaming he had a hammer to smash everything inside his mouth once and for all.

He was in his fifties, with a slight limp due to a hip malformation, and this was his second stint in Marveil. Twice for the same offence. And segregated the entire time. Kept away from the others, he had no chance to be given a nickname like Doe Eyes, Scalpel or Machine. He sometimes wondered what it might have been: the Monster? The Devil? Doucey didn't need locking up, he needed rewiring. The crimes he'd committed would have made him a target if he had been put with the common criminals. He wouldn't have lasted two days.

By nine in the evening the pain always became unbearable. A burning sensation so terrible Doucey felt he was going out of his mind, forcing him to take desperate measures. Over the previous few nights he had developed a technique. He stood up, eyes moist with tears he couldn't control. Sleep was the only way out. His back against the cell door, he took a breath, filled his lungs with air and hurled himself, head down, at the far wall. The sound reverberated down the corridor. The shock of his skull hitting the stone made him see stars, and set all the nerve ends in his body jangling. He howled with pain, but the first attempt was never determined enough. He staggered back and stood against the door once more, drew breath, and flung himself again, faster this time so that he hit the wall harder. He crashed into it and collapsed senseless to the sticky floor. Peace at last. He was back with six-year-old Leo, who was always in his thoughts. He missed him so much. If only he could hold him in his arms once more, just for a few seconds, far from his parents.

Leo.

Segregation cell No. 20
Boyan Mladic

Martineau had explained to the prison staff how dangerous the inmate in Segregation Cell No. 20 was. After that, he and only he took charge of this particular case. Given his eighteen years as chief officer at Marveil, none of the others had said a word.

As on every evening, at nine o' clock Martineau headed for Cell No. 20, cooler bag in hand. He rapped twice on the door before turning the key in the lock. A clean smell, thick mattress on the cement base, microwave, cable T.V., laptop with DVD function, internet connection. Unusual courtesies, like off-key notes in a musical score.

"Good evening, Boyan."

The detainee got to his feet at the end of the cell and approached Martineau. It was always an impressive sight: Boyan was as big as a mountain. A former Serbian soldier, decorated with many medals. Killing had made him a hero in times of war. But the relative peace the former Yugoslavia eventually enjoyed had left him without employment, and return to civilian life had completely disoriented him. Blood on his hands after objecting to being looked at in a bar, this time killing somebody made him a criminal, and so he had found refuge in the Foreign Legion. He spent six years serving the French flag before quitting to become a bodyguard. From paranoid bosses to sleazy sponsors, he had travelled the world contract after contract, until finally disembarking in France three years earlier. No-one really knew why he was in prison. And above all, no-one knew why a mere thug enjoyed such privileges in Marveil. No-one except Martineau.

The chief officer put the cooler bag down and took out three coloured plastic tubs containing Boyan's meal.

"I'll be back in an hour to clear everything away."

Boyan raised his grey, almost white eyes to Martineau and nodded his thanks. Despite this apparent calm and surprising politeness, the chief officer backed out of the cell, keeping his eyes on Mladic all the time.

"I'll leave you to eat in peace."

Boyan said nothing. In fact, Martineau didn't even know if he spoke French. What he did know was that he had to be properly looked after so that he didn't notice time going by, because for someone somewhere, Boyan was extremely important. And the amount Martineau received for looking after him confirmed that.

Segregation cell No.2
Nunzio Mosconi.

At eleven that night, Demarco was patrolling the segregation cells. He paused in front of Nano's. He opened the outer door, walked through the scanner, and stood in front of the steel bars. Inside the cell, Nano was still pacing up and down. He didn't even stop when he saw the guard.

"Evening, Mosconi. Everything alright?"

Nano came to a sudden halt and in one stride was face to face with Demarco on the other side of the steel bars. He spoke to him as if they had already been chatting for ten minutes.

"Can you lend me your watch? I need to know the time."

"It's almost midnight," the guard replied.

"No, you don't understand. I need to know what time it is at every moment. I'm getting lost."

"You have no reference points anymore. It's normal to feel lost."

As he finished speaking, Demarco searched in his pocket and took out a cigarette, a chocolate bar and a book. He passed them through the bars. *Brave New World* by Aldous Huxley.

"It's from Scalpel. He told me to tell you that you made the right choice. This is the best place for you."

Nano sniggered and lit the cigarette from the lighter, which was held out and then quickly withdrawn.

"I know where the best place is for me, but the Mediterranean is between us. With the others, I'm afraid of getting topped. In here on my own, I'm afraid of going crazy."

"I'm not sure which is better. Listen, Mosconi, I'll be honest with you. Seeing you went from the hospital wing to being

segregated, that could look like you received preferential treat-
ment. In C Wing they're already saying either you ratted or
made an official complaint. I'm not sure it's safe for you to go
back there. I'm afraid Scalpel is right. For the moment this is
the best place for you."

He jerked his chin at the book.

"That's going to become your best friend. Finish it and I'll
bring you another one."

"A book?" snorted Nano.

"Trust me."

Leaving the segregation cells, Demarco reflected on his first
few weeks at Marveil. What he had seen and what he now
understood. He remembered the T.V. interview where he had
heard the former governor himself admit the prison wasn't fit
for purpose the way it was currently organised. "A penitential
establishment is only worthwhile if it creates a fair society,"
he had declared. "One without predators or victims, where
everything is equitable and there are no special privileges or
favouritism, where there is no need for violence or envy about
what somebody else might have more of or better. Once force
is no longer necessary, prisoners can live together in a fair
community. Unfortunately, at the moment there is nowhere
more dangerous, unequal or unfair than prison. And instead of
coming out balanced or rehabilitated, the detainees leave more
violent, more cynical, more lost and more aggressive, with no
plans for rehabilitation into wider society. More poisonous, in
a way. Prison is a school for crime."

A fortnight after that interview, the governor had been
dismissed and replaced. What happens in Marveil stays in
Marveil.

12

"Can I hold your hand? I need physical contact."

It had taken Alex a week to obtain a new visitor permit. Despite spending hours on the telephone, she had been given no information by the prison authorities.

A week her brother had spent in the segregation cells, and she could only imagine what he was going through. Not knowing leads you to think the worst.

Now she was in the transparent cubicle once more. Nano sat across from her, like a lost, traumatised child. Unfinished sentences that didn't make much sense. Threats, fears, a lot of nonsense. Even Nano could grasp he was losing touch with reality. He needed something to ground him.

"Can I hold your hand? I need physical contact."

Alex held out her hand, but as soon as their fingers touched, there was the loud thump of a baton that made the plexiglass cubicle shake.

"No contact."

Alex and Nano leaped apart like two magnets with the same poles.

"Can you tell me what's going on?" Alex wanted to know.

Nano began a fresh tirade that was only half comprehensible.

"You mean being segregated? It's crazy, isn't it? It's a prison inside a prison. Scalpel says I should stay there, but it's getting to me. I read. Books. And the messages others have left. Did you know I'm my own worst enemy? Anyway, if I go back with the regular prisoners that's not good either. It seems they're out for my blood because I ratted, even though I didn't say a word. Shit, you don't know how good it is to talk. To talk to another person, I mean. How's the rest of the team doing? I miss you. I'd really like you to be here with me."

Alex didn't react. The fact that her brother imagined her inside rather than seeing himself outside, in the real world, just showed how distressed he was.

"But what did you do for them to put you there?"

"I fought back against the black guys. But they got the message – they'll leave me alone now."

Alex had protected Nano since childhood and knew her brother too well to imagine him fighting it out with his fists. She didn't believe for a moment Nano could be a tough guy. She'd been surprised when he had wanted to join Dorian and his gang in an armed robbery, and had done all she could to persuade him to change his mind. That proved impossible, and after a quick flight, he had turned up in Paris.

Alex and Dorian had been together for five years and had five armed robberies under their belt. Always jewellers'. Like so many birthday parties. She had also tried to persuade her partner not to involve Nano because he was so immature, but Dorian had insisted there were no risks. And there wouldn't have been, if it hadn't been for that stupid numbered watch.

The bell rang for the end of the regulation half hour, and Alex hugged Nano until a second thud made the plexiglass tremble once more. She watched him walk off, waiting for him to turn round so she could smile at him and cheer him up, but he didn't. Nano was already back inside his four square metres.

Out in the car park, Alex climbed into her car, and looked

the gloomy prison building up and down as though it were a person. Then she stuck her head out of the car again and threw up, shielded by the open door. When she straightened up behind the wheel, she didn't even have the strength to start the engine.

13

"I'm afraid you're not going to like it."

"I've imagined every possible scenario, Tiretto. What I need now is to know what's going on."

The lawyer picked up his notebook and read his notes.

"Things look really bad for him. I've got several clients in Marveil and their stories coincide. At first Nunzio was in a cell with a real hard case. A guy who calls himself Machine. He regularly took his anger out on your brother, but above all used him as his bitch."

When Alex didn't respond, Tiretto went on:

"Then he got a whole group of cons after him. Something about a complaint he made against them, according to rumours."

"A complaint? For what reason?"

The lawyer struggled to know what to say, until Alex lost patience with him.

"Tell me, Tiretto!"

"A gang rape. I think he's been segregated not so much as a punishment but for his own protection. He was the one who asked to be put there."

Alex almost crushed the mobile in her hand. A series of lacerating images flashed through her mind. She steadied her breathing and her nerves before they overwhelmed her.

"You know we have money. Tell your guys inside the prison

to protect my brother and we'll be grateful. You know that. That's something you can do, isn't it?"

Tiretto grimaced. He wasn't sure how safe his landline was, and this conversation was becoming risky.

"Those are not methods this practice employs," he snapped, and put the phone down on her.

He let his irritation subside, then took an almost-new mobile out of his desk drawer. It was registered to a fake name and was only used for this kind of call. Alex picked up at once.

"I'm so sorry, Maître."

"It's nothing. Where were we? We all have our Achilles heel. Yours is your brother. Even during your last robbery, he was the weak link."

Alex was more than aware of that.

"Well, do you think you can pay people inside?"

"I can ask, but money isn't so persuasive in prison. I don't know if anybody would be willing to run the risk on his behalf. Even with a bonus."

"So could we bribe one of the screws?"

"I'm not sure they're ideally placed to keep an eye on your brother. They're not with the inmates the whole time, and their shifts change. We would have to pay them all, and then some. Besides, if we have him protected by the guards, the other prisoners will notice and take it very badly. It would be tantamount to digging his grave."

"Tiretto, it's your own brain you need to dig deep into. I can't leave Nano like this!"

The lawyer sat back in his chair and, since this was the point he had wanted to reach from the outset, he cast his bait.

"Ever since your call last week, I've been thinking it over. There is a possible solution, but it's risky. Dangerous even."

"I'm prepared to do anything if it can help Nano."

58

"I wasn't thinking of merely helping him. I was more considering getting him out of there."

"An escape?"

"Don't get carried away! Our prisons might be in a dreadful state, but a breakout is still very complicated. And afterwards, he'd be on the run the whole time. Let's say what I'm proposing is a little subtler. No exploding doors or helicopters. Let's call it a legal escape."

Alex's curiosity was piqued, but most importantly the lawyer was offering her a way out that she was desperate to hear.

"I'm listening, Maître."

Tiretto's secretary came in with a strong black coffee on a tray. The lawyer frowned and put his hand over the mobile; his secretary immediately understood she wasn't welcome. She turned on her heel and went back to her computer. A lump of sugar, splash of milk, and she drank her boss's coffee herself.

Fifteen minutes later, Alex hung up, ending a conversation every word of which her partner Dorian had heard. Following the robbery, one of Alex's uncles had lent her somewhere to stay in Paris. A converted loft in a building meant for a company that had never got off the ground for lack of the necessary permits. One huge 200-square-metre room that included a spacious living room, kitchen, an immense sofa bed and some camp beds in a corner. A sliding window some fifteen metres long gave a postcard view of Belleville and the twentieth arrondissement. In the centre of the room, a table with ten or more mobiles being charged on it, a computer, and some armchairs and chairs scattered round it. Against one wall was a clothes rail with uniforms of various sizes and from different companies hanging on it. One from the French Post Office. Another from the electricity company. If the police had set foot in there, the terms "safe house" or "hideout" would immediately have sprung to mind.

Alex paced silently round the loft. Dorian watched without interrupting. Although he had carried out the five robberies, she had been the brains behind them. He knew he wouldn't have pulled off any of them without her help and her family's logistical support. So he kept quiet and let her make the decisions concerning this new operation.

Dorian had met Alex six years earlier. It had taken him more than a year to persuade her to have a drink with someone from Paris, from mainland France. The first time she had taken him to Corsica, her parents and cousins had given this scion of the French capital a cool reception. But thanks to his black suit and white shirt that fitted him like a second skin, his square John Wayne jaw and his second-hand car salesman's gift of the gab, he was soon accepted, appreciated even. Just as long as he treated their Alexandra properly. Back then he had been a petty criminal, specialising in burglary and quick swindles that weren't particularly profitable. Alex turned him into a jewel thief, an expert in alarms, locking systems and security screens, with an unapologetic weakness for old-fashioned safes. The full team included two others. Franck Mosconi, a first cousin, was the driver. He had a map of Paris stored in his brain down to the last millimetre, from the widest avenues to the narrowest dead-end streets, including all the underground garages with multiple exits. Expertise that is only fully appreciated when you have flashing blue lights closing in on your getaway car. But to describe him solely as a driver didn't do him justice. Franck was also an excellent administrator who took care of the link between their stolen goods and the receiver, between the mainland and Corsica, via the private airport at Le Bourget. He knew how to find the best vehicles and weapons that had no history. Above all, he knew how to make them disappear so they could never be traced back. He was like a butler with a Swiss army knife.

Finally there was Rhinoceros, pint-sized at one metre sixty tall, but bristling with energy and solid as an oak, with a splendid scar from cheek to cheek. He was the one who took care of the "Everybody be cool, this is a robbery". The most important part. Alex figured an operation could only succeed if everybody was listening carefully and preferably if they were scared stiff. So, once they had introduced themselves, there was usually at least one broken nose or fractured jaw. Fear paralyses, and that was what Rhinoceros could guarantee.

After the robbery, the stolen goods were flown to Corsica, where a trusted fence was waiting. Three weeks later, Alex and her team received half the value of the jewels and luxury items in cash. Business was booming. That is until Nano decided he was too smart to pay attention to basic security measures, like never wearing stolen goods. Ever.

Her decision taken, Alex joined Dorian on one of the comfortable armchairs, lying across his lap.

"Do you think we can trust him?" he asked.

"I think he knows it's better not to cross us. Besides, I don't see why he would want to cause us problems."

"Do you want to go ahead?"

Alex pulled Dorian's shirt out of his trousers and slid her hand up to his chest.

"If that's what it takes to get Nano out . . . Think of it as a kind of burglary. Probably the most daring kind imaginable, but a burglary nonetheless. I reckon it's doable."

"Yeah. But it'll be crawling with police. It must be one of the best guarded places in Seine-Saint-Denis. And first we have to find a way in."

"The lawyer will take care of that. You heard that as well

as I did. He says he'll have the name and address of a contact within forty-eight hours."

Dorian still didn't seem keen.

"Afterwards, we'll have all the police in the region on our backs . . ."

Alex's hand moved down from chest to groin, and Dorian began to feel aroused.

"We can do it. I know we can. And since when have you been worried about the police?"

"You know, it only takes one determined officer . . ."

The lawyer called for his coffee. His secretary quickly poured another one and took it in to him. As she left the room he was dialling a number on his secure mobile. After a few rings, the person on the other end took the call.

"Good morning, Monsieur Darcy. Maître Tiretto here."

"Do I have problems?" the man replied, from force of habit.

"The opposite, I should say. An opportunity. Does Boyan Mladic concern you as much as ever?"

"It's what I've made him do and what he knows that concerns me."

"And yet you told me he was loyal."

"Boyan is a soldier. A Foreign Legionnaire and a mercenary. I'm sure he wouldn't talk under torture. But incarceration can test the strongest loyalties, and the investigating magistrate is a very tempting Faust. I'm afraid if there was an appealing offer, he would squeal. How do you intend to go about this?"

"By getting him out. And having others do the work."

"And there's no chance of it being traced back to me or my companies?"

"Don't worry. They won't even know they're doing this on our behalf."

PART TWO

THE RANSOM

"Make no mistake, it's up to us to make sure this mess has a happy ending"

CAPITAINE VICTOR COSTE

14

Coste rang the bell a second time. Still no answer. Then the handle turned slowly and the door opened. He had to look down to see a little scrap of a girl with bright eyes. When she saw who it was, her whole face lit up. She wheeled round and vanished inside the house, shouting:

"Maman! It's Victor!"

Coste was left on his own, loaded down by a bouquet of flowers and a bottle of wine. Eventually Johanna De Ritter appeared.

"Hello, boss."

Johanna's husband came into view behind her and greeted him with teasing respect.

"Good afternoon, Monsieur Coste."

"Oh no, Karl! I prefer Victor! Monsieur Coste is my father."

Johanna embraced him warmly on the doorstep. Despite his broad shoulders, Coste almost disappeared in her arms. Karl pretended to be upset.

"That'll do, you two. It's not like you don't see enough of each other."

Coste handed him the flowers.

"Don't be jealous. I chose your favourites."

Casting a half-sad, half-amused glance at her husband, Johanna invited Coste in. Beyond the living room and hallway, a door gave on to the garden. Stone steps led down to a well-kept lawn, with a wooden table and chairs. Perfectly ripe strawberries, a laden cherry tree, a barbecue in the middle. Coste took a few seconds to survey his team: Groupe Crime 1 of Seine-Saint-Denis Police Judiciaire.

His deputy, Ronan – open-necked shirt and sunglasses – was drinking a cold beer as he busied himself with the barbecue's glowing embers. Sam, the team's computer nerd, was sitting with a little boy on one knee and a laptop on the other. He was concentrating hard, his brow furrowed. That left Johanna, the only feminine element in the group, although "feminine" wasn't the first word that came to mind to describe De Ritter.

"So it's true you don't have any anti-virus protection?" Sam asked incredulously, hunched over the computer screen. He turned to Johanna, who had just reached the garden table.

"Jo? Malo's new P.C. doesn't have any protection. I'm not surprised it packs up every week."

Ronan lifted his eyes from the huge slab of beef he was carefully grilling.

"No anti-virus? Even I know that's not a good idea. It's like going to Thailand without rubbers."

Johanna gave him a motherly clip behind the ear.

"Hey, Ronan? Can't you adapt your language to suit your audience? Malo is seven; Chloe five. You can be such a pig sometimes."

"Who's Rubbers?" Chloe asked as innocently as if she was talking about a unicorn.

"Bravo, idiot."

As Coste stepped down onto the lawn, he was almost knocked over by Johanna carrying her daughter to the T.V. corner, to prevent her growing up too quickly. As she passed by, she jerked her chin at Ronan.

"Seriously Victor, you know I adore Ronan, but promise me that if he malfunctions you won't buy another one."

Sam burst out laughing. So did Malo, and everyone greeted Victor with one voice:

"Hi there, boss."

Plates empty but glasses still full, conversation continued in small clusters. Johanna, Karl's hand in hers, was talking about the planned improvements to their new home, and the fact that Chloe and Malo could at last each have their own bedroom. Ronan and Sam were giggling in their corner like a pair of kids who'd found a copy of *Playboy* in the attic. Coste, with Chloe perched on his knee, was patiently listening to a surprising but never-ending story about a monster under a bed. Touched, Johanna looked over at him.

"It suits you."

Karl unwittingly put his foot in it.

"Anyway, Victor, you were welcome to bring a plus one."

Johanna aimed a kick at him under the table, whilst admitting to herself she wouldn't be able to bruise the shins of everyone who made a gaffe this Sunday afternoon.

"It's complicated," an amused Coste admitted.

"And because it's complicated, I get landed with all the autopsies," Ronan complained.

They all knew about the roller-coaster love affair between Coste and Léa Marquant, a forensic pathologist at the Institut Médico-Legal in Paris. An affair that had recently reached its nadir. Karl took advantage of the embarrassment he himself had caused to slip off to the kitchen to fetch dessert and coffee. As soon as he had gone, Johanna turned to Sam and Ronan.

"Okay, smartasses, now Karl's out of the way, do you mind telling me why you were laughing like a pair of hyenas?"

Ronan couldn't help revealing what only a few days earlier Coste had advised him to keep quiet.

"You asked us just now if we had trouble finding your place."

"So?"

"So there wasn't much danger of that," he snorted.

Johanna thought it over for a few seconds, before working it out for herself.

"No, really? Around here?"

"In this very street. Two doors down."

After twelve years in the Seine-Saint-Denis Police Judiciaire, it was rare for them to hear a street mentioned without recognising it from a rape, abduction or murder.

"Tell me."

"It was a Norwegian guy. A man around sixty we found with his wrists and ankles tied to a bed. He'd overdosed on ecstasy and poppers. It was his young male lover who called us. When we tried to contact his family, we discovered he was in the country for a project to twin two churches in France and Norway. He was a priest. I know they're very open-minded up there and like to bathe naked in freezing water, but even so, the news must have come as a shock to them."

"Fine," said Johanna. "Thanks for ruining the first days in my new home. But please, Ronan, don't say a word to Karl. It's enough for him to be married to a policewoman, he doesn't have to put up with all the rest."

"I could tell the kids, though, couldn't I?"

"Did you know I have a soundproof basement here?" Johanna threatened him.

At that moment, Karl arrived and put a stop to the team's whispered conversation. He was carrying the coffees, Malo the chocolate cake.

"What's going on?"

"Nothing," Coste said. "We were just blessing your new home."

Johanna placed her hands on her son's shoulders and winked at Karl before launching into an emotional speech.

"I was the last to join the group. I replaced a good friend of yours, Victor, and yet you immediately made me feel at home. Karl wasn't too pleased about moving to Seine-Saint-Denis, but that was where I was posted, and he knew I wanted to be a police officer. Friends of ours were supposed to join us, but that didn't work out. The husband is a childhood friend of Karl's, so we intended to ask him to be Malo's godfather. As time went by, we dropped the idea, and now Malo is seven and still doesn't have one. So, well, we wondered if you would do us the honour."

Sam raised his eyes to Coste, who was already looking at him, then turned to Ronan, before finally realising he was the one Johanna was talking to.

"I'm sorry?" he stammered.

"You're here every other weekend to fix his P.C. You two spend hours together. You invent programs for him, and you've given him your model toy collection. He talks about you all the time. And Karl and I know you'll look after him better than anyone."

"Of course," Ronan said mockingly. "It's because you're an orphan and people feel sorry for you. I would have been able to teach him to fight and pick up girls."

"When you put it like that, I'm starting to regret our decision," Karl retorted.

Sam laid down his chocolate-stained fork, while Malo stood there open-mouthed, staring at his possible future godfather.

"Well?" Johanna insisted.

"Er, yes, of course. I'd be delighted." Malo ran round the

table and flung his arms around him. Equally moved, Sam wrapped him in a skinny embrace. He knew if he shed a single tear, Ronan would be cracking jokes about it for weeks.

"There we are. One problem solved," Ronan said. "Now, are we going to sort out that cat or not?"

Johanna turned to him in surprise. Ronan reminded her of her incessant complaints these past few weeks.

"Well? You told us there was a stupid cat that came over the fence to deliberately shit in your garden, didn't you?"

"Not just anywhere in the garden: always in Chloe's sandpit. He also eats all our strawberries, though he's as fat as a manatee. So what? What about him?"

Ronan rummaged in his backpack and pulled out four small cardboard boxes with pictures of air pistols and small yellow pellets on them.

"So what? It's hunting season."

Comfortably installed in the garden loungers, Coste, Sam, Ronan and Johanna loaded their pistols with the pellets, happy to find such an agreeable firing range. With small glasses of brandy at their feet, and Karl putting the kids to bed, the garden was left to them. All that was missing was the cat.

An imposing cement-grey tom slipped a paw under the fence, then bounded onto the lawn freshly mown by Karl that morning. Not in the least bit fearful, the cat stared at them before advancing as nonchalantly as if he were a tiger.

Sam's pellet exploded a juicy strawberry. The cat raised an ear. Sam was the only one in the team who would struggle to hit a barn door. Unfortunately for the tomcat, Coste and Ronan were good marksmen, while Johanna was part of the police elite when it came to shooting. The three of them peered at their target, aiming for its backside. The small yellow projectiles

zipped through the air and struck home. The cat leaped verti-
cally upwards, meowing in surprise. Then he sped off, allowing
the strawberries and the sandpit a temporary respite. Ronan
burst out laughing.

"Result! What a stupid cat!"

They sat expectantly a while longer, over-estimating the cat's
bravery. It never reappeared, and so, tired of waiting, Ronan
picked Sam as his new target. By now, excited by all the day's
events, the children were sleeping like logs. As the light was
beginning to fade, Coste picked up his jacket.

"I'm off, Jo. Thanks for this wonderful afternoon. Get some
rest, all of you. I don't want to see anyone in the office before
ten tomorrow."

Handed the prospect of a lie-in, Ronan uncorked the bottle
of brandy and refilled their glasses.

15

Seine-Saint-Denis regional headquarters.
Police Judiciaire offices
5.45 a.m.

Coste walked down the corridors and passed by Groupe Crime 1's office without stopping. He took the glassed-in walkway separating the two wings of the building, heading for the spot where he knew he would find his team: the cafeteria. At this ungodly hour, no-one would entertain filling the office coffee machine with water, pressing the ON button, and waiting an age for it to percolate while they fell asleep on their feet. Especially given that the previous evening they had all pushed the boat out with several glasses of a brandy that was as treacherous as a blind corner, and so were all in desperate need of caffeine as quickly as possible. Coste gently opened the door.

"Well then, my little lambs? You look somewhat green about the gills."

Ronan put a coin in the machine.

"Whoa there! Don't tell me you're full of the joys. That'll only make me feel even more tired."

When the plastic coffee cup was full, he handed it to Sam. Then he put more coins in the machine and gave another cup to Coste. Johanna was sitting, elbows on knees, massaging her temples.

"Like to tell us why we're here?" Ronan asked Coste.

"Because I was woken by a magistrate at half past four. And she was in a bad mood. But you know what she's like."

Although his brain wasn't yet in gear, Sam seized his chance.

"Oh yes, Ronan, tell us what it's like to wake up next to Fleur Saint-Croix. "

Embarrassed, his colleague stirred his coffee. Fleur Saint-Croix was the one who decided when he came and when he left, usually in the middle of the night. To wake up beside her was a rare occurrence. Because she was a powerful woman? Because he was only a police lieutenant? Because she saw him as little more than a sex toy? Ronan regularly asked himself these questions. His tender heart was hooked on the only woman who treated him badly.

"Do you get off on other people's private lives?" he snapped in his defence.

Her mental fog lifting, Johanna spoke for the first time.

"O.K., so did we get up at the crack of dawn to talk about willies, or is there work to do?"

Coste took the reins and adopted a more professional tone.

"Here's what Saint-Croix told me. David Sebag. Aged nineteen. On Saturday night, his friends saw him leave the nightclub they were at. Apparently to buy a gram of coke from a guy who didn't want to sell it to him inside. None of them saw him again that night. On Sunday afternoon, David's father, Marc Sebag, started to get worried and called his son's friends. At first the kids fobbed him off, but when they realised he was really scared, they owned up about the coke."

"Hang on, he's been missing less than forty-eight hours. Your David must have crashed with a girlfriend. The local police can deal with it," said Sam.

"Okay, but at two this morning, the father received a text."

"Shit," Ronan muttered.

Johanna didn't follow. "What? What text?"

"Ransom demand. Not exactly good news," Coste explained. "But it's nothing new either. We know how to deal with it."

16

Before six, Victor Coste had given each member of his team their tasks. Sam and Ronan were calling in David Sebag's friends; Johanna was struggling to convince the owner of the nightclub to send the C.C.T.V. footage. Coste himself was interviewing the father, Marc Sebag, whose drawn face showed the effects of a sleepless night. He was wearing jeans, a baggy old T-shirt and trainers with no socks, as if he had rushed out after finding his house on fire. He handed over his mobile when Coste asked him for it.

"I got this text at two o'clock precisely this morning."

Coste swiped the screen, and the message appeared:

74 Rue Favan BR 616 VE rear wing Tombola 16.03.90 Samuel. No police if you want to see him alive again.

Coste continued his questions, eyes still on the phone.

"Where is your wife now, Monsieur Sebag?"

"At home in Stains, in case David reappears."

As when informing people of a death, Coste knew from experience there was no point beating about the bush or trying to sugarcoat things. The only way was to be short and sharp.

"Monsieur Sebag, unfortunately I'm going to have to confirm what you already suspect. My team and I believe your son has been abducted. On Saturday night, somewhere near the V.I.P. Room, a Parisian nightclub."

David's father buried his head in his hands and breathed heavily, trying to release the rush of fear and worry that threatened to engulf him. Coste didn't give him time to think too much.

"I imagine you went to the address in the message?"

"Of course, but I couldn't see any car with that number plate there. I don't understand: should my son have been in it? Did I do something wrong?"

"No, don't worry. Even if the car had been there, your son wouldn't have been in it. The address and number plate are only a test. What I think it means is the kidnappers have left a mobile phone under one of the rear wings of car BR 616 VE at 74, Rue Favan in Stains. The rest of the message is personal information to prove to you they have your son. You're the only one who can confirm that it's correct."

"Tombola is the name of my son's pet ferret. March 16, 1990 is his date of birth. Samuel is his second name. It's all correct."

Coste wrote this down, then continued:

"The mobile would have been your means of contact with the kidnappers, so they can let you know their demands."

"You mean a ransom?"

"That must never be paid, Monsieur Sebag. You should only make them believe you intend to do so. But we'll take care of this, if you're willing to collaborate with us."

"Whatever you say, but what about the car?"

"As for that, I can only see two options: either it was stolen or it's in the pound."

"I don't understand. If they have my mobile number to send me a message, why do they want me to use another phone to contact them?"

"They're known as 'burner phones'. They're only used once. They'll change it each time in case you've been to see us and we try to locate them or intercept their calls. For now speed is our ally – and you need to trust us."

Coste's words seemed to bounce around the room without reaching the ears of this broken father whose world had just collapsed.

"You should also ask your wife to join you. The way things stand, sitting patiently at home will get you nowhere."

This police officer he'd never seen before was asking to be trusted to find his son. The message warned "no police" and Marc Sebag would have respected that if the car had been where they had said it would be. But it wasn't. Now, against his wife's wishes, he had come to see the Police Judiciaire and this capitaine Victor Coste. Sebag didn't know whether it was the other man's calm attitude or shrewd expression, but for a few fleeting seconds, he felt reassured. From this moment on, the capitaine was taking full responsibility on his shoulders.

17

Seine-Saint-Denis car pound.
6.15 a.m.

A scruffy-looking guy with trousers low over on his backside led Costa and Johanna to the most recently towed away cars. The pound received vehicles from several municipalities, including Stains, the town where the Sebag family lived.

Mountains of rusty wrecks gave the immense yard a post-apocalyptic air. In a white 4x4 with all its windows smashed and its bonnet concertinaed in an accident, a dog had recently had puppies, ruining the beige leather seats. Now her attention was on the new arrivals. She was protective of her litter, but the intruders seemed to be looking for something else, and she calmed down.

"Got it! 616 something, isn't it?" Johanna shouted on her radio.

"Bravo Romeo 616 Victor Echo, is that it?"

"Yeah, that's the one. I'm at the far end, behind the burnt-out postal van."

As Coste headed for the torched wreck, he almost fell over the dog, who had abandoned her shelter for a moment. She was wagging her tail and begging. Coste stroked her flank.

"I've nothing for you, my beauty. Go on, off you go."

When he reached the car, a badly beaten-up Twingo, he

found Johanna on her knees searching under the left wing with her gloved hand. She found something, pulled at it, and recovered the mobile wrapped in double-sided Scotch tape.

"Just as well they stuck it on securely."

She straightened up, patted the dust from her jeans, and handed Coste the mobile. He had already produced an evidence bag to wrap it in.

"Capitaine Coste?"

He whirled round. Two men, apparently parachuted in from the eighties, were standing there. One, leather biker jacket and red bandana, still blond despite his fifty-something years; the other, a paunchy forty-year-old who had the nerve to wear ankle boots in the twenty-first century. Though their outfits bordered on the criminal, Coste knew at once he was facing two fellow officers. It was as though the profession left an aura, or a smell.

"Commandant Tissier and Capitaine Matin, Parisian Brigade Anti-Gang."

Tissier, the blond one, stepped forward and took the evidence bag from Coste.

"That's for us . . ."

He handed Coste his own mobile.

"And that's for you."

Johanna quickly grasped what was going on; Coste frowned and put the phone to his ear.

"Victor Coste here."

A few seconds, long enough to have the case snatched from them. Coste tried to win round the magistrate on the other end of the line.

"You can't be serious, Saint-Croix. You put us on the case, then change your mind in less than two hours? The victim is from Saint-Denis, and the father came to our office. Paris won't do any better than us."

"It's not my decision, Victor. If it had been, I'd have warned you earlier."

"A kidnapping can be dealt with in twenty-four hours when there's a ransom demand. It's not like we're novices."

"This has nothing to do with your abilities, capitaine. It's just that the prosecutor prefers to have the Brigade Anti-Gang take care of it."

"O.K., but that doesn't explain anything. We could perfectly well deal with it—"

He broke off in mid-sentence when he recalled the victim's name, and realised there was nothing to be done.

"Oh shit! Sebag. Of course. It's because he's Jewish, isn't it?"

"You'll never get anyone to admit it, but yes. Marc Sebag opened his third computer store in Saint-Denis this year. His business is doing very well, and that has put a target on his back. Local jealousy. Whatever the truth, when the press gets hold of it, they're bound to frame it as an anti-Semitic attack, and it'll be national news. So let Paris deal with it, and stay well away, Coste."

Saint-Croix hung up just like in the movies without giving Coste the chance to reply. It was an order anyway, and she was the one he reported to.

"Can you give us an office in your headquarters?" Tissier asked Johanna, as he aimed a back-heeled kick at the dog, which had made the mistake of sidling up to him.

"Of course. We'll do all we can to facilitate your work."

The dog bore Tissier no ill will, and approached him again, tail wagging furiously. Tissier bent down to pick up a stone to throw at her, but Johanna wasn't going to let him get away with it a second time.

"I promise you, you don't want to do that."

Tissier had to look up to take the measure of this big,

military-looking blonde woman. Having done so, he let the stone drop.

"We'll be in the blue Mégane at the pound entrance," said Matin, in an attempt to defuse the situation.

The two Parisian officers walked away. Johanna dropped her hand to the butt of her pistol and glanced at Coste.

"Come on, Victor. We're in a car pound and there are no witnesses. We could put the bodies in the crusher, and no-one would ever know."

Coste smiled.

18

Two hours had already gone by without Matin and Tissier so much as poking their noses out of the office they had been lent. A police car had brought Sandra Sebag to join her husband at Police Judiciaire headquarters. They were now ensconced with the two Parisian negotiators and the mobile, waiting for the first proper contact with the kidnappers.

Two anxiety-filled hours, and though they were no longer on the case, Coste and his team were alert to the slightest hint of a development. A life was in the balance and the stress was almost tangible.

Sam and Ronan had been joined by four other officers to speed up the interviews with David Sebag's friends. Nothing new had come to light: they had all been out together that evening. Vast quantities of alcohol, David the worse for wear, and the same phrase: "I'm going to buy a gram, the guy's outside, I'll be back." But none of them had seen the dealer. Judging from the C.C.T.V. footage Sam had viewed, David left the V.I.P. Room on his own at half-past one in the morning and never came back.

When Commandant Tissier finally came out of the office, all eyes turned his way. He walked down the corridor to the coffee machine and came back with a steaming cup in his hand, apparently with no intention of telling any of them what was going on. Coste caught up with him before he disappeared again.

"Do you mind if I join you? I know it's your case now, but I established a rapport with the father. It's always good to have someone they trust."

"That's cool. You two should fix up a date together when all this is over," Tissier sneered, slamming the door in Coste's face.

Left standing in the doorway, Coste couldn't help smiling.

"I think he's got a soft spot for me."

After three hours' silence, even Commandant Marie-Charlotte Damiani, Coste's direct superior as the head of the two Groupes Crime in the Saint-Denis Police Judiciaire, was growing worried. She called Victor into her office and closed the door. The bare walls and stacked boxes indicated that she was soon moving out. Dressed in a charcoal-grey suit that matched her cropped hair, Damiani had the haughty, snobbish look of a university professor. This was only a facade however; it quickly peeled away whenever one of her teams was in the firing line.

"This is annoying, Victor."

"Too right. We could easily have handled the case."

"Well . . . it makes no odds. You're not short of work, are you? But this is my last week – I hoped it would be nice and quiet so I could enjoy your company and arrange my leaving do. Instead, I've got a kidnapping on my patch and the Brigade Anti-Gang nesting in our building."

"Enjoy our company? That's rich, Marie-Charlotte."

"Don't be crass, Victor. You know I'm going to miss you."

"I can see that. You've already postponed your retirement for six months . . . How long have you've been saying you're going to take all these boxes down to your car?"

Glancing round her office, Damiani chose not to answer.

"Anyway, I still have a week to go. Seven days to get through. I don't want to sign off with a botched case."

"If it's botched, it'll be the Paris lot's fault. You can order the cakes now."

"I wouldn't be so sure. If they pull out, they could well hand their mess back to us. And three hours with no contact with the kidnappers already smells fishy to me."

"So?"

"So, prepare to be landed with it and keep your team up to speed. Meanwhile, I'll make sure those two clowns give us a full report. They're our guests here, dammit."

It was only after more than three hours of waiting that Matin and Tissier deigned to organise a meeting in the conference room. Groupe Crime 1 was there, as was Groupe Crime 2, led by the plump, authoritarian Capitaine Lara Jevric, Coste's counterpart. Also present were several members of the Brigade Anti-Gang, wellaccustomed to this kind of stand-off. From the start, Tissier let it be clearly understood that the idea of sharing info hadn't come from them.

"Apart from wasting precious time, I really don't see what we're going to gain by this, but so be it."

With this one sentence, Tissier succeeded in putting everyone's back up. A rare quality that he nonetheless shared with Lara Jevric. He repeated the story about the nightclub, the unknown dealer, David Sebag's kidnapping and the text message his father had received, now eight hours and fifteen minutes earlier.

"We should have received instructions ages ago, but apparently we're dealing with amateurs. They may even have got cold feet and bailed, but we're still hanging in there. We don't get offered hospitality like yours every day."

"More than eight hours without contact. Something's wrong.

No call, and no info on the mobile taped to the car. It doesn't make sense," said Sam.

Sam was sitting next to Matin, and his comment seemed to disturb the Parisian officer. Matin leaned over to Tissier and whispered something in his ear. The commandant's face became as pale as his colleague's. The pair closed their files and stood up, but Coste had noticed their embarrassment.

"Hey, this is the police! Nobody moves. Why are you two looking so shifty? Is there something you haven't told us?"

"We just need to check a detail," Matin stammered, drawing a black look from his superior.

An icy silence descended on the room. No-one dared say out loud what they were all afraid of. Coste took the lead.

"I don't believe it! Please tell me you've checked the mobile! Tell me you haven't been staring at it for four hours waiting for it to ring without ever thinking the instructions might already be on it?"

Matin and Tissier opted to stare at the ceiling. Coste ordered:
"Johanna, get the phone."

Matin took a step backwards.

"Wait, we'll—"

"Shut it," Johanna warned him, her hand already grasping the mobile.

She tossed it across the room, and Coste caught it in mid-air. Pressing a few buttons, he opened the Messenger app. Nothing. A few more buttons, and he was in Notes. The screen showed one entry. He read out loud:

80,000 euros. Nine o'clock. Le Millénaire. Main entrance.

"Fuck. We missed the drop-off by an hour and a half," groaned Coste. "That's definitely not good."

Tissier lowered his head, Matin swore, and Sam was already typing on his tablet.

"Le Millénaire shopping centre. Aubervilliers in Seine-Saint-Denis. 56,000 square metres of retail space, 12,000 square metres of green amenities – 130 stores in total. Far too big to stake out."

"And to get away from?"

"It's perfect: twenty or so entrances and exits, not counting the car parks, two Metro lines, two bus services, four tram lines, the Périphérique, a main road, a smaller road. Even river boats along the Seine quays. It's a sieve the size of fifteen football pitches, surrounded by a maze of entry points."

Coste re-read the message before tossing the mobile to Sam.

"Find out all you can about this, and about the number. Who sent the father the text message last night? You have ten minutes. Ronan, get hold of the C.C.T.V. footage from the shopping centre for between eight o'clock and nine-thirty. Just the main entrance. With 56,000 square metres, we won't have time to check the others. Johanna, get in touch with examining magistrate Saint-Croix – no doubt she'll be delighted with the new developments. I'll try to explain what's happened to the parents."

Coste turned to Tissier and gave him a beaming smile, just for the hell of it.

"I have a good rapport with the father; he trusts me. You don't mind, do you?"

19

The news ricocheted like a stray bullet around several police and justice departments: the Brigade Anti-Gang was up shit creek. For the head of the Parisian Police Judiciaire it was unthinkable that his elite corps should leave Seine-Saint-Denis with their tails between their legs. For the head of the Police Judiciaire in Saint-Denis, it was out of the question that they should remain on her turf without her own men being included. Whether this was a battle of different forces or of competing egos, the decision was taken out of their hands and resolved at the highest level in the Interior Ministry, with the agreement of the state prosecutors in Seine-Saint-Denis and the city of Paris. A lot of oil was poured on an already slippery surface. The result: a lukewarm compromise that didn't really solve anything. The Brigade Anti-Gang was to go on waiting for further contact from the kidnappers, and to direct the Sebag parents in their negotiations, while Capitaine Coste's team were authorised to investigate all related matters.

"Related matters? What the hell does that mean?" Johanna complained as she stuck photos on the office whiteboard: one of David Sebag on the beach with his then girlfriend, another of him in a light-grey suit at some university celebration or other.

"On the contrary," Coste told her. "The vaguer the orders, the greater scope we have. Our new buddies are stuck with the mobile, secretaries waiting for a call. The rest is our responsibility. Make no mistake, it's up to us to make sure this mess has a happy ending. With kidnappers who've just been stood up and must be seriously hacked off."

"Let's hope they don't take it out on the kid," Sam thought out loud.

A summer shower beat at the picture window in the office where Marc Sebag and his wife Sandra were waiting patiently, stomachs churning with fear. As short-lived as it was violent, the rain left buildings and pavements gleaming. The interior garden of the Seine-Saint-Denis Police Judiciaire headquarters had been refreshed; raindrops glistened on the leaves of trees and neatly trimmed bushes.

Coste had asked for a private talk with the Sebags, which Tissier and Matin didn't dare refuse. Faced with the couple, he could see justified scepticism in their eyes.

"You asked us to trust you," Sebag's father protested.

Coste could have hidden behind the other officers' mistake, or shifted the blame on to the prosecutor who had taken them off the case, but there was no point. The Sebags saw the police as a single institution, and the secrets of how it worked and its chains of command meant nothing to them. So Coste made no excuses.

"It's our fault entirely," he said. "But I promise you none of my team will rest until we've got David back."

"You think they'll be in contact again?"

"Absolutely. And the Parisian negotiators will be here to accompany and advise you. For example, the kidnappers are going to wonder why you didn't appear at the shopping centre. You need to give them the correct response, Monsieur Sebag."

"I'll tell them the truth. That I didn't find the car where they said it would be. It was in the police pound."

"No, absolutely not. There's no reason you should have known where to find it, and besides, there's no way you could have got anywhere near it and searched it without being the owner."

"So what do I say?"

"The other truth. That you didn't think to check if the instructions were already on the phone."

"I'd have to be really stupid, wouldn't I?"

Coste took the blow on the chin.

"Not all of us are just waiting around. My team and I are going to concentrate on the kidnappers – try to identify them, get a step ahead."

David's father winced at that. He and his wife were holding hands, comforting each other just by being there. No hysteria, no floods of tears. A dignified fear, kept under wraps in a way that astonished Coste.

Hair hastily tidied, traces of fatigue . . . even if she had been tossing and turning most of the night, Sandra Sebag was wide awake now, and wasn't going to let these police officers take any risks with her son's life.

"Chase after them if you wish. All we want is to have David back. And we're going to pay."

"I completely understand, but—"

"I couldn't give a damn if it's a mistake. If they want money, let them have it, as much as they want. I called our accountant, and he's already got it together. We will pay, do you hear me?"

In this particular case, paying the ransom would probably secure a favourable outcome, but the news would spread like wildfire round the estates and could give others the same idea. Be that as it may, Coste understood perfectly that at this point in time the Sebags couldn't give a damn about any possible future victims, so he didn't insist.

20

Ronan had sped to Le Millénaire and back in record time on his motor bike. He brought the C.C.T.V. footage from the main entrance on a U.S.B.

"According to their security people, between thirteen and fifteen thousand people come to push their trolleys there every day. Viewing all the tapes will be a waste of time if we've no idea who we're looking for."

"I know," Coste said. "But the way things stand, we need any evidence we can get."

Sam was in his element. New technologies and mobile telephony. Unfortunately, the kidnappers had been unusually careful, and had made no mistakes. The mobile the text message was sent from had been bought two days earlier, using a fake identity.

"How can you be sure of that?" Ronan said.

"Look, unless our guy really is called Bruce Willis, my instinct tells me it's fake."

"Bruce Willis? Shit, now they're just taking the piss."

"The message the father received pointed to another mobile, taped under a car, the one Tintin and Snowy from Paris were staring at for hours, waiting for it to ring. But that one was only used to communicate their demands. That is, the amount they're demanding and where it was to be dropped off. So they burn a phone each time. No point intercepting them, because they never re-use them. I found its serial number, it was bought with a fake I.D. too."

"Who did central casting come up with this time?"

"Christopher Walken. Two actors who've played Mafia god-fathers."

"Shit, with all the checks mobile phone salesmen are supposed to face, it shouldn't be so easy to buy phones with fake I.D. now," said Johanna.

"That's why they used Arbatel, one of the companies that specialise in calls to other countries. They sell their prepaid mobiles in tiny stores, just a few square metres, which are hardly ever checked. They're usually run by Pakistanis who can't tell a real I.D. card from a fake."

"Bruce Willis? 'Die Hard'? That film was everywhere, wasn't it? It must mean something even in Pakistan."

Coste collapsed on to the big red office sofa. He looked out through the windows at the town below. Somewhere out there, maybe just a couple of streets away, was a kidnapped youngster who must be putting his trust in God as much as in his parents. And thanks to the Brigade Anti-Gang's fuck-up, he would be wondering why his family hadn't paid the ransom, at the mercy of kidnappers who no doubt were beside themselves with rage. Coste let his mind wander, trying to imagine who they were up against. The kidnappers would need one man to guard David Sebag, another roaming the shopping centre to collect the ransom, and at least one more to head up the team, his hands free to respond as needed. So there must be at least three of them. Three unknown individuals in different locations who would have to be constantly in touch with one another. A thought crossed his mind.

"Sam, can you trace where the two mobiles were purchased?"

Sam leafed through the notes he had taken.

"Easy Phone Shop in Drancy. I see where you're coming from, Victor, but if our guys bought them two days ago, how can you expect the shop owner to remember their faces?"

"And more to the point, will he want to remember?"

"I'm not bothered about the salesman's memory," said Coste. "If, as you say, the kidnappers have burner phones for contacting the father, they'll be careful enough not to use their own phones to communicate with one another as long as this lasts. So they won't have bought only two mobiles, but a lot more."

"At least one each."

"And since we know where they bought the first two, with a bit of luck they'll have bought the others there as well. So we'll know what numbers they're going to use, and—"

Like a school kid with the right answer on the tip of his tongue, Sam didn't have the patience to let him finish.

"And we can get ahead of them! We can intercept their calls and track them down. As soon as they call or text each other, we'll be listening!"

A fresh lead. Coste tapped his hands together.

"Right. Car. Siren. Flashing lights. Drancy. Let's go!"

21

At the wheel of the Peugeot 306, Ronan ran several red lights and was hooted at a couple of times on the way, despite the police siren and the flashing blue light – these no longer impressed many people in Seine-Saint-Denis. In the passenger seat, Coste was explaining to the magistrate Fleur Saint-Croix how he was hoping to steal a march on the kidnappers thanks to their mobiles.

Ronan switched off the siren, drove up on to the pavement and parked directly outside the mobile phone store. As discreet as a barge on dry land.

A bell rang when they opened the door to Ravisha Kumar's shop. The walls inside were covered in posters of Lollywood film stars and lined with shelves offering pirated D.V.D.s, beauty creams, biscuits and, almost as an afterthought, mobile phones. Sitting on a high stool, Kumar looked up from his computer as the two men entered. He lowered the sound on his radio and raised his arms in welcome like a ringmaster presenting a circus show. His strong accent seemed to make the words roll round his mouth and stumble before they emerged.

"Good morning, police!"

The sixth sense of those with a guilty conscience.

"Good morning," replied Coste, taking a sheet of paper from his breast pocket and sliding across to the salesman. He pointed to one particular paragraph. "These are two lines you opened two days ago. We don't have much time. I'd like you to find them for us in your sales register."

The Pakistani waggled his head, still smiling on the outside.

"And client secret? Police warrant?"

Coste noted that even if the man didn't have a great deal of French, he did at least know the essentials. He put a restraining hand on Ronan's shoulder before he could proceed from words to actions. The salesman changed his mind and decided to collaborate.

"O.K. No warrant. No problem."

Pressing on the mouse, Kumar scrolled up the list until he came to the date they were looking for.

"Yes. Bruce Willis and Christopher Walken."

Ronan was livid.

"Are you joking? You can say that with a straight face? Did you at least ask them for a signature? Did your Americans show you their I.D.s?"

Kumar waggled his head and smiled once more, hoping a display of good humour could get him off the hook.

"Obviously not," Ronan concluded. "I don't even know why I'm asking."

Coste took the lead again.

"I want you to tell me how many pre-paid phones they bought, and how they paid for them."

"Warrant?" Kumar tried one last time. It seemed he was as scared of reprisals from locals as he was of them.

Ronan, who knew the limits of courtesy, seized him by the collar, shook him a little to straighten out his ideas, and added softly:

"Do you really want to be arrested, with that silly smile of yours?"

Kumar returned eagerly to his list of clients. As he read through them, he hesitated and slowed down, apparently trying to buy time. Coste walked round the counter, shoved him out of the way, and took his place. He found the first two purchasers: Willis and Walken. He scrolled down the page to see the others. Hollywood again, this time with a French touch.

"Pacino, Brando and . . . Delon."

Three new lines. Ronan glared scornfully at Kumar, who was lost in the contemplation of the tips of his shoes.

"I'm willing to believe you're no film buff, and I'm willing to believe you don't even know what that means, but for fuck's sake! It's thanks to small-time operators like you that we're always two steps behind."

Coste sent the relevant page of the register to the printer. As he looked up, he saw a C.C.T.V. camera in a top corner, pointing at the entrance and till. His hopes rose. He called the salesman and pointed at the camera.

"Does it work?"

Kumar beamed at him once more.

"Camera? Fake. Plastic. Twenty euros. You want present?"

They left the store before they did anything they might regret.

22

As they were rushing back to headquarters, Coste relayed all the new information to Sam, who was already on the edge of his seat. The fake identities and identification codes for the three new mobiles, which, of course, had been paid for in cash. The interception and geolocation were on hold, just waiting for these details.

The head of the two Groupes Crime was kept abreast of the developments in the case. She watched her subordinate return to the building with a sense of pride. Marie-Charlotte gave Coste a friendly wink as he walked past her towards his office. Perhaps her last week wasn't going to be such a catastrophe after all.

Sam didn't even give Coste time to hang his jacket on the back of his chair. He turned two laptop computers towards him, and explained:

"The three lines you've just discovered are already under surveillance. On the left-hand screen there's a map of Seine-Saint-Denis. There's no reason for them to be up to their monkey business anywhere else, unless they're not from around here, but I doubt that. Their sort usually shit on their own doorstep. So as soon as any of the three mobiles is switched on, even for a simple SMS, it'll be picked up by the mast and we'll be able to locate it. But if they do us a favour and talk to one another, it'll show up on the right-hand screen, and in that case, bingo! We'll be connected directly to them and we'll hear everything. They're tagged like an endangered species."

"Have they used the phones since they bought them?"

"Yes. Delon called Brando at eight-thirty this morning. A ten-second call. Brando pinged a mast near Porte de la Chapelle in the eighteenth arrondissement, and Delon activated one in Aubervilliers, close to the shopping centre. But as we hadn't begun intercepting them then, I don't know what they said to each other."

"O.K. So Delon must have told Brando he was at the shopping centre, waiting for the ransom. That's normal. And I imagine there was another call when the money didn't arrive."

"Right. Delon contacted Brando again at half-past ten. Twelve seconds. Delon was still in the shopping centre, but this time Brando was near Porte Maillot."

"And neither of them has called Pacino?"

"Nothing on the screen."

Coste straightened up and looked away, pleased with their progress.

"Perfect. So that's the entire team. Delon is at the shopping centre: he's the receiver. Brando is constantly on the move: he's the leader. And Pacino stays under the radar. No-one calls him, and he calls no-one. He must be guarding David Sebag."

Sam sat in front of the two screens, all eyes.

"Come on, you lot. Don't be shy. Talk to one another."

"We're going to have to be patient. I hate the waiting game," groaned Ronan, pacing up and down the office, a lit cigarette in his mouth. "I don't know how you manage to just sit in front of your screens, Sam."

"I'm used to it. Did you know that, laid end to end, a normal computer user will spend three months of his life staring at downloads. For a geek like me, you can multiply that by four or five. So yeah, I'm used to it. And by the way, it's forbidden to smoke in the office."

"That's funny, you never tell Coste that."

Sam was about to respond when the door was flung open by Matin, the Anti-Gang capitaine, visibly excited.

"They're calling. Do you have anything?"

Sam turned back to his computers. The mobile mast transmitted the information and the screen lit up.

"It's Marlon Brando, the organiser."

"We're off," Coste said.

In the adjoining office, the first ring on the mobile had caught the Sebags and the Parisian officers unawares. The ringtone was new to them: an imitation of an old-fashioned landline.

Matin had gone to warn Coste's team, while on the second ring, Tissier held the phone out to Marc Sebag, who took it with a trembling hand.

"Stay calm, Monsieur Sebag. We've rehearsed everything, it's going to be alright. Let them talk, and when you hesitate with your reply, look at me. You can do it. It's going to be fine."

At the third ring, Sandra Sebag went up to her husband and whispered that she loved him and that it was up to him to bring their son home. He took the call.

"Marc Sebag here."

"Are you alright? Did you sleep well? Don't you think you forgot something?"

The parents still had a faint hope this might all be a ridiculous joke. It seemed so improbable, something that "only happens to other people". But now, hearing this voice with its Paris suburbs accent, at once aggressive and yet amazingly measured, the threat became real, personal. It was all true, and it *was* happening to them.

"I'm sorry. It didn't occur to us to check what was on the mobile. That's why we missed the meeting. But I promise you we'll do everything you ask. How is David? Can I talk to him?"

"You're saying we give you a mobile and you don't look through it? Are you stupid or something?"

Sebag gave Tissier a black look and didn't reply. The kidnapper continued:

"You realise this is a conversation we shouldn't even be having?"

"I'm really sorry."

"You can apologise to your son's grave, moron. And tell yourself you were the one who pulled the trigger."

At this, even though she was sitting down, Sandra Sebag nearly passed out. Her husband was so distressed he almost dropped the mobile. Tissier waved his hands to encourage him. The kidnappers were merely showing their teeth, to make clear who was in charge.

Meanwhile, in Groupe Crime 1's office, Coste's whole team was focused on Sam's two screens. They heard the conversation start, the voices sounding slightly metallic.

I'm sorry. It didn't occur to us to check what was on the mobile . . . Marc Sebag was saying.

"O.K. Got it. Brando's mobile has just pinged a mast in Les Lilas, Seine-Saint-Denis."

You realise this is a conversation we shouldn't even be having . . .

Each of them was listening intently to see if the kidnapper's voice or attitude could help them in any way. An accent or intonation, the words used, the way he was conducting things, any background noise. Anything they picked up could be useful. Then another red dot appeared on the screen.

"Brando's on the move. He's just activated a new mast in

the twentieth arrondissement, towards Bagnolet. He's moving too quickly to be on foot."

The telephone conversation continued. They all frowned when it reached a critical point: *You can apologise to your son's grave . . .*

Sam was astonished how quickly Brando was moving.

"We have a problem: he's arrived at Vincennes in less than a minute."

No stranger to speedy journeys, Ronan studied the last red dot on the screen. Sam got up and went over to the map of Paris and Seine-Saint-Denis that took up half of one wall.

"From the twentieth arrondissement in the north-east of Paris to the Porte de Vincennes in one minute – that's impossible, unless he's going straight through buildings," said Sam.

"That's because he's not in the city. He's above it," Ronan concluded.

"In a plane?"

"Don't be an idiot. Not in a plane – he's on the Périphérique. Going round and round so he can't be traced."

"The bastard!"

In the adjoining office, the tension had risen another notch following the kidnapper's threats. What came next made the poor father even more anxious.

"Listen. You asked for eighty thousand. I can go as high as a hundred. Agreed? I already have the money for you. I just want to hear my son's voice."

"That's impossible. I'm not with him. You'll have to trust us."

Trust us. This was the second time that day Marc Sebag had heard those words, and the first hadn't turned out so well. The voice continued:

"But can I trust you?"

"Of course. I'll do whatever you ask."

"I hope it didn't occur to you to go to the police?"

"I swear I didn't."

This promise was followed by an icy silence, as if the kidnapper was weighing up its credibility.

"You understand the risk if you're lying?"

"I'm not lying."

"I just wanted to check. I'm going to trust you then. Stay smart. I'll call back in an hour."

He hung up. Frozen to the spot, Sebag kept the mobile pressed against his ear. His wife approached, gently took the phone, and wrapped her arms round her husband. He burst into tears.

"You did very well," Matin complimented him.

Tissier made sure his colleague was looking after the Sebags, left the office and rejoined Groupe Crime I.

"Well, Coste, you got anything?"

Coste looked up from the screens and gestured for him to come closer.

"No, nothing we can use. He's on the Périphérique, going round like the hands of a clock. But he'll have to call his men to tell them the operation is on again. That'll give us more opportunities."

"I'm not telling you how to do your job, but kidnappings are usually done by people well aware of their victims' financial means, so often they're close to them, or former employees."

"So you'd like Sebag to listen to their voices?"

"He didn't recognise the first one, but maybe we'd have more luck with the others."

"O.K. . . . Bring him in. Brando will have to contact his people again. Shouldn't be long."

As if the kidnappers had heard Coste's words, Brando's

mobile became active. Sam, who was in the front row, asked them all to pay attention.

"Alright, here we go. But it's not a call. Brando is sending a message."

He turned to the second screen and read the text out loud.

919 235 #1# LOC

"Some kind of code? Who's he sending it to?"

Sam pointed to the message on the screen. It wasn't for either Delon or Pacino. It had been sent to someone else. A fourth man on the team?

"What is all this crap?" Ronan exploded. "They're passing info under our noses and we don't understand a thing!"

Coste wouldn't allow himself to be deterred.

"Johanna, put the number into the directory. There's no harm trying."

They weren't given a moment's respite: the screen flashed once more. Sam explained what was going on.

"It's Brando again. This time it is a call. And it's to . . . Delon, who's still at the shopping centre."

"That makes sense," Coste said. "He's calling the receiver to tell him the ransom is on its way, and to stay where he is. Listen carefully and see if you can pick up anything useful."

Delon took the call, and the now familiar voice sounded harsher.

"O.K., where are you?"

"Millénaire, boss. Haven't budged an inch."

Delon had an accent from the Seine-Saint-Denis estates. He sounded younger. A minor? Interference. Sounds of a crowd.

"Alright, you can beat it, the deal's off," Brando ordered.

The police officers stared at one another in bewilderment.

"What's happened?"

"The son of a bitch is with the cops," said Brando.

"How do you know?"

"I can see it. He's not at Stains. His signal is coming from Rue de Carency in Bobigny, Police Judiciaire headquarters."

"Are they on to us?"

"No, we used burner phones, so they can't trace them. Just throw away the S.I.M. card and the battery and get out of there."

There was a click as he hung up. Stunned silence in the Groupe Crime office. Coste and Ronan were amateurs when it came to new technology, so they turned to their official expert.

"What just happened, Sam?"

"Hang on, give me a few seconds. I've lost track as well. We've traced Brando to the Périphérique, and yet he says he can see Sebag here. I don't get it."

Johanna had been asked to trace the unknown number that had received Brando's coded S.M.S. It had responded immediately. When she saw who it was, she alerted Coste.

"Brando sent an SMS to Arbarel, his service provider. But why would he want to get in touch with them in the middle of a kidnapping?"

Sam was mentally sifting all this information, trying to form a coherent picture. When everything made sense, it was like a slap in the face.

"Oh shit! If that's what they've done, they're really clever."

"Like to share it with us?" Johanna asked impatiently.

"You say he sent an S.M.S. to his service provider, and then seconds later he knows, from a distance, that the mobile they left for Sebag connects here and not at their home in Stains. That's easy. 'Find my Phone'. All providers offer that now."

He read the message again, now he understood it.

"919 must be his username, 235 his password, and #1#

LOC his inquiry. Basically, to be sure Sebag hasn't gone to the cops, Brando sends an S.M.S. saying he's lost his phone, and the service provider sends him a geo-location. We thought the mobile was just a means of communication between Sebag and the kidnappers, but it was a tracker we kindly brought in here. A Trojan Horse, and I didn't see it coming. We've been screwing them for fifteen years thanks to their phones, it's only fair they should use the same weapons against us. It was bound to happen some time."

"I'd have preferred not to be the first," Coste groaned. "This case is a nightmare."

Ronan's eye was caught by the right-hand screen, which warned there was another call. He tapped Sam on the shoulder, and he immediately refocused.

"Watch out! Another call. Brando again, and he's calling . . . Yes! He's calling Al Pacino."

"The one who's guarding David Sebag!" exclaimed Johanna. "It's our first chance to find out where he's being kept."

"And our last," Sam fretted, "because he's bound to tell him to dump the phone."

A click as the connection was made. Metallic voices again.

"Yes, it's me."

"Everything O.K.?"

A new voice. Almost adult. Stressed. Background impression of echoes and depth, like in a church.

"No, he's with the cops. Deal's off."

"Bastard."

"He's responsible for the consequences. We warned him."

"Yeah, I know, but I'm not so keen anymore."

"You'd better not let us down. You know what you have to do. We chose a Jew on purpose to get attention. If we let him go, no-one will take us seriously. We've no choice. We'll make dough on the next one. They won't dare go to the police. But if you don't follow through, you know what I'm capable of."

They could hear Pacino's ragged breathing. Brando didn't give him time to hesitate, barking out his orders.

"Dump the mobile and get out of there. But first, take him out."

These last words hung in the air in the Groupe Crime 1 office. David Sebag's life would be extinguished in the next few minutes, if it wasn't too late already. They had to act fast. Coste stood up and turned to his team, ready to give instructions, and found himself face to face with a haggard-looking Marc Sebag. David's father was standing petrified in the doorway. Like the others, he had heard the fatal words: "Take him out". Wild-eyed, unable to make sense of anything, he stared at the cops one by one. Whatever the outcome of this case, they would never forget his desperate, reproachful gaze. Marc Sebag's legs gave way, and he let his body slide gently down the wall until he was slumped on the floor. Commandant Tissier helped him back to his feet, linked arms with him, and led him out of the room. There would be time for excuses, to face the parents' anger or get a richly deserved punch in the face, but for the moment Coste pushed aside all these thoughts and focused once more on their last opportunity to find David.

"Sam, which mast did Pacino activate?"

"Mast 2347. It covers Rue Jacques-Samsey in Pantin."

"What is there on that street?"

Ronan sat at his computer, typed the address into Street View, and described what he could see.

"Not all that much. A four-storey block, Pantin town hall, a primary school and a public swimming pool."

"We can rule out the town hall, the primary school and the

pool; I can't see them keeping David Sebag in such busy places. That leaves the block of flats, but definitely not in one of the flats themselves, that wouldn't be safe enough. A neighbour could have seen them arrive or heard David's cries for help. Maybe in the basement?"

Sam was busy checking to see if any of the buildings on the street were closed, or if there were strikes or construction work going on: anything that could have opened the way for the kidnappers. On the town hall site, he found the opening hours for the public swimming baths, and what he read offered a glimmer of hope.

"The swimming baths! They've been shut for a year. They weren't used enough. The land is for sale. Do you remember when Pacino was talking? There was an echo, like he was in a big empty room."

"We need to decide right now," Ronan insisted. "Basement or swimming baths? Blue wire or red?"

Instinctively, the three of them turned to Coste. He allowed himself a moment's reflection, gazing one last time at David Sebag's face among the photographs on the white board.

"Sam and Ronan, you come with me to the swimming baths. That would be their best choice. Johanna, gather all available officers and search the block of flats. Break down the doors if necessary. We'll apologise later."

23

"How long will it take to get there?"

"It's fifteen minutes away," said Ronan, buckling his seat belt. "I can do it in six."

Coste picked up the radio, adjusted the frequency, and contacted Johanna, who was in the car right behind them.

"Johanna, we're going to step on it. You stay on our tail, O.K.? Ronan will clear the way."

"Fine by me. I won't lose you."

Everyone in the street turned to look as the police vehicles sped past, sirens wailing. Pedestrians jumped to one side and cyclists wisely put a foot on the ground.

As they neared their target, Johanna veered off left towards the block of flats and Ronan turned right. Outside the public baths, he swerved round on the handbrake and came to a halt parallel to the wire fence blocking access. Behind it, the old red-brick building was covered in protective netting to guard against falling masonry. It looked like an insect caught in a huge spider's web.

The three men hurled themselves out of the car and ran along the fence until they came to the entrance. The padlock had been sliced open and lay useless to one side.

"We're not the first."

Coste, Ronan and Sam slipped beyond the fence, passing in front of a dilapidated plastic sign announcing the start of renovation work on the site, the cost of the project, and the name of the company who should have carried it out two years earlier. They reached the nine steps up to the main entrance. The door had been forced as well. The lack of any security for a building where there was nothing to steal had made the kidnappers' job that much easier, and had probably led to them choosing it.

Although the building was long out of use, when they eased open the glass front door the three officers were met with a smell of chlorine and bleach that was probably encrusted forever in the walls and tiled floor. Their footsteps rang out in the deserted vestibule. All three had pulled out their guns and held them in front of them, pointing downwards. They went past reception and pushed open the swing doors that gave directly on to the pool. Above them were three levels of changing rooms and showers running all the way round the abandoned baths.

They stood motionless for five seconds, holding their breath, listening for the slightest sound. Coste took a few steps forward and peered down into the pool. Then he holstered his gun.

The outlet must have been clogged up with tissues, plasters and clumps of hair, because the water had not completely drained out. The hundreds of litres left in the pool formed a scummy dark red pond. In it floated a body face down, arms spread-eagled. Stunned, Ronan sat down on one of the starting blocks. Sam fell to his knees, still clutching his weapon.

Costa took off his jacket and laid his gun on it. He removed his bullet-proof vest and dropped his handcuffs to the floor. He descended the metal ladder to the dry part of the pool, headed towards the deep end and stepped into the filthy water. First up to his ankles, then his knees, finally to his waist. He grasped one of the lifeless hands and pulled the seemingly weightless body towards him. There was a bloody, viscous hole in the nape of the neck.

Sam's radio crackled, and Johanna's voice echoed off the walls.

"We've searched two thirds of the basement. Still nothing."

Sam looked at Coste half-submerged in the water, and pressed the answer button.

"You can stop your search."

Johanna knew her colleague well enough to realise that if David had been found alive, Sam would have given a different reply, in a different voice.

"Shit. O.K., we're on our way," she said in a subdued tone.

Reaching the dry end of the pool, Coste turned the body over. Despite the damage to the face, with the left cheek completely smashed, he recognised the youngster from the photographs pinned to their office whiteboard. One of him on the beach, the other at a university reception. David Sebag. Son of Marc and Sandra Sebag. Nineteen years old.

He sat down next to the dead boy and leaned back against the pool wall. Johanna and her team would arrive in a minute or two. By tacit agreement, the three cops decided to do nothing, simply remain there, together. Ronan on his block, Coste in the dry shallow end and Sam sitting on the edge, his legs dangling into the abandoned pool.

24

At half-past six that evening, Yassine Chelli parked his car in
Stains, in the middle of the Clos Saint-Lazare estate, one of the
most troubled in Seine-Saint-Denis. He used a cloth to meticu-
lously clean the steering wheel, gear stick, rear-view mirror, the
entire surface of the dashboard, and even the wires from the
starter that were hanging loose and that he'd used to steal the
vehicle that morning to constantly loop round the Périphérique.
No trace of fingerprints.

A youngster in a tracksuit pedalled several times round the
car on his bike. He soon recognised Yassine, greeted him, and
sped off towards the group of hooded dealers who had been
worried by Yassine's presence.

On the passenger seat lay the three mobiles for Brando,
Pacino and Delon, which he was to get rid of as quickly as
possible, either by destroying them or by selling them at a flea
market. Snatching them up, he checked the interior of the car
one last time to make sure he hadn't forgotten anything. Then
he took a fire extinguisher from the boot, pulled the pin out
and emptied the contents over the seats, door handles, head
rests and floor mats. The interior looked like a snowstorm.
Goodbye D.N.A.

Slipping the mobiles into his backpack, he slung it over his
shoulder and walked to his tower block several streets away.

The iron shutters pulled down on the shops he passed gave the impression these were the dog days of summer; life on the estate could be read in Braille from the tower block windows, splintered by stray bullets. Eleven dead that year from accounts settled by sub-machine gun in broad daylight. An amorphous municipality and a weary police force continually blaming one another in the second poorest area in Seine-Saint-Denis, ten minutes from the city of Paris. The local public security director had even admitted how powerless he was in a T.V. interview he must still be regretting: "Why don't the police stop the drug trafficking? Why don't the police stop the crimes? And why does the world keep on turning?" Cringeworthy.

A place people left at the first opportunity, without looking back, with no sense of nostalgia, like a village hit by fallout after a nuclear disaster. Those unable to escape were imprisoned, shutting themselves away, withering, slowly dying.

A place where the success of someone like Marc Sebag did not go unnoticed.

Yassine arrived at the foot of his tower block. He pushed open the smashed front entrance with his foot, skirted the open doors of the broken lift, and walked up four floors, stepping round the abandoned, torn apart rubbish bins. Even before he opened the front door to his flat, he could smell his mother's cooking.

A quick shower and he sat down at the table. His father, a construction worker, had spent years removing asbestos from Parisian universities; then it was the doctors' turn to try to purge the asbestos from his lungs – unsuccessfully, in this case. Now Yassine's family consisted of his mother Souila and his twelve-year-old brother Saïd. At the age of twenty-two, Yassine was the man of the family. With no qualifications, he did the best he could to keep their heads above water.

Souila filled their plates with *chorba* soup, and it was only as Yassine was sitting down that he noticed his brother's gloomy expression and saw on the table beside him the correspondence notebook from Pablo Neruda school.

"What's the matter?"

Souila was only waiting for an excuse to launch into recriminations.

"Go on, Saïd. Tell your brother. Tell him what you've done. Tell him your teacher is sending you to the school's prison."

"What's this nonsense?" Yassine growled.

"No, it's not that," Saïd said. "I've been given three hours' detention on Saturday."

"What did you do?"

"I arrived late. I couldn't help it – I have to walk to school. The bus doesn't come anymore: the driver was attacked two day ago, so now they're on strike. It's not my fault."

"Is that all? Is that why you have to stay behind?"

Souila glared at her younger son in such a way that he no longer dared to embroider the truth.

"Someone called me when I was in class, and I didn't have my mobile on vibrate. I got thrown out."

Like a racing car, Yassine went from zero to a hundred in seconds. Grabbing Saïd by the hair, he pinned his head back and thrust his face at him.

"What is it with you? How do you think you're going to get on without school? Do you want to end up like the little rats from round here, selling shit to Parisians? Haven't you got it through your head that school's the only way you're going to escape from here? If I have a problem, who's going to look after Maman?"

"Go easy, Yassine, let go of him, that's enough," said Souila, trying to protect her little one.

Yassine felt a fool threatening his brother, who – teeth gritted and eyes brimming with tears he wouldn't let fall – held his angry gaze. He had flung himself at Saïd and vented his own fears and frustrations. Embarrassed, he let his brother go.

"Forgive me, Saïd. But you have to understand that I'm done for. All I do is mess up. It's you Maman and I are counting on."

"I know," the boy whispered.

"Give me your mobile."

"Oh please, not that . . . *pleeze*, not my phone."

Seeing his brother's hand reach out across the table, Saïd stood up, rushed into his room and came back with his mobile. Taking it from him, Yassine looked the family's hope up and down.

"I'll drive you to school tomorrow. This time you won't arrive late."

"Have you got a car?"

"Don't worry. I'll find one."

25

Damiani searched through one of the boxes strewn around her office. Among all the mementoes of a lifelong police career, she found an old brown bottle with a torn label. A vintage cognac she had never given herself permission to open.

"That's not going to make us any sharper," said Coste.

"That's not the intention."

After midnight, the Police Judiciaire offices were deserted, the gloomy passageways lit only by emergency exit signs. Judging there was no longer any real urgency, Coste had sent his team home. The only sound in the building came from the hum of the photocopiers and computers. Every now and then, a telephone rang in an office, persisted for a while, then fell silent.

"What about forensics?' asked Damiani.

"They've gone over the swimming pool with a fine-toothed comb. For fingerprints and D.N.A. They'll examine the mobile tomorrow morning. With a bit of luck there'll be some trace on the battery or S.I.M. card. Besides that, the bullet was found in a corner of the pool. Completely crushed, so it's no use for ballistic testing: we'll never trace it back to the weapon that fired it."

"What about our American movie stars?"

"They dumped the phones. No chance of geo-locating them, all the intercepts have gone silent. They've vanished and we have no leads."

Coste emptied his glass. The slightly sweet cognac scorched his throat.

"I didn't run into the parents when I got back. I thought I was going to get it in the neck."

"They went straight to the morgue. I told them there was no point, but they wanted to be close to their son. I can understand that."

Coste thought of Léa Marquant, forensic pathologist at the Institut Médico-Légal, who must have received the body that afternoon. He hadn't seen her in months, and both hoped and feared she had found herself the man she deserved. Someone better than him at any rate.

"I'm going to take a few days off, Marie-Charlotte."

"And leave your team in the midst of an investigation?"

"We'll catch them. They're bound to slip up, they always do. It's just a matter of time. You don't need me: Ronan can take over. He'll soon be promoted to capitaine, so he needs to learn how to lead a group."

"Do you trust him?"

"Yes, and so do you. I know you like him. Even if he gets wound up occasionally. If he's heading up the team, he'll restrain himself."

"Alright, but before you go, could you supervise the autopsy tomorrow morning?"

"No, I really couldn't."

"You established a good relationship with the parents, and I'm sure they'll be at the Institut. They need to know we're still on the case, that we're not dropping it."

"For the moment, I don't think they give a damn. Hatred and the need for revenge take time to surface."

Damiani surveyed her subordinate. Forty well-spent years, reassuring salt-and pepper-hair, an officer she could rely on, a man whose decisions she respected even if they weren't always strictly by the book. And yet he seemed absent, as though detached from everything. She could distinguish between being weary and being burnt-out, and she was concerned at what she saw.

"You'll take a few days off and then return?"

"I'll take a few days off."

This laconic reply didn't exactly fill her with confidence.

"I'll be gone by the end of the week, Victor. The Groupes Crime need someone to take over until my replacement is announced. As you can imagine, I'm not going to ask Jevric to fill in. With her diplomatic skills, she risks blowing the place sky high. Stay."

"For how long?"

"A week, ten days max."

Coste raised an inquisitive eyebrow.

"You mean I'll not only lead my group but I'll also be in charge of Jevric's? Do you know how much she's going to hate that?"

"You see, Victor, you're having fun already."

Midnight. The intercom rang. A silhouette Ronan recognised appeared on the screen, and he pressed the button. Leaving the front door to his apartment ajar, he returned to the living room. Fleur Saint-Croix closed the door behind her and dropped her coat on the white sofa. She sat a metre away from him, not yet sure of the welcome she would receive. A young examining magistrate, parachuted into Seine-Saint-Denis at the age of twenty-five, she had had problems at first and some friction with Coste's group, until she'd realised she would never learn as quickly as with Ronan. The violence she encountered in her job soon put paid to her slightly immature, priggish attitude.

Pushing a blonde curl behind her ear, she lit one of Ronan's cigarettes and kicked off her high heels.

"Is Coste angry with me?"

"No, he knows you're part of a hierarchy too."

"How do you feel?"

"As well as could be expected. Coste always tell us 'they're not your loved ones, it's not your grief', but in this case I find that hard to swallow."

"Can I stay the night?" Fleur asked tentatively.

Ronan was taken aback. Normally in their relationship the decisions weren't his to make.

"If you sleep here, you won't be able to send me packing in the middle of the night. You'll have to see me at breakfast."

"Stop it. I just want to be with you."

Ronan stole the cigarette from her. Part of him was still sitting on the edge of an abandoned swimming pool. Fleur Saint-Croix came closer and ran her fingers through his hair.

"We don't have to fuck, you know."

"Being crude doesn't come as naturally to you as it does to me, but I'm delighted to know that's not all you want me for," Ronan said.

Johanna De Ritter's husband Karl pushed open the door to his daughter Chloe's bedroom as gently as possible. He skirted the bed, sat down on the carpet, stretched out his arm and laid his hand affectionately on a shoulder.

"Jo?"

Johanna opened her eyes with a start, as if caught out. She had wrapped her arms round her daughter to protect her from bad dreams.

"You went to tuck Chloe in and fell asleep."

"Shit, I'm sorry. What time is it?" she stammered, not yet fully awake.

"A little before one in the morning. You've still got your gun in your belt."

Johanna stood up and sat on the edge of the bed. Karl held out his hand.

"Give it here, I'll put it away."

Without watching what her hands were doing, Johanna took her firearm and handed it to him. She kissed him on the mouth and whispered that she was going to bed. Karl went downstairs to the living room and, as calmly and professionally as any policeman, took out the magazine, pulled back the breech to eject the last cartridge, and put everything back on the top shelf of the cupboard. There were two other guns in their holsters besides Johanna's service revolver. Competition weapons, one of which had allowed her to carry off first place in the prestigious police marksmanship championship.

At one metre eighty-five and with certain Viking traits, Karl De Ritter himself could have joined any police force. And he was always keen to leave aside his profession as a civil engineer and join Johanna on the shooting rage, firing off rounds at the paper targets.

"Are you coming?" Johanna asked impatiently from upstairs.

Karl double-locked the cupboard and hid the key on top of it.

"Coming."

He climbed the stairs and went past Malo and Chloe's open doors. He listened to make sure they were asleep and switched off all the lights on the way to his bedroom. Johanna's silhouette was visible by the faint light from a bedside table lamp.

"Are you tired?" she asked.

"No."

She got up, stood in front of him, and looked at him as if for the first time.

"Undress me then."

*

Sam's three-room flat was in semi-darkness, lit only by an anglepoise lamp on his desk. Not so much a desk as a work bench. The bulb cast Sam's slender shadow onto the right-hand wall. He was bent over a tangle of electrical and mechanical parts.

Picking up a S.I.M. card, he studied it under his magnifying glass, muttered to himself, and tossed it to the far end of the table. On his computer screen, he again checked the instructions he had found on the internet to help him build a G.P.S. tracker – if he could only find the parts he needed in all this mess.

Being a godfather made him feel more responsible. Well, responsible for someone else. Given the dramatic conclusion to their kidnapping case, he wanted to give Malo a small device that would always pinpoint where he was, even if the idea did smack of "Big Brother". Of course, he could have bought one for eighty euros from Montgallet in the twelfth arrondissement, but making it himself was far more interesting.

Working long into the night, he assembled a 3G G.P.S. module with a S.I.M. card on a mini-controller transmitter the size of a sugar cube, powered by a small lithium-ion battery. Once the S.I.M. card was activated, all that would be required to locate his godson was to send an S.M.S.

When he had soldered everything together, he put the device into a container the size of a matchbox. Malo would be able to fit it into his jacket pocket or school satchel easily. All he had to do now was persuade Johanna to allow her son to be tracked like a stolen vehicle.

He picked the remains of a joint out of the ashtray, took three puffs before burning his fingers, and stubbed it out. He'd promised to give it up. Just as he'd promised to give up video games. Promised who, anyway? Sam lived alone and didn't regard that as a hardship. He enjoyed his solitude. Or he'd grown used to it.

His neurons slightly dulled, he stretched out on the sofa, with the T.V. on mute. It was showing a series about cops who had yet again managed in less than three quarters of an hour to put a stop to a serial killer's mad rampage across the United States. He switched the set off, leaving the sounds of the city as background noise. A shout in the distance. A car engine racing. The squeal of tyres. A shop alarm going off. Another problem for other cops.

26

Paris Institut Médico-Légal Institute
8.00 a.m.

In the morgue, the body was lifted out of its refrigerated cab-
inet, placed on a trolley and taken upstairs in a lift. Wheels
squeaking, it went down a passage, turned into the X-ray room
and was pushed round under an X-ray machine. When the
photo-sensitive plate was at the correct angle, the technician
took images of the front and side of the skull. Whenever there
was a bullet wound, a search had to be made for the projectile or
for any metal splinters left behind. The completed X-rays were
slipped inside the folder and the body was sent on another trip,
this time to the autopsy room where Doctor Léa Marquant had
already been waiting for several minutes.

Once the assistant had left, she pulled back the white sheet
covering the body and walked round it. For the moment, the
aluminium table, the face visor, protective gown and the different tools that cut, crushed or sawed were all spotless. In less
than an hour they would be covered in blood, as if a haemo-
globin grenade had exploded in a closed box.

Léa read the folder accompanying the corpse. David Sebag.
Premeditated homicide by firearm. Relevant police service:
Seine-Saint-Denis Police Judiciaire. The X-rays showed no
extraneous material. A bullet to the head. Very effective.

The intercom crackled and told her the Police Judiciaire officer had arrived. Léa went down the corridor and when she arrived at the building's entrance she recognised him, even from the back. As she walked along, she adjusted her auburn hair in its tight ponytail, looked at her reflection in a window – and immediately scolded herself for her reaction. When she reached the newcomer, she deliberately spoke in a flat, distant tone.

"So you remembered the way? I'd got used to working with Ronan."

"Good morning, Léa," he replied, turning round.

"Hello there, Victor. Follow me, will you? I've got a heavy workload today and I can't spare you much time."

Considering his attitude in recent months, he could hardly have expected a warmer welcome. Her actions matching her words, Léa set off two paces ahead of him. He followed her, unable to see the little smile of satisfaction on the pathologist's face.

Like two dancers meeting up again and instinctively following the familiar steps, Coste and Léa immediately took up their positions in the clinically white room where they had seduced one another professionally before getting to know one another far more intimately.

Léa exchanged her slender oblong glasses for a pair of protective goggles and pulled on a pair of reinforced latex gloves. She removed the sheet to reveal the naked body, its skin grey, arms and legs rigid. Part of the left cheekbone and cheek were missing, like pieces removed from a puzzle. Coste knew the ritual, and the two of them stood still and silent for a few seconds above the young man's body. A final token of respect before cutting him open from neck to groin.

"Have the parents been here?"

"Yes. They stayed all day yesterday, wandering around the corridors."

"Did they see the body?"

"No, I refused. First I'll do the autopsy, then I'll sew him up again. I also need to find a bandage big enough to cover what's missing from the face. It's an image that will stay with them for the rest of their lives, so I prefer it to shock them as little as possible."

Léa picked up a scalpel from the instrument table next to her. Reflecting the white neon light, its blade winked at them.

"As for this one, I can give you my conclusions already. Entry point the nape of the neck from point-blank range. The bullet went through the skull and exited, taking everything inside with it. What with the shock of the explosion and the bullet's trajectory, the brain must have been instantly shattered. Cause of death, a bullet to the back of the neck. Your kid probably didn't even know what hit him. He was simply unplugged."

Léa was a forensic pathologist. Bodies were her raw material. Her apparent lack of sensitivity and plain-speaking were nothing more than a way to help her forget their humanity. Coste knew this and he had never been upset by it. Today though, with David Sebag, it was different.

Léa could see he was troubled and studied him closely for the first time that morning. Coste looked as if he had spent the night on a park bench. His face was as frayed as his suit, his three-day stubble suggested there were three more to add to them, and there was a faint smell of alcohol on his breath. His blue eyes and expression were sadder than ever.

"You look in about as good a shape as my clients, Victor. Is there something I should know? All I have is 'premeditated homicide' on my file."

Coste raised his eyes from the corpse and consulted his watch.

"Exactly twenty-six hours ago, his father came to see us to

123

report his son as kidnapped. I told him to trust me, we messed up, and you have the result in front of you. A kid who has to be covered in bandages to be shown to his parents. All for eighty thousand euros."

This astonished Léa. She put the scalpel down and pushed the goggles up to rest on her forehead.

"I don't get it. Lara Jevric, your colleague from Groupe Crime 2, is bringing in another case in less than an hour. Some guy shot his neighbour with a hunting rifle over some stolen mail. That's nowhere near eighty thousand euros. You know very well that in Seine-Saint-Denis death has no price tag. Since when did you start to take things personally? What happened to all your good advice? To take three steps back? Not to contaminate an investigation with your own feelings? You're acting as if you were a new recruit."

"Unfortunately, I've been doing it for almost fifteen years, and I'm starting to get tired. I imagine that after scraping up fifty or so corpses a year, one day you get to saturation point. Alright, so their faces are different, and so are the clothes they wear and the motives that led to their deaths, but when it comes down to it, it's the same old rigmarole."

"You always got too close to the victims, but up to now you knew how to leave that behind in the office."

"There's no room anymore. It's spilling out. I get residual images, like when you drive on the motorway all night and you still see the white line flashing by hours later. I have the same feeling now. When I talk to someone, whether they're a stranger or someone close to me, my mind strays and I end up imagining what they'll be like afterwards. Their withered skin, their waxy, almost oily complexion, their taut features, the veil that death draws over their eyes. It's involuntary. It just happens."

"Yes, I know what you mean. It's a lot to deal with. Do you want to take five minutes for a coffee?"

"No, thanks. I want to be done with this."

Léa had thought she would make him pay a little more dearly for ending their relationship, but now that impulse had evaporated. She laid the tip of the scalpel on the boy's skin, then effortlessly slit the body open before cutting deeper into the muscles.

An hour later and they were outside in the fresh air, sitting on the steps at the entrance to the Institut, coffee in one hand, cigarette in the other. This too was part of their shared ritual.

"I'll email you my preliminary conclusions this afternoon."

Coste tossed the remains of his cigarette into the remains of his coffee.

"Send them to Ronan instead. I'm going to the country for a few days."

"A few days without T.V. or radio, far from the storm. That's all I ever used to ask of you."

There was nothing Coste could say to that, no attenuating excuses. He simply had no idea how to live as a couple.

"Which station are you leaving from?"

"I'm going in that," he said, pointing to a battered wreck in the Institut car park, a black Ford Taunus parked at an angle.

"Christ, that's ugly. You have a car in Paris? I didn't think there was any point."

"It's my father's. He wanted to get rid of it, but I didn't have the heart. We used to take it on holiday when I was ten. I'm sure you can still find grains of sand from Vieux-Boucau between the seats."

Léa was about to add a sarcastic comment when her eyes darted behind Coste. Her mood changed instantly.

"Victor . . . his parents."

Victor turned his head, put his coffee cup down on a step, rose to his feet and smoothed down his trousers as if he were on parade. The Sebags came level with him and Coste took a step forward, preparing to greet them and assume responsibility for whatever followed. Marc and Sandra Sebag walked on by without any gesture or look of recognition. They pushed open the wooden double doors to the Institut and disappeared inside. Victor stood stock still, dazed. Léa reacted angrily:

"Shit, it's too easy for them to lay all their grief at your door. I can understand them, I feel for them. But it's too easy."

"So who should they blame?"

"I don't know. They guy who pulled the trigger, for example?"

"He's still faceless. For now, mine suits them just fine."

Léa went with him to his Ford. He threw his rolled-up jacket into it, and she fished with feigned innocence:

"Are you leaving straightaway, or do you have to pick up . . . a passenger?"

"I'm leaving right now. On my own. How about you? Are you seeing someone?"

"That's none of your business," she replied coyly, pleased by his interest.

27

Ronan threw his helmet and biker's leathers onto Groupe Crime 1's sofa. He had arrived early at eight o'clock sharp, only to find he was the last one in and had a coffee waiting for him. Johanna and Sam were concentrating on typing up their statements about the previous day's events; seeing them, he realised that getting down to work was the last thing he wanted to do. He went over to Sam's two computers – one for listening in, the other for geo-locating.

"Did any of them use the phones overnight?" he asked no-one in particular.

"No, nothing. I get the impression we'll never see them again. We have to ask Coste if he wants us to wind up the surveillance."

"Where is he anyway?"

"Not back from the autopsy yet."

"He's been landed with it?"

"Apparently. It was agreed with Damiani."

"I don't feel like doing anything this morning," Ronan said. "It's all too much." He collapsed on the sofa.

"Did you two get any sleep last night?" asked Johanna.

The two men glanced at each other and, slightly embarrassed, shook their heads.

"We just have to hope the boss has enough juice to get us all going," said Ronan, trying to convince himself.

At that moment, Marie-Charlotte Damiani flung open the door, a file under her arm.

"Ronan, Victor is taking a few days off. You're in charge of the group. Don't do anything stupid, I'm keeping my eye on you. Get to it."

The order reverberated round the office as loudly as the door Damiani slammed as she left. There was a moment's stunned silence. Sam and Johanna smiled broadly at Ronan. His usual self-assurance had vanished; he was close to panicking.

"Shit, I hate it when Coste does that."

"If you think for a second I'm going to call you boss, you can forget it," said Sam.

"So there's a new sheriff in town," Johanna quipped.

"Thanks a lot. I can tell you trust me, and that's a big help. Plastic friends and cardboard colleagues: I don't know which recycling bin to throw you in."

Sam buried the hatchet and returned to their investigation.

"O.K., so do we suspend the surveillance or not?"

"Give me thirty seconds, if you don't mind. I'm going down to admin to see what's new. I'll be right back."

Ronan got up from the sofa and left them to their statements. He made his way quickly past the administration office and headed for the toilets. He opened the cubicle doors to make sure he was alone, stood in front of the big mirror, and splashed some water on his face to clear his head. Coste had left him at the controls for the next few days, and the responsibility this brought intimidated even a big thirty-five-year-old kid like Lieutenant Ronan Scaglia.

When he opened their office door again, there was no mistaking his attitude. No more fatigue, still less any desire to nap on the sofa.

"So, what about the surveillance?" insisted Sam.

"Keep it a day longer."

"I really don't see the point."

"Is this your father's bar? Are you the one paying? No. So stop pissing me off."

Sam and Johanna exchanged smiles. They could see that Ronan was taking his role seriously. What came next confirmed it.

"Alright, if there's nothing new, we'll go over what we have. We'll listen to David Sebag's friends again. Watch the tapes from the nightclub and Le Millénaire shopping centre. Push forensics on the results of their findings. And I want a list of all the employees of Marc Sebag's businesses, past and present. Bring in Kumar, the owner of the mobile phone shop, and show him the photo file until he goes blind or spurts blood from his eyes. I want a lead before Papa gets home, got it?"

"You see, your balls were there all the time," Johanna teased him.

28

Saïd was accustomed to promises that were never kept. "I'll drive you there", "We'll do this", "I'll teach you that" . . . So many empty memories . . . A useless big brother whose absence would make no difference to his life. Even so, at eight o'clock that morning he tried several times to wake Yassine. All he received was a grunt and a few insults. So much for the lift to school he'd been promised the previous evening.

About to leave his brother's bedroom following a final refusal, Saïd passed his desk – an incongruous piece of furniture that Yassine had rarely used for study. Among a jumble of overflowing ashtrays, gamepads, counterfeit brand glasses and watches, there were four mobile phones. In the semi-darkness, with the blinds three-quarters down, Saïd checked them all, but none was his. That meant a day without a phone, with no possibility of calling or being called. Apparently, that was how things used to be, back in his parents' day. Unless he took . . .

In the Groupe Crime 1 office, the morning had sped by, giving way to a sunny afternoon. "Nothing more pointless than a sunny day in the suburbs," Johanna said to herself. "It merely reminds you that the beach or the mountains aren't there for you to enjoy, just concrete buildings that warm up uselessly."

The C.C.T.V. footage from the nightclub and the shopping

centre had been analysed second by second, but no suspect had been identified. There were just a few loose ends to tie up. And a few hours to go before their day was done. Sam stood up to stretch his arms and legs. He tilted his head left and right to crack his neck vertebrae. Johanna recognised this tic.

"Oh, so you're the one Malo gets that lousy habit from . . . He does it all the time. Funny how he imitates you."

Malo . . . Sam suddenly remembered the device he had spent the night assembling. He searched in his pockets and then in the backpack at his feet. Taking out the G.P.S. tracker in its box, he placed it on Johanna's desk.

"A plastic box," she said. "Sam, you shouldn't have. I'm touched."

"It's a tracker. For Malo. If you slip it into his coat, I'll know where he is at all times."

"Er . . . thanks . . ."

Ronan butted in.

"I can't decide if that's a perfectly normal idea or a seriously worrying one."

"Yeah, I know. I asked myself the same question while I was making it. But I was thinking about David Sebag. When we couldn't locate him, I had these weird ideas about surveillance and tracking people. Listen, do what you want with it."

Johanna picked up the box and slipped it into one of her pockets.

"You're a sweetheart. I'll talk to Karl about it. Can you tell me how it works?"

Sam came over to show her what to do. As he was passing in front of the computer screens, his eye caught one of them flashing. He turned up the volume, muted the previous evening.

"Is this a joke?"

"What?" asked Ronan.

"It's Brando's line. It's been activated. He's using the mobile again."

The three of them focused their attention on the screens. Clicks as the phone connected. New voices. Maximum concentration.

"Yeah, who's this?"

"It's Saïd."

"This isn't your number."

"I know. My big brother took mine, but I removed the S.I.M. card. I nicked one of his. Weren't you in class?"

"Nah, I'm ill."

"Is it catching?"

"No, I'm not really sick. It's cool, you can come over if you like, I'm on my own. I've got the console to myself."

"O.K., I'll be there."

The call ended. It had been a mine of unexpected information, and yet despite this stroke of luck Ronan hesitated.

"Aren't families great? Thanks, little brother," said Johanna.

"Do you want us to ring Coste?" asked Sam.

"Fuck you."

"What then?"

Ronan snapped out of it.

"Which mast did the call ping?"

Sam pointed on the screen to Mast 2231 and the three streets it covered. By now, Ronan was back in full control. He barked his orders.

"Find out which school covers that patch and get down there with Johanna and make a list of all the Saïds. Get me their full details and we'll target those with a big brother. After that, we'll pull on the line and see what's on the other end."

"If we identify him, should we bring him in tomorrow morning?" asked Johanna.

"No, for the moment we only have one of them. If we arrest him the other two will vanish off our radar and we risk losing them. Everything clear?"

"We're on our way, boss," the other two replied with one voice.

Boss. That sounded good. Ronan decided not to call Coste, but to let him have at least twenty-four hours' rest, just to show he didn't need a chaperone.

29

Night was falling by the time the ancient Ford left the main road, passed through a village and then followed a dirt track that led to the brow of a hill. On the hillside, several kilometres from any neighbours, stood an old converted barn surrounded by massive trees.

The car crunched across the gravel, startling a deer that Coste caught only a fleeting glimpse of as it glided away into the wood. He parked outside the windows of the kitchen, the only room with lights on. As he switched off his headlights, the outside light came on. An old man with a shock of white hair appeared, wearing a pullover and corduroy trousers.

"You could have warned me."

"I changed my mind en route. I didn't really know I was going to end up here."

The old man stared in astonishment at the car.

"So you didn't get rid of it?"

"Who knew?"

He slammed the car door shut and the two men kissed each other briefly on both cheeks.

"Good evening, Papa."

"Good evening, Victor."

*

Monsieur Coste unwrapped a gingham tea towel protecting a barely touched rustic loaf. He placed a plate of cheese and charcuterie in front of his son and poured some wine into glasses that didn't match.

"So the deer are back?" said Victor.

"Yes. They're lovely, but they eat all my flower buds. Still, there's no way I'm going to shoot them."

"No, you mustn't."

Victor's eyes darted round the room, searching for something that was missing.

"Wasn't there a photo of Maman on the windowsill?"

"Yes. It's in my bedroom now."

"It's time you two got closer."

"Don't start, please."

It only took a couple of spiteful remarks or a clumsy comment for Victor and his father to turn the house upside down and set it on fire. Monsieur Coste decided the furniture should stay where it was and didn't fan the flames.

"How are you?"

"Fine," his son said evasively.

"Obviously. Why else would you drive five hundred kilometres and show up without warning. How's Léa?"

"I only ever told you about her once. I'm surprised you even remembered her name."

Monsieur Coste clutched the loaf to his chest and cut a slice.

"Because she's the only one you ever told me about."

"It lasted five months. We're not together anymore."

"Cretin," his father sighed.

"Oh yes, you think so?"

"You don't escape being lonely so easily when you're my age. And you haven't got that long to go."

"Listen, for the moment it suits me well enough."

"Obviously. When you're on your own, you're not responsible for anything. Unhappiness or happiness."

"Why? Do you know that many happy relationships?"

"Of course, you police are experts at knowing how rotten the world is. Leave the rest of us a bit of hope; who knows, we might have some to spare for you."

Monsieur Coste picked up the bottle of wine, but Victor put his hand over his glass as a sign he didn't want any more.

"Can I use my bedroom?"

"It's always ready for you."

"Shall I see you tomorrow?"

The old man nodded. Victor picked up his jacket and stood up. As he passed behind his father, he put his arms round him, feeling the wrinkled skin on the backs of his hands.

30

At eight the next morning, force of habit woke Monsieur Coste. The house was silent. He filled his old Italian coffee pot, ignoring the capsule coffee machine his son had given him the year before. On the table behind him, Victor's mobile was vibrating, shuffling forward a few millimetres among the breadcrumbs with each ring. Curious, he looked to see who the call was from: *Ronan, Police Judiciaire.*

An hour later, the mobile began its dance again, and the same an hour after that. Four hours later, Monsieur Coste knocked gently on his son's door and went in.

"The police have found you, poor lad."

"How often did they call?" Victor mumbled, sitting up in bed.

"Four times."

"I'll have a shower and be right with you."

After twenty minutes under a scalding hot shower, Victor gulped down a strong black coffee that left him wide awake.

"You see what a good cup the machine I gave you makes," he said proudly.

"Yes. I wouldn't be without it now. I'm going down to the village: is there anything special you'd like to eat?"

The mobile began to ring again on the table, and Victor picked it up, leaving his father's question floating in mid-air.

Monsieur Coste left his son to his own business – he'd never been particularly interested in it anyway. A flood of words in an over-excited voice poured from the phone.

"Calm down, Ronan. I've only just got up."

"Sorry. I was saying we've located one of the guys in the gang."

"That was quick. How did you do it?"

"Brando's line was re-activated yesterday afternoon. It was traced to the Pablo Neruda school in Stains. And the kid even dropped his first name: Saïd."

"A schoolkid? That's a bit young to organise a kidnapping, even in Seine-Saint-Denis. Have you followed the lead?"

"Yes. There are three Saïds in the school. One has a younger brother, the second only has sisters, and the third has an older brother. He seems the likely candidate."

"I'm listening."

"Yassine Chelli. Twenty-two years old, twenty-six offences to his name. A month in Marveil prison for extortion. Three months in Fleury-Mérogis for burglary. Robbery and violence fit the bill exactly."

"One out of three. We have to identify the others before we bring them all in. Otherwise we'll scare them off."

"That's what we thought. Look, I don't know where you've hidden yourself, but if you want to come back, I wouldn't mind in the slightest."

"It's true, I've had twenty-four hours' rest. That's a bit much, isn't it?"

"That's not what I meant. It's just that . . ."

Coste cut him short.

"I was teasing, my little lamb. You've done a great job. I'll be there in four hours."

"Do you know how to reel in the others?"

"I've got an idea, but you'll have to prepare a few things for me."

Monsieur Coste laid two brown paper bags on the kitchen table. His jacket potatoes had comforted Victor when he was little, and though he'd forgotten how to prepare them, this seemed like a good occasion to relearn. Monsieur Coste had devoted his entire life to his profession and had had little time for anything else, always replying "tomorrow" when anyone asked him about today.

Time was something he had plenty of now – it was Victor who found it in short supply. As the years went by, the son had turned into the father.

Monsieur Coste emptied the contents of the two bags and called out:

"Victor?"

His bedroom was empty, and the old Ford had gone. There was a scribbled note on the windowsill where his mother's photograph had once stood. Monsieur Coste unfolded it, read it, and smiled sadly.

His son really had become just like him.

31

Following three weeks of stakeouts and tailing, Groupe Stups had that morning seized two hundred kilos of a new genetically modified cannabis that had been selling like gold dust. There hadn't been enough room in the department's safes, so an office had been commandeered to hold the rest. Ever since, an enticing smell of peppery chlorophyll had been wafting around the building. A further problem had arisen when the Groupe Stups had learned from various wiretaps that certain criminals were already discussing how they could recover the booty when it was being taken for incineration. As a result, police headquarters had been turned into a bunker, with four armed men at each entrance, submachine guns and pump-action shotguns at the ready.

Coste drove into the garage and was immediately stopped by one of the policemen on duty. Lowering his car window, he greeted the man.

"Oh shit . . . Is this car yours, capitaine?" the uniform apologised. "It's so beat up I almost opened fire on you."

"I keep it for sentimental reasons. That excuses any lapse in taste. What's going on?"

"Groupe Stups have brought in a haul. A new drug. That's all I know."

"Okay. So will you let me through, or do I have to run you over?"

Coste parked his car in the underground garage, lit in poor patriotic taste by blue, white and red neon strips, and bounded into the lift.

When he pushed open the door to Groupe Crime 1, he found everybody there. No-one had been brave enough to take David Sebag's photos off the whiteboard. The young man appeared to be watching them, reminding them they had a job to finish, and scum to deal with. Alongside the photos of the victim was a black-and-white shot of Yassine Chelli, the team's prime suspect.

"Afternoon, Victor. You look rested. Your little holiday seems to have done you good," Sam joked. "Where did you go?"

"To say hello to someone I hadn't seen in a long while."

"Want to tell us more?"

Coste threw his jacket on the arm of the long red sofa.

"Not especially. Did you make the enquiries I asked you to?"

"Yes, we've just finished. The photo album is on your desk. There are seventeen candidates, together with C.D. recordings of their interviews. But unless you identify them by intuition, I don't really know how you're going to do it."

"I'm going to make them talk."

"All seventeen? We'll be here all night."

"Don't worry, it'll be much faster than you think. What time is it?"

"Twenty-five past four."

"It shouldn't be long now."

The young man who presented himself at Seine-Saint-Denis police headquarters went to the front of the queue despite the grumbled complaints of all those who felt they had been waiting patiently for far too long. Laying his black case on the ground, he rummaged in the inside pocket of his hoodie and pulled out a card striped with the French national colours.

"Good morning. Julien Degrève, from S.C.I.T.T.* Groupe Crime 1 is expecting me."

Embarrassed, the desk duty officer asked him to repeat himself.

"S.C.I. . . . what?"

"Don't worry, forget it. Nobody knows what it means. Capitaine Coste is expecting me."

He was escorted upstairs and along corridors until he got to Groupe Crime 1's open door. Seeing him, Coste rose from the sofa.

"Morning, Julien."

"Hi there, capitaine. Nice smell in here. Do you grow your own weed?"

Turning to his team, Coste made the introductions.

"This is Julien Degrève, from S.C.I.T.T. . . ."

Sam leaped up, hand extended and smiling broadly. At last he was meeting a colleague on his own level, someone with similar interests, from a leading unit he had long been envious of.

"S.C.I.T.T.? No way! Have you come all this way from Lyons?"

"Yes. You usually have to come to us, or send us your findings, but this seemed urgent and . . . it's hard to say no to Coste."

Degrève finished the round of handshakes, and Coste took

---

* S.C.I.T.T.: Service Central Informatique et des Traces Technologiques: Central Office for Computing and Technological Tracing, based in Lyons.

him over to the coffee machine, arm round his shoulders. Ronan whispered to Johanna:

"I think I'm seeing double. Sam and Degrève are identical twins. What a couple of nerds."

He turned towards Coste and the new arrival:

"O.K., you two lovebirds, will you tell us how you first met? The boss has never mentioned you."

Degrève drained his coffee and satisfied their curiosity.

"As I remember it, about eight years ago Victor was looking for a new member of his team. He already had the tough guys and he wanted a technical expert. I was on his list, but then I got an opportunity to join the S.C.I.T.T. Not the sort of offer you can refuse, so I made my choice."

About eight years ago. Sam had no need to count on his fingers to calculate that he had been part of the team for exactly that long, and if he remembered correctly Coste had faced a choice between him and this Julien Degrève. The idea that he might have been second choice gave him a little stab of jealousy in the pit of his stomach. All of a sudden, he wasn't so keen on this skinny little nerd in his delinquent's hoodie.

"Tell me more about this case of yours," Degrève said.

Victor picked upthe photo album and C.D.s from his desk and handed them to him.

"We're working on a kidnapping that went wrong."

"The kid in the swimming pool? It was on the radio this morning."

"We've identified one of the gang: Yassine Chelli. But we know there were three of them altogether. We also know that a kidnapping like this is complicated and requires a certain level of trust. So it was probably planned by people who know each other well. I asked Sam to put together a photo album of all Chelli's known accomplices. That's what I've just given you."

Opening the album, Degrève saw seventeen not exactly pleasant mugshots of disgruntled suspects, each more sinister-looking than the last. The photographs were all taken just after the subjects had been arrested, which explained the dearth of smiles. Degrève was quick on the uptake:

"So, you think the two other members of the gang are among your Yassine's former accomplices? That is, among these seventeen."

"That's what I hope, because for the moment we don't have much to go on – we're relying on instinct. These seventeen characters have all been questioned over the past few years, either by us or at different police stations in Seine-Saint-Denis, and their interviews were filmed. They're on those C.D.s. The question is, do they match with our recordings of the voices of the three members of the gang?"

"You had their phones tapped in advance? How did you manage that?"

"Instinct again, but it would take a while to explain. Anyway, that's where we need your help."

Degrève took a laptop out of his briefcase and switched it on.

"I can't do much myself, but Batvox could be useful. It's our voice recognition software. I can compare the voices of Yassine's accomplices with the ones you've recorded. If any match, they're your men."

Sam raised a doubting eyebrow.

"Is it reliable?"

"Batvox? It was used in the Cahuzac affair*. We compared

---

* Jérôme Cahuzac was Minister for the Budget during François Hollande's Socialist government. In 2013 he was tried and convicted of money laundering and fiscal fraud thanks mainly to secretly recorded telephone conversations where his voice was identified.

his voice when making a speech with the recording of him discussing his Swiss bank account and income tax avoidance. That was how he fell."

"Oh, so Cahuzac fell, did he?" said an astonished Ronan.

"Obviously not," Degrève admitted. "He's a politician. They totter, they reel, but never actually fall."

Launching the program, he asked impatiently:

"Shall we get started?"

Degrève only needed seven seconds of a clear voice recording to identify the essential elements. He began with the conversation with Pacino. He put it in a loop and compared it to extracts from each of the seventeen interviews of Yassine's known accomplices.

The first interview showed no similarities. On the screen, the sound waves of the two recordings rose and fell without ever coinciding. The same was true of the next nine; it wasn't until the eleventh interview that they hit a perfect match. Pacino was no longer a movie star, but instead one Sofiane Badaoui, with a police record for armed robbery, burglary and fraud. For starters. He was the one waiting for the ransom payment at the shopping centre.

Degrève went back to the beginning, this time comparing the seventeen interviews with Delon's voice. There was a perfect match with No. 9, who was revealed as Lorenzo Weinstein: sexual harassment, violence against his father – whom he had put in hospital on more than one occasion – and several snatch thefts in his youth. He was the one who had guarded David Sebag and had carried out the order to shoot him.

Degrève had arrived at four-thirty, and by the stroke of five he and Batvox had identified Yassine Chelli's accomplices. By a process of elimination, Chelli must be the gang leader. Feeling pleased with himself, Degrève was finishing his comparative report under the admiring gaze of Johanna and Ronan. Only Sam refrained from congratulating him. He could have shit a gold brick and Sam still wouldn't have applauded.

"Bravo for your instinct," Degrève told Coste. "But enjoy it while you can, because with D.N.A., digital fingerprinting and speech analysis, plus social media and soon body-odour tests, it will soon be as obselete as a cassette recorder. To be a policeman in ten years' time, all you'll need will be a good computer, a technical expert and a few laboratory rats. You can kiss old-fashioned investigators goodbye."

"I hope you'll lay some flowers on my grave," Coste responded gruffly.

Ronan leaned over to Sam and whispered:

"I don't know about you, but I shan't miss this guy when he's gone."

Convinced that his audience was all ears, Degrève continued:

"You know, your investigation has given me an idea. I'll have to mention it to S.C.I.T.T. If we had seven seconds of all the interviews filmed at every police station in France, and compared them with the wiretaps where we haven't yet identified the suspects, it could solve at least a thousand cases at a stroke."

"A thousand, eh? I hope you'll wait until I've retired before you suggest the idea. Are you staying the night in Paris?" asked Coste.

"No, there's a train at six o'clock. But if you ever find your-self in Lyons, come and visit us. Maude will be delighted to see you again."

The two men left the office; the others were unsure what to make of him. When Coste returned, Sam asked him, in as casual a voice as he could muster:

"How many candidates were on your list when you selected me?"

"Two. You and him."

"And is it because he went to S.C.I.T.T. that you chose me?"

Coste pretended not to have heard, and instead began to print the photos of the day's two jackpot winners – Lorenzo Weinstein and Sofiane Badaoui – then went to pin them on the whiteboard. Ignoring all protocol, Sam rounded on him.

"Spit it out, Victor! Was I second choice or not?"

Coste would have enjoyed stringing him along a bit longer, but he remembered just in time that Sam was an orphan and that their group was the nearest thing he had to a family. That curbed his enthusiasm. That and the murderous look Johanna gave him.

"You were the one I chose, and when Degrève learned that he went off to join S.C.I.T.T. He just likes to say the opposite. I suspect that over time he's even come to believe it."

"So why me? He's obviously better qualified, isn't he?"

"A better technician, maybe. But that doesn't make a good officer. And he's a cocky little bastard, as you all saw."

"And yet you asked him if he was staying the night in Paris. Were you planning to spend the evening with him?"

"No way. I saw the return ticket in his briefcase."

Sam found it hard to conceal his satisfaction. Ronan restrained himself from coming out with the ten or more jokes on the tip of his tongue. He was pleased to see his colleague happy – besides, he didn't like anyone else getting a rise out of him. Coste went on:

"O.K., it's five o'clock now. Ronan, you stay with me to organise the arrests. Sam and Johanna, you can go home. I want you here tomorrow morning at five o'clock sharp."

He pointed at their three targets on the whiteboard.

"Yassine, Sofiane and Lorenzo. Tomorrow they're done for. This is their last day of freedom."

Johanna and Sam left the office and headed down the corridor to the lifts. Sam ventured:

"I acted like a child, didn't I?"

"Not at all. Your little tantrum reminded us all how important our team is. That's a good thing."

"Where are you going now?"

"To collect Malo from school."

Sam seemed to hesitate, concerned he was imposing or taking advantage, then blurted out:

"Can I come?"

"I'm sorry, but I've already asked Degrève. Some other time?"

Then, before he could blow his top, she tossed him her car keys.

"You drive. I'm tired."

32

Clos-Saint-Lazare Estate (Stains)
6.00 a.m.

A tidy bedroom, apart from a few schoolbooks scattered on a desk and a pile of clothes underneath it. On the wall, a football club scarf and several photos from a school trip the previous year. The typical bedroom of a young boy who has never been in trouble. Sam approached Saïd's bed without a sound and kneeled down. He shook his shoulder gently, and the boy opened his eyes. Placing a hand over his mouth, Sam whispered that he was from the police, flashed his I.D. and asked him to stay calm for the next few minutes.

Thinking he had won the boy's trust, he removed his hand. Against all expectation, Saïd sprang upright and shouted his brother's name to warn him.

"Yass—"

As if he'd received an electric shock, Sam seized the kid by the arm, pulled him against his chest, and clamped his hand over his mouth again, this time so tightly Saïd could only breathe through his nose. In the struggle, both of them fell onto the bed.

"Stop it, for God's sake! There's no point. Calm down."

Even so, he kept up the pressure with his hand. He could

sense Saïd's breathing gradually slow down, while against his arm he could feel the boy's still wildly racing heartbeat.

"Calm down, please."

They had not switched on any lights, and the layout of the flat was a mystery. Only their torch beams helped reveal what was in the rooms. A passage led from the front door to the bedrooms. Sam had been given the task of taking care of Saïd in the first one. The second was empty, the bed unmade. Souila was already on the train that took her every morning to clean the offices in the twin towers of a big bank, along with all the other black and Arab mothers among France's early risers.

In the last bedroom, Yassine was sleeping like a log. Saïd's strangled cry had reached him, but he had merely groaned and turned over.

In the semi-darkness above him, the three menacing silhouettes had tensed for an instant. But Sam had reacted quickly, and Yassine remained fast asleep, lying on his front. After the moment's alarm, silence reigned once more. Coste and Johanna levelled their guns at their target's head. A pair of handcuffs in hand, Ronan was waiting for the signal to throw himself on him. Coste nodded.

Johanna tore back the sheet, revealing that there was no hidden weapon he could grab. Yassine woke with a start. His first word of the day was a loud "Fuck!"

Ronan leaped on him, thrusting his knee between his shoulder blades and forcing his left arm backwards into an unbreakable lock. Yassine's yelp of pain was stifled by the mattress.

Coste quickly felt under the pillow in case there was a weapon concealed there. Ronan attached the cuffs to both wrists, then hauled Yassine into a sitting position. They all returned their guns to the holsters, and the tension ebbed away.

"It's two minutes past six. You're under arrest for kidnapping, illegal confinement and being an accessory to murder. You have the right to keep your trap shut."

Scowling, Yassine looked at each of them in turn, his jaw clenched, his mind in a whirl. Images of what was to come flashed through his mind like a bad movie he had seen too often. Arrest, questioning, transfer to court and, if things went badly, prison. Above all, he was trying to work out how they could have traced him so quickly. Had someone squealed on him? Had he slipped up? Until he knew the answers, he adopted the attitude recommended by every defence lawyer he had met.

"I don't know what you're talking about. I haven't done anything. You've got the wrong guy."

In Saïd's room, Sam had heard the sounds of the violent arrest. Then the storm passed.

"I'm going to take my hand away, alright?"

The boy nodded.

"I'm sorry about all this, kid. We won't be long. Can you tell me where the mobile you used yesterday is?"

Saïd stared defiantly at him but said nothing. Sam understood he was only trying to protect his big brother, and wasn't annoyed. Everybody had their role to play, and he stuck to his, even though it wasn't his style.

"Tell me, or we'll turn the flat upside down. Your choice."

With Yassine eyeing them uneasily, Johanna and Ronan made a careful search of his bedroom. Coste radioed the other two teams taking part in the operation; they confirmed the other two arrests had gone as planned. In two separate flats in Stains, Sofiane Badaoui and Lorenzo Weinstein had been arrested, though the latter had fought back briefly and suffered a broken finger. Coste gave instructions for the three teams to rendezvous back at headquarters.

Coste, Johanna and Ronan escorted Yassine outside, his hands cuffed behind his back, leaving behind them a ransacked room that was somehow even more of a shambles than when they had arrived. As they walked down the passage to the front door they passed Sam, his arm round Saïd, who was still in his pyjamas. The two brothers glanced at each other: Yassine miserable and humiliated, his little brother scared and lost.

"Did you find the mobile?" Coste asked Sam.

"Yeah. In the kid's backpack," he said, showing it to them.

So Yassine understood how, and above all why, the police had come for him so quickly. He should have got rid of the phones as soon as their operation had been aborted, but either because he was lazy, or more probably because he hoped he could make a bit of cash by selling them, he had hesitated. A few euros against several years in prison. A high price to pay.

In the same instant, Saïd also realised the consequences of his actions. He didn't entirely understand the butterfly effect, but it seemed clear enough. Borrowing his big brother's phone had brought the police down on them. And it was entirely his fault.

"I'm sorry," he muttered, head bowed.

With a twist of the shoulder, Yassine freed himself from Ronan. He wasn't aggressive, so Ronan let him be. Yassine kneeled down until he was at eye level with his little brother, who took him in his arms and hid his face in his neck.

"I'm sorry."

Yassine gritted his teeth.

"It's nothing to do with you, Saïd. I always fuck things up. You're in charge of the family now."

Ronan pulled Yassine to his feet and propelled him through the front door. Coste and Johanna followed. Sam turned to Saïd.

"We used a locksmith to force the door, but it's not broken. Don't forget to lock it after us, will you?"

His words didn't seem to reach the bewildered boy. Sam stayed with him for a few more moments.

"What time do you start school today?"

"Half-past eight."

"You should go back to bed. We'll let your mother know what happened within the next few minutes."

Sam left the flat too. In the wake of the police hurricane, Saïd found himself standing in the middle of the dark corridor. Abandoned, choked with guilt, he sat on the floor and began to cry softly.

33

First a series of brief interviews, in which all three denied the facts and repeated the line they had learned: they were innocent. Next came the overwhelming evidence, received by each of them like so many scissor cuts in the fabric of their alibis. This made them adopt a second position: accusing one another. Not so much to protest their innocence as to insist they had only played a small part in the crime. Their already fragile house of cards came crashing down.

Criminals only collude when the offence is taking place. Confronted by the police, they put their own freedom first.

By two in the afternoon, the case was sewn up. Yassine, Sofiane and Lorenzo were as good as convicted. When Ronan emerged from the office following one final interview, he found Coste busy talking to Damiani.

"Yassine says it's not his voice on the recordings. He says he found the mobiles downstairs in the tower block."

"Naturally, he'll deny everything right to the end, whatever the evidence against him." Coste was not in the least surprised.

"I'll show his lawyer out. Take Yassine down to the cells, and I'll call Saint-Croix to bring her up to speed."

"Do as you wish with the lawyer, but leave me his client. I want a minute with him."

Coste entered the office and asked Sam to leave. Sitting down facing Yassine, he took some time to study him. Twenty-two years old according to his file, light-brown eyes and an attractive, almost gentle face.

"You're not a bad-looking lad," Coste said. "I didn't picture you like this."

"And you seem less stupid than your colleague. Can you tell him I didn't do anything and that you're going to leave me alone?"

Coste lit himself a cigarette then stowed the packet in his jacket.

"Don't bother, we're not recording anymore. You can speak freely; it'll stay between these four walls."

It was Yassine's turn to study Coste. He recognised him as one of the three cops who had given him such a rude awakening that morning.

"Well done for tracing the mobiles. We should never have bought them all at the same place."

"Thanks," Coste replied drily.

"Frankly, I thought you'd be a bit happier. You've nabbed us, you've solved your case, you must be over the moon," Yassine scoffed.

This unsettled Coste, and he replied in a confidential tone somewhere between introspective and a confessional.

"Pleased? Shit, you don't know what you're saying. I don't even know where to start, but you're way off the mark. We fucked this case up right from the beginning. After that we were simply trying to redress the balance, but whatever happens, it'll always be in your favour. Normally I wouldn't even notice you. You're just a murderer, you're not a real person. If you died, I wouldn't even bother to put my cigarette out."

"That's more like it. I prefer it when you insult me like your pal. But why are you telling me this: is this personal then? What have I done to you?" Yassine was getting worried.

"You made me drop my guard. You almost made me give up. You're the last straw for me. It's all a matter of timing. It could have been any scumbag, but it just happened to be you."

Coste pushed his cigarette butt into an empty soda can.

"Yeah . . . you're my last straw."

"I haven't got a clue what you're talking about," muttered Yassine.

Coste stood up and made to leave the room.

"It doesn't matter. I wasn't really talking to you."

Yassine Chelli and his two accomplices spent the night in custody, in separate cells. When all the formalities were completed, the examining magistrate Fleur Saint-Croix had them transferred to the law court cells.

Two hours later, their respective lawyers appeared before the judge, who refused bail and sensibly had them remanded to three different prisons, Lorenzo Weinstein to Fresnes and Sofiane Badaoui to Fleury-Mérogis. When Yassine Chelli, accompanied by his lawyer, came up before the judge, he told him the news:

"I see you've already been in Marveil. You know the place. So now you're going back there."

Yassine broke down. For an instant he was almost a child again. Marveil had that effect on even the toughest thugs.

"No, please, not there, your honour."

Astonished, the judge raised his eyes from the file.

"This isn't a travel agency. I'm not asking you to choose between the Maldives and Morocco. I'm sending the three of you to prison, full stop. And you are going to Marveil."

Yassine tried to persuade him, but fear made him aggressive, shouting and swearing in dangerously close proximity to the judge, until the two officers who had escorted him had to step in, grabbing him by the arms and forcing him to the floor. Seeing him restrained, the judge regained his composure.

"Get this piece of shit out of my office."

The clerk didn't take down this last sentence and, considering his client's attitude, the lawyer didn't dare lodge a protest.

34

At seven precisely that evening, the caterer hired by Damiani for her leaving drinks was arranging the tables and setting out the cakes in the meeting room. When everyone was assembled, Commissaire Divisionnaire Stévenin launched into a speech that covered her entire career. Damiani winced as she heard her life flash past her eyes, from her first posting to the last as she approached sixty. For a moment she was afraid the fast-forward button had got stuck, and that the commissaire would speed on from the present to the day of her death. There was always an air of a funeral oration about these speeches, and a few glasses of champagne were required to dispel it.

Those who had attended out of politeness or a sense of duty slipped away by about ten o'clock, leaving Damiani with the officers she was directly in charge of. Charming and friendly, she went round them one by one. She tried her best to disguise how sad she felt, but Coste knew her too well to be fooled.

"So what does tomorrow have in store for you?" he asked, handing her a stiff whisky and Coke that Ronan had poured.

"Oh, you know. All the things I've never had time to do. And more besides."

"I see you've given it some thought."

"You can joke, but you'll be in the same situation soon enough. You give your all to this job, then one fine day you're too old, and since you haven't had time for anyone, you find there's no-one around."

"I should introduce you to my father; you've got a lot in common. Are you going to your house in Cahors?"

"My house . . ." Damiani repeated thoughtfully. "It's been ready and waiting for twenty years. Then I cheated on my husband. I was ditched, of course, and had to go through an ultra-messy divorce, and my daughters were on my husband's side and loathe me to this day. Yet I got to keep the house. But shit, it's so big and I've got so little to do there . . ."

Coste drew a little closer to her. Throughout her career, Damiani had kept a polite, professional distance from her officers. Over the years she had spoken as a close friend only to the capitaine, and then strictly in private. But when he gave her a hug for the very first time she didn't pull away, allowing herself to give in to it, eyes closed.

"My dear," Coste whispered. "I don't really know what to say."

"I know, Victor. There's nothing to be said."

Damiani stayed until two in the morning to accompany the most determined partygoers. When even they succumbed, she walked down the silent corridor to her office, where one last small box awaited her.

In the lift down to the underground car park she caught sight of her reflection in the mirror. All she saw was a tired-out woman. She turned her back on it, as if to leave the image a prisoner in the glass.

Outside in her car, she glanced in the rear-view mirror. The back seats were piled high with her things; on top lay her smart midnight-blue dress uniform, with its ribbon of medals. The uniform to be worn when you're being congratulated by the regional Préfet, or in your coffin if the profession has proved too much for you.

She switched on the ignition, let the engine run, then switched it off again. She rested her head in her hands on the steering wheel and took a deep breath before telling herself there was nobody left she had to keep up the pretence for, and let the tears fall.

35

Tiretto was afraid his Audi TT might be damaged in the twentieth arrondissement, which to him was already the dangerous suburbs. The taxi dropped him at the foot of an office block. He went up to the brand-new videophone where none of the buttons as yet had a name, and pressed the top one, as instructed.

"Maître Tiretto."

"Top floor," came the voice from the speaker.

Alex Mosconi had assembled the whole team for the meeting. When the doorbell rang and the lawyer entered the huge loft, he found himself face to face with Rhinoceros, with his small shifty eyes and slashed scar.

"Hi there, maître. Your mobiles, please."

Tiretto did as he was told and held out his two phones. Rhinoceros switched them off and slipped them into his pocket.

"Unbutton your jacket and raise your arms."

The lawyer did not complain, allowing the burly man to search him until he was sure he wasn't carrying a microphone or a weapon.

"He's clean."

"Of course I am," Tiretto said, buttoning up his jacket and stepping into the room.

He laid his briefcase on the big central table among several other mobiles and a computer. He wasn't particularly pleased to see these people again, but it had to be done. He sighed and studied them.

Dorian the ex-burglar was as impeccably dressed as ever in a black suit and white shirt, as though he were going to an exhibition opening. Without rising from his armchair, he greeted the lawyer with a nod.

At the far end of the room, out of earshot, Alex and her cousin Franck were talking in front of the picture window, with Paris a screensaver in the background. They shared an obvious family likeness, although Franck looked more like Nano, a more robust version, with added glasses. Franck looked worried, and Alex was trying to reassure him.

"Don't get a bee in your bonnet. Let the shyster talk, then we'll decide."

Putting an arm round his shoulder, she led him to the centre of the room where the others were waiting.

"Afternoon, Tiretto."

"Mademoiselle Mosconi."

Dorian brought over his armchair for Alex to sit in, and Rhino put out four chairs so the meeting could begin.

"Any news from your brother?" the lawyer began.

"Yes. I saw him a few days ago. He's become friendly with the shrink in Marveil, who gives him drugs to keep him out of it all day. He's lost ten kilos; he refuses to be put back with the ordinary prisoners, and if we don't do something he'll go completely crazy. So now's the time for you to reveal your plan."

Tiretto picked up his briefcase. Before it was properly open, Rhinoceros seized it from him and searched it roughly.

"You can carry on playing with it; all I need is that thick blue folder."

Amused rather than annoyed, Rhino removed the folder and

tossed it onto the table. As it slid across to the lawyer, some of the contents spilled out. Tiretto tidied them up, then turned to Alex: he always preferred to talk to the one in charge.

"There's a flaw in the case against your brother."

"And you've only just spotted it?" Dorian protested.

"Because it's only now that it can prove useful for us. Shall I go on?"

Alex nodded, and Dorian leaned back in his chair.

"There was no expert verification. I won't go through the whole story again: your brother was stopped by the police wearing a luxury watch. Its serial number linked it to the hold-up at the Van Cleef and Arpels jewellery store in Paris. The jeweller identified the watch, and although normally it's up to the Van Cleef and Arpels official expert to certify it, that was enough for the police and the courts to put Nunzio away."

"Who gives a fuck?" Dorian interjected. "That was the watch he was wearing. An expert verification will only confirm it."

"That's right. Unless the watch disappears, that is. I know the jewellers have asked for it to be handed back. That the request is in the pipeline and about to be agreed upon, but for the moment the watch is still in the high court building at Bobigny, in the evidence vaults. Since everyone seems to have accepted the jeweller's pseudo-identification, I intend to demand a proper expert judgment. But if the watch isn't there anymore, the whole case collapses. No-one will be able to swear that what your brother had on his wrist was a watch from the hold-up. And they'll have to set him free."

Franck Mosconi pushed his chair back out of the circle and leaned over to whisper in Alex's ear, making no effort to be discreet.

"You're telling me not to worry when we're talking about breaking into a courthouse? It must be crawling with cops – C.C.T.V. everywhere, security like a nuclear power station. This is absolutely not a good idea."

Tiretto closed the folder.

"You're right, Franck. That's why you won't be going."

The entire team turned towards the lawyer, intrigued. Up to that moment, his audience had been rather distracted, but now Tiretto had their full attention.

"If I ask for an expert verification, the examining magistrate will have the evidence bag brought to them the previous evening. So the watch will be in their office overnight."

"O.K., so we know where the watch will be. That doesn't solve the problem of how we're going to lay our hands on it," Dorian objected.

"I'm coming to that. There's a man at the law courts who could be very useful to us. Simply because he's worked there so long he's become invisible. He's the one in charge of the evidence bags. He's the one who'll receive the magistrate's request. He's the one who'll go and check the watch is in the vaults and take it to the magistrate's office. That way we can be sure where it is. Thanks to his position, this man can come and go from the court building, even stay there late, without arousing suspicion. All he'll need to do is wait for all the legal people to go home, return to the magistrate's office, force the lock, steal the watch, and hand it over."

"How much?" Alex interrupted him.

"I don't follow."

"How much is your guy asking for taking such a risk?"

"Ah I haven't the faintest idea. Besides, he doesn't even know we're talking about him. I give you the plan. It's up to you to carry it out."

"Does your guy have a name?" Franck wanted to know.

"I spend much of my time at the law courts, so it wasn't hard to learn his name. His address was even easier. And he has a family. I say that because . . ."

He turned to Dorian.

"If I'm to believe your criminal record, you can break into any building?"

Dorian accepted the compliment with a nod of the head.

"And you, Monsieur Rhinoceros, I imagine that once you're inside, you'll be able to persuade our man to help us?"

Rhino gave a broad smile that transformed his horizontal scar into a lightning flash.

"It's what I do best."

Tiretto took a folded piece of paper from his briefcase.

"Here's his address."

The expensive suit gave some idea of the person wearing it. So when the client had asked the taxi driver to wait as long as it took, he had agreed. When the man plunged back into the taxi half an hour later, with the meter registering a sky-high fare, the driver was more than satisfied. Returning to Paris during the afternoon rush hour meant he wouldn't do more than twenty kilometres an hour, so he was on course for a three-figure sum.

No sooner had the driver set off than Tiretto was busy on his secure mobile phone.

"Monsieur Darcy."

"Good afternoon, Maître."

"Boyan Mladic's future is looking brighter, if that reassures you."

"It does. The Corsicans seem to trust you."

"They don't really have a choice. The longer this goes on, the worse the state their relative is in. The plan I outlined was vague, but they don't know anything about the internal workings of a courthouse. That helps."

"We still need them to make a mess of it."

"True. It all depends on them failing. After that, they'll be so caught up in things they'll have no option but to plough on."

36

Marveil Prison

Perched on piles of refuse stretching the length of Marveil prison, rats, cats and pigeons fought with beak and claw under the thousands of cell windows to recover the detritus thrown out by the prisoners. Occasionally, when the prison administration launched a surprise inspection to demonstrate their authority, the inmates had no choice but to jettison their alcohol or shit. This meant the refuse-pickers could enjoy an alcohol-cannabis trip that left them squeaking for hours with their paws crossed, or zig-zagging through the air before impaling themselves on a barbed-wire fence. No surprise then that this kind of news sped rapidly from drain to dump, and any fresh piece of garbage was soon fought over by a host of scavengers.

A pigeon luckier than the rest alighted on a slice of pistachio-flavoured dessert and tried laboriously to fly away with it. After only four wing beats, another bird swooped on him to steal the booty, which fell uselessly to the ground. Thus began an aerial battle that ended in a huge blur of flying feathers outside Chief Officer Martineau's window. He jumped up, swore, and the interruption reminded him of something he had to do.

With the heavy bunch of keys at his belt, he opened the grille to the segregation cells, carefully closing it behind him. Walking past the first doors, he came to a halt outside No.

20, where he knocked politely before entering. Alerted by the sound of the key turning, Boyan Mladic got to his feet. The neon light in the ceiling made his shadow so huge it swallowed Martineau up entirely.

"Good morning, Boyan. I have a letter for you."

The envelope was still sealed. The chief officer had no idea of its contents or the language it was written in. He didn't even know if Boyan spoke French. He passed it through the bars. In the prisoner's hands it looked no bigger than a post-it. Boyan tore it open, took out a quarter of a sheet of paper and read it closely. Then he crumpled the letter up, put it in his mouth and chewed it like a cow chewing its cud. Closing the cell door again, Martineau wondered what news could justify such precautions. Then for his own peace of mind he decided not to think any more about it. A turn of the key in the lock, and back to his office. In the corridor he ran into the new guard.

"What are you doing here, Demarco?"

"I'm going to Cell 13, Antoine Doucey. He has his weekly appointment with the shrink."

"Come and see me afterwards. We have a new arrival, Yassine Chelli. We need to find him a bed."

Without waiting for a response to an order that didn't really require one, Martineau walked on.

Demarco waited for him to disappear completely before making a detour to Cell No. 2, which was in complete darkness.

"Hello there, Nano. I can't see a thing in here. Have you smashed the bulb again?"

"It's your lot's fault. That stupid light of yours drives me crazy. It's like being in an operating theatre."

Demarco reached into the pocket of his uniform and pulled out a battered book with dog-eared pages.

"Come over here, Nano. Get up."

"What for? I'm fine as I am."

"I've got a new book from Scalpel."

"He can go fuck himself. He's with them. The ones who want to do away with me. Have you checked inside it? You never know."

Despairing, Demarco closed his eyes for a moment. Nunzio Mosconi was obviously losing his mind, and there was no-one who could prevent it. He tossed the book into the middle of the cell's four square metres the way people throw food to zoo animals.

"Yes, I've checked, there's nothing dangerous in it. And I'll ask for someone to come and change your bulb."

He closed the door. Nano left Scalpel's present on the floor: *The Man Who Walked Through Walls* by Marcel Aymé.

Walking further along the corridor, the guard stopped outside No. 13. He unlocked the door.

"Doucey. Session with the shrink."

The prisoner stood up and limped over to the cell door. As he did so he repeated a few words of encouragement to himself:

"Leo doesn't exist. I don't think about Leo anymore . . . Leo? Who's that?"

The psychiatrist thanked Demarco and invited Doucey to sit down across the desk from him.

"How are you, Antoine?"

"Quite good. And you?"

"Not bad, thanks. What about your teeth?"

"I saw the dentist. He pulled out three, so my nights are calmer."

"And your dreams?"

"I dream less and less."

The shrink had fifteen minutes per patient, so he had little time for chit-chat. And no appetite for it.

"Leo?" he asked abruptly.

"I've understood that was bad. I don't think about him anymore."

"That's probably the medication."

"Or I've seen reason. I hope to be as much part of my own cure as your drugs are."

"Of course," the psychiatrist reassured him. He detested seeing Doucey sitting opposite him. He knew all about his record and his deviant behaviour. Above all, he knew these brief sessions were completely useless, and that this monster would leave prison just as dangerous as when he had arrived.

On the way back to his cell, escorted by a new guard, Doucey wondered whether the shrink had children. Maybe a little boy? He also wondered whether he gave him showers or if they took baths together. Rubbing hard everywhere. That's important. Under the arms. The thighs. Between the legs. Between the buttocks. Carefully and methodically. To be really clean. Leo, who had never been far away, flooded back into every corner of Doucey's mind.

Minutes later, Demarco led the way for the new inmate, who, laden down with a stinking blanket and a toilet bag courtesy of the prison administration, was looking anxiously left and right. Demarco opened the cell door, showed him his bunk, pointed to his cellmate, and vanished.

Yassine put his load down on the mattress with its thick blue plastic undersheet. He peered round the cell; wherever he looked he was left disgusted. His cellmate politely allowed him to get settled before striking up a conversation.

"What's your name?"

"Yassine. And yours?"

"Me? I'm Machine. But your name now is Doe-Eyes."

Taken aback, Yassine looked at him. The brief explanation was not long in coming.

"Because you're a queer."

"But . . . I'm not at all queer . . ."

Machine got up and took a step towards him, already amused.

PART THREE

HOME INVASION

*We've terrorised the guy. If I told him to
eat his own arm, he'd ask which one.
He'd do anything for his family. We have
that much in common at least.*

ALEXANDRA MOSCONI

37

Staked out in his car a few metres from the house, Franck
had spent the last forty-eight hours watching the comings and
goings of the Alves couple and their sixteen-year-old daughter.
She left the house at eight o' clock precisely, backpack slung over
her shoulder, earbuds in place, and as soon as she was round
the first corner, lit a cigarette. At half-past eight, the husband
appeared on the doorstep and kissed his wife goodbye, leaving
her to the housework. The wonderful daily merry-go-round of a
perfect 1960s couple. For her, the day passed in a comfortable if
dull routine of chores, cooking and German series on daytime
T.V. At about three o'clock, a trip out for errands or perhaps
to window-shop, to get some air. At seven p.m., the three of
them met up again for an evening in which the T.V., an active
member of the family, filled the hours before sleep.

To avoid any unpleasant surprises, Franck had waited until
the second day to pay a flying mid-afternoon visit. Carrying
perfume samples packaged as though for an advertising cam-
paign, he had appeared wearing a postman's uniform bought
on eBay. Noting there was no spyhole, he rang the bell. Isabel
Alves opened the door and invited the postman in while she
searched for a pen to sign his delivery note. All she saw was the
uniform, ignoring the person wearing it. Franck only stayed a
few minutes, long enough to make sure there was no alarm,

dog or bodybuilder friend he had failed to spot from outside. No sign of anything like that. He concluded that the Alves family was so vulnerable they almost deserved what was in store for them.

Alves family home
Monday, 7 p.m.
Home invasion: Day One

"Not even a spyhole?" Dorian seemed disappointed. "Frankly, they're asking for trouble. It's as if they were just waiting for us."

"So we knock on the door and I do the presentations, is that right?" Rhinoceros said. "I know how I'm going to introduce myself, anyway."

Dorian scowled. "Why do I think it's bound to be something vulgar? You're going to behave like an ass yet again."

"I'll be polite if you like."

None of them believed him. They all knew that in this kind of situation the first few seconds are essential – they needed to make an instant impression to discourage any revolt or heroic act.

Alex checked both ends of the street, not very busy at this time of day, then gave the go signal. The four of them got out of the car. Dorian and Franck walked round it and took two black canvas bags from the boot. They all strode towards the house. Franck instinctively raised his hood.

"You shouldn't do that, you can't see what's behind you," Dorian warned him.

Franck shrugged like a teenager exasperated by his grand-father's advice and took the lead.

"I can see perfectly well what's going on behind me, and besides . . ."

Rhinoceros silenced him with a tap on the top of his head.

Franck wheeled round, but as he didn't know who had done it, he had to swallow his anger.

"O.K., so I didn't see that coming. Alright, I'll pull the hood down."

They pushed open the wooden garden gate, went past the flowerbed, climbed the few steps up to the house and laid their black bags on the porch. Now Rhinoceros came to the fore. He stood in front of the door, cracking his knuckles with his hands behind his back. The others stood to one side.

Isabel opened her oven and saw her gratin wasn't yet sufficiently golden. The front doorbell rang and she asked one of the others to get it. Her request fell on deaf ears; the bell played its tune a second time. By now Isabel was seriously annoyed.

"I'm in the kitchen. Can't someone else go?"

A loud voice from the first floor responded to her aggressive tone.

"I'm in my room! I'm on the phone!" her daughter shouted, as if her conversation was the most important thing in the world.

Tomas Alves saw the funny side and got up from a sofa misshapen by time and use. Beyond the frosted glass door, a vague outline. He opened it trustingly.

"Good evening?" he said.

Rhinoceros stared at him for a couple of seconds. No danger would come from this chubby-cheeked forty-year-old, all spark extinguished by a lifetime of habit.

"What can I do for you?" Tomas asked when the visitor made no reply.

"The head butt has to come from here," Gérard Depardieu once said in *"Les Compères"*, tapping his torso. Tomas's nose exploded with a snapping sound. The shock made him stagger

177

three steps back before he fell to the floor, hands clutching his face. The four intruders entered the house and Alex quickly shut the door behind them. Rhino grabbed the man by the hair, lifted him up and through gritted teeth threatened him with the opening line he had rehearsed as thoroughly as any actor

"Listen to me, Papa. You're going to do exactly as I say, or I'll make you fuck your daughter in front of your wife."

Tomas went limp, petrified by fear. Dorian raised his eyes to the heavens. He never ceased to be amazed at the perverted imagination of his colleague, who was now dragging the father into the kitchen.

"Who is it?" asked Isabel, still with her back to them.

She turned round, teacloth on her shoulder and wooden spoon in hand. She soon realised the evening had been ruined.

Background music from her earphones, skimming through her homework with a bored expression, the family adolescent hadn't yet noticed a thing. A silhouette passed in front of the pendant light in her bedroom, casting a shadow on her schoolbooks.

"What now?" she asked in her permanently irritated whine.

She hardly had time to turn round before she received a resounding slap that left her ears ringing and her cheek bright pink.

"And you, you little slut, you're going to learn to treat your elders with respect."

Rhino came downstairs with the teenager in a painful arm lock. He slammed her down onto a chair at the table where her father and mother were already seated, Isabel in tears and Tomas paralysed, unable to overcome his fear. Alexandra sat facing them and explained the situation in a calm, level voice.

"I hope you'll excuse my friend. I myself find him a little violent at times, but from now on I'm in charge. If you behave yourselves, he should keep quiet. "

United in their panic, parents and daughter exchanged terrified glances, as if to make sure all this was really happening. Four intruders had broken into their home, and they were at their mercy.

"My name is Alexandra, and if we're not hiding our faces or our identities from you, it's because I'm sure I can trust you. Am I right, Tomas?"

The father looked across at her, his voice quavering as his jaw trembled uncontrollably, his nose still out of joint, blood on his lips and chin.

"We'll do whatever you want. You can take everything. I have some money upstairs if that's what you're after."

Alexandra folded her hands on the tabletop before addressing mother and daughter.

"You must be Isabel . . . and you, Aurélie."

Hearing their names pronounced by a stranger, they both stiffened in their chairs.

"If everything goes well, we'll have left by tomorrow evening. In exactly twenty-four hours. But first, hand me your mobiles."

Tomas laid his on the table. Dorian accompanied Isabel to the kitchen to collect hers. Thick smoke was pouring from the oven, and he urged her to save the gratin, which would now be for them as well. He watched as Isabel, a petite brunette as appetising and shapely as a warm brioche, nervously came close to spilling the dish. He picked up a cloth.

"Leave it. I'll do it."

He put the dish down on the hob. As Isabel was reaching for her mobile on the worktop, right next to the open knife drawer, her hand wavered close to a long blade. Dorian came up behind her, pressed himself against her back, and whispered in her ear.

"And then? What would you do next?"

Isabel trembled, then let her hand drop to shut the drawer. She picked up her mobile and gave it to him.

Rhinoceros accompanied Aurélie to her bedroom to get her mobile, with Tomas looking on despairingly. When they were upstairs, the teenager went over to her desk and searched underneath her schoolbooks. Aurélie's body was as appetising as that of her mother, but twenty-five years younger. Seeing her bra pressed against her chest under the T-shirt, Rhinoceros felt a surge of desire. He laid a rough hand on her buttock.

"Wait, I'll help you. Maybe it's here, in your back pocket?"

Knocked off balance by his crude gesture, Aurélie gripped the desk with both hands, gritted her teeth and closed her eyes. Behind them, another voice made itself heard.

"What are you doing?"

Turning his head, Rhinoceros found Franck confronting him.

"Would you like a piece?" he asked.

"And you? Would you like me to tell Alex about this?"

Rhino withdrew his hand as if he'd touched a hot electric plate.

"She's all yours. Two little virgins, you should get on well together."

Now that the danger had left the room, Aurélie had the courage to turn round and hand Franck her mobile. Their hands met inadvertently, and for a split second she noticed the green of his eyes, while in turn he was impressed by the deep black of hers. She almost said thank you, until she remembered what was going on and changed her mind. She walked towards the door, and as she passed Franck she tugged down her T-shirt in a confused adolescent gesture.

All three mobiles were now on the table. The whole family looked round at Rhinoceros when he tore the internet cables from the wall. Just in case. Alex resumed the conversation where she had left off.

"Tomorrow, Aurélie will be ill. Isabel, you're going to call her school and explain."

Alex broke off, annoyed at the mother's constant sniffling.

"Shit, have a bit of self-respect. Stop blubbing! You're going to have to get used to the idea, sweetie. We're here in your house and you have no choice. Get a tissue and listen to me."

Isabel wiped her tears on her sleeve. The smudged mascara left black panda circles round her eyes.

"O.K., so you'll call the school, then the two of you will spend the day with us, waiting patiently for Tomas to come home. That's all there is to it. You simply have to wait."

Alex turned to the father.

"As for you, Tomas, it's obviously a bit more complicated. But I know you love your family enough to do as we say. This is going to be a long night for all of us, so I'll have time to explain everything."

She laid her hand on his forearm.

"You're responsible for the sealed evidence bags at the law courts, aren't you?"

38

Tuesday 8.30 a.m.
Home invasion: Day two

In the hall, Tomas took down his coat and put it on carefully, first one arm then the other. He looked back into the living room. On the floor were two mattresses they had tried to sleep on, under constant surveillance. Isabel and Aurélie had managed to close their eyes for a few hours in the middle of the night. He himself had been awake the whole time, his nose a burning agony.

A few feet from the front door, Alex was finishing her coffee. What would she do if she were in Tomas's shoes, and four intruders were threatening her family? She'd prefer to die rather than submit. There would be blood on the walls. Nobody touches the Mosconis. She went up to Tomas and opened the door for him. The cool morning air wafted in.

"Your nose is still swollen. Good job it's not broken. You can say you have a head cold; that should do the trick."

"No-one will notice," muttered Tomas, picking up his briefcase.

"I get the impression not many people notice you."

"You did. More's the pity."

"Do what you have to. I'll keep an eye on your family. No-one will harm them. Unless you force us to."

She handed him back his mobile.

"From now on, it's up to you . . ."

Outside the house, clutching his briefcase, Tomas ran through all the different scenarios. Only one of them seemed to guarantee his wife and daughter's safety. To collaborate. A police car sped by in the distance. He ignored it and got into his own.

Alex sat down at the table where Isabel and Aurélie were already seated, holding hands. Their panic had passed. Hostages in their own home for more than twelve hours, their fear had given way to resignation and a wish to survive. They were docile prisoners.

"We're going to need more coffee," Alex ordered.

Isabel got up and disappeared into the kitchen. Franck searched in the pocket of his hoodie, took out a cigarette and offered it to Aurélie.

"It's time for your fag, isn't it?"

She was so surprised she didn't know what to reply.

"I watched you for two days. I know you want one."

Aurélie tilted her head in the direction of the kitchen, hesitated for a moment, then accepted the cigarette and lit it from the lighter Franck was holding out. She inhaled deeply, as if it were pure oxygen. Her mother reappeared, a full cafetiere in her hand. Aurélie tried in vain to conceal the cigarette under the table while her mother was filling the cups. When she had finished, she turned to her daughter.

"Give me a drag."

"I didn't know you smoked."

"I hide it, like you do."

This moment of complicity brought them closer. Just then Rhinoceros, fresh from his shower, came downstairs and joined them. His lascivious gaze lingered on their bodies and their stress and anguish resurfaced. A white quiff, his hair still wet, he had used Tomas's cologne and he smelled like him. This intermingling of the two men brought Isabel's heart into her mouth.

"You O.K., Tomas?"

He realised he was still holding the document he needed to make twenty photocopies of, and that the machine was spewing out blank pages. His colleague, carrying a heavy folder under her arm, surveyed him with amusement.

"Rough night?"

You can say that again, he thought. A bunch of criminal lunatics are keeping my family hostage, and I have to break into an examining magistrate's office.

"No, no, I was just miles away," was his only reply.

He had still not received any request from the third floor. At ten, he'd told himself to be patient. At eleven, he'd had a panic attack, and shut himself in the toilets. But now it was three in the afternoon, and the stress manifested itself on his livid, sickly-looking face.

To calm himself down he repeated the instructions he had received the previous evening.

"Take one of our canvas bags in your briefcase. A magistrate will call you at some point in the morning to ask you to bring him a sealed evidence bag. Make sure it's a watch he wants, and that it relates to the Nunzio Mosconi case. Take it to him as instructed, then wait for the end of the day when everybody leaves your floor. Say you're behind with your work, or whatever you like, but make it credible. In our bag you'll find a small iron bar. One end has been flattened. You're to use it as a crowbar to break into the magistrate's office. The same for the desk drawers. Recover that evidence bag, but not just that one. You have to confuse things. Steal another ten or so files at random, as well as the hard disk with their details. The police must think stealing the watch was an afterthought. Almost by chance, a coincidence. Playing by our rules is the only way to save your family."

"The only way to save your family." Like a tune that becomes an earworm, these words went round and round in Tomas's head, until at six in the evening he decided to call Alex.

Apparently seated only centimetres from his telephone, the lawyer picked up at the first ring.

"I've just heard from our man at the law courts," Alex said accusingly. "No news from the examining magistrate guy."

"From the magistrate woman, you mean. I know, she's not going to call him," Tiretto confirmed.

Alex's frustration was obvious.

"I thought she had the evidence brought up to her the evening before her interviews. Is your info a load of crap?"

"Absolutely not. The jewellery expert put a spanner in the works. He was supposed to pick up the watch from the law courts, but he's changed his mind and now wants it taken to him. So he'll examine it at the main Van Cleef and Arpels shop in Paris. If he says it's theirs, the magistrate will hand it back to them. Since the evidence bag will be taken directly from the law courts to the expert, there's no reason for her to keep it in her office."

"You mean that's the end of it? We've missed our window?"

"Something like that."

"Wait, we've terrorised the guy. If I told him to eat his own arm, he'd ask which one. He'd do anything for his family. We have that much in common at least. All I have to do is tell him to take the bag himself and bring it to us. He's the one in charge of them, isn't he?"

"Whether he's in charge or not, there are regulations. To take an evidence bag out you have to sign a register kept by a secretary who sits behind a bulletproof screen. If the watch disappears, they will only have to look at the register, and the spotlight will immediately fall on Monsieur Alves. You may have scared him sufficiently for him to want to forget you as quickly as possible, but if the police get their hands on him and start to pressure him, or worse throw him in jail, are you sure he'll be able to keep quiet? Would you be willing to jeopardise your freedom? And Dorian's? Or your brother's?"

"You sound far too calm not to have a Plan B up your sleeve, Tiretto."

The lawyer let several seconds pass.

"Unfortunately, Plan Bs always present more risks."

"Tell me in detail, because I have a team holding an entire family hostage and I'll have to explain all this to them without losing face."

Right from the outset, this was the point Tiretto had wanted to reach. Plan A had always been meant to fail, leading to the only one that really interested him. He wasn't in the least surprised the magistrate hadn't called Tomas Alves, because there had never been any question of that. But Alex Mosconi had to be compromised up to her neck, in the middle of a home invasion, so that she had no choice but to continue. The tune the lawyer was about to play was a solo piece which didn't allow for any false notes.

"You're going to have to recover the watch yourself. That's the only solution, before it vanishes for good."

It was Alex's turn to allow his words to hang in the air, as what he was saying sank in.

"You're not saying we break into the sealed evidence vaults at Bobigny law courts, are you?"

"I know. It sounds crazy, but I think you'll be surprised. Talk to Monsieur Alves. You have the best inside man possible, and the best team to pull it off. Let me send some info to your mobile."

After the day's fiasco, Tomas had been recalled home. On the way back he couldn't help imagining the worst. Had they touched his family? Hit them? Had the one with the scar gone upstairs with Isabel? What if he'd shut the bedroom door to enjoy more privacy? What if Aurélie had been his target? The thought made him slap the steering wheel in despair, and he almost ran down an old lady as he drove through a red light.

When he opened the front door, his wife and daughter flung themselves on him. Despite the disgusting mess he found himself in, he couldn't help wondering how long it had been since Aurélie had been so affectionate. Then he saw Alex's face, and Rhino's behind her. The disgusting mess bubbled up again.

"I promise you I never got a call. I even went up to the magistrates' floor. The offices have glass windows, but I couldn't see any evidence bags."

"I know," Alex said. "Everything's O.K."

Tomas put one arm round his wife's shoulders, the other round his daughter's. Were it not for their weary-looking faces and the dark lines under their eyes, it could have made a good family photo.

"You know we won't say anything," Tomas pleaded.

"I haven't the slightest doubt about that," said Alex, kicking the front door shut. "Because we're staying."

39

Not long before dawn, Alex's mobile vibrated on the sofa where she had fallen asleep. On the mattress at her feet, an exhausted Tomas had succumbed to fatigue, arms flung round his wife and daughter. Alex rubbed her eyes and opened the message she had just received: a series of names, crimes committed, and the relevant case numbers. Sent by Maître Tiretto. The first stage of Plan B.

Alex had spent a good part of the previous evening explaining the lawyer's plan. Franck had accepted because Nano was his cousin and family meant everything to him. Dorian had accepted out of love. "To hell and back," he had added. And Rhino had accepted because the operation was not only dangerous but promised to be legendary. All they had to do was to put Tomas in the picture.

A quarter of an hour later, the team were sitting round the living-room table, coffee in their cups. Tomas found himself at the centre of the meeting: his wife and daughter had been forced to stay in the kitchen.

"Describe the evidence vaults for me," said Alex.

Taken aback by the question, Tomas searched for an adequete

response. Becoming impatient, Rhino picked up the burning hot cafetière and held it above his head, the spout pointing downwards.

"Do you need more caffeine, or will you wake up on your own?"

Tomas spoke immediately.

"It's on the ground floor. There's an office with a secretary who receives and registers the evidence bags. At the far end there's a spiral staircase that leads down to a room about two hundred square metres where the bags are stored."

"And you can get in there without being checked?"

"As long as I don't take anything in or out, there's no reason for the secretary to ask me anything."

Alex slid her mobile across to him.

"Read this message. It's a list of names from different cases. Each one has an evidence bag that interests us. Today you'll have two things to do, both of them simple. Every evidence bag is marked with the number it was registered under. That's the only thing we don't know. You're to go into the vault, find them, and note down their numbers. Basta. Will you be able to do that?"

"Yes. I often check on them. There'll be nothing unusual about that."

"And we need a plan of the ground floor," Franck added. "Room by room. With all the access points."

Tomas frowned uneasily.

"All the access points? Some of them will be emergency exits. Not even I know all of them. I could do a drawing from memory if you like, but it won't be a hundred per cent accurate."

Dorian added a second sugar lump to his coffee before speaking, pleased finally to be able to use his experience.

"Don't worry, the fire service has already done the job for you. All you need do is find the fire emergency panels. They're legally obliged to have one on every floor of administrative buildings, mapped on a precise diagram."

"How many entrances are there to the law courts?" Alex said.

"One for the public, and five others for the employees."

"Which is closest to the evidence vault?"

"The one at the back of the building. We call it the stage door. That's where the police come to drop off their case files and evidence."

Alex turned to Franck.

"Today you can get some fresh air, cousin. Drive past discreetly and assess the security outside. We can deal with whoever's inside the building later on."

Aurélie appeared from the kitchen. On the table she laid what her mother had deemed a suitable breakfast.

"Are you planning on doing what I think you are?" asked an alarmed Tomas.

"Thinking is precisely what we're not asking you to do," Rhino corrected him. "Remember what's at stake and what you could lose."

Still looking Tomas in the eye, he stroked Aurélie's thigh. She backed away in disgust. Then he shouted at the entire family:

"Now clear out of here. Stay in the kitchen. Sit on the floor and keep your mouths shut."

When the family had gone, Rhino leaned towards Alex and lowered his voice.

"Why go to the trouble of stealing several bags? It'll take much longer that way."

"If only one bag is missing, that's like signing our name on the theft. If five are stolen, things grow murkier."

"And why the ones on your list?"

"A bag with twelve grams of shit or a miserable kitchen knife won't get anyone excited. According to Tiretto, the ones he's chosen are from serious crimes that landed some nasty people in jail. The kind of theft that puts pressure on the police and sends them scurrying all over the place."

"The perfect diversion," Dorian concluded.

Towards the end of the afternoon, Franck pulled up ten metres from the rear entrance to the law courts. There was a pedestrian crossing just level with it that would allow him exactly the amount of time he needed. He waited until a group of noisy, excited school kids appeared, carrying their backpacks. As they approached the crossing, Franck pulled out. He reached it at the same time as they did and stopped to let them pass. That gave him ten seconds to comfortably scan the building without any risk. Then he drove off again.

Less than fifteen metres away, in the same building, Tomas had descended the spiral staircase to the vault, where he was busily writing down the numbers of the evidence bags Alex had selected. That done, he went back up to his office on the second floor and waited for the end of the working day. At one minute to six he put on his coat, crossing the threshold of his office precisely sixty seconds later.

Alves family home
8 p.m.

The pizza delivery boy never for a moment imagined what was going on behind the door to the house. Dorian had paid and added a tip, and the boy remounted his red scooter to speed to the next address on his round.

By now all that remained of their meals were the greasy,

empty boxes. They were removed from the table and replaced by the fire emergency details, the evidence bag numbers and their approximate locations. Rhino pointed out one hastily scrawled number.

"Is this an eight or a three?"

Tomas leaned over and read: "2015/58/1. That means the year 2015, evidence bag number one, case 58. It's an eight."

"I don't like to mention it, but you write like a four-year-old."

"I know, I'm sorry. I was a bit stressed."

Isabel and Aurélie were told to move to the sofa, and the preparations continued, with Alex, as ever, in charge.

"We're listening, Franck."

Franck picked up a notebook to show them his annotated sketches of the rear entrance to the law courts. He laid it on the table so the team and Tomas could see it.

"O.K. First of all, there's a reinforced security gate with a guard post. Behind that, a small yard that leads to a security scanner. I think there's a second guard post because I saw three guys in black uniforms who must be from a private security company. According to Tomas, immediately beyond that there's a door with a digicode panel that leads to the secretary's office, protected by a bulletproof screen. There must be C.C.T.V. cameras as well, but I didn't have time to spot them. It's nothing like how Tiretto tried to sell it to us."

"It's guarded three times better than any jeweller's!" Dorian exploded.

"That scumbag!" Alex thundered. "According to him, it ought to be easy . . ."

"We're going to need more people. Weapons. Several vehicles and probably police uniforms. It'll take at least another three days to prepare. That is, if we really decide to go through with it, because between you and me, it sounds far too risky," said Franck.

Another three days ... Tomas turned to his wife and daughter. He weighed up their fear and his love for them. Faced with the complexity of the situation, his mind was suddenly clear, as if there were no other choice open to him. The best way to help his loved ones was to become part of the criminals' gang and help them make a success of it. He decided to take the lead.

"If you'll allow me . . . Your lawyer is right, and you're creating problems that don't exist."

The four intruders stared at him, dumbfounded. Alex pushed the notebook in his direction.

"That's exactly the attitude I've been hoping for from you from the start. I'm glad to hear it."

Tomas glanced briefly at the notes, then put his elbows on the table and leaned forwards, as if they had always worked together.

"Let's go through this step by step."

Stupefied, his wife and Aurélie listened as Tomas explained.

"To begin with, the first gate. You can forget about it. It's always open and the first guard post is empty."

"Is it a trap?" asked Dorian in astonishment.

"No. The mechanism is broken, and there are no funds to pay for a guard. Yes, the guards in the second control room are from a private security firm, but they don't have any weapons or means of defence. There are four of them, usually from South Africa: some don't even have residence permits. They're changed every two or three weeks, which means that none of them really knows the job. They're paid fifteen hundred euros a month to pretend. We call them the 'parking meters'. They're only there for appearances."

"But we'll have to be dressed as cops to get in, won't we?"

"Not necessarily. The Police Judiciaire are plain clothes, and court employees also use this entrance."

"So you have to show your police credentials or a security pass?"

"They couldn't care less, I'm telling you. For the amount they're paid, they don't even check their video screens. They hardly bother to look up when someone enters. Once you're through there, you come to the secretary's office. The digicode door isn't a problem, because it's only locked between noon and one in the afternoon – the lunch hour. The rest of the time it's left open. So you need to show up at two minutes to twelve. No cop would dream of bringing evidence bags in during lunch, so it's highly unlikely you'll be disturbed."

"That leaves the bulletproof screen in front of the secretary's desk."

"Well, there's a gap at the bottom to push the bags through. All you need do is slip your arm under and threaten her with a weapon. It won't take long for her to decide to press the button that opens the door, and then you're inside."

"But isn't there an alarm button as well? Hidden under her counter, for example – like in banks."

"Yes, but not under the counter. It's two metres from her chair, so there's no risk."

"O.K. What about when we're inside?"

"At the far end of the room there's a spiral staircase. You go down with the secretary, tie her up somewhere, do what you have to do, and leave."

Closing the notebook, Tomas pushed it to the middle of the table and concluded:

"To sum up, you need a gun, a car and guts. There you are – piece of cake."

Tomas's unexpected intervention led to a stunned silence. Despite the danger and their fear, Isabel was seeing a new side to her husband and realised just how far he was prepared to go for them.

Rhinoceros refused to believe him. The plan was so simple it had to be suspect.

"Impossible. It's impossible. Either you're taking the piss out of us, or you want us to get caught. Your plan is a joke."

"What about that cocaine heist from thirty-six Quai des Orfèvres, the headquarters of the elite Paris police? Was that impossible? The guy arrived with two sports bags in broad daylight. He went into the evidence vaults, took fifty-two kilos of coke and left as if he'd just been shopping in a supermarket. Since there are never any break-ins or thefts, vigilance drops until no-one gives a damn, and in the end everything is left open. In fact, it's the security surrounding our administrative buildings that's a joke, not my plan."

He had just put Rhino's back up without realising it. The henchman got up angrily and went to root through the fridge. Alex raised a hand to advise Tomas not to overdo it. Rhinoceros was a dangerous animal and Tomas was on the lowest rung of his food chain.

"Franck, go back to the loft and bring something we can scare the secretary with," Alex ordered.

"I've got the pistol and the revolver we used on our last raid."

"Find something better. Something showy. A break-in is like anything else – it's all in the marketing."

Before leaving the house, Franck, in his hoodie with the car keys in his hand, raised the corner of the curtain and glanced out into the street.

"When will you be back?"

Aurélie was standing right behind him, head bowed because she had dared speak to him.

"In an hour. Two at most."

She half-opened her mouth, thought better of it, and made to turn round. Franck caught her by the arm.

"Stay close to Alex. And make sure you're never alone with Rhinoceros. I won't be long."

He opened the door. She watched him disappear into the night. A rebellious, mixed-up sixteen-year-old, hormones running riot on top of her Stockholm syndrome. She detested Franck for what he was putting her family through. She detested him so intensely she could have kissed him . . .

40

Thursday 11 a.m.
Home invasion: Day four

Dorian was pacing between the kitchen and living room. To attempt the break-in almost empty-handed with Alex would be practically suicidal. Suicidal, and therefore romantic. Everything depended on how far they could trust Tomas, and how afraid of them he really was. A delicate balance.

In her mind, Alex was going over the roles each of them had to play. Tomas Alves, already at his desk so as not to arouse suspicion. Franck at the wheel of their car ten metres from the law courts, ready to drive off as speedily as necessary, depending on the obstacles they encountered. Dorian and herself as police officers for the day, ready to win best acting Oscars. Rhinoceros left behind to keep an eye on the wife and daughter. She watched as he did press-ups, feet on the floor and hands on the fourth step of the staircase. She only hoped he wouldn't assume the role of the bloodthirsty tyrant during the hour the break-in would take.

Aurélie emerged from the bathroom, showered and dressed. As she prepared to descend the stairs she saw her route was blocked. Rhinoceros looked up and saw her, and pushed back against the wall to make way for her. Above his head was a family photo, ski boots in the snow during a winter holiday when the girl was only eight.

"Come on down. I won't touch you," he promised with a ravenous smile he must have thought was friendly.

The adolescent came timidly down the first steps. She had dried herself hastily and regretted it now, because her T-shirt was sticking to her moist skin, showing off the contours of her body in a way that appeared to arouse Rhino. When she came level with him, he sniffed her like a dog and deliberately took up more room so their bodies would brush against each other.

Isabel saw all this and dug her fingers into the leather arm of the sofa. Rhino was amused by her helpless rage. He shouted across the room to her.

"I'd be worried if I were you, Maman. Your daughter smells of sex – she must take after you. You're going to find it hard to keep her on a leash. I bet if there were dick-flavoured gum she'd be chewing it all day long."

Delighted at his own joke, he burst out laughing.

This gratuitous humiliation hadn't escaped Franck's attention. As he took the clean clothes and disguises he had brought from the loft out of a sports bag, his eyes met Aurélie's, moist with tears. He zipped up the bag and went over to his cousin.

"Can I talk to you, Alex?"

"No need. I know."

She spoke to all of them.

"Time to go. Dorian, get ready. Rhino, bring the car up. Franck, you stay and guard the family."

Halfway up the stairs, Rhino gripped the banister and leaned over to talk to them. He was not a happy animal.

"Since when do we change plans ten minutes before we leave? I was supposed to stay here."

"What do you want us to tell them back in Corsica? That we did the job while you were here babysitting?" Alex cut him down.

Rhino looked menacingly from Franck to Aurélie and caught the keys Dorian threw to him.

"I know the address. I could always pay her a visit one of these days," he said, so as not to lose face.

Bobigny High Court of Justice
11.54 a.m.

The car came slowly to a halt at the appointed spot. Alex was wearing a blonde bobbed wig over her brown hair and blue lenses to disguise her green eyes.

"You look good as a Swede," Dorian complimented her. His disguise consisted of no more than a pair of glasses and a pencil moustache. That was all they needed for any description to the police to be sufficiently distant from their true appearance. However limited the subterfuge, it had worked for five jewellery hits, and there was no point changing it now.

"Rhino, if everything goes pear-shaped, clear out of here and pick Franck up, O.K.? Don't worry about us, there'd be nothing you could do anyway."

Rhino nodded to show he had understood. Dorian plucked at his shirt collar and smoothed his jacket. He had chosen a grey one to go with his dark blue jeans so as not to appear too smart. More police officer than businessman. A sudden doubt crossed his mind.

"By the way, what do you do to look like a cop?"

"Scowl and look down your nose at people," Rhino advised him. "That should be easy for you."

"Ready, baby?" Alex asked.

"To hell and back."

The adrenalin began pumping through their veins when, exactly as Tomas had promised, they passed through the first open gate and beyond the deserted guard post.

"So far so good, so far so good," as Steve McQueen said in "The Magnificent Seven".

The small yard. Five metres to the next obstacle. As they approached it, Alex patted her new blonde hair and Dorian pretended to be looking at his mobile. Small, natural, innocent gestures. They went straight through the security scanner and found themselves in a glass control room where six screens projected images from the surveillance cameras dotted around the building. In the middle of the room, four African colossuses, the smallest of them already very large. Alex and Dorian were given only cursory glances as they pushed open the second door and left the security guards behind.

Now they were at the heart of the law courts. Above their heads were four floors full of hundreds of police, lawyers and magistrates.

A few metres further on they came to the door with the digicode panel. Dorian laid his hand flat on it as if taking its pulse. He let a second go by, convinced that it would be locked or that an alarm would go off.

Behind them, three uniforms and a lawyer in a black gown appeared, deep in conversation. Dorian and Alexandra couldn't have felt more visible and vulnerable if they'd been dressed up as clowns, complete with red noses and size-fourteen shoes. But the three cops merely glanced at them, respectfully saluting what they took to be their plain-clothes colleagues. They continued their discussion before disappearing into a lift at the far end of the corridor. As its doors closed, the two thieves' heartbeats slowed to normal.

"As easy as that?" whispered Dorian.

"We aren't there yet."

Dorian grasped the door handle and turned it. Two steps inside the room and they found themselves facing a young woman in her twenties. Skinny, round glasses on a cord, bent over a dozen case files and evidence bags she had to register. Between her and them, a thick pane of glass. The door closed on its own behind them. The secretary looked up, already weary at the thought of more work. Checking the time, her face brightened.

"I'm sorry, it's lunch hour. You'll have to come back at one," she chirped, adjusting her granny glasses.

Dorian plunged his hand into the inside pocket of his jacket and took out what Franck had gone back to their loft to fetch. He took the pin out of the grenade and grasped it firmly so the safety lever didn't go off. He stuck his arm beneath the bulletproof screen and pushed the grenade under the secretary's nose. She stared at it, aghast.

"If you make the slightest false move, I'll blow you to five thousand pieces. Open up or I'll set this off."

Hypnotised by the grenade, the secretary pressed the button. There was a click, and the last door opened for them. Alex entered first, while Dorian carefully replaced the pin in the grenade.

"We're going down to the vault and you're coming with us. Get up," Alex ordered.

The young woman didn't move. Behind her glasses, her eyes began to flutter and her face turned the pallid white Dorian had often seen on employees in the jewellers' they had raided.

"We're losing her. Bring her round," he snapped.

Alex's slap had the desired effect. The secretary, hand on cheek, was finally paying attention.

"I said we're going downstairs, and you're coming with us. Stand up."

At the bottom of the spiral staircase, they froze on the spot, unable to believe their eyes. Two hundred square metres of tight rows of shelves, a vault the size of two football pitches. Close to five thousand evidence bags of all shapes and sizes, bags that told the recent criminal history of Seine-Saint-Denis. Dorian's head was spinning greedily.

"Take a look at it, Alex. Drugs, money, jewels, weapons, compromising documents people would pay a fortune for. It's the ultimate heist right here. We'd be crazy to only take five."

Alex produced a rolled-up canvas bag no bigger than a clementine. When unwrapped it was far bigger than it at first appeared. She took out a bunch of cable ties and threw them to Dorian.

"We stick to the plan. We never improvise, you know that. Tie her up."

Seizing the secretary by the wrists, Dorian dragged her over to one of the metal struts firmly anchored to the floor. He wrapped a cable tie round the strut and pulled it tight. A floppy rag doll, the secretary didn't react. He had fastened her low enough for her to be able to sit, and he even suggested it:

"You can sit down if you . . ."

Without letting him finish, she slumped to the floor, still unresponsive. Her neck didn't seem strong enough to hold up her head, which fell forward drunkenly.

"Leave her, she's no threat," Alex said.

She tore the list in two and handed him half.

"You have three bags, I have two, and we've got five minutes."

Pulling on latex gloves, they began to search the racks, row after row, following Tomas's description of this labyrinth of forbidden, tempting marvels. Dorian found the first two bags easily and then, almost by chance – unless it was the power of attraction – his fingers brushed against a thick transparent plastic bag containing a jewellery box. An open velvet-lined casket that resembled a nest of golden vipers, stuffed with a twisted mass of rings, bracelets and necklaces. In the centre, as if protected by the reptiles, lay a ring so large even Dorian thought it over the top. He read the attached note:

Burglary – 2015/21/9 – Case against M. Mayeras.

Professional that he was, Dorian mentally estimated its value, then picked up the heavy bag and showed it to Alex through the shelves.

"As much as we'd get robbing a jeweller's! With no effort! It'd be rude not to take it."

Despite her convictions, Alex hesitated momentarily. She came round to stand beside Dorian and like him was tempted. Then she examined the note stapled to the bag.

"It's not a hold-up, it's a burglary. You know I'm superstitious. There's too much love in jewellery that's already been worn. It would bring us bad luck. Leave it."

She turned on her heel and disappeared round the end of the row. Dorian reluctantly did as she said. He placed the bag on a shelf and carried on looking, trying hard not to think about what they were leaving behind. When he finally found the evidence bag for case number 2014/56/3, the last on his list, he took it out and put it in the canvas bag with the others. Alex came to find him in the middle of the room, holding two manila envelopes.

"Five bags including the watch. We're good to go."

They looked at each other one last time before retracing their steps.

Spiral staircase, digicode door, scanner, guard post, guards not guarding much, small yard, another post. Fresh air.

When Rhinoceros saw them walking calmly towards him, the canvas bag slung over Dorian's shoulder, he clenched his fists and punched the car roof twice.

"Impossible!" he shouted, literally overjoyed. "I didn't believe it! Right up to the last minute, I didn't believe it!"

"Calm down. Let's go, and make sure you respect the highway code," Alex said, getting in beside him. "We don't want to be stopped by the police."

Indicating politely, Rhinoceros pulled out of the parking space. Until the law courts disappeared in the rear-view mirror, the three of them held their breath, fear still palpable. When they came out onto the main road leading to the Alves family's home the dam burst and shouts of joy exploded like fireworks inside the car. Alex turned to Dorian, seized his jacket collar, pulled him towards her and gave him such a passionate kiss she almost devoured him. Even Rhino, not usually so delicate in these matters, began to stir uncomfortably.

"Hey, take it easy . . . you'll set the car on fire."

41

At two minutes past one in the afternoon, a police team approached the secretary's office. Carrying a boxful of evidence to be registered, the officer in charge opened the door with the digicode. He noted first of all the secretary's strange absence, then the open door to the vault, and most disturbing of all, several case files scattered on the floor. He put the box down, reached for his weapon and disappeared down the spiral staircase.

Three seconds later, he came bounding up the stairs and punched the alarm button. The sound echoed throughout the building. A courthouse robbed like a miserable corner shop. Tomas, who had been on tenterhooks all morning, saw the other court employees stiffen and panic. He recalled what Alex had told him: "Playing by our rules is the only way to save your family."

He prayed they had pulled it off.

Within a few minutes, the entire building was a hive of police buzzing with orders and anger at having been duped in their own back yard. The law courts were put into lockdown: all the staff had to stay on their own floors; even the magistrates were kept prisoner in their offices. The local Bobigny officers were soon replaced by heavyweights from the Seine-Saint-Denis Police Judiciaire.

By eight-thirty that evening, their report was ready and its findings were damning. No-one had seen or heard anything. The robbers, however many there had been, had entered and left without using any violence after a successful break-in between noon and one o'clock. It was impossible to tell exactly which evidence bags had been stolen. The secretary, who had been a witness to the entire operation, had not yet been able to string a single comprehensible sentence together.

As things stood, Alex and Dorian might as well have been ghosts.

Tomas opened the front door to his home and rushed into the living room. No sooner had he appeared than Alex and her team began to applaud, their faces beaming, bottles of champagne on the table. Tomas was so astonished he dropped his briefcase. Dorian came up to him and flung an arm round his shoulders. Like a master of ceremonies introducing an honoured guest, he announced in a loud voice:

"Ladies and gentlemen . . . Tomas Alves, our double agent!"

An even louder round of applause, with appreciative whistles. Still taken aback, Tomas turned to his wife and daughter. They each had a glass of champagne and looked embarrassed by this unlikely celebration. Embarrassed, but less terrified. The family were no longer victims, but accomplices.

The mattresses had been returned to their bedrooms, and the living room looked warm and inviting once more. Next to the table were the full canvas bags, ready to be stowed in the car boot. Rhinoceros poured a glass that foamed over onto the tablecloth. Then he drew up a chair and invited Tomas to sit down.

"Come on, drink! Tell us! What did the cops' faces look like? And the judges? I'd have loved to have been there. But drink!"

Overwhelmed, Tomas wet his lips in the bubbles. Since everyone was staring at him, he cleared his throat before giving his account.

"The alarm went off at two minutes past one. I know, because the wall clock faces my desk. Then the law courts were completely sealed. Nobody could come in or out. All of us – magistrates and employees – were questioned in our offices. I heard the police gave the security guards on the ground floor a hard time, asking why they were so useless. They wanted to review the C.C.T.V. footage, but most of the cameras just film what's going on without recording, so there is none. As far as the secretary goes, I don't think you have anything to fear. She's in too much of a state to say whether there were one or four robbers, whether they were men or women, black or white."

"We didn't harm her, if that means anything to you," said Dorian.

"I know. Thank you for that, she's a good girl. Oh, and tomorrow morning a commandant from the Police Judiciaire wants to interview me. Wait . . ."

Tomas took a business card from his pocket and read out loud:

"Commandant Rivière, from the Groupe de répression du banditisme."

"The G.R.B., our best buddies!" chortled Rhinoceros. "What do they want from you?"

"To know which evidence bags were stolen, and what was in them. At the moment, they think they may be hidden somewhere in the building, so they're going to spend the night searching it, supervised by the head of the examining magistrates and the police chiefs. We were told to leave our offices unlocked. It's unheard of."

"They think it's a two-stage heist. First we steal then hide the stuff and recover it later. That's not so stupid – but they're wrong. We're much better than that," Dorian boasted, depositing the bags with their haul on the table.

"I asked you to help get my brother out of prison," Alex said, turning to the three men. "And you all agreed. Without asking anything in return. Now I know who I'm dealing with. We're not just a team. We're a family."

Glasses were raised again, but three remained on the table. Dorian refilled Tomas's, and Franck did the same for Aurélie and Isabel. This was already their second, and they were slightly tipsy.

No sooner had they finished drinking than the insatiable Rhino filled their glasses once more. Tomas looked across at his wife and daughter. At that moment the only thing he wanted was to return to the life they knew – their normal, occasionally boring but incalculably precious life. With nothing more to worry about.

Yet he was still uncertain how his family's forced collaboration would end. For the time being, he played along, repeating a snatch of conversation that would flatter Alex and her team.

"As I was leaving, I overheard the commandant with one of his men. They were talking about you. They called you 'the magicians'."

Thunderous applause and laughter. Alex raised her glass, and they all turned towards her.

"Abracadabra, gentlemen."

Shortly before midnight, everything that had been brought to the Alves' family home over the previous ninety-six hours had been lined up in the hall. Just to be sure, Alex sent Franck to do a final check in every room. He inspected the living room and kitchen, went upstairs to look in the bathroom, and didn't bother with the parents' bedroom because none of them had been in there. As he was making his way back downstairs, he passed Aurélie's bedroom. The door was ajar, so he gently pushed it open. She was at the window, anxiously waiting to see them leave. When she sensed Franck behind her, she gave a start.

"Sorry, I didn't mean to frighten you," he apologised.

Aurélie gave him a disarming, ironic smile. He didn't know how to react.

"O.K., maybe we should have thought of that four days ago, when we took your home over."

He took a step inside the room, and she took one towards him.

"We're going now. And don't worry about Rhinoceros. We'll put him back in his cage tonight. You won't see him again either."

Another step. Chest pounding and stomach churning.

"Thank you," Aurélie whispered. "For defending me. You didn't have to."

"I wanted to."

From the ground floor, Alex's stern voice brought Franck back to business.

"I really must go now," he said, turning on his heel.

She took hold of his arm, bent closer, and stole a kiss on his mouth. She did this so quickly that Franck only realised it afterwards, his moist lips the only proof.

"You didn't have to . . ."

"I wanted to," she said, blushing.

Now the three men were in the car, with the engine running and Franck at the wheel. Alex was with Tomas on the front doorstep. Two globe lights illuminated the flowers in the garden

209

as she walked down from the house. The Alves family had behaved impeccably over these difficult days, but the terms of their bargain had to be spelled out one last time. She signalled to Tomas.

"Come here, I won't bite . . ."

Not entirely convinced, he took two steps towards her. Leaning forward, she whispered a compliment.

"You were perfect. Courageous. A real head of the family."

"Thank you," Tomas said fretfully.

"You and I have an agreement, don't we?"

"I know what you're going to say, but it's not necessary."

"But it is," she corrected him. "In a week's time, your fear will have subsided. You'll even think you could have done this or that to prevent us getting in. You'll replay the film in your head. And within a fortnight, you'll be telling yourself you can betray us to the police without any consquences. You may even think you know everything they'll need to convict us. Our faces and names. But one evening you'll come home and I'll have sent someone to sew your daughter's head on your wife's body, and your wife's head in that damn oven where she cooks her gratin."

Tomas looked down at the ground.

"That really wasn't necessary."

A neighbour came out of his house to take out the bins and glanced in their direction. Alex embraced Tomas as if he were an old friend, and finally left his home.

And his life as well, Tomas fervently hoped.

PART FOUR

BUTTERFLY EFFECT

"We're in deep shit, if you'll pardon the expression"

FLEUR SAINT-CROIX
INVESTIGATING MAGISTRATE
AT BOBIGNY HIGH COURT

42

Seine-Saint-Denis Police Judiciaire.
Eleven hours earlier

Almost lost in an office too big for him, camouflaged in a mundane beige suit as though trying to hide inside it, Commissaire Divisionnaire Stévenin was leafing through two thick case files that had landed on his desk. Going from one to the other to get some idea of what they were about, he eventually closed them both and looked across at Coste. Since Damiani's retirement, Coste had been temporarily in charge of the two Groupes Crime, a promotion that seemed self-evident. Except maybe to Capitaine Lara Jevric, the head of Groupe Crime 2, who still couldn't understand why she had been passed over. She had argued that she had seniority (even though there was only two months in it), brought up Coste's questionable record, and argued she was better placed for the role, because for the fourth year running she was trying for promotion to commissaire, like a puppy banging its head against a brick wall. Unfortunately for her, Damiani herself had chosen her replacement, and Stévenin had been more than happy to hide behind that decision.

"What do you think of your new office?" he asked Coste.

"It's not mine. It used to be Damiani's, and it'll soon belong to her successor. I'm only keeping the chair warm."

"How about Jevric?"

"She's never been hard to fathom. She shits on her team, competes with anyone on the same level as her, and fawns to those above her. For the moment, I belong to that category, so she more or less leaves me alone."

"Don't worry, Damiani's replacement will be here in a week. You'll be able to return to your group and get out there again."

Inside or out, that wasn't the problem. Coste didn't react, and his superior didn't insist, aware the capitaine was going through a bad patch. Laying his hands on the two files, he spoke forcefully, hoping this would motivate Coste.

"Can you bring me up to speed on these? That'll save time."

"Of course," said Coste. "Jevric's group are handling the case of a woman found in the street yesterday morning, her face bashed in with a hammer. The autopsy revealed it wasn't just her face that was in bits. Her whole body was smashed like a vase."

"With a hammer?"

"No, thankfully. The forensic pathologist reported that the fractures were consistent with falling from a great height – a cliff or tower block. Thanks to that report, all Jevric's group had to do was look up. The body was found at the foot of a tower. The one her lover lived in, where she had gone to tell him it was over. A violent argument, he throws her out of a seventh-floor window, but she survives. Sometimes the human body is . . . So he came down and finished her off with a hammer."

"My wife and I see a marriage counsellor," Stévenin mused.

"The hammer is in my office if you change your mind. We're keeping the ex in our cells for a few more hours, then he'll be transferred."

Stévenin stood up and inserted a capsule into his coffee-maker. He looked inquiringly at Coste, who mouthed a "no thank you" back.

"As for my group . . . sorry, I mean Ronan's group," Coste

corrected himself, "they're dealing with a case that came up yesterday afternoon. A little girl found dead in her bed. Six years old: no wounds, no broken bones, not so much as a scratch. Her parents called the local police at two o'clock in the afternoon, saying she wasn't breathing. At three, the Groupe Crime was on the spot with the emergency doctor. At the autopsy, the pathologist compared time of death and body temperature. Grosso modo, if you remember your courses, one degree less per hour from the third hour after death. The body was brought to the Institut Médico-Légal at six that evening, so the temperature ought to have been thirty-five degrees. It was twenty-seven. She had died the previous day or early that night. The parents were spinning a line. Ronan interviewed all nine members of the family to get a better picture."

"And the winner is . . . ?"

"The father. The little girl had bronchitis for a week. It prevented her from sleeping, so he stuffed her with sleeping pills. But two night ago, he overdid it. A senseless death."

"As if there's any other kind. As for the pathologist, she followed her intuition in both cases. Good work, isn't it?"

"Yes, you're right. That's the best way to look at it. It's good work."

"And this morning?"

"A Roma girl stabbed and left on a fly-tipping dump, two hundred metres from her camp," Coste replied wearily.

Stévenin put down his empty cup.

"These are cases, capitaine, not people."

"I know that, and yet I find it increasingly hard to compartmentalise."

"Take a few days off."

"I've tried that. It's just kicking the can down the road."

Stévenin almost asked what the problem was, but quickly

realised he didn't want to know the answer. Since his mouth was already open, he took the opportunity to politely dismiss Coste.

No sooner had Coste left Stévenin's office than he saw Jevric at the far end of the corridor. She was lumbering towards him, her face a picture of reproach. She didn't even wait until she was at arm's length before barking:

"Are you serious, Coste? Really?"

A few heads were already poking out of the adjoining offices, eager to catch Jevric's latest outburst. Though she was addressing her temporary new boss, she continued at the top of her voice:

"Yesterday you dumped the carpaccio girl on us, and now it's the gyppo on a fly-tip? What do you think we are, refuse collectors? Why didn't you assign her to your group? It's blatant favouritism!"

"I thought it was so blatant it didn't need pointing out."

Jevric almost choked at such calculated impertinence. Coste left her standing in the corridor, ready to vent her anger on whoever she bumped into next.

Once he was alone in his office with the door closed, Coste sat down and from under a pile of dossiers took out a document he had thought it wise to conceal, for the time being at least. To make it official he only had to sign it. He took out a pen and unscrewed the lid. Just at that moment his mobile began to ring, allowing him to postpone his decision yet again. Reading the name of the caller on the screen, he slid the document into a drawer.

"Hi there, Léa. I was just about to call you. Stévenin has asked me to congratulate you on your good work."

Léa wedged her mobile between shoulder and ear while

she parked the trolley she was pushing down a corridor of the Institut, then jumped on it and made herself comfortable.

"Go on then."

"Pardon?"

"Congratulate me."

Coste hesitated over what to say next. He'd been thinking it over for several days. The introspection of a forty-something man, combined with the pressures of his job and what his father had said to him. After fifteen years getting his hands dirty, he had realised there were perhaps only two real things in his life. The close bond with his team. And Léa.

"Not over the phone. Besides, we need to see each other. I'd like to apologise for my attitude, if it's not too late."

"Careful, Victor. I swear I'll give you a good punch if you're playing games with me."

"You ought to have done that long ago. Listen, I was wondering . . ."

Doors slamming, agitated cries and people running. Coste stood up in mid-sentence and stuck his head out of the office. A group of officers was sprinting towards the exit, paying him no attention. Beyond them he saw Commandant Rivière, both physically and mentally the archetypal rugby player. Radio pressed to his ear, he was barking orders. Behind him were two of his lieutenants, one putting on his bullet-proof vest, the other holstering his gun.

"Léa, I have to go. Something's come up."

He ended the call just as Léa was about to permit herself an "I miss you" she would have regretted all day. Like a stray bullet, the confession missed its target. Coste was already somewhere else, intercepting Rivière.

"In a word?"

"Break-in at the law courts' evidence vault."

"The law courts . . . ? You mean the ones over there? The ones twenty metres from here?" Coste exclaimed.

The commandant disappeared, followed by his men. Turning round, Victor stared through his office window at the court building with its red brick walls and big panes of glass. A wobbly architectural cube, as if a disturbed kid had been playing with a box of Lego.

"It had to happen some day," he said to himself.

43

The morning after the break-in Dorian, stretched out on a sofa bed, was struggling with a reflection of the rising sun that painted the loft an autumnal dark orange. He tossed and turned, and finally managed to get back to sleep. He hadn't even noticed Alex was no longer beside him. That is until she almost hit him in the face when she threw one of the stolen evidence bags at him. It was as heavy as a brick.

"Shit! What's the matter with you?" he mumbled, still half asleep.

Stony-faced, she sat next to him and held out a torn piece of paper. Dorian recognised the half of the list she had given him.

"What does it say on the third line?" she asked, like a mother reproaching a kid for a poor school report.

Dorian sat up in bed. He saw Franck and Rhinoceros sitting with their coffees in the middle of the room, staring uneasily at him. Rubbing his eyes, he read:

"2015/58/1 . . . What's the problem?"

Alex picked up the bag that had served as his wake-up call and thrust it under his nose.

"What does it say here?"

"2015/53 . . . Oh shit."

"Yes, shit! 2015/53/1. You got the wrong number."

Furious, she straightened up, then flopped into the chair opposite the sofa bed.

"Read us the case it's related to."

A bewildered Dorian did as he was told.

"2015/53/1 – a laptop computer. Case against Doucey Antoine – possession of images and videos of a paedophilic nature."

He put the bag down, still unable to comprehend why Alex was so angry. And she hadn't yet finished with him.

"I know exactly when it happened. It was when you saw the jewellery box and started drooling over it and lost concentration. You're about as much use as a concrete parachute!"

"In his defence, it wasn't very clearly written," said Rhino, half-hidden behind his coffee cup.

"You stay out of this!" Alex warned him.

Wide awake by now, Dorian could think more clearly and recover some of his self-assurance.

"O.K., calm down, Alexandra! Calm down and explain. We took five pieces of evidence to give the cops five cases to investigate. We couldn't give a damn whether they're kids in an orgy or nuclear warheads. The important thing was to conceal the theft of the watch among the others. So what does this change?"

Alex looked down at the floor, and Dorian repeated more gently:

"Alex, what does this change?"

A few moments later, they were all gathered round the table, with Alex the centre of attention.

"It had to be precisely those five bags."

"You're the only one who understands, Alex. Tell us what this is about."

"Tiretto's list wasn't just random."

"We know. Important evidence from important cases, to confuse the boys in blue."

"No, he was very specific, it had to be those five and no others."

"So you think there was a reason for it?"

"Shit, he's a lawyer: do you reckon he does things out of the goodness of his heart? Obviously there's a reason, and don't forget he still has the chance to shop us all with a simple anonymous phone call."

"O.K., wait a second. Tell us word for word what he said to you," Dorian insisted.

"We steal the watch for Nunzio, along with the four other bags. We don't touch them, and above all we don't open them. We wait for him to call to agree a place to hand them over to him."

"Do you know what he wants them for?"

"No idea."

"You didn't ask?"

"No," said an exasperated Alex. "He offered me a way to get Nano released and told me the rest would be his reward. I didn't argue."

Rhinoceros stood up, leaving the circle.

"This stinks. I say we give him nothing until Nano is released and we're all safely back in Corsica. If these bags are so important to him, that can be our guarantee to get off the mainland without problems. Especially as we've only taken four of the ones he wants, and he's apparently expecting something other than low-res photos of kids."

"We just have to hope he continues with the plan," Alex groaned. "Now there can't be an expert verification of the watch, we need him to petition the judge for Nano's release. This isn't the moment to upset him."

Franck's mobile began to vibrate in his pocket. Consulting the message, he picked up his coat and excused himself.

"I'm going to do some public relations. I'll leave you to it."

"Where and who with?"

"If you're so interested, I could make you a list of all my contacts, cousin. If you want weapons, I find them for you; the same goes for cars. But that takes trust, and for that I have to show my face from time to time. I'll only be gone for the afternoon. Anything else?"

Franck left the loft and bounded down the four flights of stairs. He opened the front door and studied each side of the street carefully before waving to the young girl sitting waiting for him on a car bonnet. When she came over, he took her by the arm and pulled her inside the building.

"Where are you taking me?" she asked.

The three bottom floors were completely empty: only the fourth-floor loft was in use. A safe place where Alex and her team could prepare their raids, and afterwards, somewhere to lie low until things calmed down.

Franck and the girl reached the first-floor landing. They pushed open the swing doors and found themselves in an immense, silent space. A series of empty offices, fitted carpets never trodden on, here and there pieces of furniture still in plastic wrapping. The visible remains of a failed real estate project. At the far end, a big room with the same huge windows as the loft, and a sofa – also still wrapped in plastic – probably intended for a boss who never moved in.

"I missed you," Aurélie whispered into his shoulder. They kissed tenderly, their hands started to roam, and they soon collapsed onto the thick carpet, where their movements became increasingly frantic. Two minutes later, they had moved to the sofa and were squeezing one another like bubble wrap.

222

"I have to be home by six," Aurélie warned him, pausing to get her breath back, her bra straps dangling down.

"I'll write your parents a note. Come back here," Franck said impatiently, pulling her towards him.

44

A few minutes before seven that evening, the phone rang on Coste's desk. Jevric had left the bags with the stabbed young Roma girl's clothes on it, as well as the findings and photos from the crime scene. The stench of over-ripe fruit and rotten meat was so strong that Coste had opened the windows to let in some fresh air. He picked up the phone, pleased to have something else to think about.

"Capitaine Coste? Fleur Saint-Croix here. I need to see you and your team."

"Right now?" he asked, looking across at the wall clock.

"Do you really want me to answer that?"

The tone of her voice told him the atmosphere over at the law courts wasn't exactly festive. Justice had been broken into the day before, and Justice wasn't amused.

"Give us five minutes."

Johanna, Sam and Ronan chose chairs some distance from the desk. Coste took the remaining one, facing the magistrate. A grey and black room completely devoid of any ornament. Fleur Saint-Croix had not even allowed herself a picture on the wall. It reminded Coste of his flat.

"We're in deep shit, if you'll pardon the expression."

"Yes, we gathered that," said Coste.

"No, it's even deeper than it was yesterday."

"We're listening, darling," said Ronan, immediately wincing at a word he only used in bed with her.

Fleur Saint-Croix didn't even seem to notice.

"If you haven't been brought up to speed, here's where we are. The person responsible for the evidence bags and his eight staff spent all day checking them, and there are five missing."

"Only five?" Sam was astonished. "All that effort for five?"

"It's not how many that's worrying us, but the absurdity of what's in them. A laptop, a luxury watch, a C.D. with phone taps, a G.P.S., and a hunting knife. Five bags from five distinct cases covered by five distinct police forces. Most of them have little resale value. And we can't find a link between the crimes. So how can I ask five police departments to investigate the same robbery?"

"It's far too random and incoherent for there not to be a link," Coste argued.

"The truth is, I've no idea what it all means," the magistrate admitted. "I get the impression someone is playing games with us, but I don't know what the rules are."

"And you're asking our advice?" Coste said.

"No, I'm asking you to take over the investigation, to be the focal point."

"It's currently with Commandant Rivière and his men. I don't see any reason to ask him to step down."

"Don't worry, I don't either. Let them deal with the technical side of the break-in. You focus on the link. There must be something. You don't go around burgling the High Court for a G.P.S., for heaven's sake!"

Coste turned to Ronan.

"Jevric is busy with the Roma girl stabbing, so if the Police Judiciaire gets involved, it'll be down to you. Can you handle it?"

"Of course," Ronan said, almost offended.

"We can't leave any stone unturned," said Coste. "I want the five original case files and all the most recent petitions from their defence lawyers."

"I'll see to that," Saint-Croix assured him. "You'll have copies of all the trial transcriptions first thing tomorrow morning. Everyone is so on edge they won't hold back any information."

Coste nodded and stood up. His team followed suit, but one of them was asked to remain:

"Lieutenant Scaglia, could you stay behind a minute?"

Johanna winked at Ronan as she shut the door behind her. Alone with the magistrate, he was quick to apologise.

"Is it because of the 'darling'?"

"Of course not, everybody in your team knows anyway. But how is Coste?" she asked, sitting closer to him on the edge of her desk.

"He's managing the groups from a distance, from his office. He hasn't left it in over a week."

"When he says you're going to take over the investigation . . . He'll still keep an eye on you, won't he? I mean, he'll get involved?"

"Don't count on it," Ronan said, frowning. "But don't worry, I'll do the best I can."

Offended by her lack of confidence, Ronan turned on his heel. With his hand on the doorknob, he emphasised his disgruntlement.

"Besides, it's not just me, if you don't think I'm up to it . . ."

Saint-Croix bit her tongue, once again regretting her lack of tact towards Ronan. For his part, when he left her office, he found himself faced by the rest of the team, looking highly amused.

"Everything alright?" asked Sam. "Did she tell you off?"

"I just have to avoid calling her 'darling' in future," Ronan blustered.

45

Night had been unable to offer any advice, and Coste had hesitated a hundred times over whether to call Léa or not. Morning didn't clarify anything either, and once again he sat staring at the form he still couldn't make up his mind to sign. The heading "Resignation Report" made him feel like a coward, a deserter.

There were three knocks on the door, and Lara Jevric burst in. Like a teenager trying to hide a porn mag, Coste clumsily dropped the form into a drawer.

"Am I disturbing you? What are you trying to hide?" she gloated.

"None of your business. What can I do for you?"

"Nothing. I've come to give you my conclusions about the young girl in the rubbish dump."

"So soon?" Coste was astonished.

"Maybe I'm not as useless as you think."

She sat down opposite him and opened the file on her knees.

"Denitza Boti, aged seventeen. The only girl with any education in the camp. All the witnesses interviewed wanted to stay anonymous, but basically she refused to accompany the others to beg in the Metro. The camp's boss didn't think much of that: he'd already taught her a lesson that put her in hospital. I found the medical report: it was brutal. But despite everything, she went back to high school, and this is the result. He wanted to make an example of her."

"Denitza Boti – that rings a bell," said Coste, repeating the name to jog his memory.

"Same here. So I looked into it. They wrote about her in *Libération*. She wanted to become a paediatrician for travellers and Romas."

Lara closed the file and stood up. Before leaving Coste's office, she felt pleased enough with herself to make one of those pronouncements that always threatened to bring him out in a rash.

"Yeah, the ship's sinking, Victor. We won't be able to save everyone."

As soon as she closed the door, Coste took out the form and signed it without hesitation. He was giving his bosses enough time for Damiani's replacement to get their feet under the desk; after that, they would have to do without him. He scanned the sheet of paper one last time, then headed for the secretary's office to make it official. As he made his way down the glassed-in walkway, he passed Groupe Crime 1's office. His heart lurched when he saw the whole team busy at work.

"No-one is irreplaceable. The ship can perfectly well sink without me," he told himself.

As promised, they had received close to four thousand pages of court proceedings. As a sweetener, Saint-Croix had added a box of chocolate muffins.

Faced with this mass of documents, Ronan wiped the whiteboard clean. He knew he would be filling it again all too soon.

"O.K., Johanna and Sam, go through the summary of each case and give me the gist."

Johanna put down her coffee and half-eaten muffin, wiped her hands on her pullover and opened the first file, her mouth still full.

"First stolen evidence bag. A laptop computer containing paedophile images and videos."

Ronan wrote the details in capitals on the board.

"A case in the Seine-Saint-Denis juvenile court against one Antoine Doucey. He was reported by the parents of a young boy. His own neighbours, if I'm to credit what's written here . . ."

Marveil Prison
Segregation cell No. 13

The memory of that afternoon haunted Doucey almost every night. The one he had spent in his flat with Leo, when the boy was ill and he'd offered to look after him. When, eight years earlier, the couple had arrived from the provinces to settle in the Paris suburbs, the wife was already heavily pregnant. Leo arrived only three months later. As the years went by, they became friends. Until that afternoon when, with Leo at his mercy, Doucey had taken advantage to get closer, more hands on. That same evening, the boy's mother undressed him for his bath. First his pullover, then his T-shirt, then his trousers, but, to her consternation, no underpants. She was paralysed by the evidence; eight years of blind trust fell away from her eyes. After a sleepless night, she phoned the police emergency number. When they searched Doucey's place, they found the underpants under two sofa cushions, and on the desk a laptop full of downloaded images and videos that would be seared into the imagination for good.

"People should never trust their neighbours," concluded Sam, opening the second case file. "The second evidence bag stolen:

a G.P.S. A Brigade Financière case against one Boyan Mladic. Arson."

"What's the connection between a G.P.S. and a case of arson?" Ronan asked in astonishment.

"Wait a minute, I'll look."

Marveil prison
Segregation cell No. 20

Only a few more days to wait. Boyan wasn't too keen for his future to be left in the hands of a lawyer, but he knew too much about Darcy to be left in this hole. It wasn't to his employer's advantage to let him think things over for too long in here. You make bad decisions when you feel you've been abandoned, even if, Boyan had to admit, he had messed up on his last contract. He had turned up at the home of a brasserie owner to explain how interested Monsieur Darcy and the real estate company he represented were in it. To no avail. So he had simply burned the place down using a few gallons of petrol. Unfortunately for him, the flames burned so brightly it allowed an eyewitness to spot his licence plate number. Taken into custody, the Serb had denied everything, but due to him being a foreigner and his past in the Foreign Legion and as a bodyguard, the judge preferred to remand him in prison while they checked his G.P.S. data to see if he had been at the bar before it was reduced to ashes. Yes, Boyan conceded, he had become less vigilant, taken fewer precautions. But it was only a few more days, he told himself, strengthening his fists by punching the cell wall for hours until they bled.

"If he was the one responsible, he must be delighted his G.P.S. was stolen," Sam concluded as Johanna picked up the next file.

"Third evidence bag," she announced. "A luxury Van Cleef

and Arpels watch. A case for Rivière's G.R.B. Against Nunzio Mosconi, for a raid on a jeweller's."

Marveil Prison
Segregation Cell No. 2.

Nano often woke in the middle of the night. Or possibly in the middle of the day for all he knew, given the lack of windows or any indication of how time was passing. Always the same images, whatever the dream: watches everywhere. On his wrist, on the ground, in mid-air, hanging from trees or hidden under pillows, round watches, square watches, melted watches – nothing but watches. Shortly after the raid on the jeweller's he had been introduced to cocaine by friends at a party. A great discovery with dreadful repercussions. Literally off his head, he had tried to start his car, but only managed to shunt into the one in front. Police on the scene and an attempt to make a run for it. He remembered tripping over his feet and landing head first in a refuse bin like an idiot. It was only at the police station that the cops realised his watch was worth two years of their salary. And that its serial number linked it to a raid on a jeweller's.

This time Nano had dreamed of a dog wearing a watch-collar urinating on his Paris–Ajaccio plane ticket. Turning over on his concrete bunk, he beat his head against the wall to get to sleep.

"So you can plan and carry out a smart burglary and still be a halfwit," Ronan chortled.

"Fourth case," Sam continued, "and this is one of ours. A hunting knife. Accusation of murder against Gabriel Rezelny, investigated by Crime Group 2 and our beloved Lara Jevric."

Gabriel Rezelny, known in Marveil as Scalpel, was standing in a corner of the Jungle, observing his companions in misfortune. He shared everything with them – boredom, violence, loneliness. Everything, with the possible exception of innocence. A builder with his own company, he had taken on a two-week job and offered a big discount to a newly separated young woman with whom he had felt such a spark it had almost electrocuted him. He had never denied cheating on his wife with her. Nor that he had deleted the messages from his besotted client when she had threatened to spill the beans. But he had always refused to admit that he'd raped her, stuffing a sock in her mouth to stop her screaming then slitting her throat with a hunting knife.

His wife hadn't paid him a single visit. Like everyone else she was convinced that as well as being an unfaithful husband he was a rapist and murderer. Abandoned, Gabriel had given in and accepted his fate between these four walls. Until an assault was reported in a nearby region, with a familiar *modus operandi*. A victim threatened with a knife and raped, silenced by a sock. This time, however, the victim fought back, managing to drive off her attacker and surviving to describe him to the police. A homeless guy, half-tramp, half-nomad was arrested. A clasp hunting knife was found on him. Scalpel's lawyer had called for the knife to be sent to the Bobigny law courts to see if it matched the wounds found on the throat of Gabriel Rezelny's client. If the result was positive, he could be released.

Scalpel couldn't bring himself to feel glad it took a second victim for his case to be re-opened, but the hope of getting out gnawed at his stomach and led him to become a model inmate and keep his head down while he waited for a possible appeal in his favour. He had only once broken this rule, when he had tried to take young Nano under his wing. A wasted effort – the youngster had gone crazy and been segregated for far too long. After that, Scalpel had sworn not to take pity on anyone. That was why, when he saw the new inmate in the middle of the Jungle, staring straight ahead, jaw clenched as he made his way towards Machine's game of poker, he decided to move away from the wall to avoid getting caught up in anything. When the newcomer reached Machine, he snorted noisily, cleared his throat and spat a disgusting yellowish stream right at Machine's two pairs of jacks and queens. Machine looked up at his aggressor calmly, then threw his cards on the ground.

"The more we look, the less I'm seeing," confessed Ronan. "I still can't find any connection between these offences. A paedophile, an arsonist, a robber and a murderer. If we have them all going into a bar, it could be the start of a bad joke. Come on, let's hear the fifth one."

"The fifth and last," said Johanna. "A C.D. of phone taps. Case against . . ."

When it came to the investigating police force and the name of the accused, she suddenly fell silent.

"Case against whom?" Sam asked impatiently.

Marveil Prison
C Wing Exercise yard

The new prisoner had just challenged Machine with a thick gobbet of spit, interrupting the game and what looked like a very promising hand. Machine had already forgotten his cards. He was on his feet, surprised at first by his cellmate's defiance, and then determined to give him a beating in front of everyone.

"Hey, Doe-Eyes, has your brain cell gone out or are you trying to attract my attention?"

Yassine Chelli made no reply, but turned on his heel and headed for the Ring. The other poker players laid their cards in front of them. Some onlookers stood back to make way for Yassine, murmuring among themselves that he didn't stand a chance. In the shade of the Ring his outline became indistinct, hidden from the guard's binoculars up in the watch tower. Yassine puffed out his chest, stared defiantly at Machine, grabbed his penis and shouted loudly at him:

"Hey, gorilla! Come over here. I've got a banana for you."

Like dogs about to go on the attack, Machine's nose and the corners of his mouth began to twitch. He was going to annihilate Yassine. He'd grab him by the neck and beat his head against the ground until all that was left was mush between his fingers. He began in slow motion, treading heavily, then the rhythm increased and he went hurtling towards him. By the time he got to the Ring he was running at full tilt. Just as he was reaching out to grab his quarry, four inmates appeared from behind an unperturbed Yassine, who had not budged a centimetre. Finally spotting the trap, Machine slowed down, but too late: the blows began to rain down on him. Jaw, ribs, cheeks, stomach, liver. Faced with this furious assault, he curled up on the ground, lifting his knees to his stomach and covering his head with his arms. Machine had been beaten up in the past and knew how to protect himself. Unfortunately for him, his arms and legs were pulled apart, and despite his strength he could do nothing to prevent himself being left spreadeagled, his groin at anyone's mercy. Yassine came up to him, all sense of humanity long gone.

"You like it when I stroke you in the cell, do you?"

Drawing back his leg, he launched a tremendous kick right in the middle of his victim's crotch, permanently crushing a testicle. Machine squealed like a pig and his eyes rolled up.

Yassine kicked him even harder. This time the shaft of his penis was smashed. He kicked him again and again, with the same question each time, screaming it as if he was reliving the experience:

"And now? Do you like it now, loser?"

By the third kick the intense pain made Machine lose consciousness; after that, he didn't feel anything. Even when his arms and legs were freed and Yassine went on kicking him until only swollen, mangled flesh remained.

If Machine had friends in the prison, Yassine had even more, and so no-one came forward to defend him. Two youngsters dragged him by the legs and left him in view of the watchtower. The loudspeaker blared:

"To the gate!"

The two kids took hold of the body again, while a few metres away a panting Yassine lit himself a cigarette.

"Case against who?" Sam asked impatiently.

"Investigation by Groupe Crime 1," Johanna said. "Against Yassine Chelli. Kidnapping, illegal imprisonment and accessory to murder."

The tip of the whiteboard marker did not move.

"Shit," Ronan muttered. "What the fuck is he doing there?"

He replaced the marker top and turned to Sam.

"Could you go and find Coste, please?"

46

As she was putting it in the signature file, Stévenin's secretary glanced over the form that had just been left on her desk. A resignation was rare enough for her to read it a second time to be sure of the bad news she was bringing the commissaire divisionnaire. She slipped it in among the other documents for his attention, fearing that yet again it would be a case of shooting the messenger. At the end of the passage, she saw officer Sam Dorfrey discussing something with Coste. It was clearly an awkward conversation.

"Oh shit! It can't be true! What the fuck is he doing in this muddle?" the capitaine exploded.

Intrigued, the secretary continued to eavesdrop.

"We don't know anything more at the moment. Maybe nothing. Ronan simply thought perhaps you'd like to . . ."

"Wait for me here," Coste said.

He turned on his heel and strode back towards the secretary. He extended his hand.

"Could I have the form I just gave you?"

"Of course."

She opened the signature file and took out the sheet of paper.

"Keep it to yourself for now."

"Of course."

"You're a sweetheart."

Then Coste returned to Sam. His weariness had evaporated; an electric storm was raging in his mind; he was as enthusiastic as on his first day in the job.

"So are we going or not, for God's sake?"

Like a play with the roles reversed, the new team leader Ronan summed up what they knew for Coste. At first he was hesitant: the paedophile's laptop; the arsonist's G.P.S.; the hold-up man's luxury watch; the murderer's knife and the kidnapper's phone-taps. The longer he spoke, with Coste listening closely, the more confident Ronan grew. Then came the brainstorming session. Theories flew round the room. Lines joining the different cases on the whiteboard, question marks, far-fetched conjecture, some more or less sensible suggestions, shaky theories. Several hours later a cathedral-like silence descended on the group, each of them with their nose in a file without the slightest hint of an idea.

"Well then?" Johanna asked hopefully.

Coste looked up and realised the question was addressed to him.

"Well then what?" he retorted. "If your three brains combined couldn't come up with anything, why should I be a miracle worker?"

Although this observation wasn't exactly helpful, Ronan was secretly pleased that Coste was proving no movie-star cop with the solution always to hand, somehow able to identify the guilty person before anybody else. He was as lost as the rest of them. When the phone rang on what had until recently been his desk, Coste picked it up out of force of habit.

"Coste."

"What are you doing on this line?" Saint-Croix greeted him.

"Taking an interest in your case."

"That's good news. Have you discovered the connection?"

"Not as yet."

"Well, I've been getting it in the neck. This robbery has repercussions no-one could have imagined. It's going to be hell. The justice system is a laughing stock."

"We'll be there."

"No, I've already got my coat on, and my arms are full of files. I'll be with you before you know it."

Since early that morning, Fleur Saint-Croix had been deluged with phone calls, and the court clerks were literally in the eye of a storm. The reasons for the break-in were becoming clearer, and three defence lawyers had shone the spotlight on them.

After joining Coste and Groupe Crime 1, Saint-Croix didn't waste any time. She flung her coat on the red sofa and studied the already full whiteboard.

"I can see you're floundering," she said, handing Ronan the marker pen. "If you don't mind, I have some fresh info to add."

Opening her file on the nearest desk, she took out the first sheet.

"Five evidence bags have been stolen. Each one an exhibit for the prosecution or defence that allows us to get at the truth and if need be put the accused behind bars. Sorry to give you this lecture, but it explains a lot. For example, why the lawyers of those accused are suddenly so interested in these bags, and why the court clerks are facing a wave of demands for corroboration and second opinions."

"What does that mean in practice?" asked Sam.

"It means a stormy day with red alerts. First, Boyan Mladic's lawyer. He'd called for an analysis of the G.P.S. data from the car his client was said to have been seen in immediately after the arson attack. Without the G.P.S., we can't prove Mladic was there."

"What about the witness who saw his number plate at the scene?"

"He withdrew his statement last week. He's no longer sure he saw the plate properly. Either that or he's received a persuasive visit – we'll never know. Be that as it may, Mladic was in jail on remand, because his dual French-Serb nationality meant he was a flight risk. Now we're empty-handed the request for his release won't be long in coming. You can cross him off your list."

Ronan did as she suggested.

"From the same lawyer, but this case is only a fortnight old: a request for the expert examination of a Van Cleef and Arpels watch stolen in a robbery. Apparently, the jeweller himself identified the watch, but that doesn't qualify as an expert opinion. This was supposed to be carried out by Van Cleef and Arpels, who created it. But if there's no watch, there can be no expert verificiation, and the accused benefits from reasonable doubt. So you can cross Nunzio Mosconi off too; he'll be released soon. I can go on, but I imagine you're beginning to get the picture?"

"Slowly but surely," Coste agreed disconsolately. "Evidence disappears, so the lawyers wake up. They check and seize the opportunity if it can help their client. And for the moment, that appears to be the case. Are the others equally bad news?"

"Pretty much. Before noon, Antoine Doucey's lawyer presented the receipt for the purchase of the second-hand laptop. Now he's sure we can't check anymore, he's claiming the child pornography photos and videos were already on it. He says he wanted us to verify the dates of the downloads, but since there's no computer, that can't be done. So yet again there's reasonable doubt as to his client's guilt. Together with the receipt, he lodged a petition for Doucey's release. He'll soon be able to have a soft drink in a park surrounded by children."

"But the underpants of the neighbours' little boy were found on his sofa, weren't they?" protested Johanna, who was even less tolerant than the others when it came to this kind of thing.

"Yes, but the boy never testified against him because, and I quote: 'he's my neighbour and my best friend'. Young minds are easily manipulated."

"It's as clear as day," Sam snorted. "The legal shysters are seizing on any loophole that can get their clients released."

"They've being handed that opportunity," Coste clarified, disheartened. "If they didn't seize it, their image would suffer. They're all trying to outdo one another, and for now it's working."

"And there's more," Saint-Croix continued. "At one this afternoon Gabriel Rezelny's lawyer showed up. The modus operandi of a tramp in the Somme region fits with the murder Rezelny is accused of. Moreover, the knife found on him perfectly matches the wounds on the murdered woman. To speed things up, the evidence bag was sent a month ago to the Bobigny law courts for expert comparison. This is possibly the most disturbing case of the lot. Now the weapon has disappeared, we have no chance of exonerating Rezelny. That means there could be an innocent man in prison. But beyond that, in the Somme there's a monster who'll only be accused of rape. The average sentence for rape is seven years, whereas for a serial killer it's thirty. Just think about that! And all because we're incapable of guarding our own evidence?"

Johanna was so taken aback she couldn't stay silent.

"Listen, I hate criminal lawyers as much as you do, but to go from that to imagining they would use the break-in to downgrade a serial murderer to an ordinary rapist for the sake of their own reputation: that's demonising them a bit too far, isn't it?"

Coste was amused by her innocence.

"They do it because the law permits it. That's something they say that always revolts me. If a lawyer discovers evidence that goes against their client, they're under no obligation to inform the police. If it were anybody else, that would be criminal complicity. But for them, it's the famous right of the defence. As a result, they regularly secure their clients' release even though they know they've committed a crime. Because the law permits it. But if lawyers are allowed to hold back the whole truth, I don't know why we should ever believe them."

"O.K., but here we're talking about a serial killer. It's not in the same league."

"I could give you ten examples," said Coste, "but I'll just choose one from this year. A woman was sentenced to thirty years for poisoning her four husbands. Her lawyer lodged an appeal and since that process took its time – more than a year in fact – he dusted off an article in the Penal Code which states that an accused has to be tried within a reasonable period. So the black widow was released. When a journalist asked him if he could understand the feelings the release of a serial killer like her could arouse, especially in the victims' families, he replied tranquilly that 'the law permitted it'. Where's the morality in that?"

"I've always wondered if lawyers have mothers. I can't imagine it," Sam said sarcastically.

"Or if they do, they can't have loved them much," said Johanna, dismayed.

Coste saw Saint-Croix hesitating over the last dossier, then make up her mind and open it.

"I'm sorry, capitaine, for not having realised earlier. Yassine Chelli was one of yours, I believe."

"For a while. Then he was Marveil's problem."

"Given everything we charged him with, I'd be really surprised if he got out," Ronan boasted.

Hearing this, Saint-Croix lowered her gaze imperceptibly,

and Coste understood Yassine was going to be part of the job lot as well. When the magistrate spoke again it was less firmly, as if she was slightly ashamed by what she had to say.

"His lawyer has a nerve, to say the least. You used voice recognition software to identify Chelli, the same program used in the Cahuzac affair. Unfortunately, that politician is still at large, and your software is only ninety-five per cent reliable. The lawyer is trying to use Cahuzac as a precedent; he's calling for an expert second opinion. Which will be difficult without the C.D. of the phone taps. You didn't happen to make a copy, did you?"

"As you know, that's illegal."

"Just a thought. For once I wouldn't have minded if you had bent the Penal Code a little."

"What about the mobile phones found at his place that were used to plan the kidnap?" asked Sam.

"Yes, I agree we found them at his flat, but he could have bought them from anyone, at any time. That doesn't make him a criminal."

"And his two accomplices?"

"Your investigation proved Lorenzo Weinstein had powder traces on his clothes and hands. So he'll stay inside. On the other hand, even if Sofiane Badaoui was seen coming and going for more than five hours on the shopping centre C.C.T.V., he could always claim he was waiting for his girlfriend. Luckily though, he attacked a guard in Fleury-Mérogis and broke his arm, so for the moment he'll be staying put."

Her explanations were almost at an end. The whiteboard was so full of crossings-out that someone looking in would have struggled to understand a thing. Saint-Croix decided she was ready to voice a conclusion:

"The break-in at the law courts is freeing four criminals. That's the link."

"I don't think so," Coste said. "I'm sorry if what I'm about to say sounds stupid, but there's no link because there is no link. And that itself is the link."

"Will you take me for a moron if I say I'm not following you?" asked Ronan.

"A gang can't have four different objectives," Coste explained. "Whoever carried out the break-in is deploying a smokescreen. Right from the start, they only wanted to get one person out. The others are lucky – they're decoys to send us running all over the place. The real question is who the original target was: Doucey, Mosconi, Mladic or Chelli?"

"What about the one with the hunting knife? Rezelny?"

"Rezelny isn't aimed at us, but at public opinion. He's the cornerstone of the whole operation. Justice could have dug in its heels and kept the other four in prison, but it will have enough on its hands with this Rezelny affair and a possibly innocent man being locked up. They won't want to risk a whole series of judicial errors."

"The only way we can find the evidence bags is by finding the robbers," said Saint-Croix. "But as you say, with four different targets, if we don't find any D.N.A. or other traces on the spot, we haven't got a hope."

"It sounds like the perfect crime," sighed Johanna.

"Because it is the perfect crime," said Coste. "Enjoy it. It's not often we're so completely screwed."

No sooner had he finished than the Police Judiciaire secretary stuck her nose in the doorway, looking doubly embarrassed at interrupting a meeting *and* being the bearer of bad news.

"There's a journalist who wants to talk to you, Victor."

"Tell him I don't want to talk to him."

"It's Farel," she added, aware this information could change things.

And Coste's attitude did change; the secretary vanished.

"I hope you don't plan on telling him about this business?" Saint-Croix bridled.

"He's more than just a journalist. Marc Farel* is a legal reporter I trust, and if he's calling us it's bound to be more of a favour than anything else."

Coste picked up the phone on the first ring, and after the usual greetings Farel broached the news that had his profession in a spin.

"It seems it's open day at Marveil, capitaine?"

"Something like that. We're dealing with prison over-crowding any way we can. Are you after information?"

"No, I have all the info I need. I was calling simply to tell you it's hitting the headlines in the morning."

"Can you hold it back?"

"Impossible. Everyone already knows about it."

"Obviously. Who gave you the scoop?"

Their conversation continued without Coste putting it on speaker. When they had finished, he hung up and answered the question no-one had asked him:

"It'll be on every news stand tomorrow morning. The lawyers have leaked to the media to lend weight to what they're doing. With all the noise that the right is making about the administration of justice these days, they want public opinion on their side."

"What about us?" said Ronan.

"Us? We've got nothing."

Coste stared at the sun outside, seriously unimpressed.

"It's really beautiful weather for such a crap day."

47

Scalpel was taking nothing with him: he didn't want anything that would remind him of this hole. He'd leave behind three years of patient hoarding: toiletries, a few cans of food, a little money and a tiny ball of cannabis he kept for difficult nights. He would even leave his T.V. set to Chef, his cellmate, who had taught him the Marveil codes, who had protected him. The guard banged twice on the cell door.

"Rezelny, visiting room."

Scalpel lowered his head and bit the inside of his cheeks to avoid smiling. That was enough to upset his friend.

"I forbid you to hold back, for fuck's sake! Jump, shout, thank the Lord. What do you think you're doing? Protecting me from your happiness? Shit, it does me good as well. I didn't think it existed anymore."

The old Turk went over and hugged him.

"I'd even say you smell good, you bastard."

"That must be a foretaste of the outside world."

All the transparent cubicles in the visiting room were empty apart from one. As he approached, Scalpel recognised his lawyer's arched back. They had been through many storms together and known some dark moments, but today was another day, and a day like no other. Today was Scalpel's last day as a murderer. When he walked round the cubicle, he finally saw the man's face. Bleak, eyes lowered, avoiding contact. Scalpel's heart lurched and a black hole formed in the pit of his stomach, sucking in the light, hope and infinite possibilities he had believed in only a fraction of a second earlier. As he sat down opposite his lawyer the plexiglass door swung shut behind him.

"Look me in the eye, at least," Scalpel muttered between gritted teeth.

The man didn't react. Scalpel slapped the table with both palms, making him jump.

"Look at me, for fuck's sake!"

The guard gripped the top of his baton and came a step closer.

"The evidence bag with the knife has disappeared. That means there won't be any tests. I'm sorry really sorry I don't know what's happened Gabriel," the lawyer gabbled without pausing for breath, as if his words stung as they passed his lips.

"That's impossible," Scalpel protested. "That can't happen. Not now."

As best he could, the lawyer explained the ins and outs of a story that cast Scalpel as collateral damage.

"You have to tell my wife all this. Got it? She has to know. That's what's most important."

As tactfully he could, the lawyer explained to Scalpel that Lola Rezelny had been refusing to take his calls for six months now. From the moment she had moved away, with someone else. Far from Seine-Saint-Denis, which she didn't imagine would be safe for the child she was expecting. Scalpel listened calmly, sitting stock still, his hands flat on the table, far beyond fury and tears.

Chef knew it only too well: hope is the worst thing to have in prison. His cellmate had come back and sat down without a word. A searing silence that the Turk immediately understood. Scalpel was not violent by nature, still less towards him, but everybody has their breaking point, and Chef decided his questions could wait.

Night fell and Gabriel was still staring at the cell floor, as if he could see Hell thousands of kilometres below. When it was so late the T.V. set was showing repeats of the day's programmes, Gabriel stretched out on his bunk, staring at the ceiling. Chef sat up on his bed to keep an eye on him. He'd stay there, wide awake, however long it took. He'd do so day after day if need be, and the wound would heal, not completely of course, but sufficiently at least to be able to breathe. He would be there and . . .

A stab of panic jolted him awake. How long had he been asleep? The T.V. was on standby and the cell was in darkness. He groped for the remote and found it in his tangled sheets. He knew the right button even in the dark, and switched the set on again. It was showing an advert in which a family was riding bikes through the fallen leaves of a new spa hotel only ten minutes from Paris, built for city dwellers in need of chlorophyll. Now the ad showed the same family in the park's wave pool. The artificial waves cast a bluish light on Scalpel, hanging from a sheet tied round one of the window bars.

The weight of the body had tightened the slip knot, and Chef wasn't strong enough to pull him down. He hammered on the cell door until his wrists ached, shouting for help and waking up the whole of C Wing.

Alerted by his cries, Demarco was the first to arrive. He cut the sheet with a knife and Gabriel's body fell to the floor. The guard pressed two fingers to his jugular, looked across at the old Turk, then sat on the floor himself, helpless.

Over the next few minutes, the news spread from cell to

cell. Scalpel had never attacked anyone or stolen; he had never lowered his eyes. He was one of those rare prisoners everybody respected.

Demarco left with the stretcher. Silence returned to the cell, as if Scalpel had merely decided to move out. Only the coiled sheet on the floor remained as proof that this was more than a nightmare.

Chef took his metal cup and banged it against the window bars. Again. And again. Then every second. The two inmates in the next cell took up the rhythm and the metallic clang rang out louder and louder. The message spread through every cell in the wing; soon the whole prison was shaking to the rhythm of the banging. It was as if a giant was hitting Marveil with a ten-ton metal bar. The inmates' prayer for an innocent man.

The scene would have touched Gabriel. Not because a thousand prisoners had shown their respect for him, but because it would have reminded him of happier times. He would have told his Turkish friend of the day in Vietnam when, under a tree, he had asked Lola to be his wife. The tree where the fireflies sheltered. As night fell, one of them would emit a first winking light, little more than a green glow. Then one close by would do the same, and another. The light would grow brighter. At first the tree was lit at random points, but soon the fireflies' tiny glowing tails merged like the instruments in an orchestra until the tree was aflame, alternating between intense green and deep black, as regular as a slow heartbeat.

That night in Marveil prison the inmates played at being fireflies for a whole hour, in memory of a man who, even within those four walls, had been able to remain good.

That night in Marveil, Scalpel had chosen the freedom he'd been denied.

48

Dorian pushed open the loft door. He was laden with cups of coffee and provisions for the day; rolled up in his back pocket was that morning's newspaper.

Franck had gone to see someone he knew at a scrapyard to dispose of the car they'd used for the break-in. Rhino had gone off somewhere – "what the fuck does it matter to you?" – without giving any details, and so Dorian found Alex on her own. She was sitting at her laptop, busy with a Skype call to her father in Corsica. Skype did after all allow you to speak to the whole planet without the risk of being overheard or intercepted by the police. Dorian put his purchases in the fridge, only catching fragments of their conversation. Monsieur Mosconi was wondering impatiently how much longer all this was going to take, and Alex was trying to reassure him without giving any definite response. Dorian didn't like hearing her talking to her father: she sounded on the defensive, as if apologising for everything she had done.

The call ended, but he hesitated for a moment before approaching her. He knew he had something in his back pocket that would ruin her day still further. He made a couple of sandwiches so that he could enjoy her company before she blew her top.

"Did you get a newspaper?"

So much for a few moments' calm. Dorian laid the paper

on the table. The headline immediately caught Alex's attention: INNOCENTS?

Beneath this one word, photos of four men: Doucey, Chelli, Mosconi and Mladic. Alongside the other unsavoury-looking characters, Nano looked as if he had been miscast. Alex read the article that followed, bylined Marc Farel, taking in every word. As she did so, she finally realised they been puppets in Maître Tiretto's hands.

"We didn't just help your brother," said Dorian. "Each of those stolen evidence bags helped release someone."

Alex pushed the newspaper away. Dorian was surprised at how well she was taking it.

"I can't say I'm surprised. I suspected Tiretto had his own agenda. But getting us to do his friends' dirty work is a step too far – he's taken me for a ride."

"Taken us for a ride, if you don't mind."

"I don't think you should play the victim, Dorian, especially as there's a paedophile among those being released simply because you can't read a case file number."

"Tiretto will know what to do to send him back inside. Call him."

"No. We have a phone call at nine o'clock tomorrow morning, exactly three days after the robbery. That's what we agreed."

"He screws us over and we still respect the rules?"

"While Nano is still inside, Tiretto holds all the cards."

Dorian went back to the worktop in the galley kitchen to fetch the sandwiches he had made. From there he tried to excuse himself.

"You know, that guy might only like to watch. Somebody who's aroused by kids must have a problem getting it up or something. He's just a peeping Tom. They download photos of kids at the swimming pool and jerk off into a wet glove."

"But it's because of people like him that there's a market for that stuff. It's because of people like him that others abuse children. And given how long he's spent inside in the company of perverts, who's to say that photos will be enough for him once he's released? It's common enough to move on to action. Take me, for example: I spent years admiring jewellery in shop windows. Then I started stealing it."

"We'll find a way to put it right. You're worrying over nothing."

"If you say so," Alex sighed.

Franck had agreed to spend the evening with his scrap-merchant friend for a family dinner. Scrap metal is a dirty and not exactly elegant business, but it brings in good money, and Franck was surprised at the lavish house his friend had been able to buy. Unless that had more to do with his sideline in receiving stolen vehicles.

For his part, Rhinoceros had succeeded in persuading his latest conquest not only to stay in their hotel room, but for only a few additional banknotes, to consider it an excellent idea. As a happy consequence, Dorian and Alex had the loft to themselves. When supper time arrived, an exchange of amorous looks meant not only were they no longer interested in food, but their clothes became superfluous.

Appetites satisfied, Dorian unfolded the sofa bed. He removed the mattress and laid it on the floor in front of the huge window overlooking Paris. Alex was quietly staring out. Seen from behind, naked and in silhouette, she seemed to be hovering above the city streets. He lay down, held out his hand towards her, and she joined him. One of the windows was slightly open, and a few minutes later they fell asleep to the capital's distant rumble.

In the middle of the night, Alex woke with violent nausea, ran to the bathroom and vomited. She splashed her face, then poured herself a glass of cold water, lit one of the small table lamps and sat down. Turning to Dorian, she saw he was still asleep. Her gaze fell on the pile of evidence bags in front of her. It seemed like a sign that the one closest happened to be Antoine Doucey's. She rubbed her stomach, hesitated, then made up her mind. Tearing open the wax seal, she took out the reinforced envelope containing the laptop and its lead. She had been fighting against this impulse since reading the article that morning, knowing she wouldn't be able to resist it forever. If it was her fault a sexual predator had been released, she needed to know the details.

The screen flickered then settled down, showing a screen saver of green hills. On one of them was the only folder. She double clicked on it, and two files appeared: PHOTOS and VIDEOS. No protection, password, or any other kind of security. Afraid of what the other file might contain, Alex opened PHOTOS. An endless list of numbers. Scrolling down, she saw there were more than a thousand. She clicked on photo number one. Exotic scenery, a blue sea and a flaming sunset. On the beach, smiling sadly as if he'd been ordered to pose like this, a young boy sitting fully dressed on a plastic chair. Dark-haired, ten years old at most, with tanned skin and pinched, exhausted features. She clicked on the second photo. The same background, the same boy, but this time completely naked and no longer smiling. Alex clicked on the ninth photo to make sure. The boy was sitting next to a man in a hood who was also naked. The sight of this hooded man on a beach was as shocking as his nudity. She didn't dare go any further, and instead opened a different file. A new background: this time a forest with a river running through it. On a path, another boy. A little younger, but a similar Mediterranean type to the first one. She clicked on photo number 14. The boy was on his knees, still fully dressed. What was being stuffed in his mouth was so huge it looked as if his jaw was about to break. The camera's automatic flash had succeeded in the artistic feat of making the tear on the boy's cheek glitter like a diamond. Alex leaped up, sending her chair flying. Dorian turned over in bed. She closed the PHOTOS file, drained the glass of water, and, morbid curiosity getting the better of her, opened the VIDEOS file. A hundred or so icons came up, each one a short film. Alex clicked on the first one. She didn't really understand why, except perhaps that she felt she had to. A shiny stainless-steel table covered with a white sheet. A silhouette laid a baby down on it, its chubby arms flailing in all directions. Alex covered her mouth with her hands. A man in a suit wearing a white Venetian mask came into shot. He separated the baby's legs to caress the soft skin on the inner thigh. Then he licked his middle finger and covered it with a thick layer of saliva to lubricate it. As if she could really put a stop to the scene, Alex snapped the laptop shut before the worst occurred and ran again to the bathroom. But she had made the lid bounce against the keyboard without shutting the computer down properly, and from the bathroom she could hear the baby start to wail. Alex wiped her mouth and rose to her feet. She saw Dorian standing in the centre of the loft, woken up by the noise. He was staring at the laptop, his face lit by the images. Swallowing hard, he shut the computer correctly and turned to Alex.

"What time is the call with Tiretto tomorrow?"

"Nine o'clock," Alex whispered.

"I'll set the alarm."

49

A sleepless night. Coffee over and done with, Dorian massaged Alex's shoulders, feeling the tense neck and muscles as tough as teak.

"Don't fly off the handle at him, O.K.?"

Her only response was to lay her hand on his, without turning to look at him. At one minute past nine, her mobile began to buzz on the table, making a spoon vibrate against its cup. She took the call.

"I imagine you've seen the papers?" Tiretto began.

"The day your car explodes, you'll have a millisecond to recall the moment you took me for a fool."

Dorian's brow furrowed. Even when Alex seemed in control of her emotions, she always had an inner Rottweiler ready to pounce.

"I can imagine how annoyed you are, and that's fair enough. But don't lie to yourself. You knew perfectly well I wouldn't have done all that without getting something out of it."

"I like to know what the stakes are from the start, otherwise I feel vulnerable. And when I feel vulnerable, I need to be protected."

"Meaning?"

"That until my brother is released and all my team are safely back in Corsica, I'm keeping the evidence bags. As insurance. Is that clear?"

"I wouldn't do that if I were you. It wouldn't go down very well."

"With who? I wanted to get Nano out, but is that what you want for the other three? Not No. 58, I hope, because we slipped up there."

"Yes, I read about that. Bravo. A mistake that could see a paedophile go free. Don't worry, it doesn't change anything. You can keep the evidence if you like, as long as you respect the rules."

Alex unfolded the previous day's newspaper and read the name under one of the photos.

"I'm willing to wipe the slate clean if you tell me how we can send Doucey back where he belongs."

"That's quite simple. All you have to do is return the evidence bag untouched to the law courts. You haven't opened it, have you?"

Tiretto took her silence as an admission.

"The wax seal carries the imprint of the police department that collected the evidence. If the seal is broken, it's no longer admissible evidence. You could have put anything inside it, made a switch. So I'll ask you again: you didn't open it, did you?"

Fresh silence. Fresh admission.

"Well then, you can throw it way. It's useless. You'll have to live with yourselves. But don't worry, Doucey is classified as being non-aggressive, if that salves your conscience. On the other hand, for your security and mine don't open the others. Keep them safe wherever you like, but don't lose them."

"You seem preoccupied. That's almost good to hear."

"That's because you don't know all of those involved."

"About that: when's the grand opening?"

"The petitions for release have gone to the examining magistrates this morning. They have five days to give a ruling or pass them on to the appeals judge. That adds another three days. So it could be any time between tomorrow and eight days' time."

Growing calmer, Alex leaned back in her chair.

"Any more surprises?"

"That would be abusing your trust, Alexandra."

Franck appeared an hour later, surrounded by a vague cloud of alcohol. He collapsed onto the sofa, a washing machine drum spinning round in his head.

Dorian slipped the evidence bags into one of the big canvas holdalls. Alex tapped her drowsy cousin on the head.

"What have you got for us?"

He rummaged in his coat pocket and took out a set of keys, a present from his scrap-merchant friend.

"A Volvo. Ugly but discreet."

"Great! You shouldn't have," muttered Alex.

"I also got a new supply of mobiles, with new numbers. Help yourself – they're over by the door. One each."

Then he saw Dorian, bag slung over his shoulder.

"Where are you off to?"

Alex threw the evidence bag with the Van Cleef watch onto Franck's lap.

"Gare du Nord. We're storing the other three in left luggage lockers. And I want you to get rid of this. You can melt it down, eat it, send it to another planet, but I never want to hear another word about it. Ever."

50

Seventy-two hours later
Marveil Prison
6 p.m.

Boyan Mladic signed the release register, closely watched by the clerk. Mladic was the last of those already dubbed the "four-leaf clovers" to be legally walking free. The lucky ones.

"You ought to play the lottery, you're on a winning streak," the clerk said, thinking he was being funny.

Boyan raised his whitish-grey eyes to him, and any thought of humour flew out of the window. The Serb was leaving Marveil without ever opening his mouth. He picked up the bag with his personal belongings and stepped through the heavy iron gate. Outside, he took a deep breath of fresh air. As he went past a rubbish container, he lifted the lid and threw the bag in. Not the slightest hint of nostalgia for anything in it. He walked over to the taxi waiting, engine running, and clambered in. The taxi set off, still without Mladic uttering a word. He turned in his seat and watched the prison recede in the distance. The taxi sped through the town of Marveil, then into a kind of no-man's-land between built-up area and countryside, with farmland alongside big warehouses. It emerged onto a main road that cut a field of rapeseed into two huge yellow rectangles, then came to a halt in the middle of nowhere. Mladic got out, slammed the door, and the taxi set off again. Without any transition, Boyan had gone from his four-metre-square segregation cell to being surrounded by this sea of yellow flowers, with no-one in sight. A small crop-spraying plane caught his attention for a moment. It flew overhead in the distance, released a thick cloud of fertiliser, sped up and was gone.

Ten minutes later a dot appeared at the far end of the road. As the dot grew, it turned out to be a metallic grey Bentley, which drew up alongside him. The door opened, he plunged in, and sat next to the man in the back seat.

"Good morning, Boyan."

"My respects, Monsieur Darcy."

So Mladic could speak. And what's more in accentless French. Darcy signalled to the driver; the Bentley set sail again through the rape fields.

"You should have left me in there. You're taking a risk."

"What sort of friend would I be if I abandoned you at the first mistake?"

Turning towards him, Mladic nodded his grateful thanks. Darcy gave him a fatherly smile, then stared out over the fields. That day he was wearing exactly the same suit as the one he wore on his business's advertising hoardings. Charcoal grey, a black shirt with a red tie, silver hair brushed back off his forehead. Forty billion euros' annual turnover, and still he wanted more, always more, until he choked on the money.

"This is an amusing coincidence. We're currently driving through my latest acquisition. Two hundred hectares of fields I'm going to cover over with concrete to welcome my latest little scheme. The hundred and sixtieth Darcy supermarket."

Half of which were built illegally, and for which he was supposed to be paying a fine of ninety-four billion euros that the State never dared demand, such was the nature of the man, with his network of influence and the reach of his empire. It was hard to tell which of the two on the back seat of the Bentley was more dangerous.

"I don't even know what I'm going to destroy. It looks pretty though," Darcy went on pensively.

"I think it's rapeseed," Boyan said. "Your father would be very proud of you."

"My father was a small, unambitious commercial traveller. A washing powder salesman. I'm a powerful businessman, and that should make you happy. My father wouldn't have been able to get you out of Marveil."

"Now you mention it – how did you do it? If you don't mind my asking."

"I made the G.P.S. disappear and sent someone to get the person who saw you at the blaze change his mind."

"You've already replaced me?" Boyan asked anxiously.

"For the G.P.S. I took advantage of an opportunity. As for the witness, the poor guy was seventy years old. Philippe here took care of him."

"Thanks, Philippe."

The driver twisted round, his face sombre at the mention of that unpleasant incident.

"It's nothing, but I've already told Monsieur I don't like doing that kind of thing."

Darcy's lips curled in a sardonic half-smile.

"You see, Boyan, not everyone has your tolerance level for violence. However, I see it as a normal part of any negotiation. That's why I get on so well with you, even though I would have imagined that as a military man you'd prefer good old-fashioned maps to a G.P.S."

Boyan took note. He knew perfectly well that beneath the polite facade Darcy was furious with him. He was also aware that in Philippe's glove compartment there was a 9mm gun he knew how to use, even if afterwards he told Monsieur he didn't like it. Boyan tried to excuse his costly lapse.

"I fought in the Ivory Coast and Chad. I was a Foreign Legion sniper in the former Yugoslavia. But working for you over the past three years I've been scaring vegetable whole-salers, building foremen and lawyers, who all have a low pain threshold. I think I dropped my guard, went soft. And I was caught. You should have left me with the common criminals; I could have got back into training."

Darcy tapped Boyan benevolently on the knee. Anyone but him risked losing two fingers doing that, but the entrepreneur had feelings for Boyan that as a professional he kept in check – and that Boyan pretended not to notice.

"I've got something that will help get you back in shape," said Darcy.

"I'm listening."

"Alexandra Mosconi. Yes, a woman, but don't let that fool you. She's the one who recovered our evidence."

"So I ought to be thanking her."

"Except that now she's being selfish. She still has the G.P.S. and doesn't seem to be in any hurry to return it."

"You want me to get rid of her and recover what's ours?"

"I haven't decided yet."

Stains – Clos-Saint-Lazare Estate
7 p.m.

No-one had been waiting for him beyond the Marveil prison gates. Yassine climbed aboard the free bus taking released prisoners to the nearest railway station, and after a two-hour journey through grey city suburbs he finally dropped his bag by his front door. He raised his arm, but hesitated to ring the bell. Perhaps he already knew what was awaiting him on the other side.

His mother would slap him, then embrace him, with just as much love in both gestures. His brother wouldn't dare look him in the eye at first, and Yassine would have to set his mind at rest, tell him it wasn't his fault. He would also swear it had all been a mistake, that he'd never got mixed up in any kidnapping. He would lie just as he had done ever since he was fourteen, when he was first arrested. He would see the doubt and resignation in his mother's eyes. Feelings she wouldn't express, preferring to lie to herself, to pretend that everything was fine and that life could begin again. Until the next time.

Yassine took a step back, then turned on his heel. At the end of the corridor, he removed the wooden cover on an electricity conduit and stowed his bag there. He looked out of the window towards the foot of the neighbouring tower block. He recognised several faces among the youngsters leaning back against the wall as if they were propping it up. He would show off to them, polishing his local legend by telling them how he had survived Marveil.

Up until the last moment, Nano was convinced it was a trap. When Demarco came to tell him he was being released. When his cell door was opened. And even outside the prison, where a taxi was waiting for him. Everything had happened so quickly he found himself in the road, bag in hand, like an evicted tenant. In his pocket was a tube of anti-depressants, courtesy of the Marveil shrink.

Out of a mixture of paranoia and professionalism, Alex had decided they would only meet up two days later at the airport, with plane tickets in hand. Meanwhile, she had organised everything for him, and an hour later the taxi pulled up outside the Hotel Banville, a four-star establishment a few streets from the Arc de Triomphe.

Grand piano in the lobby, receptionist and porter ready and waiting: Nano's arrival didn't go unnoticed. He was accompanied to his room, paid with cash in advance. Given Nano's clothes, the bad smell he gave off and his bewildered air, the bellboy didn't even dare wait the four embarrassing seconds that usually oblige people to rummage in their pocket for a tip.

A few moments later, the porter reappeared with a letter. Nano immediately recognised his sister's neat round handwriting. Tearing open the envelope, he took out a sheet of paper and unfolded it.

We'll meet in two days' time. Get some rest. Go out as little as possible. Ask for whatever you like from reception. You deserve it. Pamper yourself. No drugs. No girls. Stay cool. We'll soon be back with the family. Love you. Basgi and Forza. Alex.

Nano dropped the note, which fluttered down onto the impeccably white sheets of the deep, welcoming bed. Clean: everything was so clean. He surveyed the bedroom and the little sitting room where a bottle of champagne awaited him on the frosted glass table. The hotel's royal suite was eighty square metres, exactly twenty and a half times bigger than his cell in Marveil. His head started to spin, and a panic attack made him shut himself in the bathroom, which was a more manageable size. He felt in his pocket, opened the tube and tipped three pills into the palm of his hand. He swallowed them without any water.

Antoine Doucey had arrived in his neighbourhood towards the end of afternoon, at a time when people came home from work or school, kids close on their heels like a line of ducklings. Not exactly the ideal moment to show his face, especially when there was a risk of it being bashed in by any one of his neighbours. He waited for darkness to offer him deep enough shadows to remain hidden, and walked to his flat with his head bowed.

In the downstairs lobby he saw his letter box stuffed with junk mail. He was about to empty it and throw everything away, but stopped himself when he realised that would only announce his return. No need to do that, the news would spread quickly enough without his help. Six floors higher up, he prayed the lift doors wouldn't open on a face he knew. A similar prayer as he walked down the corridor to his flat. He noticed the name had changed on his neighbours' doorbell. Above all else, he'd feared bumping into Leo and his parents, and yet he couldn't prevent a stab of disappointment in his stomach. Evidently his former friends had chosen to leave behind not only the difficult incident but also the betrayal of trust that on good days left them feeling gullible, and full of self-loathing the rest of the time. On Doucey's front door in red marker pen: LEAVE OR KILL YOURSELF, BUT DON'T STAY HERE.

The news had obviously preceded him: maybe he had already been in the papers. He rubbed at the writing with his sleeve, but it made no difference. Turning the front door key, he was met with a stale, musty smell.

It had been more than a year and a half since daylight had shone on the furniture, and all that time the same air had circulated round the rooms. His dusty possessions and books were strewn all over the floor, just as they had been since the police search that had condemned him. The cops had gone to town, with Doucey looking on, as stipulated by law. Even the sofa cushions were still scattered around the flat. He recalled how his stomach had clenched whenever one of them went near the kitchen or happened to look down at the white tiled floor. Then they had opened his computer, examined some photos, and concentrated all their attention on its contents. But that was only the tip of the iceberg.

Doucey took a knife from a drawer by the kitchen sink, kneeled down and, twenty centimetres from the fridge, slipped the blade under one of the tiles. It came loose without any effort. Waiting for him underneath were a key and a French I.D. card which, even though it bore Antoine Doucey's photo, was not in his name.

At the foot of Doucey's building, in a Volvo with its headlights and engine switched off, Dorian threw his cigarette out of the half-open window. He blew out the smoke, which had fogged up the inside of the car.

"I know you've been thinking of nothing else for the past three days, but as you can see, he's not doing anything. What were you expecting? For a school bus to pull up outside his place and for him to come out with a camera, dick in hand?"

Alex didn't even look in his direction, preferring to keep her eyes on the building entrance.

"According to Tiretto, he was in Marveil for twenty-one months," she said. "Can you imagine? He must be straining at the leash. We're leaving France in forty-eight hours, so you can do whatever you like, but I'm staying here. I want to know who he is. I want to know who we set free."

Dorian felt partly responsible for the situation and so told himself to keep his mouth shut. An hour later he was glad he'd done so when Doucey poked his nose out. He looked as nervous and jumpy as a rabbit on the first day of the hunting season. A taxi with a green light on passed the Volvo and came to a halt. The indicator changed to red when Doucey got in. Alex pulled out behind him.

"I told you he'd crack."

Bobigny – police judiciare headquarters
9 p.m.

Like an enthusiastic estate agent, Commissaire Stévenin showed Commandant Ventura round the whole service. Office after office, team leader after team leader. Damiani's replacement was getting his bearings in his new fiefdom; he had also been obliged to endure Lara Jevric for more than two hours. Seated on her chair like a sea lion on its rock, she had presented him with an endless list of demands and happily gone on and on, pleased at the look of her new immediate superior, with his slightly mafioso Italian appearance. In his fifties, black beard trimmed to the millimetre, short tousled brown hair, the first signs of a paunch, all encased in a dark brown suit. Ventura had only been expecting a quarter of an hour's chat, but Jevric had literally got her teeth into him, and it had taken the arrival of the head of Groupe Crime 1, announcing the welcome drinks in the meeting room, to release him.

"A thousand thanks – Coste, isn't it? I thought I was going to have to taser her to shut her up."

"I interrupted you too soon then," joked the capitaine.

"I'm sorry we haven't had a chance to talk, because you're the one who really interests me. It's your group who's in charge of the most pressing case, isn't it? The four-leaf clovers."

"Yes, unfortunately it is. But it's not going to show us at our best."

"Can you bring me up to speed in thirty seconds, or did you go to the same school as Jevric?"

"Thirty seconds should do it. No traces at the crime scene. No D.N.A., no fingerprints, no C.C.T.V. footage and no reliable witnesses. Four suspects because there were four people who benefitted, but for now they all have the best possible alibi: they were in prison, watched over by guards and behind walls two metres thick, forty kilometres from here. Their stay behind bars has left them as pure as the driven snow: no phones that we know of, no bank accounts, no social media – so no weak points. I passed the word to border control so we can follow their movements, but for the moment they're lying low. That's it: I've got a few seconds left, but I wouldn't know how to fill them. We're clueless."

"They weren't helped by complete strangers. You need to look among their former accomplices," suggested Ventura.

"As you can imagine, for security reasons they won't be contacting anyone for weeks. If that. As far as Nunzio Mosconi goes, it was his first time in Paris. Before the break-in he had no police record. And with Doucey, I tend to believe paedophiles act alone, or with the protection of the elite."

"You need to scotch that urban myth," Ventura warned him. "Paedophile parties with kids rented for the enjoyment of a few wealthy perverts."

"I reckon they're sufficiently well-known to have a name, but we can talk about that some other time. Then there's Boyan Mladic. A former legionnaire. You could say everyone in the Foreign Legion is his accomplice. Those guys are welded together so tight you'll never get anything out of them. And finally Yassine Chelli – the problem there is that we've already arrested his gang."

The two men left the glassed-in walkway linking the two sections of the service and headed for the drinks.

"Fine. Send me the details of your line of enquiry. I might

have a different approach that could be useful. But I imagine we'll have plenty of time to discuss it over the coming days."

"As for that . . ." Coste tried to say.

Stévenin saw them at the end of the corridor and waved his arms in the air, as if they might not see him.

"I think we're going to have to wrap things up for now, Coste."

The arrival of a new colleague is usually only an event within his or her department, but when a new Groupes Crime boss takes over, there is more interest. So the meeting room was thronged with Police Judiciaire officers, a handful of investigating magistrates including Fleur Saint-Croix, and members of the Group de répression du banditisme, as well as an array of regional commandants and commissaires.

"They've put on quite a show," Ventura said with a hint of satisfied pride.

He accepted a glass of champagne and an unidentifiable canapé. He downed the former and got rid of the latter without tasting it. He shook a few hands, then drew Coste's attention to a young woman with her back to them.

"Fantastic! Even my little cupcake is here. I worked with her on quite a few cases in Paris before I was transferred to Seine-Saint-Denis. I've been after her for years. Six months ago she almost gave in, but we never got beyond first base. Mind you, I like it when they put up a bit of a fight."

Ventura took hold of the young woman's arm, and she turned round. He dropped his hand to her hip and kissed her noisily on both cheeks.

"Léa Marquant! My little cupcake! The sexiest forensic pathologist in all Paris. With a twenty per cent rise in crime in Seine-Saint-Denis we're going to see twenty per cent more of each other. Isn't that good news?"

Léa saw Coste and pretended to ignore him, focussing all her attention on the Italian charmer, who was continuing with his blandishments. Coste felt awkward at having to witness this spectacle, but a team is a team, and Johanna and Ronan appeared as if by magic.

"Good evening, Commandant Ventura," Johanna greeted him, all smiles. "We've seen you doing the rounds of the top brass. But if you only speak to them, you won't understand a thing about the Police Judiciaire."

"Most important are the worker bees who make the honey," added Ronan, taking his arm to lead him away from Léa. "Come on, we'll introduce you."

The three of them moved off, leaving the pathologist alone with Coste.

"You've got them well-trained," she said.

"Normally they would have pinioned him on the ground, but I suspect there's no reason for me to be jealous."

"Especially since you apparently had something so important to tell me . . . six days ago . . ."

"Maybe my guys were a bit heavy-handed. Do you want me to take you back to Ventura?"

Léa reached for Coste's breast pocket and took out his packet of cigarettes.

"I've heard you have a rooftop with some deckchairs where you can enjoy the night in peace."

"You're going to miss the party."

"I only came for you."

Ventura watched intrigued as they left the meeting room and climbed the spiral staircase to the roof.

"Cupcake?" said Coste, still upset at Ventura's familiarity.

"I'll explain," laughed Léa.

*

The taxi came to a halt in the suburbs near Noisy-le-Sec, in an area where the streetlamps lit only deserted streets. Doucey paid the fare, got out and stood in front of a huge self-storage depot announcing in bright neon letters: MXR: MY EXTRA ROOM.

Dorian parked some metres back.

"You can see he's not on the hunt. It's only a storage unit. If he left a kid in there, he'd have a pretty empty stomach after twenty-one months, don't you think? O.K., can we go and find the others now?"

His words had no effect on Alex. She was as stubborn and determined as ever.

"If he's coming here, it's because the cops never found it."

"Great. So you want to steal his ski clothes and communion garb? What else do you think you leave in a storage unit?"

"What if he didn't have everything on his computer? If we go in and find more photos and videos, he's going back behind bars. Don't you get it? We tie him up, scatter the evidence all round him, and call the police. They have to have their uses sometimes."

Dorian was still hesitating, which annoyed Alex even more.

"Besides, we have no choice. If you hadn't screwed up that case number . . ."

"And if you hadn't opened the evidence bag."

"That's why I'm here," she said angrily. "But are you with me?"

Dorian took a bundle of cable ties from the glove compartment and stuffed them into his pocket. He felt for his pistol under the seat and pulled back the breech to load it with a metallic click.

"To hell and back, baby."

The night watchman saw a young woman come stumbling past, straw-blonde hair and eyes on the ground as if looking for signs to guide her home. He came out of his cabin to help or, who knows, to take advantage of the situation. He only got as far as saying "Mademoiselle" before the first blow from a gun butt left him staggering. Dorian watched him sway to left and right, then hit him again. The man dropped to one knee, dully rubbing his scalp but already seeing stars. Dorian hit him a third time, finally knocking him out.

"Shit! I don't know how they do it in movies! Usually one blow to the back of the head and that's it."

Alex entered the cabin to check the man's computer.

"Last unit opened, number 297."

At last Doucey was back in his Neverland. When he raised the shutter a bulb came on automatically, casting a bright light on his collection. Thirty square metres dedicated to his inadmissible passion: boys under sixteen. On a table pushed back against the wall lay piles of photograph albums, chests full of old Super-8 films bought on the dark net, and boxes of video cassettes. In the centre of the room was a 1980s video recorder connected to a T.V. set; opposite it an old leather armchair with broad armrests. Linked to a monitor beside the television, a computer was hidden under a stack of C.D.s. High up on the left-hand wall, on the right-hand one and the one at the back, were three rolls of canvas, held in place by ropes with slip knots. Under the middle roll, a brown teddy bear with big black eyes hung as if dangling from a scaffold.

Before plunging into his favourite perversions, Doucey went to the far end of the unit where a mobile was plugged into a charger. Switching it on, he opened the only file on the screen and checked the contents. Then he slipped it into his trouser pocket and breathed a sigh of relief.

Next he dipped his hand into one of the boxes, rummaged around, and eventually took out an album he had especially missed. Comfortably installed in the armchair, he opened the album wide on his lap. After turning only a few pages, he ejaculated straight into his trousers without even touching himself. He controlled a rush of butterflies behind his eyes and twitched ecstatically several times. He had soaked his underpants and was enjoying the sensation of the warm liquid on his belly when the shutter opened wide once more.

"Stay where you are, you pervert," said Dorian, wearing a black balaclava, a finger on the trigger of his gun.

Doucey dropped the album, which fell open on a series of photos of little boys clutching their downy privates.

The bottom half of her face concealed by a scarf, Alex also entered the unit. The first thing she noticed was the big stain between Doucey's legs. Then she saw the eight yellowing photos on their dog-eared pages. Her first reaction was to slap him, hard.

"You bastard."

"Wait . . ." Doucey began.

A second slap cut him short.

"I can't guarantee we're going to let you live," Dorian told him. "So I'd advise you to keep your trap shut."

Alex grabbed Doucey by the arm and forced him to stand up.

"Listen carefully. You're going to take all this filth and pile it up in the middle of the room. That way even the cops will understand."

Doucey begged and sobbed, gulping in the middle of his sentences like children do when their hearts are breaking. This only served to fire Alex up more.

"Take it all if you want," Doucey pleaded. "It's worth a lot of money. I can even tell you who you could sell it to."

Now it was Dorian's turn to see red.

"Who do you take us for, you scumbag?"

Gripping his gun by the barrel, he lashed out at the corner

of Doucey's eyebrow. Doucey staggered, almost fell, but managed to grab the rope holding the rolled-up left-hand canvas. The slip knot came loose, and the canvas dropped until it filled the entire wall. It showed a sublime sunset on a deserted beach. Recognising the backdrop, Alex was frozen to the spot. Horrified, she looked round at the other two rolls of canvas. She pulled on the nearest slipinsert spaceknot and a snowy mountain scene appeared. Striding to the back wall, she did the same and the canvas took them to a river and a path bordering a forest. Shrinking back, she bumped into the table, still piled high with boxes. As she turned, she saw a flash of light under one of them. She swept the cassettes and photos off the surface, leaving a spotless steel table as shiny as a mirror. The baby's cries lanced through her memory.

"Just a peeping Tom, is he?" she raged at Dorian.

He was as shocked as she was to discover the monster they were dealing with. He lowered his eyes, horrified at having been so mistaken about Doucey. He hauled the paedophile up, threw him back onto the armchair, then kneeled to bring his hands together and bind them with a cable tie. He did the same with his ankles, then linked this tie to the first one. Hunched on the chair, Doucey could twist and wriggle like a worm but was unable to escape. There was no avoiding it: once tipped off, the cops would find him. Soon he'd be back inside Marveil.

"Please, please don't call the police," Doucey implored. "I can't go back to prison. We can come to an arrangement. I have money. Not on me, but I could get it, lots of it."

Already sickened at having to touch him, Dorian made no reply.

Alex had a flashback to the image of a baby with its mouth wide open. Then another, of the masked man licking his middle finger. She ripped the scarf from her face.

"However long his sentence, he'll get out some day," she hissed.

Dorian felt a tug in the small of his back as she pulled out his gun. He stood up, realised it was too late, and stepped back.

"Life."

She shot Doucey twice in the head. Flung back, he bounced against the soft upholstery and collapsed to the floor. At first there was nothing, then hot blood began to gush from the two holes, spreading over the photos in one of the albums.

Desperate for air, Dorian tore off his balaclava and took a deep breath.

Up on the roof of police headquarters, Victor and Léa had swapped the deckchairs for the ground, and were sitting on his jacket. Léa was nestling between the capitaine's legs as they gazed down on the city.

"One day, I don't know why, I don't even remember the conversation, but I sort of said I liked cupcakes. After that at every autopsy he brought me a box of them. It's called 'courtesy' and it's supposed to make a woman's heart melt."

Coste held out his lighter and the pathologist lit a cigarette. Amused at the silence that followed her words, she said nothing more. It took Coste a few seconds to recover.

"He led me to think you two knew each other."

Léa burst out laughing.

"I don't believe it! You met him for the first time today, and that's all you could find to talk about?"

"Whoa! All he said was that he'd got somewhere with you – something about a first base. That must be a sporting metaphor. So did you . . . I mean, did you . . . ?"

Turning her head, Léa blew smoke in his face.

"Capitaine Coste, you don't even have the right to ask me

that sort of question. You dropped me as if I was surplus to requirements. What was I supposed to do?"

"I'm sorry. You're right, completely right. But . . . what did he mean by 'first base'?"

She reached up and stroked the back of his neck.

"Don't worry. First base means a fancy restaurant, clumsy chat-up, accompanying me home, and of course the obligatory blow job in the doorway to get rid of him."

Coste almost choked. The cigarette fell from his grasp.

"Something wrong?"

He gritted his teeth so as not to explode. Léa felt his body stiffen.

"Don't be silly. He didn't even touch me."

She turned and gave him a gentle kiss.

"I still hate you, you know . . ."

Feeling her lips on his, Victor relaxed a little. "I know. But I'm going to change. Really and truly."

"Was that the important news you wanted to tell me?"

Coste held her tighter, and she snuggled closer.

"Have you ever seen the Northern Lights?" he asked.

"Yes, on screen savers and Ikea paintings."

"You can see them for real in Canada or Norway. I get the feeling one can find peace there."

"I've always dreamed of Canada, and I'm happy to talk about the wonders of nature with you, but what are you trying to tell me?"

He was on the edge of the precipice. So he jumped.

"For you, does it have to be Paris and Seine-Saint-Denis?"

Turning towards Coste, she pushed him flat on the ground, wriggled on top of him and kissed him more passionately.

"I hope you're not playing games with me, Victor."

*

When they got back to their car, Alex was trembling all over. To kill is to kill yourself a little. Something had gone awry in her soul.

Dorian had not uttered a word since he pulled the metal shutter down to hide the lifeless body. He should have known how Alex would react. He should have known that in her condition she wouldn't be able to bear it. Before driving off, he laid his hand anxiously on her stomach.

"Everything alright?"

On the verge of tears, she looked across at him, and put her hand on his.

"We won't tell him anything, O.K.?"

Dorian was about to comfort her with the notion of the universal balance between good and evil, which she had undoubtedly tipped a little in the right direction, when her phone began to vibrate. An unknown caller, so she hesitated. Strangely, and without consciously being aware of it, she was afraid it could be Doucey calling from beyond the grave to tell her he would be waiting for her, however long it took. She accepted the call. The man on the far end sounded stressed and agitated, though he was impeccably polite and professional.

"Good evening, Madame Carat. We're extremely sorry about this, but there's a slight problem with your friend."

Alex covered the mobile with her hand and whispered to Dorian:

"It's the hotel. Nano's in trouble."

"We heard loud noises from his room," the receptionist went on, "and he refused to open the door. If you think you can sort this out yourself, it would avoid us having to call the police."

"Please don't. I can be there in less than thirty minutes, if that's alright."

"That would be perfect. Could you come with Monsieur

Demarco? Your friend keeps shouting his name and banging on the door. He says he'll only open for him."

Alex frowned, wondering what mental maze her brother was lost in this time.

"I'll take care of it myself. I'm on my way. Thanks again."

She ended the call, and seeing Dorian staring at her in bewilderment, explained:

"Nano's as high as a kite. We'll have to take him with us."

"Are you sure? We said that . . ."

"I don't care what we said," she snapped. "I don't care, do you hear me? I want to be with my brother."

The receptionist and the hotel security manager led Alex down the red carpeted corridor on the top floor. As they passed, several reproving heads poked out of their rooms. They came to a halt outside Nano's room. The hotel employees said he'd been quiet for five minutes. The security man agreed Alex could go in alone, and slid his pass card over the electronic pad.

The room had been turned upside down. Alex saw Nano on the far side of the bed, which had been dragged nearer the wall, together with a table and an upended mattress. Nano was sitting with his back against the wall, the window open on his right, in the centre of a child's fortress measuring about four square metres. The floor was littered with the remains of sandwiches in their cardboard packaging.

"Hi there, little brother."

Nano turned towards her. His eyes were red and the corners of his lips were white, his mouth dry from all the tablets.

"Alex!"

"Is this a joke? I tell you it's all-inclusive here and you order from Maccy D's? It's worse than I thought," she said, trying to lighten the mood.

276

She scrambled over the bed and approached him.

"Can I?"

"Yeah. Sit down and listen."

A few dozen metres below them the noise from the Périphérique at Porte de Champerret was clearly audible. The throb of engines was like a lullaby to Nano. His befuddled mind transformed the automobile sounds into waves breaking on the city. First, a distant rumble as a car drew near, then a thunderous crash as it arrived, followed by a gentle caress on the sand as it pulled back.

"Can you hear it?"

"What?"

"The sea."

Alex's eyes crinkled with fear.

"Oh yes, now you mention it. Let's go, shall we?"

"Have you been in touch with Demarco?" Nano asked anxiously.

51

From the moment the door was opened Léa never touched the floor. Arms and legs wrapped round Coste, she bumped against all the walls leading to the bedroom. Their clothes were flung off in an embrace that lasted well into the night.

At five in the morning, Coste groped for his mobile before it rang a third time and woke Léa up completely. He answered and was greeted by Ronan's wide-awake voice.

"The clover's lost one of its leaves."

Coste made a mental note of the address where the team was to meet and ended the call.

"At this time of the morning, I don't even need to ask if it's work."

He turned round, and Léa coquettishly hid part of her face behind her long brown hair.

"I can still see you're beautiful."

"No, you're just guessing. Do you have to leave right now?"

"Doucey has been shot."

"The paedophile? That's almost good news."

"It's a new lead in an inquiry that was going nowhere. So you could say that."

He got out of bed, picked out some clean clothes, and disappeared into the shower. Shortly afterwards the curtain parted and Léa joined him, pressing her body against his under the steaming hot water.

"I'm going to find it difficult to walk away from this case."

"No-one's asking you to."

Coste pulled up at the luminous MXR sign. He didn't need any help finding the exact spot: he had only to follow the line of police cars until he came to unit 297, cordoned off with yellow tape. For once, Sam had agreed to enter a crime scene, probably calculating that the horror was more bearable when it had been wreaked on a monster, which meant Coste found his entire team already there.

Trussed up like a pheasant, Doucey lay crumpled on the floor in the midst of a patchwork of photographs, surrounded on three sides by canvas backdrops of a forest, a deserted beach and a mountain scene where a splash of blood was staining the snow. Johanna came over to Coste and handed him a pair of latex gloves.

"I know it's not a priority, but did you go home alone last night?"

Sam and Ronan looked up in amusement.

"Don't you think we've got more important matters to deal with?" said Coste.

Johanna looked down at her wedding ring, at the dead body on the floor and then at Coste.

"No, actually, I don't."

"Ronan? What have we got?" Coste said, avoiding her question.

"Antoine Doucey and his paedophile empire. It'll take us days to go through it all. I've contacted the Aid to Parents of Child Victims people, they'll send someone to headquarters to look for any match with missing kids. I've also called the

Brigades des mineurs at Quai des Gesvres in Paris. They'll cross-check with current cases, but it's already obvious that Doucey wasn't just a passive observer."

Sam handed Coste a photo he considered to be among the more bearable. A little black boy playing on a beach that Coste recognised as the one on the left wall. Johanna came up to him again.

"What with the cassettes, C.D.s and photos, there must be hundreds of different kids. How could he have found so many victims without ever attracting attention?"

"There are more than a thousand unaccompanied minors in Paris and the suburbs that we know about," Sam informed her. "So you can bet there are three times as many we are unaware of. Throw in the Roma street urchins roaming the capital who'll get into any car for ten euros – if it's not their camp boss offering them to you himself, whatever age you like. Then there are forty-five thousand runaways every year, and the known child prostitution sites at Porte Dauphine and Bois de Boulogne. It's a real supermarket. It's not that complicated, and there's no need to travel to the Philippines."

Ronan had opened one album, then another, before giving up and throwing everything he found into big boxes without even looking at what he was picking up. His disgust prompted a theory.

"Do you think it could be one of the parents?"

"I think I'd be capable of it," Johanna confessed. "However long his prison sentence, it could never be enough."

A uniform came up, asked who was in charge, followed their gazes and addressed Coste.

"There's a couple with their little daughter who'd like to get into their unit. I told them it was impossible, but they need some things to take on holiday."

"Keep them waiting a few seconds. We'll shut this place: bang twice once the coast is clear."

Ronan reached out and pulled down the shutter. As it closed, the ceiling light went off.

"Oh yes, of course," said Sam. "It came on automatically when we opened it, and it's the same when it's being closed. There must be a contact somewhere."

Three piano notes rang out in the darkness.

"Does that belong to any of you?" asked Ronan, switching on his Maglite.

None of them replied. There were two bangs on the shutter. Ronan grasped the handle and raised it again. As he did so, the light came on once more, and the brief sonata sounded a second time. They looked at one another, then down at the body on the floor.

"Have you searched him?"

"Not yet. Forensics have just finished taking samples."

Already wearing his latex gloves, Ronan crouched down and felt Doucey's jacket, then his trousers. He stopped when he felt a solid, rectangular object in one of the pockets. He took out a mobile and handed it to Sam. He examined it quickly, because there wasn't much to say about it.

"There's no operating system. No way of calling or being called. I can't really see what use it is. There's only an app I've never seen before. Shall I open it?"

The other three gathered round, and Coste nodded. Sam touched the screen and a calendar appeared. Under today's date there were seven entries. The previous day, four. Pressing with his finger, he opened that day's folder. To their surprise, Ronan appeared on the screen, arms raised as he opened the shutter to the unit. It took Sam a few seconds to understand.

"He's got a camera on his own burrow, the jerk. Ronan, you

were the last one to open the shutter. There must be a trigger somewhere that activates the camera."

He swiped to the other photos, and this time Johanna appeared.

"That's when the three of us arrived."

He flicked through the previous images.

"Those are the cops who got here first. And shortly before that, the nightwatchman on his rounds when he came to check."

"Are you telling us that if we go back in time we'll have a picture of our killers?" Ronan asked excitedly.

Sam opened the folder containing the four files from the previous day. He swiped back through them.

First photo: Doucey opening the unit.

Second photo: a shot of Doucey from behind as he shut himself in.

Third photo: a man in a balaclava and a blonde woman, face covered with a scarf, opening the door. Opposite them, Doucey in his armchair.

Fourth photo: the man and woman, balaclava and scarf removed and a gun in her hand. On the floor, Doucey, wrists and ankles bound, in a pool of blood.

Sam pinched two fingers on this last photo and zoomed in on their faces.

"Hi there, you two."

"Do we know them?" asked Johanna.

"Not that I'm aware of."

"A couple," Ronan said with surprise. "Maybe Sam was spot on with his theory: parents dispensing justice."

Coste was studying the photo to see if he could identify where the camera was positioned. Hanging from a rope at the back of the unit was a brown teddy bear with big black eyes.

He walked over and unhooked it. He unzipped the toy to reveal a tiny digital camera, the lens replacing the bear's right eye.

"You're a first-rate informer," he said, stuffing the bear into an evidence bag.

52

An hour after his return to headquarters, Coste decided it was time to report in to his boss. He headed for his office, but saw him out in the passage, shouting furiously at the officer in charge of supplies, an elderly man wounded in action who had never managed to leave the service.

"I couldn't give a damn about your budgets. I want a computer I can take round with me, not one of your clunky desktop monstrosities. I had one in Paris, and I want one here. Period."

The older man walked away, almost in tears. He gave Coste a helpless look – unless he bought it himself, he'd never get the laptop the new commissaire wanted.

"I'm glad I caught you in a good mood," Coste said, taking a risk.

"Ah! It's you. Good. I wanted to see you. In my office."

Coste accepted the invitation, recalling how his father had advised him never to start a conversation with someone already in a temper. He had hardly closed the door behind him when Ventura went on the attack.

"O.K. Tell me . . . Are you going to let them be gunned down one by one, or are you planning to get your act together?"

Taken aback by this open hostility, Coste had to remind himself of the previous night's discussion with Léa about their future, and resolved not to let a petty dictator spoil his last few weeks. Unusually for him, he took it on the chin.

"I suppose that's your way of asking me for a catch-up on the case? Ronan is depositing everything we found in the storage unit in the meeting room. As you know, Doucey had set up his own photographic surveillance system, so Johanna is sending round photos of Bonnie and Clyde. We also found an I.D. card on Doucey. Fake. Probably the one he used to open a bank account to pay for the unit during the months he was behind bars."

"He must have had an accomplice," raged Ventura. "I have to change my camera batteries every month. Those things don't run on oxygen."

"The camera comes on when the door opens, then clicks off. There are only eleven photos on it, and he rigged up an adapter so he could use the same batteries they use in smoke detectors. They last more than five years."

"I see. We're not going to have these four-leaf clover scum hanging round our necks until next spring. Usually a case is solved within a week, otherwise it becomes a ball and chain. Things slow down, everything drags on, and soon you're skiing in July. I hope you'll make more rapid progress than you used to under my predecessor."

Coste had been willing to forgive this excessive display of aggression from a commandant who was finding his feet. As long as it was only directed at him . . . but at Marie-Charlotte? That was another matter.

"You mean Damiani? With respect, commandant, if one day you come up as far as her ankles, you'll be able to say you're a big boy."

Ventura went from scarlet with rage to a vision of sly calm, his lips curling in a smile.

285

"You're not a team player, are you? Am I right?"

Coste raised an inquisitive eyebrow. Ventura had just lobbed a hand grenade at him and he had no idea why. It didn't take the commandant long to enlighten him.

"I tell you the Marquant girl is off limits, and you don't bother to tell me you two are together. Do you enjoy making me look like a fucking idiot?"

Now Coste understood why he was the commandant's favourite target today.

"We weren't really together. I mean, we weren't at that moment."

"Better still! I tell you I'm pursuing her, and you decide to go and fuck her up on the roof?"

Coste's hand was tingling with the desire to punch Ventura on the nose, but just at that moment Johanna burst in.

"Can I see you, Victor?"

Out in the corridor, Johanna could see how agitated her boss was.

"Everything O.K.?"

"Never better."

"Then stop gritting your teeth so hard. You'll break one."

It was only then that Coste realised how tightly his jaw was set. He relaxed, puffed out his cheeks and moved on. They entered Rivière's office, where the commandant of the Group de répression du banditisme was staring at his computer screen. On it, the face of Clyde.

"May I present Dorian Calderon," said Johanna proudly. "He was in our mugshot records."

Coste sat in the nearest chair and invited Rivière to tell him more.

"I can't say I saw this coming. My unit investigated him a couple of years ago. His name came up on intercepted calls relating to the hold-up of a jeweller's. A Corsican family was involved. The stolen jewellery was supposed to slip out of the country through Le Bourget airport. We staked it out for several days, but nothing happened. Meanwhile, since your Dorian Calderon is only known as a small-time house burglar, we took no further action against him. We had so little on the gang, the investigating magistrate closed the case."

Rivière clicked on the mouse and a second photo came up: a man with a prominent scar, built like a tank.

"He was caught once with this charmer, a certain Michaël Mention, alias Rhinoceros. They spent two months inside together, and that creates bonds."

"And the woman?" Coste asked.

"She's pretty. That's all I can say about her."

Rivière printed the photos and Coste took them back to Groupe Crime 1's office. He pinned them to the whiteboard, pointed at Dorian's photo and turned to his team.

"I want to know what this guy had against Doucey. And get me the private and public C.C.T.V. footage from around the self-storage depot. Dorian Calderon and Michaël Mention, his only known accomplice. I want their entire networks – professional, personal and financial. I want to know everything about them. The places they go, who they go there with, their cars, their jobs, any known addresses present or past, their properties, trips, what they eat, what they wear, what they like. We're turning their lives upside down. I want to know more about them than their girlfriends. I'll have their photos pinned up in every police station across France. It's noon now, report back in two hours. Get to it."

"Do you think there's a connection with the break-in at the law courts?"

"I think it's our only lead, so I don't even ask myself the question."

53

In the loft the mood was gloomy. And yet up to that moment everything had been going smoothly. They had successfully raided their fifth jeweller's. They had broken into the law courts with panache. They had got Nano out of prison, and now all they had to do was to wait to board a plane like ordinary tourists.

"We took every precaution," Alex said in her defence.

"No, you didn't," snapped Franck, the team's logistics expert. "It takes us three weeks to prepare a heist. Timetables, security systems, procurement, exit strategy. But you, Alex, without a word to anyone else and without any preparation, you went and took that pervert out. The planet is crawling with perverts, so why the avenging angel routine this time? What got into you?"

"It wasn't planned," Dorian objected.

"Great," said Franck. "You acted on impulse. Nothing good comes of using your guts instead of your brain. You two make me sick. I've half a mind to call your father, Alex."

Alex lowered her eyes, realising Franck was in charge now. The only girl in the Mosconi family, she'd had to work a hundred times harder than the menfolk to win respect and permission to form her own team. The return to Corsica wasn't going to be as triumphal as she had hoped.

"Nobody leaves the loft," Franck continued. "Leave your

phone on the table. We don't get in touch with anyone. We barely breathe. Tonight I'll change cars again and get two days' shopping in. I'll be back in the morning. Until then, no-one moves a muscle."

As he was leaving, he looked unsympathetically across at the sofa bed where Nano was still fast asleep, face down on the pillow, a crust of saliva around his mouth.

"And if he has another meltdown, knock him out."

Following two hours of fruitless investigation, the galvanising effect of a new lead was beginning to wear off. Dorian Calderon and Michaël Mention seemed to have vanished into thin air. Sam went through the checklist, crossing out each dead end.

"No known jobs, no registered cars, and I've checked all their addresses going back ten years – nothing. No telephone accounts either – they're not even on Facebook. They both claim state benefits, paid into accounts that show no transactions for weeks. As far as I can tell, they could be living abroad. The only proof Dorian Calderon is in the country is the photo taken yesterday in the storage unit."

"About that . . . Have we had any news from the border force?" asked Coste.

"No, but they have to check every place one by one, so it can take time," said Ronan, who had been assigned that task.

"This means they're being very careful. To the point of being non-existent. Finding nothing is already finding something. It looks very much like a pair who are hoping to pass under the radar. Anything from the C.C.T.V. footage?"

"Yes, there are about sixty cameras in Noisy-le-Sec. A new neighbourhood security police initiative. The street where the self-storage depot is situated has intersections at both ends. Between the time codes on the photos when Doucey's unit was opened and when the couple were coming out, seventy-three vehicles were filmed. None of them stolen. I checked on their owners, but there was no-one very interesting, and definitely no Calderon or Mention. I got all the female owners to send me their driver's licences, but none of them looked anything like Dorian's Bonnie."

"They wouldn't have gone to kill Doucey in their own car. They must have used a stolen car and swapped the number plates. We'll split the list in four and call all the owners. When we find someone who wasn't in Noisy-le-Sec between half past nine and ten last night, we'll have our registration number. It's a start."

"Then what?" Ronan asked. "Instead of chasing after a face, we'll be chasing a number. Have you any idea how many cars there are in Seine-Saint-Denis?"

Coste turned to him and patted him on the shoulder. Ronan got the message, and Groupe Crime 1 became a call centre. For three hours, while Sam distributed landline numbers from the Yellow Pages and mobile ones courtesy of the various service providers, the others punched them in and explained why they were calling. Without success until they stumbled across a young Breton woman living in Brest who stammered:

"Noisy le what?"

"Noisy-le-Sec," Johanna repeated. "Yesterday evening."

The young woman pulled back the lace curtain on her kitchen window and checked that her Volvo was where it should be.

"No. Neither I nor the car left Brest."

Johanna thanked her, hung up and put an end to her colleagues' now pre-empted conversations.

"A blue Volvo 740. A Breton antique that stayed in its parking spot all night. Licence number AB 344 CA. What do I get?"

"A ridiculously large wage packet," Ronan quipped.

Coste picked up the list of police stations and thrust it at Sam, who almost dropped it.

"We have our target. Ronan, make sure it goes onto the list of stolen vehicles a.s.a.p. Sam, call all the stations in Seine-Saint-Denis and get them to put all the A.N.P.R. vehicles on the road now, this afternoon and all night. I want them spinning round like tops until they locate it. But tell them not to touch it – that's our job."

Despite being part of the group for two years, Johanna had to confess her ignorance.

"What are A.N.P.R. cars?"

"One of you explain. I'm off to Doucey's autopsy."

54

Léa used the blade to prise the flesh from the breastbone. A smaller bone got in the way, so she snapped it with a flick of her wrist. A thick liquid oozed out, which she decanted into a bowl. Coste took out two plates and put them next to the meal. White meat for her, thigh for him. Léa had listened closely to how the inquiry was going and made some suggestions, but stumbled over the same thing as Johanna.

"A.N.P.R.?"

"Automatic Number Plate Recognition. We have thirty patrol cars with the equipment in Seine-Saint-Denis. They can easily cover the area. They have six cameras placed under the flashing light that can record thirteen hundred number plates a minute. Each one is automatically compared with the list of stolen vehicles. The kind of equipment that can do the job of a hundred cops.

Later that evening, Léa nestled against Coste's shoulder on his sofa and dipped into a book while he watched the rolling news to see if there were any repercussions from the paedophile's death.

Closing the book gently on her chest, she tapped a finger on its cover. Coste could sense that several thoughts were whirling round her brain.

"I'm not really watching, you know," he said.

"That's good. Because I'm asking myself a lot of questions right now."

"I'm listening."

"You're a cop, Coste. You've never done anything else. It's the only thing you know how to do."

"And look where it's got me."

"You know I'll follow you anywhere. With my qualifications, work isn't really a problem for me. But you – once you've taken stock and spent three months freezing your butt off under those Northern Lights of yours – what are you going to do?"

"You're a pain in the arse," he joked. "First you tell me my work takes up all my time and now you're worried you won't love me when I give it up."

"I never asked you to resign. And if your job takes over your life, that's because you give it too much importance. No-one is forcing you to spend twelve hours a day at work."

"That's what everyone in the Police Judiciaire does."

"Exactly. Take time to think it over. You know there are a thousand other ways to be a police officer, and none of them are anything to be ashamed of. A quiet little police station in a small town, like your friend Mathias[*]? We'd be happy like that, wouldn't we?"

"I need to think it over. Let's make a start with the Northern Lights, shall we?"

Appeased, Léa shifted position, stroked his face with the back of her hand and opened her book once more. Her breathing slowed and became more regular, and Coste realised she had dozed off. He looked down at her tranquil face and saw her top lip moving as if she were dreaming of being a singer. Though

---

[*] Lieutenant Mathias Aubin, Coste's closest colleague in *The Lost and the Damned*.

293

she didn't weigh much, she was deadening his shoulder, but he wouldn't have spoiled this moment for anything. He used his free arm to lower the sound on the T.V., channel surfed for a few minutes, then also fell asleep.

At five in the morning, his mobile rang. A few short sentences were enough to send him sprinting to the shower.

"Capitaine Coste? Unit TN 316 in Saint-Denis. We've spotted AB344 CA near a car breaker's yard. What are your instructions?"

The stolen car had just been used for a murder, so it made sense to get rid of it, and what better solution than a scrapyard?

"Call your crime prevention people and get them to send out an unmarked car. They're not to make a move, but take note of everything going in or out. We'll be with them in less than half an hour."

55

Ronan parked the police Peugeot 306 twenty metres from the entrance to the breaker's yard. Switching off the lights, he left a slit open in his side window so their breathing wouldn't form condensation and give the game away. Sprawled on the back seat, desperate to continue his night's sleep, Sam was struggling to keep his eyes open.

Coste and Johanna passed them in the second car and came to a stop just beyond a black Renault Mégane. Coste jumped out on the driver's side and ran towards it, crouching down so that he was hidden by the car's bodywork. He tapped on the windscreen and the rear door opened.

"Gentlemen."

"Capitaine," the three officers responded in unison.

"What can you tell me?"

"At 04.50 hours, the Saint-Denis A.N.P.R. picked up your target and followed it from a distance until it pulled up here."

"For a long while?" Coste asked.

"No, only for one street. After that they kept on going so as not to be spotted. They saw the car turn into this breaker's yard in their rear-view mirror. They contacted you at 05.00 hours, and we replaced them at seven minutes past. It's 05.32 now, and no-one has come out."

"That's very precise. Do you know who the owner of the yard is?"

"Yes, he's a big fat gypsy guy. He fired buckshot at us last week. We reckon he receives a lot of stolen vehicles. If you have a breaker's yard in Seine-Saint-Denis it must be tempting."

"Thanks. We'll take it from here, but I need you to stick around."

"No problem, we'll inform base."

A few minutes before eight, Sam felt a resounding slap on his thigh. He woke with a start, and it took him a few seconds to realise he wasn't at home in his bedroom. While he was coming to his senses, Ronan seized the radio and spoke to the other car.

"See it?"

A dark green Renault Clio emerged through the morning mist on the dirt track leading from the yard to the road. Before pulling out, Franck looked left and right, leaning forward into the windscreen. As he did so, the streetlamps picked out his face.

"Coste to A.N.P.R.," Coste said into his radio. "Does he look like your big fat gypsy?"

"Negative," came the response. "Ours is three times his size."

"Great. Don't move. Let us leave first, then you can return to base. Thanks for your help."

Coste organised the operation with Ronan and Sam, well aware that nothing is more delicate than following someone who is on the lookout.

"O.K., listen up. No-one went in after the target at five o'clock. Ten to one says it's our guy in a fresh car. Johanna and I will start to tail him. We can take advantage of the light traffic at this hour. You stay well back, and we'll let you know how we're getting on. We'll swap places every three minutes."

The streets slipped by as Coste followed the Clio, concealing their car behind vans and trucks. After three minutes, he indicated to turn off, and left the main road. Immediately behind him, Ronan's Peugeot took his place and continued the tail for the next three minutes. They continued to switch in this way until the scenery around them became all too familiar. Still lying low on the back seat, Sam contacted Coste.

"We're approaching Bobigny. He's taking us back home. We're just going past the bus depot. Will you take over?"

Ronan turned off and disappeared. Coste took up the dance. He saw the Clio pass the buses parked outside the depot and then pull up on the road bordering the Darcy shopping centre. Johanna pointed to a space about ten places behind him, and Coste swerved into it. Their target got out of his car and headed for the stone steps leading to the esplanade outside the centre's main entrance. Two beggars, one of them a musician, fifteen or so kids on their scooters, smoking, swapping insults or whistling at pretty young girls, and even those who weren't. And a constant flood of anonymous citizens, going inside empty-handed and coming out laden with shopping bags. Behind the supermarket stood a semi-circle of imposing tower blocks, as though the Darcy building was merely their entrance hall.

"Coste to Ronan. I'm parked too far away. I don't know if he's going into the shopping centre or not. If he's buying provisions, we might get lucky and he'll lead us to the others, but I can't spot him."

"I'm right opposite the entrance, on the same road as you. He's coming towards me, so I'm signing off."

Ronan slid down in his seat, and even though it made no difference, held his breath. Sam tried to bury himself in the back seat as Franck Mosconi walked past their car. The tension eased when he reached the esplanade, and Ronan switched the radio back on.

Their target approached the shopping centre entrance, slowed up, and walked over to the kids on scooters. One of them, hoodie down over their eyes, left the group and went up to Franck.

"He's made contact with someone," said Ronan.

"Do we know him?"

"Impossible to tell. Not from where I am."

Coste hesitated. With the little info they had, their target's contact could very easily be part of the gang. Blue wire, red wire? He gave his orders.

"Tell Sam to kit up and go in. He's to enter the shopping centre and exit at the rear, nothing more. I want to know who this new guy is."

Ronan punched open the glove compartment and took out another radio. He passed it back to Sam, who added an earpiece and pushed it into his ear. Unfortunately, delinquents have long since learned to look for these devices and recognise them straightaway. So Sam covered the earpiece with a bulky pair of headphones that were impossible to hide but more in keeping with his surroundings. To blend in even further, he raised the hood on his sweatshirt before he got out of the car. Ronan lowered his window and called to him.

"Lower your hood. You won't be able to see to the sides."

Sam did so, then headed for the esplanade. He stuffed his hands in his pockets, adopted a scowl, and swayed his head to the rhythm of imaginary music. He sauntered over to their target and his contact, who turned away from him at the last moment. Sam slowed down, hoping to get a better view. Franck turned his head as well, and for a split second their eyes met. Cool as a cucumber, Sam looked away, then entered the already crowded shopping centre.

"Sorry, I couldn't see who the other guy was. Want me to go out again?"

"Negative. Find a shop with mirrors in the front window and try one more time."

The first shop Sam came across, directly to his left as he entered, was a jeweller's with shiny mirrors that allowed him to keep an eye on every exit. He pretended to be interested in the watches, peering cautiously into one of the mirrors, and caught sight of scooter wheels and trainers. Raising his head a little, he found himself eyeballing their target, who was staring straight at him. That left him no choice but to continue with his charade and enter the boutique. The sales assistant came over and asked what she could do for him. Sam ignored her and raised his hand to his ear, panting a little.

"O.K., we've locked eyes twice now. He'll get suspicious if I keep on like this."

The assistant wondered who he could be talking to and Sam obliged by raising his top and showing the gun in his waistband. Franck meanwhile whispered something under the youngster's hood, then the two of them parted and he walked back across the esplanade. He seemed in no hurry. On the contrary, to Ronan it looked as if he was going far too slowly.

When he reached their pavement, Franck walked calmly along the line of parked cars to rejoin his own. As he passed by Ronan's Peugeot, he glanced casually at its roof. Sam received a fresh order from Coste in his earpiece.

"Stay where you are and keep the scooter kids in sight."

Ronan let their target carry on for a couple of metres, then spoke to Coste with the radio between his thighs.

"He's heading towards you. Slowly. Too slowly. I don't know what he's doing but he's getting edgy."

Good thinking. Franck's radar was on, and he was scanning everything around him for the slightest suspicious person or conspicuous detail – anything that jarred. He had already been spooked by the guy in the shopping mall, but people around here seemed to stare at one another openly, so he had dismissed his fears as paranoia. Now, though, there was something about that grey car's roof he didn't like: his antennae were working overtime. He carried on walking, peering at all the car roofs. He reached one with a couple inside, holding hands lovingly, deep in conversation. She looked a bit masculine with her cropped blonde hair; the man was in his forties, with salt and pepper locks. Franck was about to walk on when he glanced at their car roof and for the second time, on the same road, saw the same scratches. Deep grooves made by police on an adrenalin rush flinging the magnetic rotating blue lights willy-nilly on top of their speeding vehicle. Coste and Johanna heard Ronan calling them.

"Shit! I know what he's doing! He's looking for marks left by our lights, the son of a bitch. He knows we're on to him. What do we do?"

Coste watched their target draw nearer the Clio and, like Johanna, stretched a hand to the door handle, ready to leap out.

"I hope you're wrong. We're holding tight for the moment. If we go for him, you and Sam deal with his contact up on the esplanade."

Franck Mosconi rested his hand on the side of the Clio and took a deep breath. A thin film of sweat covered his back. He calculated that if he tried to do a U-turn he would find a bunch of guns stuck to his windscreen, pointing straight at him. He looked across at the nearby tower blocks and their labyrinthine entrances, and made up his mind. Taking another deep breath, he sprinted towards them.

"Strike!" yelled Coste.

Johanna and he were out of the car in less than a second. They sprinted as fast as they could to make up the ten-metre lead Franck had on them. As he ran, Franck seized the mobile in his jacket pocket and at the first corner threw it down an open drain. He turned his head and saw the female officer had already halved the distance between them. He dashed across the pedestrian crossing towards the towers, failing to see the van that piled into him with a deafening screech of brakes until it was too late.

The traffic came to a halt on both sides of the road. A few curious drivers got out of their cars, while the van driver, paralysed by shock, was already tormented by the question everyone who's been in an accident asks themselves: "Was it my fault or theirs?"

Franck was lying flat on the ground. At first when he opened his eyes everything was hazy. Two shadows leaning over him. Recovering slightly, he could make out the police couple more clearly. The question of whether or not he'd gone to heaven was no longer relevant.

"You gave me a fright, fuckwit," Coste said mockingly. "I thought you were dead."

"Strike!"

As soon as he heard this from Coste, Sam ran out of the jeweller's, just as the kid in the hoodie was entering the shopping centre and mingling with the crowd. Sam pushed his way through the shoppers, immediately drawing attention to himself. Hoodie ducked into the supermarket, trying to lose Sam among the aisles.

When Ronan arrived at the jeweller's he turned full circle before realising he couldn't see his colleague.

"Sam? Where are you?" he shouted into his radio.

"In the middle of Darcy's. I've lost contact!"

Just then at the far end of an aisle, Sam saw a hooded

silhouette turn left. He ran towards it, narrowly missing a trolley, skidded round on the tiled floor, and ended up in the middle of frozen foods. It took him a few seconds to check the twenty or so customers all busy planning their week's menus – no sign of Hoodie. Tired of being led a dance, he clambered up on top of the freezer cabinets to get a proper view of the surrounding aisles. He caught sight of his target next to shower gels and toothpastes, constantly looking over his shoulder. If Sam ran up the parallel aisle, he could cut them off at the corner. To the astonishment of the shoppers, he jumped down and ran to the end of the aisle, coming face to face with Hoodie. The youngster turned tail, and although Sam was no athlete, he could sprint five metres. He caught up and launched himself. The pair of them crashed into a pyramid of organic jams on special offer. The pots shattered on the floor in a strawberry-and-fig-coloured abstract masterpiece. They both slipped trying to stand up, but Sam pulled the suspect down by the legs. During the struggle the hood fell back, and a shock of long brown hair tumbled out.

"Shit! Who on earth are you?" Sam exclaimed, taken aback at having had such trouble collaring a teenage girl.

At that moment Ronan arrived and discovered them in a sea of glass, covered in jam. Sam quickly checked the girl's pockets. He found a cloth wallet and handed it to his colleague. Ronan opened it and came across an I.D. card. He read the name out loud.

"Aurélie Alves. I don't know what the fuck you're doing mixed up in all this, but you're under arrest, sweetheart."

As a voice announced on the loudspeakers a 3-for-2 offer on organic jam, Sam handcuffed their new suspect.

56

Brought in with no I.D. on him, the male suspect was escorted to Forensics to have his fingerprints taken.

"If you want to know who I am, you only have to ask."

"But you might lie," the technician retorted, as he prepared the black ink and the fingerprinting form.

"My name is Mosconi. Franck Mosconi. Tell that to the others; it should make them sit up and listen."

Surprised at this, the technician signalled to his assistant, who went to pick up the phone.

Sam hung up. He was confused but excited.

"I don't know why he wants to save us time, but he's just told Forensics his name: Franck Mosconi."

As he said this, Sam was already consulting the national offenders' database to discover Mosconi's record. He read it out to the others:

"Arson, several convictions for assault and extortion. All in Corsica, nothing in mainland France. Nice fellow."

"Mosconi?" Coste repeated, going over to the whiteboard.

He looked first at the photos of Dorian Calderon and the unknown woman coming out of the storage unit, then at the names of the four-leaf clovers and their lawyers and the various addresses and number plates that had cropped up during the investigation. An organised jumble that made it difficult to spot connections – even for them.

"So that's two from the same family then. We have Franck Mosconi driving the Volvo seen at the time and place of the murder of one Antoine Doucey, a paedophile released thanks to the break-in at the law courts. Nunzio Mosconi was freed in the same operation. I'm not saying it's completely clear, but it's beginning to take shape. How long since he was brought in?"

"Thirty-seven minutes," said Johanna, consulting her mobile.

"So we have twenty minutes before we legally have to interview him. We'll need an empty office – there's too much info on the walls here."

Blinds down; a desk with a computer on it. No other decoration in the beige office they'd managed to commandeer. Coste was sitting across from Franck.

"Do you want to see a doctor?"

"Just because I was run over by a van?"

"Would you like us to inform anyone of your arrest? A loved one? A wife? Or even an accomplice – we're not hard to please, but we'd need their name and telephone number."

Franck looked at him, a faint smile on his lips. His silence was taken as a no.

"Do you want to see a lawyer? The duty one here? Your own counsel?"

"My own lawyer," Franck replied without hesitation. "Maître Tiretto, of the Paris bar."

"The same lawyer who got your brother Nunzio Mosconi released?"

"Nunzio is my cousin. And Tiretto is our family lawyer. You're going to have to do a bit of work, lads, I'm not going to give you everything gift-wrapped."

Coste slid the photo of the couple leaving the storage unit across the table.

"Well, just between the two of us, would you like to tell me who this pair are? This morning, you were seen in a car linked to them."

Franck thought back to the stolen vehicle that must be a Rubik's cube in his scrap-merchant friend's crusher by now. The police would need a lot of patience to find the slightest trace of D.N.A. there.

"Just between the two of us," he said, "why don't you leave me in peace and take me back down to the cells?"

"Are you upset because I called you a fuckwit when we brought you in?"

"It wasn't the highlight of my day," Mosconi admitted.

"Oh, I'm sorry, I thought you knew it already."

"We won't get anything out of him," muttered Coste as he watched Franck, hands cuffed behind his back, being led down to the holding cells on the ground floor.

"Not before his lawyer has told him what to say," Ronan agreed. "What I don't understand is why he told us his name. He could have gained a few hours before his fingerprints told us who he was. We didn't find any I.D. on him. All he had to do was keep quiet."

"But he didn't. That's because he wants to see his shyster lawyer as quickly as possible. He knows Tiretto will tell his accomplices he's been arrested."

"In other words, as soon as he's talked to his lawyer, the rest of his gang will find out and stay well hidden."

"That leaves the girl," Coste thought out loud. "She might not be as tough. And she might know something."

"Except that Tiretto will be able to see from the charge sheet that Aurélie Alves was brought in together with Franck. I don't know the connection between them, but even if Mosconi's accomplices trust him not to give them away, I doubt they'll be as confident about a teenager. Which means they're not going to stay put. Wherever they might be, they'll be sure to move, and then nobody will know their whereabouts, not even Franck Mosconi."

"Unless we neglect to mention Aurélie Alves in our statements," Coste said.

"You want us to tamper with them?" said an astonished Sam.

"I want us to wrap this investigation up," replied Coste. "Put the kid in our cells on the third floor and keep Mosconi down below. They mustn't catch sight of one another."

"Do you want to see a doctor?" asked Johanna.

"No, no, I'm alright," the teenager stammered.

"A lawyer?"

She almost burst into tears.

"Why? What have I done?"

"I have a whole list of offences. Do you know that your friend Franck might be an accomplice to murder, which means you could be as well? And when we wanted to talk to you, you shot off like a champion sprinter. So, do you want a lawyer? They're expensive, and it's only guilty people who need one," Johanna said, to confuse the young girl.

"No then," said Aurélie, increasingly lost.

"You're underage, so I have to contact a legally responsible adult. Who do you want to choose?"

"My father. Tomas Alves."

"What's his telephone number?"

It took Tiretto fifteen minutes to reach police headquarters. He was received by a certain Capitaine Coste, the officer in charge of his client's case. Watched over by Sam, who had modified the arrest report as rapidly as possible, he leafed through the pages, noting down whatever seemed to him useful.

"It's awkward having someone perched on my shoulder while I read," he objected to Sam.

"I don't suppose it's the most awkward thing in your line of business, but this is my office, so it's where I work. If you like, I can put a chair out in the corridor for you."

Tiretto didn't respond to the provocation. He was accustomed to this kind of welcome in police stations.

"May I see my client now?"

Mosconi was taken from his cell and accompanied to the room set aside for lawyers. Tiretto soon entered, and when he saw him, Franck's shoulders drooped. No more play-acting. The arrogant attitude and impassive mask he had put on for the police had vanished.

"So?"

"So nothing. You were seen by the Saint-Denis police in a stolen car. You'll be accused of theft or receiving stolen goods at most. Regardless of the fact that the vehicle," the lawyer continued, "may have been involved twenty-four hours earlier in the death of Antoine Doucey, the paedophile whose release you obtained by mistake. I imagine that was down to Alex?"

"She did that off her own bat, without telling any of us. If she had, I would have stopped her. I knew she'd land us in the shit with those moral scruples of hers."

"That's why I don't have any. Keep quiet and you should be out soon."

"What about the car?"

"Don't you remember?" Tiretto said in astonishment. "You

found it in Saint-Denis, engine running and doors wide open, so you took it to a scrap merchant to make a bit of money."

"That's a bit far-fetched, isn't it?"

"Maybe, but it's up to the police to prove you're lying. So we'll stick to our story."

"Talking of the police, who are we up against? Do you know them?"

Tiretto took out his notebook and found the page where he had made notes.

"Groupe Crime 1 led by Capitaine Coste. If you ask me, that's not exactly good news. He's said to be determined and occasionally obsessive. The same goes for his team. Wait a second . . ."

He turned the page and read the names he'd seen in the report.

"Lieutenant Ronan Scaglia, Lieutenant Johanna De Ritter and Officer Samuel Dorfrey."

Franck seemed to hesitate over what he was going to say next, then made up his mind:

"Was I brought in on my own?"

"Why? Were you with someone?"

"Shit, Tiretto, did your mother never tell you not to answer a question with a question? Was I brought in alone or not?"

"Yes, Franck. You're the only one mentioned in the police report. But you're worrying me. You do know I have to be told everything if I'm to defend you?"

"There's nothing else to tell. Get word to the father."

"Not Alexandra?"

"She's sidelined herself. From now on, we deal directly with Monsieur Mosconi."

Coste himself accompanied Maître Tiretto to the exit. He opened the big glass doors and let the lawyer go first.

"Obviously you have the right to be present at all your client's interviews."

Tiretto assumed a pained expression.

"There's nothing more to this than a stolen vehicle, capitaine. He's not got too much to say about it, so I'll be happy to read the transcript tomorrow. Thank you for your understanding. However, you should call a doctor as soon as possible – don't forget, my client was in an accident. It would be a shame if a procedural error undermined your investigation."

Coste watch him walk over to his Audi saloon, illegally parked in a space reserved for the police. When he reached it, the lawyer picked up the penalty notice from under his windscreen wiper and tossed it away. Ronan joined Coste at that moment.

"In two minutes he'll have warned everyone else in the gang."

"Everyone but Aurélie. Tell Johanna to start the officially recorded interview. I want her to discover the connection between her and Franck Mosconi. With a bit of luck she knows who the others are, addresses, their safe house – or any tiny crumb that will help us progress."

They left the reception area and headed for the lift. On the way they passed a chubby little man with a worried look on his face. He stopped at the front desk, where the duty officer was stifling a yawn.

"Good morning. I was called in by Lieutenant De Ritter. It's about my daughter."

His anxious voice reached the two policemen at the far end of the lobby.

"Monsieur Alves? Capitaine Coste and Lieutenant Scaglia, Police Judiciaire. We're in charge of proceedings against Aurélie."

Tomas almost exploded.

"What has she done? Is it those kids on scooters at the shopping centre again? I told her they were no good for her, that they'd only get her into trouble. But I don't understand. Usually it's the juvenile police who contact me."

With a sweep of the arm, Coste invited him to follow them.

"Let me explain."

In the interview room, Tomas Alves shifted uneasily on the uncomfortable chair he was offered. Coste opened the dossier on the table in front of him, while Ronan looked on, leaning against the wall.

"Name and first name?"

"Alves. Tomas, with no 'h'."

"Date and place of birth?"

"July second 1969 at Orleix, in Hautes Pyrénées."

"Profession?"

Under the impression he had been called in for another adolescent misdemeanour – though these officers weren't the ones he usually dealt with – Tomas responded without considering the consequences.

"I'm an employee at Bobigny High Court."

Coste's fingers paused above the keyboard.

"What kind of employee?"

"I'm in charge of the evidence bags."

Coste turned towards Ronan, who, message understood, left the room briefly, then came back carrying all the case files with him. Alerted to this unexpected turn of events, Sam and Johanna also appeared. Surrounded by four police officers, Tomas was more concerned than ever.

"I think you're obliged to give me the reasons for my daughter's arrest," he protested feebly.

In response, Ronan opened the folder and slid Franck

Mosconi's photo across the table. Right under Tomas's nose. He froze: the cops had uncovered his link with the gang, and it was Aurélie's arrest that had brought it to light, though he had no idea how. In his mind's eye, he saw Rhino grabbing her by the hair and dragging her into the living room. And Alex warning him she would put Isabel's head in the oven . . .

Coste clicked his fingers and Tomas returned to the room. "Monsieur Alves?"

He closed his eyes and tried to control his breathing. That morning on their front porch, Isabel had given him a gentler and longer kiss than usual, as if to prepare him for something like this.

"I don't know this man," he said, raising his eyes.

Ronan took over, in a more aggressive tone.

"Franck Mosconi. Your daughter was arrested with him. He's the cousin of Nunzio Mosconi, one of the inmates released following the theft of evidence bags from your workplace. All our enquiries lead to your doorstep. You're going to have to do better than that to wriggle out of this one."

Aurélie with Franck Mosconi? The news landed like a kick to the stomach. What was she doing with him only a few days after he and his gang had broken her father's nose and kept her family hostage and threatened to kill them?

"I'm sorry. I don't know this man," he repeated mechanically, his fists clenched.

After that he refused to say anything more. Coste weighed him up and in his attitude saw a mixture of fear and resignation. Ronan took Tomas by the arm, lifted him from his chair, put his arms behind his back and handcuffed him.

"Monsieur Alves, it is 10.15 hours, and you are under arrest for aiding and abetting an armed robbery."

Tomas made no objection, although a thousand questions

were pricking his brain like red-hot needles. Coste watched him go with the distinct impression they had missed a trick. Sam confirmed his impression.

"We're wide of the mark somehow, aren't we? You saw how he reacted when Ronan showed him the photo. I thought we were going to lose him. He obviously knows the guy. What I don't get is why he'd prefer to be arrested and leave his daughter in here just to protect Mosconi."

"Unless it's not Mosconi he's protecting. Johanna, you've done a first interview with Aurélie. How many are there in the family?"

"We now have two thirds of them in our cells. Then there's the mother, Isabel. The parents have no police records. Aurélie has committed a few adolescent offences, but nothing serious. I really can't see those three pulling off a robbery like that."

"But if we're going to uncover anything, it'll be thanks to them," said Coste, "so carry out the usual checks. Sam, I want all their bank transactions for the past two months: father, mother and Aurélie. Their phones, too: get hold of detailed bills for the same period. Johanna, send a forensics team to their address – you and Ronan can join them there. And bring Madame Alves back with you. We've got the gang on one side, and on the other a family with no police record. I want to know how those two worlds came into contact."

57

Rhinoceros was growing impatient. Being a baby-sitter or carer had never been part of the plan, so he complained to Dorian.

"Nano's been stuck in front of the box all morning, and I'm not even sure he understands what he's watching. If we keep stuffing him full of drugs, he's never going to have a clear head."

"I know," Dorian agreed, "but he's been on medication for weeks. We can't take him off it in one go – that would be dangerous. He needs to behave himself in the airport. Alex says to wait until we're back in Corsica, and that everything will be easier over there."

"And I say it's time for you to grow a pair and go and tell her to look after her brother herself."

Dorian glanced across the room at Alex, who was sitting at the table in the middle of the loft, staring at her phone. He went over and sat next to her.

"Is there a problem with Nano?" she asked in alarm.

Dorian knew her well enough to appreciate this wasn't the moment to bother her with Rhinoceros's injured pride.

"No, everything's fine. It's just that we need to think about feeding him something other than antidepressants."

Alex hardly seemed to hear him. She couldn't take her eyes off the phone.

"Any news from Franck?" Dorian asked.

"Nothing. He should have been back two hours ago with a new car. I've called him four times and left four messages. Something's gone wrong, I can feel it."

"Wouldn't you like to spend some time with Nano? I think Rhinoceros is getting restless."

Alex hesitated, then decided to go and see what the problem was. Halfway there, a tune suddenly filled the air. Skype was announcing that someone was trying to get through. She turned round, sat at the table, and frowned when she saw it said "Mr M." in a corner of the screen. She clicked to take the call and her father's face appeared. Suntanned skin, furrowed brow, shaven head, a white shirt with several buttons undone. Behind him, a window giving on to a bright blue sky. The top half of another man appeared briefly, placing a glass of sparkling water on the table next to him.

"Papa?"

The connection was poor and there was half a second's delay, so her father's angry scowl remained on screen, even as his voice came through the speaker.

"I should never have allowed you to get a team together. You don't know how to protect your men," he spat, his strong Corsican accent adding force to the reprimand.

Momentarily taken aback by his violent outburst, Alex reacted by once more becoming his little daughter.

"What are you talking about, Papa? Nano is here with us. We got the job done and we're leaving from Orly tomorrow morning."

"With Franck?"

"Of course with Fr . . ."

She trailed off mid-sentence, realising her father knew more than she did.

"And after the hold-up to release your brother, are you

314

planning on hitting the Police Judiciaire to get your cousin out?"

By now, Rhinoceros and Dorian were standing behind her, though sufficiently far back to avoid finding themselves in Monsieur Mosconi's line of sight or a target of his anger. Alex chose not to reply, knowing she would only choke on the words.

"Franck was arrested at ten this morning," her father continued. "Tiretto has just left the police station."

"Do we know what happened?"

Waiting for the question to reach him in Corsica, Monsieur Mosconi took a sip of cold water.

"Something about a stolen car; you'll have to explain it to me."

"We . . . we're quite safe. He won't talk," Alex ventured.

"I know that. I trust him. But vehicle thefts are dealt with by the local police, not the Police Judiciaire, and especially not their groupes crime. The lawyer tells me we shouldn't underestimate them. So now we have to assume you've all been identified. Your current hideout is still your best bet. But you won't be able to leave France on any official airline. You'll have to take the same route as the jewels."

"Le Bourget airport?"

"I'm busy organising your return here. I've booked a flight. This evening, a Parisian friend of mine will be in touch. He has passports for you all. I suppose you're also short of cash. He'll see to that. And after this conversation you're to wipe clean your computer. Your plane leaves tomorrow at one in the afternoon. Until then, do you think you can manage not to set the continent alight?"

Alex looked down at the floor. Since the age of eight she had fought to have her father treat her the same as her brothers, but had only ever received criticism and scorn. Suddenly, though, Monsieur Mosconi's voice became calmer, almost paternal.

"Alexandra. I hear you killed a man."

That loudmouth Tiretto, thought Alex. He must have learned about it from Franck, and like a little lap dog he'd gone and told the patriarch everything. She gritted her teeth and, standing by her decision, for the first time dared meet her father's eyes.

"It was necessary."

"I know. I've heard who he was. You did the right thing. But it was an operation within an operation. You should have come back here, made sure your team was safe, and then planned what you were going to do. We could have thought it through properly together."

"Franck gave me the same advice. I didn't listen to him."

"And now he's in the hands of the police."

Acknowledging her guilt, Alex let her father finish.

"Come home. We'll talk about your future."

58

For the third time that afternoon, Tomas, Aurélie and Franck had been grilled by Groupe Crime 1. For the third time, each of them had stuck to their story, and the printed transcripts of the sessions amounted to no more than half a page.

Franck admitted stealing a car he had found unlocked, sitting there like a birthday present on the public highway. He was patiently waiting for the cops to grow tired and for the hours he could be held to slip by.

To protect their family, Tomas and his daughter would have sworn they weren't related to each other, and Aurélie was even more determined to save Franck.

Isabel Alves had been brought in and had made her statement. If her husband had turned pale when he saw Mosconi's photograph, she had gone to pieces, and in a very poor piece of playacting had insisted she did not know him, her voice close to cracking. Afterwards her mobile was taken from her and she was put in a locked office in unofficial custody.

Coste and Johanna allowed themselves a coffee, leaving Ronan to wade through all the answers to the enquiries they had made that morning.

"What did you find?" asked Coste, putting down his cup.

"As far as I can see, there weren't any suspicious bank transactions. If Tomas Alves was paid, it must have been in cash.

But their phone records are more interesting. Aurélie and her mother's weren't used at all on the day of the break-in or the three preceding it."

"If a teenager doesn't use her phone for ninety-six hours, I'd be checking her pulse," said Johanna.

"On the other hand, Tomas definitely used his. He received several calls he immediately diverted to his voicemail, and made just one, to a number that was immediately wiped. I'll have it checked."

"Either they used other phones during the robbery, or they were prevented from communicating," Coste mused.

"Our search of the house revealed nothing, and nobody is saying a word," Johanna added. "What shall we do with the mother?"

"I don't know whether we should protect her or treat her as a suspect. Maybe both. So she stays where she is."

"Aren't we going to arrest her?"

"On what charges?" Coste said. "Look at the three of them: Dorian Calderon, a known thief, Franck Mosconi, a Corsican villain, and an unknown blonde, gun in hand – and what are we doing? We're focusing on a father, his sixteen-year-old daughter and his wife? The only way this business makes sense is if Tomas was forced to help carry out the break-in. It seems to me all we have is another bunch of victims."

"So why would Aurélie carry on seeing Franck Mosconi days afterwards?"

"Maybe she knew him from before. She might be the one who told them what her father's job was. She could even unwittingly have given Mosconi the idea for the break-in."

"And apart from the Volvo he was driving, how do we link Mosconi to the couple leaving the storage unit?"

"Give me a break, Ronan. I'm as lost as you are. I'm casting around, turning somersaults, making hypotheses. O.K., we'll take a minute's rest and then question them again."

Since the discovery of the body in the storage unit, Coste and his team had slept six hours in two days. Their exhaustion was palpable.

"So we ask the same questions indefinitely?" said Johanna.

"Yes, indefinitely and more and more insistently," snapped Commandant Ventura. None of Coste's team had noticed him appear in the doorway.

He took a step inside and added:

"When somebody's in custody, you wear them out, you break them, you push them to the limit. Threaten them with hell, make them cry, but above all, get them to talk. You've got a family in here. Threaten them in front of each other. You're being too soft on them! If you don't feel up to it, I can draft in Jevric's team. You were quick to do them down, but she gets results. So . . . pull a miracle out of your arse and get this case moving."

As he was leaving the office as stormily as he had come in, he almost knocked over Sam, who had a stack of papers in his hands. Coste watched Ventura leave, wondering who among the management instructors at the police academy had advocated for his particular brand of motivational speaking. Sam took his place on the sofa and picked up on the last thing the head of Groupes Crimes had said.

"Does it count if the miracle comes from the fax?"

"The Lord moves in mysterious ways . . ." said Johanna. "What have you found?"

Sam laid his documents on the low table in front of them.

"Two days ago, Rivière identified Dorian Calderon for us. We saw there was nothing in his bank accounts, and he didn't use his phone, as though he was on standby. The kind of silence that precedes a crime. Victor, you asked us to investigate his movements, so I did. And our border police have come up trumps."

He sifted through the sheets of paper looking for the information.

"They found his name on a Paris–Ajaccio flight two months ago. I managed to get hold of the passenger list, and guess who was with him, in the row behind? Michaël Mention. In the window seat, to get a good look at the Mediterranean."

"Who?" asked Ronan.

"You really do have the memory of a goldfish, don't you? Michaël Mention, his only known accomplice. The guy he spent two months in jail with after a series of robberies. Rhinoceros: does that mean anything to you?"

"O.K., so they see a lot of each other, but that doesn't get us any closer to solving the break-in," Johanna said.

"And they were travelling to Corsica," said Ronan, whose family name, Scaglia, showed that, like Franck and Nunzio Mosconi, he had roots there. "Not everyone who comes and goes from the island is *mafiosi* or a terrorist. We need something more solid."

"Comes and goes – that's exactly what I told myself," Sam responded. "So I checked when they came back."

He turned over some more sheets until he found another passenger list. He had highlighted several names in yellow.

"So a week later we have an Ajaccio–Paris flight. Dorian and Rhinoceros again, this time on opposite sides of the aisle. And here's our miracle."

"I really feel like punching you when you drag it out," Ronan groaned. "This had better be good."

"See for yourself," said a confident Sam.

Handing Ronan the list, he read from his own notes.

"Seat 36, Franck Mosconi. Seat 59, Nunzio Mosconi. And Seat 71, what can you see?"

Ronan ran his finger down the list.

"Alexandra Mosconi?"

Sam, fast becoming an expert in the art of creating suspense, took the very last piece of paper from his dossier. A blow-up of Alexandra Mosconi's passport photo on one side, and the couple leaving the storage unit on the other. They all leaned in to get a good look.

"Dyed hair?" suggested Coste.

"A wig," Johanna corrected him.

"Wouldn't you say they were a team?"

"Good work, but let's not rest on our laurels," Coste told him. "We're off to see Rivière. He seemed to know a lot about that family."

As they were getting up to leave the office, Johanna's mobile buzzed in her trousers pocket. Checking who the caller was, she pursed her lips guiltily and sent the call to voicemail.

"A problem?" asked Victor.

"No, it's just my son. That's the third time . . ."

Sam, the brand-new godfather, looked at her inquisitively. She reassured them both.

"It's nothing, I promise you. We've rented a cottage in Normandy for the weekend, leaving tonight. It's nearly six o'clock, but it looks as if this case isn't finished with, so Malo must be afraid I'm going to let them down."

Just then, Sam's mobile also rang. The icon of the tracking device he had made for his godson after the David Sebag affair was jumping up and down on the screen. Johanna gave an apologetic shrug.

"If I don't pick up, he tries you. Makes sense."

Sam dialled the De Ritter family's landline. A child answered.

"Hey, Malo! The tracker is only if you think you're in danger."

"Yeah I know, but I'm in danger of not going away for the weekend. And there's a swimming pool and a pirate ship."

"Listen, we're on a tough case with real villains. You ought to be proud of your mother."

"I am proud of her," said Malo. "But isn't there anyone else who can do the work? Just for two days? Can't you ask Victor?"

"Ah no, that's just it, matey. There's no-one half as good as Johanna here. Without her, we're all lost. Including Victor Coste."

"O.K, I get it," Malo conceded.

"So you pack your things and leave with your dad and your sister. We'll try to wrap this up as quickly as possible, alright?"

"I guess so."

"And above all, don't forget your tracker. If you get attacked by Captain Hook, I'll be right there with Tinker Bell."

Sam hung up and Johanna kissed him on the cheek.

"No-one half as good as me?" she said with a smile.

"Don't get carried away."

"The Mosconi family? Shit, you do choose your suspects," Rivière whistled. "I'm not surprised no-one will talk. Franck would prefer to die with his lips sealed, and your little family must be terrified."

Coste's team were squatting in Rivière's office, seeking expert advice. One on a chair, the other on the edge of a table. Coste was standing facing the commandant.

"I told you we had them down as suspects for a jewellery theft, didn't I?"

"Yes. You also said you hadn't managed to pin it on them," said Coste.

"We spent several days and nights staking out Le Bourget airport, but there was nothing doing."

"Why there in particular?" asked Sam.

"Because it's only used by the rich, and the border checks are run by private companies, not the police. The same companies who sell airline tickets to the same rich people. It's all very cosy. They barely glance at your passport, and as for the luggage . . . It was from there, according to our informer, that the Mosconis were going to smuggle out their loot."

"But his info was useless, if I remember correctly."

"Judging by what became of him, I'd say it was accurate. The Ajaccio police found little bits of his body after his house had been sent on fire. With his five-year-old son on the first floor."

Johanna shuddered at the idea of her home going up in flames with one of her kids inside. Coste meanwhile was putting two and two together and formulating his conclusions on the fly.

"Nunzio Mosconi was nabbed for wearing a watch that came from a hold-up at a jeweller's. He was remanded and ended up in Marveil. Then someone pays a visit to the evidence vault at the High Court and he's released. Next we find Franck Mosconi linked to the Alves girl, whose father is in charge of those evidence bags."

"So did Tomas Alves take part willingly or did they force him to?" said Rivière. "Either way, he's not going to say a word. The Mosconis settle things either with lead or petrol – and that dissuades people from spilling the beans."

"Shall we suspend the questioning?" Ronan said.

"For the moment," Coste agreed. "We concentrate on someone we haven't so far investigated: Alexandra Mosconi. Dig up everything you can. We'll report back in an hour."

59

Ventura was staring at the clock oscillating from right to left on his screen saver. He contained himself for a few more seconds until it showed seven o'clock, then gave in to his impatience.

He walked down the corridor towards Groupe Crime 1's office, where Coste was facing Alexandra Mosconi's photo on an almost entirely filled whiteboard, adding the fresh information Sam, Ronan and Johanna had dug up on her.

"Might I know why each of our four suspects isn't being grilled right now?" barked Ventura.

"Three suspects. Isabel Alves is helping with our enquiries but she isn't being held officially," replied Coste. "As far as the others go, we think we can find more information ourselves than by keeping on asking them the same questions."

"This is no time to be treading softly! I told you to get me results, for fuck's sake! That means breaking them down by attacking the others. We're dealing with a close-knit family: that's the easiest thing to smash."

"We also run the risk of putting them in danger. You should get Rivière to fill you in on the people we're after. It seems they have short tempers. But thanks to Ronan we're following up on a telephone number Tomas Alves contacted once. He's never called it before or since, and as it was immediately taken out of service we think there could be a connection to the thieves."

"I've traced it," said Ronan. "It was used in the days leading up to the break-in, and points to the twentieth arrondissement, in the Belleville area."

"Belleville," an irritated Ventura repeated. "High-rise buildings everywhere. Even if it is their number, it'll take you days to get a precise fix on their location."

He snorted with indignation, resolving to take charge himself. Coste seemed to him to be playing things too much by the book – he wasn't aggressive enough. Ventura considered shaking the team up a bit more, then changed his mind.

"Where's the mother?"

"Next door."

He gave them one last withering look, like a teacher disheartened by a class of slow pupils, and left the room. He headed straight for the Groupe Crime 2 office, where he found Jevric in the midst of a briefing.

"Lara, with me. I need you to speed things up."

Following Ventura's unpleasant rant, the bewildered Coste and his team had gathered in their office doorway – just in time to see the commandant return, followed closely by Jevric, obviously delighted to finally be called on. Ventura flung the door open on Isabel Alves so violently she jumped.

"Capitaine Jevric, I'd like you to place madame under arrest. But first I'll take her on a tour of the establishment."

Grasping her arm, he forced Isabel to stand, then pulled her towards the holding cells so violently her feet hardly touched the ground. Johanna turned to Coste and asked anxiously:

"What's he going to do?"

"He's going to use her to soften up the girl. This could get messy. Sam and Ronan, you stay here and investigate that telephone number. Johanna, follow me."

When Ventura reached the cells, he glanced at the video screens and asked the duty officer:

"Do your cameras record?"

"No, they're only for surveillance, commandant."

"Fine, then look away."

Tightening his grip on Isabel's arm, he literally dragged her past the cell where Aurélie was being held. When she saw how her mother was being manhandled, the young girl leaped to her feet.

"What are you doing?" she cried. "Let go of her! She hasn't done anything!"

Ventura came to a halt in front of the plexiglass rectangle giving a view of the cell's interior.

"You can keep your mouth shut. Take a good last look at your mother, because in a few hours from now I'll be sending you all to different prisons."

He tugged again at Isabel's arm, almost pulling her over, then had the adjoining cell opened and shoved her in.

"Don't move," he spat at her.

Coste and Johanna kept their eyes peeled, ready to step in. While Isabel and Aurélie tried to comfort one another through the thick walls separating them, Ventura rushed to the end of the corridor, opened the last door and hauled Tomas out. He pushed him roughly towards his daughter's cell. Then he took his prisoner by the scruff of the neck and pressed his face against the plexiglass. Terrified, Aurélie raised her hand, trying to stroke his face. She had cried so much already that day, and her puffy red eyes were making her look ill. "Papa," she whispered in despair. Ventura launched into another tirade.

"Take a good look at your father too. Make the most of it. Have you any idea what they do to chubby little guys like him in jail? They make them squeal. Do you know what that means?"

Pulling Tomas back a few centimetres by his shirt collar, he dashed his face against the plexiglass.

"And you, Papa, take a good look at your daughter! She's going to get you sent to prison, you and your wife. Accessory to a serious crime like this means twenty years. All because this little whore has fallen for a piece of shit. How does it make you feel, knowing your daughter is fucking a criminal?"

Ventura yanked his victim back, and Tomas sank to the floor, eyes brimming with tears. Rhinoceros hadn't been any more brutal than this policeman. He caught sight of Isabel and was overcome by a sense of shame. Neither of them could do a thing faced with Ventura's violent outburst. Ventura left him lying on the floor, ignoring him as if he was a piece of trash. He took a step forward and stood facing Aurélie, who was distraught with anger and sorrow.

"Did you know your Franck Mosconi was married?" he bluffed. "He has two kids, one of them a girl almost your age. Do you think he's going to want to protect you? Do you think that when you're out of here he'll call you to go to the movies or for a romantic picnic? Are you a complete fucking numbskull, or what?"

He pointed to her father, who was still slumped on the floor, humiliated in front of his family.

"Look at him, for fuck's sake! How long is he going to be in jail for? And if I get your mother sent down as well, do you know you'll be put into care? So talk to me. Did you and Franck Mosconi get in touch to arrange to meet? Where? When? How?"

Ventura turned round, hauled Tomas up, and crushed his face against the plexiglass once more. He repeated the three questions, banging his head against the glass each time. Where? When? How? The cell door shook with every blow.

Aurélie flung herself at the door and beat at it with both hands.

"Let go of him! I'll do it!"

Silence in the eye of the storm. Ventura had succeeded. Johanna turned to Coste, furious that the commandant's technique had worked. Crushed, Tomas allowed his daughter to save them.

"Leave him . . . I'll talk," she mumbled, giving in.

Ventura let go, and her father fell to his knees. The commandant addressed Jevric.

"Pick this thing up and throw him back in his cell. Take the girl to Coste's office for an interview, and if she hasn't come clean within five minutes, charge the mother."

With that, Ventura stepped away from the chaos he had created as if nothing had happened. Tomas in a heap, Aurélie huddled in a corner of her cell, unable to keep back the tears, Isabel paralysed by a scene she never imagined she'd witness in a police station.

Coste could see a smirk of satisfaction on his commandant's face as he left the cells.

"You're a real piece of shit, Ventura."

"Maybe so, but you've got a new lead."

"Everyone knows you can get confessions if you use torture."

"Don't play the innocent! Admit it — I've helped you save time. Use the Alves girl while she's still hot. Either you take advantage of the situation or all this was for nothing. You choose."

60

"I went to their hideout once . . ."

Back in their office, Johanna had brought Aurélie a glass of water, but even though Coste's tone was nothing like Ventura's, she was still shaking. Ronan put a double row of photographs in front of her, showing the entire Mosconi clan.

"Do you recognise them?"

Aurélie studied them one by one, then pointed to each of them in turn.

"The woman is Alex. This one is Franck; they're from the same family. That one is nicknamed Rhinoceros, and he's a friend of the other one, Dorian. Dorian and Alex are a couple."

"Which of them is the leader?"

Ronan and Sam had wagered it was Franck. Coste and Johanna's choice was Dorian. When the young girl pointed to the last photograph, they all had to swallow their sexist assumptions.

"She's the leader. Alex."

Coste continued with the interview.

"And it was you who told Franck about your father's job?"

"Never!" Aurélie protested. "They came to our house one evening. They already knew everything. They forced him to co-operate."

"Can you explain why you're still seeing Franck days later?"

Aurélie fell silent for a moment, then asked her most urgent questions.

"Is it true he's married? Are you going to release my parents?"

"In that order?" asked Johanna with dismay.

Meeting Room: 8.30 p.m.
Operational briefing
Groupes Crime 1 & 2, and the Group de répression du banditisme

With the episode down in the cells, Ventura had taken over the inquiry and he didn't seem to want to relinquish it. He organised the teams and set up the operation.

"It's number fourteen rue Levert in the twentieth arrondissement. A four-storey building. Apparently the kid was given the honours on the first floor, and says it was all empty offices. So we'll take the upper ones. Groupe Crime 2, floor two, O.C.U. third floor, and Groupe Crime 1 the top floor. Synchronised actions. Any questions?"

Sitting next to Rivière, Coste knew Ventura wouldn't listen to what he had to say and so passed his colleague his notebook, on which he had written a single word: Hideout. Rivière read it and became his spokesman.

"Wouldn't it be better to keep the building under surveillance for a while? Even if it's just for a night. That way we'll know who's in there, and see if the lights go on and off, and on which floor," he suggestion.

"No." Ventura rejected the idea. "Mosconi has seen his lawyer, and he will have informed all the other accomplices. Either they're already long gone or they're on the point of making themselves scarce. We can't waste time; we'll catch whoever we can."

Rivière pushed the notebook back to its owner. On it he'd scrawled an obscene caricature that made Coste smile.

The three groups split up to get equipement. Firearms, battering rams, tear-gas canisters, bulletproof vests and protective shields in case things got hot. Before leaving, Rivière took Ventura aside to speak to him, equal to equal.

"I get the impression you have it in for Coste."

"It's purely professional. If he messes up this raid, I'll take him off the case and hand it to Jevric."

"Coste is a good officer. I'm not sure Lara would do any better with it. Has no-one warned you about her?"

"I don't like good officers. I like officers who are loyal to their superiors."

Hearing this, and knowing that some personalities will never be compatible, Rivière realised there was no point insisting.

61

They had been waiting impatiently for the call from Monsieur Mosconi's trusted ally – a man they called "The Artist" back in Corsica – since late afternoon, Dorian in his tailor-made suit, and Alex a lot less presentable in a pair of jeans and a baggy sweatshirt. Dorian ran his hand over Alex's belly; he was the only one who knew why the baggy sweatshirt was becoming increasingly necessary.

"Do you want me to go on my own?" he asked.

"No, he doesn't know you. I'm the only one he'll give the passports to. My father's orders are clear."

"He really doesn't care for me, does he?"

"I do, and that's enough."

Touched, he bent down to give her a kiss. Just at that moment, the mobile began to vibrate on the table. Alex pushed Dorian aside.

"Get out of the way. It's him."

She muttered a string of yeses and alrights as she took in the information and then hung up.

"In twenty minutes at the newspaper stand by Jaurès Metro station."

"Why doesn't he come here?"

"He doesn't even want to meet us. He's an old friend of the

family, so he knows my face. As soon as he spots me, he'll put the envelope with the passports between some magazines."

"He's taking a lot of precautions."

Following her father's instructions, Alex had placed two heavy magnetic disks on the computer to completely erase its contents. It was obvious Monsieur Mosconi was taking no chances when it came to securing their smooth return home.

"With all the cops buzzing around, my father must have told him we weren't a hundred per cent secure. It's good of him to offer to do this."

Dorian took his raincoat and Alex chose a jacket from among the assorted outfits and uniforms hanging on the rail. She opened one of the black canvas bags and hesitated over two handguns.

"You want to go armed?" asked Dorian in astonishment.

"We've come too far to take the slightest risk."

Her hand caressed a black metal pistol, then a silver revolver, before returning to the pistol. She took it out and tucked it into her waistband behind her back. She turned to her brother, who was still fast asleep on the day bed with the T.V. on, and called to Rhinoceros.

"Just be patient a little longer, O.K.? It'll soon be over."

Rhinoceros muttered something and watched them leave.

As if on cue, two minutes later Nano woke up.

"Where are we?" he asked, completely disoriented.

"In the loft. We're safe here," said Scarface.

"What about Alex?"

"She'll be back in less than an hour."

Nano leaped up as though he'd been given an electric shock.

"No! She never leaves me on my own. She promised she'd never leave me alone again."

He started pacing hysterically up and down the room,

looked in the toilet and bathroom, and when he couldn't find his sister, headed for the front door. Rhinoceros shouted at him:

"Fuck's sake, where do you think you're going?"

Nano took a step outside. Rhinoceros grabbed him round the waist to pull him back in and threw him down on the sofa.

"You stay where you are!" he ordered.

Nano got up and, as though he had no recollection of his first attempt, headed for the door a second time. He stumbled and almost fell, but clung on to the table and straightened up. He vomited a stream of brown liquid that pooled on the floor.

"Shit! This had to happen now, on my watch! I don't believe it!" raged his babysitter.

Nano wiped his lips on his sleeve.

"I'm not well. Not well at all. I need my meds. I can't breathe. I'm suffocating."

He fell to the floor. His eyes rolled back in his head and an acute panic attack convulsed his body. Rhinoceros slid one arm under his knees and the other under his shoulders, picked him up and carried him to the shower. He switched it on full, and a few seconds later Nano's trembling ceased.

"Please, I need my meds. It feels like somebody's crushing my chest."

Rhinoceros ran over to the sofa. He found the tube of tablets by the armrest. He shook it – empty. Nano's moans from the bathroom were growing louder and louder. There was no way he could leave him like that for an hour. Then he remembered how Dorian had cut his arm on a broken pane of glass during a robbery, and the medical care he had needed. He picked up the black bag Alex had been looking in and laid it on the table. He took out the cable ties, the grenade they'd used to threaten the secretary, and the small five-shot revolver, until finally he found the prescription pad he was looking for. In certain situations, going to hospital or to a doctor wasn't exactly wise, especially if the wound looked as if it had been made by a bullet or knife. So the prescription pad they'd stolen from a quack had proved very useful. Reading the name of the medication – Clomipramine – on the side of the empty tube, he wrote it on the pad and added a scrawled signature.

As he entered the bathroom, Rhinoceros opened his mouth to apologise for what he was about to do, but found Nano passed out on the floor, gasping for breath. He wrapped a cable tie round his right wrist and attached it to the joint between the tap and the inlet pipe. There was a pharmacy on the corner of the street. He could be there and back in two minutes at most.

Everything would be alright.

PART FIVE

OUT OF CONTROL

"A member of my team is dead. It was my responsibility.
It amounts to the same thing."

CAPITAINE VICTOR COSTE

62

At nine that evening, a line of unmarked police cars pulled up a hundred metres from the entrance to 14 rue Levert. A man in blue overalls carrying a leather satchel emerged from Rivière's vehicle. He walked up the street, stopped at the number he had been given, looked in both directions, then kneeled down and with two jabs of his electric drill perforated the door's lock. A few moments later the locksmith stood up and walked off. As he passed the parked cars, he nodded and left the rest to them.

The three teams climbed silently out of their cars, quietly closing the doors. They entered the building, agreed on a thirty-second countdown, and split up. Jevric's group stayed in front of the double swing doors on the second floor. Twenty-five seconds. Rivière and his men climbed to the third floor and took up position. Fifteen seconds. Coste and his team reached the fourth floor. Ronan raised the battering ram. Five seconds . . .

Nano woke with a start. The panic attack had seriously affected his befuddled brain and erased all memory of the previous ten minutes. He found himself in a bathroom, dressed but soaked to the skin, one wrist tied to the plumbing. He panicked again, thrashing around and cutting himself on the plastic restraint. He chewed at it like a rabid dog, so ferociously he loosened a tooth. He spat it out, then looked around for any sharp object he could use. His gaze fell on a toilet bag on a glass shelf. He kicked out and smashed the shelf. The toilet bag fell a few centimetres from him, and he managed to pull out a small pair of scissors. He had to attack the plastic repeatedly until he cut it through. Staggering to his feet, he slipped on the floor tiles, almost splitting open his skull, but finally managed to emerge from the bathroom, just as the front door was splintering from the impact of the battering ram. Ronan stepped to one side to let the rest of the team in, guns levelled.

In front of Nano, on the big central table, was Franck's black canvas bag. Scattered around it were more cable ties, a grenade, a prescription pad, an empty tube of anti-depressants. And a silver revolver.

The sound of the front door being smashed to smithereens, together with the sudden appearance of four strangers in a place he had no memory of, left Nano in fear for his life. In a reflex action, he reached for the revolver, scooped it up and waved it in front of him. He was so close that all he had to do was pull the trigger and he would hit the first police officer facing him. And since that officer was Victor Coste, Johanna's heart exploded with adrenalin. She fired two shots. Exactly as she was taught to do on the firing range. Head. Heart. Nano's body twitched. He collapsed onto the table, then crashed to the floor.

Out on the street, Rhinoceros had almost broken into a run clutching the pharmacy bag. As he reached the building, he took out his keys and was about to insert one in the lock when he realised there wasn't one. Metal shavings on the ground confirmed the door had been forced. He took to his heels, tossing the tubes of Clomipramine into the first dustbin he passed.

*

On the fourth floor, their ears were still ringing from Johanna's two shots. Synapses boosted by the tension, his mind completely clear, Coste weighed up the consequences. He ejected his gun magazine and took out two bullets.

"Jevric and Rivière will be here in three seconds. I need you all to trust me and not question my orders."

Sam and Ronan barely reacted. Despite all their experience, this was the first time they'd seen anybody shot in front of them. Johanna still had her arm extended. She was paralysed, her eyes staring blindly ahead.

"Johanna, listen to me."

No reply. Coste shook her and she slowly returned to the loft.

"Quick, give me your gun."

Obeying his order, she handed it to him mechanically. Coste slid open the magazine and pressed his own two bullets into it. Then he tilted the gun and energetically rubbed the mouth of the barrel against his wrist before handing it back to Johanna.

"We came in, he took aim at me, and I fired. Do you hear me, Johanna? All of you – I was the one who shot him, got it? That's all there is to say."

Before any of them could object, Groupe Crime 2 and Rivière's team stormed in, guns trained, ready to respond. Seeing Nano Mosconi lying in two litres of blood, they holstered their weapons. Lara Jevric took out her radio.

"Crime 2 to headquarters. We need an ambulance."

Rivière walked calmly over to Coste.

"Victor? You alright? Do you recognise him?"

"Yes, it's the little brother. Nunzio Mosconi."

"He was in prison at the time of the break-in, wasn't he?"

"I know. We're wide of the mark again."

63

Forty minutes later, Dorian and Alex, fresh passports and money in their pockets, were walking back towards the loft. Just one more bend in the street and they would be within sight of the building. Just as they were going by, a wide doorway opened, and Rhino jumped out at them. He'd had plenty of time to prepare his story. A story that had to be convincing if he didn't want to become Alex's next target when she learned he'd left her brother trussed up like a gift for the police. He pulled the two of them inside the dark inner courtyard, away from prying eyes.

"What's going on?" shouted Alexandra. "What are you doing out here? Where's Nano?"

"The cops found us," Rhino whispered.

"And you abandoned my brother?" Alex accused him, chin quivering with rage.

"Calm down, there was nothing else I could do. They smashed open the ground floor entrance and we could hear it up in the loft. I wanted to gather all our things to leave no traces behind, but that's when Nano lost it."

"So you're saying you can't control a kid off his face on medication?"

"He started shouting. He was going to give us away. He was saying you had promised never to abandon him, that he wasn't going to leave without you. He yelled your name, saying you'd come for him. There was nothing I could do. I left the loft, hid on the third floor, and when I saw the cops going up, I got out of there. I'm sorry, but what else was I to do? Let myself be caught with him?"

Rhinoceros wasn't very smart, but when it came to saving his own skin, he could find the right words. Words that cut deep wounds of guilt like a jagged piece of glass. Justifying his actions by a promise Alex hadn't kept had probably just saved him from a bullet in the head courtesy of the Mosconi clan.

Alex's legs gave way under her. Dorian caught her just in time.

"All that for what?" she panted. "It's not possible. It's not fair."

As she straightened up, an engine roared in the street outside, together with a siren whose sound she recognised. She turned to Rhinoceros in a rage.

"That's not the police! That's an ambulance! Why do they need an ambulance?"

Dorian tried in vain to hold her back, but no-one could stop Alex once she had decided to do something. Still less when it concerned her little brother. She opened the street door a crack and pointed to the café on the opposite corner. They would have a good view of their hideout from there.

"It's risky," Rhinoceros objected.

In a café some fifty metres from their building, Alex and the two men sat at the window table. There were more customers at other tables, so they would not look too out of place if the police came sniffing too close.

"What can I get you?"

None of them paid the waiter any attention, so he repeated his question.

"Three coffees," said Dorian.

"Is it the cops you're watching?" the waiter said chattily. "It's rare to see them going in like that. I wonder who they're after. Terrorists perhaps?"

An ambulance, unmarked cars, patrol cars and a swarm of plain clothes and uniformed police were blocking both sides of the street. The crime scene technicians went in carrying their forensic equipment.

A big saloon car was authorised to make its way through this hive of activity. It parked and Commissaire Divisionnaire Abassian from the Police Inspectorate got out. Long dark overcoat, raven black hair, he climbed the four floors and joined the group of officers in the loft. Coste stood apart from the others, facing a man in a white coat who was taking a swab from the skin on his wrist. Abassian approached as the technician was placing the sample in a hermetically sealed capsule.

"Good evening, capitaine."

"I wouldn't call it that, but good evening anyway, commissaire."

"Have you followed the guidelines?" Abassian asked, wasting no time.

"Yes, my gun is already bagged up."

"Perfect."

"And Forensics have just taken a swab."

"Good. All that remains is to prove it was self-defence."

He turned to look at the lifeless body the police photographer was aiming his camera at.

"In any case, with an attacker still holding his weapon, that shouldn't take long."

"What next?"

"It's ten o'clock. I'm taking you into custody until you've

been interviewed and had a blood test. Your team should remain at our disposal."

Coste turned towards them, then followed Abassian. Out in the street he ducked into the saloon car. As it was disappearing down the street, two paramedics carried their burden out of the building. On the stretcher, a dull black body bag zipped up to the top left no doubt as to the state of the victim.

When Alex saw it she leaped to her feet, knocking over two of their coffees and attracting the attention of several customers. Rhinoceros was the one who took it upon himself to act, grasping her arm and forcing her to sit down again.

"What are you hoping to achieve, Alex? Shoot the lot of them? There are too many cops and you don't have enough bullets. Are you going to finish them off with those little fists of yours?"

As the stretcher was being loaded into the ambulance, Alex felt a wave of sickness come over her. Dorian accompanied her to the toilets, leaving Rhinoceros alone at a table swamped with coffee.

Alex raised her head from the bowl and allowed her face to be wiped like a child. She burst into tears right there, in the filthy toilet, surrounded by obscene graffiti and a disgusting smell of urine.

"Get me out of here, I'm begging you."

64

Back in their office, Ronan, Sam and Johanna felt orphaned. They had all completed stress management courses; they knew that using a weapon was an occupational hazard – even if every police officer prays it will never happen – and yet none of them could properly return to earth.

Being authorised to kill in self-defence takes nothing away from the fact of ending a life, or of being a witness to it. They were shocked, disoriented; none of them had spoken. They could still hear the gunshots, the sound of the body toppling, the blood gushing out. Johanna stood up, shut the office door and finally allowed herself to show her emotions.

"I'm the one who fired . . . I don't understand. I'm the one who fired! I should never have let him do what he did. It was self-defence for me as well, wasn't it? Why did he take my place?"

"Don't you have any idea?" Sam asked gently.

She stared at him uncomprehending, so he went on.

"Nunzio Mosconi is in prison. They risk everything to get him out by breaking into the law courts, showing they're not afraid of anything. For some reason we haven't yet fathomed, they despatch Doucey, proving they're capable of killing as well. Remember Rivière's warning: 'The Mosconis settle things either with lead or petrol'. And think what happened to the informer in Ajaccio. His five-year-old son burnt to a crisp in their home? That was what you were risking."

Shaking her head, Johanna turned to Ronan.

"Tell me that wasn't the reason."

Feeling awkward, Ronan lowered his eyes, but he didn't deny it.

"It was classic Coste."

At that moment, Commandant Ventura burst without knocking into an office he regarded as his own.

"Everyone alright?" he asked.

Since none of them bothered to reply, he went on:

"None of our colleagues was wounded, that's the main thing."

"But if we'd staked the place out for a while, I still think we'd have caught more of the gang. Maybe even avoided a cadaver."

"Don't go soft on me, Lieutenant Scaglia, otherwise you'd better change profession. But right now, I want you to sort out the case files and hand them over to Jevric's group."

"I get the sense we're being thrown out of our own birthday party," muttered Ronan.

"You can't pursue this inquiry until you've been interviewed by the Inspectorate. Coste will be with them for most of the night; your appointment is for eight-thirty tomorrow morning. The three of you will be questioned together. And as for your last remark, this operation has been botched because your boss dragged his feet. To be an effective policeman you have to play by the rules of the bastards you're chasing."

Seeing Ronan clench his fists, Sam sat upright on the sofa.

"You shouldn't say things like that. Now's not the time. We're all feeling a bit raw, if you must know."

Ventura chose to ignore the warning.

"If a cop doesn't have the balls to get his hands dirty in this job, no-one is going to stop me saying so, and if Coste—"

Ronan's left hook caught him full on the mouth. Ventura staggered back and had to steady himself against the wall.

"I did warn you, Commandant," said Sam. "We're all a bit raw."

Ronan was still confronting Ventura, chest and head thrust forward, fists clenched to repeat the punishment if need be. Ventura, eyes blazing and his face contorted with rage, cupped his cheek in a daze, like a child unjustly slapped.

"Scaglia, you've just sunk your career! I'll make you pay until the day you retire."

Now it was Johanna's turn to confront him, in an office where Ventura was beginning to feel less and less secure.

"Like hell you will. You're going to wipe your mouth and forget it, the same way I'm going to forget your little torture session down in the holding cells on a family of victims with an underage daughter. And now, please, get out of here."

65

Hotel de Banville —Paris, seventeenth arrondissement
II p.m.

The receptionist recognised Alex at once, and the memories of the previous disturbed night made him stiffen. Dorian greeted him and tried to mollify him.

"I know we may have seemed somewhat eccentric a few days ago," he said, slipping a folded five-hundred euro note across the counter.

The receptionist glanced at the banknote, then at Dorian, before making the money disappear into his pocket and recovering all his hospitable charm.

"If there were no place for eccentricity in four-star hotels . . . How many rooms do you need?"

"Two. Adjoining. On the first floor. With an interconnecting door."

They emerged from the lift and came to a halt in front of Rooms 7 and 8. Rhinoceros opened the door to the first, but when Dorian made to follow Alex into the second, she pushed him back firmly.

"I'm going to call my father. I prefer to be on my own, if you don't mind."

She had not opened her mouth once during their taxi ride.

Wrapped up in her thoughts, she was extraordinarily calm, as if her feelings of distress and anguish had been replaced by another, more insistent emotion. Now Dorian didn't dare argue with her, so he followed Rhinoceros.

Alone in her room, Alex closed the door behind her and sat on the edge of the bed. Even though she wasn't in the suite Nano had occupied, she recognised the exact same décor, and her stomach churned. Taking the envelope with the passports out of her jacket pocket, she looked for Nano's and opened it at the page showing his photograph. His face looked happy and innocent, the way it did when they were children and the beach was their playground. It had taken no more than seventy-two hours for her to lose control of the situation. All that remained now was to salvage what she could. She consulted the search engine on her mobile and dialled the number that flashed up.

"Le Bourget airport, Prime Flight here, good evening," a female voice crooned.

"Madame Carat speaking. I'm calling to make a change to our reservations."

After a few seconds checking her computer, the airline employee spoke again.

"Carat . . . Three seats on the flight for tomorrow, Saturday, at one p.m."

"Now we will only need two. Instead I need an open ticket for a later flight. The same destination."

With that settled, she tapped on the interconnecting door.

In the neighbouring room, Rhinoceros was sharing his considered view of recent events with Dorian.

"This is getting heavy. Nano dead, Doucey dead, and Franck arrested . . . Are you sure your bitch isn't a one-woman shit-storm?"

Dorian turned towards him, eyes flashing.

"It's funny how you never seem to learn when to keep your trap shut."

There were two taps at the door. Dorian went over to it.

"How did it go?" he asked anxiously.

"Badly, of course," replied Alex. "I've had new instructions."

"We're staying?"

"No, I'm staying. You two are leaving tomorrow as planned. I'm keeping an eye on Tiretto while he sorts out the repatriation of Nano's body."

"I don't see what difference it makes whether you're here or in Corsica," Dorian objected.

"Really? You can't see it?" she replied cuttingly. "Can you see me returning home without my brother? Think of the shame if I left him behind. Can you see me confronting the clan and telling them that I've abandoned him?"

"Then I'll stay too."

"You're starting to piss me off, Dorian. If the cops managed to trace us back to the loft, that means they've identified us. So they're looking for three people. It's better for us to split up. And I prefer to settle family matters myself."

This last remark hit Dorian hard. He was hoping to create a family with Alex, and to find himself excluded hurt him more than he expected. For his part, Rhinoceros still considered her a shitstorm, and was delighted to be putting distance between them. But Alex pulled him back from these private thoughts.

"I'm going to need you tomorrow morning. There's one last thing we have to deal with."

She took her mobile out of the back pocket of her jeans, removed the cover and revealed a slender left-luggage key. It was their only means of putting pressure on Tiretto, so she'd kept it safe. Rhino recognised it at once.

"The evidence bags? You want me to go and leave the key at the lawyer's office?"

"No, let's stay well away. They've searched our hideout, and I know Franck will never talk. The only ones who know about them are my father and Tiretto."

"Then he can go fuck himself with his bags."

"We don't really have a choice. They're of interest to others, and this is no time to make new enemies. I still need the lawyer."

66

Lara Jevric had spent most of the night reading the thousands of pages of the Mosconi case files, when at nine o'clock sharp Tiretto appeared in her doorway.

"Commandant Ventura has just informed me you're in charge of the case now."

"Which I'm not going to discuss with you," she snapped. "Do you want to see Franck Mosconi?"

"No, I'm here for Nunzio."

Jevric raised an eyebrow, uneasy at having to tell him the bad news.

"That could be complicated. He died last night."

"I know. But even the dead have the right to a lawyer. His family are considering taking civil action against the police, and in the meantime they wish me to see to his repatriation. Well, as soon as you've finished the autopsy. Which is why I'm here."

"The forensic pathologist is planning to carry it out today. I'll be in touch. And now if you don't mind, clear out of here."

Tiretto didn't budge.

"Say hello to Capitaine Coste from me. I imagine that even for a professional it must be unsettling to have to use one's weapon."

"That's not exactly a subtle approach, but you won't get anything from me."

"The case changes hands, and I've learned that Coste has just finished being interviewed by the Inspectorate. The conclusion is obvious. I'll be in my office all morning, should you wish to call."

Coste stepped out of the shower, his body steaming, a towel wrapped round his shoulders. He felt cleansed after a sleepless night spent endlessly repeating the same story to Commissaire Abassian.

He put on a clean T-shirt and a pair of jeans, then went into the kitchen and put a capsule in the coffee maker. After four days without sleep his brain was playing tricks on him: he saw a black cat sitting on the edge of the sink. He had to blink several times before he realised it was nothing more than a shadow. He felt a desperate need for a few hours' rest, but he had just received a text from Ronan telling him that their interviews with the Inspectorate had finished and they were all heading his way. Ronan must have sent the message en route, because at that moment the intercom buzzed downstairs.

The four of them were now in his living room. Johanna was the first to demand an explanation.

"I blame myself for going along with it."

"You didn't go along with anything. I didn't really give you a choice."

"Sam said it's because you're afraid of the consequences."

"You have a family, Johanna. I'm sure nothing's going to happen, but I don't want to run any risk."

Sam stepped forward, somewhat embarrassed.

"It's not much good saying it now, but I think if I'd had your presence of mind, I'd have done the same."

"We're police officers," added Ronan. "We signed up for

trouble. But neither Karl nor Malo nor Chloe should be dragged into this."

Both touched and annoyed at being mothered like this, Johanna was torn between thanking them and telling them to go to hell.

"You know," Coste went on, "killing someone is the worst thing that can happen to a police officer. I'm not talking about the sense of guilt or the psychological repercussions, but the legal process you have to face. It can take years, and there's an indelible mark on your record that you can never erase. The institution abandons you completely, and lots of officers suffer from depression and quit. Some have even committed suicide."

"None of which applies to you?" said Ronan.

Coste made no reply. Johanna sat on the sofa and went on the attack.

"It doesn't apply to him because he couldn't give a damn. Or am I wrong?"

Intrigued, Sam and Ronan turned to look at her.

"What are you talking about?"

"Victor's resigning."

Silence descended on the room. No-one wanted to believe this bombshell.

"How did you find out?" asked Coste eventually.

"Through Léa. Don't forget, I was the one who consoled her when you dumped her. She spent entire evenings at home with us, as though it somehow kept her close to you. Now we often meet and talk. About everything, your resignation included."

"So when were you thinking of telling us, Victor?" said a deeply offended Sam.

"Once I'd accepted the idea myself. Do you think it was an easy decision?"

355

"I knew the David Sebag affair had affected you, but I thought you'd get over it," said Ronan.

"I've been getting over things for fifteen years – after every case, every victim, every murderer. I have to stop. So I thought that taking responsibility for Nunzio Mosconi's death would make a good final bow. One last thing I could do for the team. Your team now, Ronan."

There was the sound of a key turning in the lock, the front door being closed, and then Léa appeared in the room. Ignoring the others, she addressed Coste directly, without even taking off her coat.

"I've just finished Nunzio Mosconi's autopsy. Lieutenant Jevric tells me it was you who shot him. Is that why I haven't been able to get hold of you? You could have called me, couldn't you?"

Sam and Ronan stared at the floor, and Johanna was careful to avoid catching her eye. Léa realised she had burst in on a meeting unbidden and uninvited, but rather than inhibiting her this only increased her curiosity and anger.

"I can tell at once when you lot are on edge. You all look like guilty brats. What's happened?"

An awkward silence descended on the group.

"It was me," Johanna said faintly.

The pathologist turned towards her. The expression on her face demanded an explanation.

"I'm the one who shot him, Léa."

67

Tiretto's secretary had never seen him so nervous. She had carried out his instructions to cancel the last two appointments that morning, and had even been told to take her lunch break earlier and not to hurry back. Perhaps this was due to the presence of the man who had been in his office for more than half an hour now. A man who instantly reminded her of a strongman you might see in circuses snapping steel chairs or bending iron bars. She gathered her things and let her boss play ringmaster.

"What time is she supposed to call?"

"At ten. She's usually punctual."

"She has one minute to live up to her reputation."

"You shouldn't have bothered coming. I would have sent you the evidence bag as soon as I had it. Doesn't Monsieur Darcy trust me?"

"Monsieur Darcy never trusts anyone," said Boyan Mladic. "And neither do I. My best friend shot me in the back when we were in the Tibesti gold-mining region in Chad. A stupid squabble over a gold bar he wanted to keep for himself. So, when it comes to trust . . ."

Still no phone call, so Tiretto tried to keep the conversation going.

"Since you're here with me, I suppose your friend has been arrested."

"No, I shot him from two hundred and ten metres using a telescopic sight. He never knew who pulled the trigger. I like that idea."

Mladic's matter-of-fact tone made the lawyer realise that sometimes silence is preferable to curiosity. Just then his secure mobile rang and saved him from this awkward exchange. On the other end of the line, an equally troubling individual didn't even give him time to say hello.

"Do your friends still want their evidence?"

"Good morning, Alexandra. And yes, I have to say they're growing impatient."

"Well, now it comes at a price."

Tiretto smiled at Boyan as though he had the situation under control, but a bead of sweat suddenly appeared on his top lip. Seeing him squirm, the Serb leaned over the desk, pressed the speaker button and dropped back into his chair, which creaked under his weight.

"How much are we talking?"

"I don't want money. That doesn't matter anymore. I want the name of the cop who killed my brother."

Boyan raised an appreciative eyebrow as if he considered this only logical. Tiretto breathed a sigh of relief, grateful that he merely had to give her a piece of information.

"Coste. Capitaine Victor Coste, of the Seine-Saint-Denis Police Judiciaire. He's the head of the group that's been after you all week."

"And his home address?"

Tiretto suddenly had a clearer idea of his client's intentions.

"You're going too far, Alex. Revenge never stops, it simply changes sides. You'll have the entire police force on your back, and you'll set them on to me and my friends."

"I understand. If that's your decision, tell your friends the evidence bags will be left at the law courts later this morning. I'm being considerate: that will give them a few hours to throw a trunk into the Seine with you inside it."

"Alex, the police aren't in the Yellow Pages. Their home addresses are in their files, and they're kept at headquarters. Even for—"

She cut him short, angry at having to hear problems rather than solutions.

"So what do you do when you're looking for a witness or a debtor? Start bawling because they're not in the Yellow Pages? I thought you were smarter than that."

Boyan nodded gleefully, as if Alex and he were on the same wavelength. He considered her a worthy adversary.

"I'll give you two minutes," said Alex, and hung up.

Tiretto put his mobile down and hurriedly consulted his contact list.

"Only a minute and fifty seconds to go," said Boyan.

"I get the impression you're enjoying this."

"Very much so. It's always instructive to watch a proper negotiation."

Tiretto's finger came to a halt next to a name. A year earlier by a feat of magic he had secured the acquittal of a government employee accused of fraud. Only the lawyer knew he was guilty; he had even managed not only to save the man's job, but to win him compensation for defamation.

He dialled the number. A voice bordering on depression answered.

"Office for taxes and public finances. Good morning."

"Good morning. Monsieur Dorin's extension, please."

A click and the call was transferred. A different voice, as unenthusiastic as the first.

"Paul Dorin, litigation department."

"Tiretto here. I need a tax reference."

"I've already told you I don't want to do that anymore," the man said, embarrassed.

"I'll pay double. And keep what I know to myself."

A slight pause to show he disapproved, but Dorin knew he had no choice and he didn't hesitate for long.

"Tell me."

"Victor Coste. In Seine-Saint-Denis."

The sound of typing, a few seconds to bring the address up.

"Here it is. Coste, Victor. 10 rue Victor Hugo, 93500 Pantin. And please don't call me again."

There were ten seconds left when Tiretto's mobile rang once more.

"Are you in a trunk?"

"No, I've got what you want. Victor Coste, 10 rue Victor Hugo in Pantin. What about our evidence bags?"

"They're at Gare du Nord. Locker 68."

"And the key?"

"It's on its way."

Out in the street came the sound of breaking glass, then the alarm on the lawyer's car echoed throughout the neighbourhood. Mission accomplished, Rhinoceros disappeared round a corner.

Tiretto and Boyan rushed through the spacious entrance hall of the town house where the lawyer's practice was situated and ran to the Audi. The right front window was smashed and on the leather seat lay a small, slender key. Boyan tapped the lawyer on the shoulder.

"I get the impression they don't trust you any more than you trust them."

"Shit, they could have put it in my mailbox or under the

windscreen wiper! There was no need for them to damage the car . . . "

"Yeah . . . They don't trust you . . . and they don't much like you either."

Tiretto didn't react, simply handing him the key.

"Good. You've got what you came for. You can tell Monsieur Darcy."

Boyan recalled the telephone conversation.

"But that Alexandra of yours mentioned several bags, didn't she? Don't you want them all back?"

"I couldn't give a damn about them. It was just to confuse the police. Besides, one of them is dead, and the other one isn't a client of mine, so . . ."

68

Thirty minutes later, Boyan Mladic was setting foot in Gare du Nord, ignoring delinquents, tramps and train passengers. On red alert since the beginning of the year, the patrolling soldiers with their assault rifles reminded him of his past, and the police of his present.

He descended the escalator to the basement and walked along the row of lockers until he came to Number 68. He inserted the key, turned it, and saw three brown envelopes awaiting him. Satisfied, he took out his mobile.

"Monsieur Darcy, I have our problem in my sights."

"And the clouds are clearing. Good work, my friend."

"But apparently I've also recovered other people's problems."

"That doesn't change anything. Get rid of them."

"Both of them? We're getting mixed up in things that don't concern us. Wouldn't you prefer me to leave the other bags where they are?"

"If ours is the only problem to vanish, that wouldn't be very prudent. Did everything go as planned?"

"More or less. That little Corsican girl is tougher than I thought."

"Did you meet her?"

"Not really. I heard the phone conversation between her and Tiretto. She asked him for the name and address of the cop who shot her brother. I don't know what she intends to do, or if she'll really go ahead, but she has the guts for it."

"You seem to think highly of her."

"She's not bad. I'd have liked to have her on our side."

"Unfortunately, she's too close to Tiretto, and therefore to us. This is no longer about a little G.P.S. that could land you in jail for three years. Tiretto masterminded a raid on a state institution, and if that ever gets out, we're his accomplices. We can't allow the police to arrest her – she knows too much."

"You should have left me in Marveil," said Boyan, without a hint of irony.

"I would have left anybody else there," Darcy admitted. "We've been trying to find that Mosconi woman for days. Now that you know where she's headed, don't let her out of your sight."

Standing under the first six statues outside Gare du Nord, Boyan tore open the envelopes one by one. He snapped the C.D. of phone taps effortlessly in half and threw it in a bin. Then he weighed the hunting knife in his hand, felt its heft, and slipped it into his pocket. Finally, to the astonishment of a homeless man in a sleeping bag, he twice smashed the G.P.S. against one of the columns of the main entrance and tossed it into the same bin.

Without realising it, Boyan had just committed the sin of leaving Gabriel "Scalpel" Rezelny a killer for all eternity and of definitively acquitting Yassine Chelli of David Sebag's murder.

69

Sam and Ronan had been sent back to their office to write their reports. Though they had been taken off the case, they were the only ones able to account for what had taken place in the loft during the four seconds after the battering ram had smashed open the door. Johanna had been allowed to go home to say goodbye to her children for the weekend. Coste had stayed in his apartment to face Léa's reproaches.

"What were you thinking?"

"I thought I could protect you both. Johanna by saying I fired the shots—"

"And me by keeping me out of the picture?"

"I'm not keeping you out of anything. I'm only asking for us to stay apart for a month or two to see how the Mosconis react."

"I've had it up to here with coming second to your group. This is the last time I'll have you playing the big protective cop."

"You've never come second. You know very well I've always thought of you as a member of my team."

He put his hand on Léa's thigh, but her hackles rose like a cat's and she brushed him off.

"Don't touch me. God, you really infuriate me! What you did wasn't noble, it was stupid. You put yourself in danger, and I'm left wondering if you'd have done the same for Sam or Ronan."

"Are you suggesting I have a weakness for Jo?"

"I'm not suggesting anything," Léa grumbled. "I know it. I can see it."

Coste burst out laughing. Although Léa resisted, he put his arms round her until she calmed down.

"You drive me crazy, you really do!" she whispered.

He kissed her gently on the neck.

"I'd like you to take all your things and go home. I'll call you a taxi."

"Stop it. I can do that perfectly well on my own. Besides, the others don't need you. Spend the day with me, Victor."

"I have to go back in to sign the report about the death of the Mosconi brother, and our group has to brief Jevric's team on the whole case. That's going to take up most of the day. And I do want us to be as careful as possible at least for the next few weeks. That doesn't mean I'm cancelling the Northern Lights. I don't think the Mosconis have any informers in Canada. I'm pretty sure they won't bother us."

"And afterwards, that's it?"

"That's it. No more Police Judiciaire. No more stress, no more lousy hours. Afterwards it'll be just us, somewhere else."

"Coste just for me?"

"That's all I want."

He picked up his coat and was heading for the door when Léa caught him by the waist. As she was about to kiss him, Coste saw a black rabbit hopping down the passage to the bathroom. Léa also turned, but obviously couldn't see anything.

"Is there something there?"

"No, I seem to be transforming shadows into little animals."

"How long is it since you last slept?"

"It's been hard since David Sebag, and it's only got worse. I don't know, more than four nights, I think."

"Ninety-six hours is the limit. What you see are called pareidolias. Your brain is making shadowy shapes into things it recognises."

"Either that or I've got a rabbit and a cat squatting in my apartment."

Johanna had become Mummy Bear, with Chloe clinging to her right leg, Malo her left, and the telephone pressed against her ear.

"I'm sorry, it's a bit noisy here. Say again: what time is the briefing?"

"Two this afternoon, in the meeting room. Groupe Crime 1 and Groupe Crime 2. You'll even have time to get some rest if you like."

"I'm not sure that'll be possible."

Karl came to the rescue, lifting off the two baby bears, and Johanna shut herself in the kitchen.

"Have you told Karl?" asked Sam.

"No, otherwise he would have insisted on staying with the kids. I'm going to take this weekend to recuperate. Normandy would be too much for me. I want to be with all of you. I'll tell him later."

Johanna heard a flurry of shouts and tears in the background and was jerked back to her role as a mother.

"I have to go now. See you shortly."

Karl had done what he could to organise the weekend on his own, and their three suitcases were lined up in the front hall. The kids were sulking; it took Johanna several minutes to get them to agree to leave with their father.

"I'd like to know if they'd protest as much if I was the one sneaking off," Karl wondered.

Johanna put a hand on his backside and snuggled against his shoulder.

"I'm not sneaking off anywhere; I've got a case to deal with. And to be honest, I reckon I could take them on holiday for three weeks without them noticing you weren't there. You'll have to get used to it – I think your children hate you."

They embraced so lovingly that Chloe and Malo gave indignant yucks.

"You haven't forgotten anything, have you, kids?"

"Yes," Malo moaned. "You."

Watching the car pull away tugged at her heartstrings. Now the house was calm once more, Johanna was left alone with her thoughts. Far too alone. She smelled of gunpowder and sweat, she smelled of the city and the patrol car. She decided to have a bath. She removed her gun and laid it on the kitchen table. Took off her jersey, dropped it on the living-room carpet, left her shoes on the stairs, slipped off her belt. As she passed by the children's bedroom, she caught sight of a small black box on the bedside table. Malo's tracker. She snatched it up, slipped it into her jeans pocket and rushed downstairs in the hope that some last-minute hitch had brought the car back to the house. But when she opened the front door, the street was empty. Malo would be annoyed with himself for forgetting it, and she could imagine him making a fuss, even asking Karl to turn round.

She closed the door and continued stripping off until she reached the bathroom.

70

Le Bourget private airport
Prime Flight Airlines

The plush armchairs sank into the V.I.P. lounge's thick purple carpeting. On the right-hand wall, an impressive blue departures and arrivals board. The whole left side was a window that allowed them to watch the intricate ballet of jets and air taxis manoeuvring on the ground, taking off and landing. Dorian immediately felt at home in the midst of all this luxury and had accepted the flute of champagne offered by the hostess. Rhinoceros preferred to keep a sharp lookout, studying the room and every new traveller who came in, swivelling round at the slightest movement.

"Calm down, Michaël, we're in no-man's-land here. Nothing can happen to us."

"Nothing can happen to us . . ." Rhino repeated. "You realise that's how all disaster movies start?"

"Take a good look – we're not in the real world! Everyone you see here is only too happy to spend eight thousand euros a pop not to have to mix with the rabble. Remember the passport control?"

"What control?"

"Exactly. We're going to board a plane for Corsica and nobody has really checked who we are. Simply because we've purchased peace of mind. This is the way we transport the loot from our heists, and the receiver has never once had problems. Think of this place as a magic bubble. A bubble where you can meet tax exiles, terrorists, migrant smugglers, drug traffickers . . ."

"And criminals on the run."

"Them too."

This time, Rhinoceros did not refuse the glass held out by the seductive hostess in her mouse-grey uniform and little blue hat. Firstly because Dorian's words had reassured him, but more importantly because, after accelerating so fast they were flung back against their seat rests, the aeroplane had lifted off and the dark clouds were now beneath the fuselage rather than above their heads. He would scarcely have time to relax before the descent into Ajaccio. The flight would be quick, the champagne still sparkling in his glass on arrival.

71

Léa went into the bathroom to gather up what Coste had referred to as "all your things". That is, two nighties, a few books, a toothbrush and some moisturiser. Then she stole one of his T-shirts and a pullover and stuffed everything into a big bag she had seen in his bedroom wardrobe.

She typed the address into her mobile, and the app told her a taxi would be waiting outside in between five and seven minutes. After six, a confirmation text told her it had arrived. She picked up the bag, crossed the living room, opened the front door – and found herself with the barrel of a gun pointing straight at her forehead.

"If you make a sound, you're dead. Turn round."

Léa did as she was told. Alex encircled her throat with her left arm and pressed the gun against Léa's temple with the other.

"If you're on your own here, nod."

Terrified, Léa obeyed.

"Who are you? His wife? His sister? His maid??"

Still threatening Léa with the gun and crushing her windpipe until she could hardly breathe, Alex dragged her round all the rooms to check. Then she pushed her into the centre of the living room.

"I asked you a question . . . Who are you?"

"His . . . wife," Léa managed to reply, gasping for breath.

"Perfect; you'll do. Call him and tell him to come home. If your voice changes, if you try the slightest thing, it'll be your last conversation."

Léa didn't move. There was no need for introductions.

"You're Alexandra Mosconi, aren't you?"

Alex struck her hard on the forehead with the gun barrel, and Léa fell to the floor. The gash began to pour blood; it trickled over her eyebrow, round the eye, down her cheek to her lips. Léa could taste it.

"With every question you ask, every second you make me lose, I'll spoil your cute face a little more. Got it? So if I tell you to call Coste, just do it."

Léa wiped the blood on her sleeve. She took a deep breath, thought of the Northern Lights and Victor, then stared Alex in the eye.

"No."

Alex remembered what Rhino had taught her and decided to be more direct in her approach. The first vicious kick she aimed at Léa knocked all the air out of her. The second and third made her double up on the floor. Alex stood on her left ankle and stamped on it with her heel. It sounded like a biscuit being crushed. Léa howled with pain. Alex kneeled down beside her.

"Do you know what he did to me?"

"He simply defended himself," Léa responded as best she could, trying to ignore the agony and stay focused so as not to pass out.

The swinging gun barrel hit her between cheek and eye, which in less than five seconds started to swell and close.

"Wrong answer. Anyway, I've changed my mind. I reckon you're so much in love you would bleat down the phone that you're not alone. I'm not going to run that risk. No problem, we'll wait for him."

She took one of the armchairs, dragged it almost to the entrance, and installed herself comfortably in it facing the door, gun on her lap. Coste would open it, she would give him time to show his stupefaction, then say the name of her little brother, and fire.

Behind her, Léa's breathing came in a rattling whistle. Mentally transporting herself to the slab in the morgue, she performed her own autopsy. Smashed ankle. Gash in her scalp. Windpipe crushed. One or possibly two broken ribs. Not life-threatening, unless the whistling in her breathing wasn't due to being strangled but to a pneumothorax or collapsed lung. In which case she had more or less forty minutes' respite before things became really complicated.

"We're going to wait for him, and you'll see everything. You'll have a front-row seat."

72

Ventura had enough sense to leave Groupe Crime 1 in peace and turn all his attention and repellent manners on Jevric's team. Coste took the opportunity to read his group's reports and correct a few mistakes and omissions here and there.

On the office's red sofa, Ronan was finding it harder and harder to keep his eyes open as he watched Sam taking down all the photos and notes from the whiteboard. The case was in other people's hands now, and there was nothing left to say. They could only follow orders.

On his desk, next to a stack of pending files, Coste's telephone buzzed. When he saw Léa's name he picked up, not knowing whether he would have to explain himself again or apologise for his decision. To his consternation, a stern male voice came on the line.

"Coste?"

He would have preferred to hear a "Capitaine" or a "Monsieur".

"Speaking. Who are you? What are you doing with this mobile?"

Sam and Ronan turned to look at him, trained by now to distinguish different tones of voice, such as hesitation, impatience . . . or anguish.

"I'm sorry, sir. This is Lieutenant Guillaume, from the fire brigade. Do you know the owner of this phone? Your number was the last one dialled. Your neighbours heard noise and . . ."

It took Ronan only a few minutes and several smashed wing mirrors until he screeched to a halt outside Coste's apartment block. A patrol car and a rapid response vehicle were already on the spot.

Coste ignored the lift and raced up the three flights of stairs, followed closely by Ronan and Sam. At the end of the corridor, his front door was wide open; a uniform was standing with his notebook and three paramedics were clustered around a stretcher. The usual scenario for a murder or assault. Except that this time it was happening in his own home.

The uniformed officer stepped aside, and Coste saw Léa stretched out on her side, an oxygen mask over her mouth.

"She has stabilised, but we need to take her to Emergency," he heard a paramedic he didn't even look at say. "Respiratory failure – she's losing consciousness every ten seconds. A rib probably pierced her right lung. Would you like to come with us?"

Coste dropped to the floor and took Léa's hand. She opened her eyes, peering up at him with a look that was impossible to define. Her voice was almost inaudible.

"I'm so sorry," she whispered, barely conscious, into the mask, which misted over.

"Sorry for what? I'm the one who was stupid."

She passed out again. Coste squeezed her hand tightly as the uniform gently edged him away so the paramedics could raise the stretcher.

Ronan gripped Coste roughly by the shoulder and forced him to take three steps backwards into the living room.

"Forgive me, Victor. I know this isn't a good moment, but there's nothing you can do here. You can see that, can't you?"

Coste struggled to switch his attention from the paramedics and Léa. He tried hard to become a police officer once more.

"What are you talking about? Mosconi found me sooner than I expected, and I left Léa—"

"Stop it, for chrissake!" Ronan interrupted him. "If it was Mosconi who came here, why is Léa still alive? Why didn't she wait for you? Don't you get it yet?"

At that moment, Sam's mobile buzzed, and the tracker symbol bounced up and down. He swiped it and a map of Seine-Saint-Denis appeared, gradually zooming in on a neighbourhood, then a street. He went over to the other two, his face white as chalk.

"Victor, Ronan – Malo's tracker has kicked in. And it's nowhere near Normandy. It's at Johanna's."

Suddenly everything became clear to Coste. Léa had done everything she could to protect him. Everything, including shifting the blame. Everything, including telling the truth. He turned to the stretcher where she was conscious once more, and finally understood what her indefinable look meant: a mixture of shame and guilt.

"I'm sorry," she repeated, her eyes brimming with tears.

Furious and appalled at the same time, Coste couldn't control his voice. He bellowed at her, his hands grasping the side of the stretcher as if he wanted to shake her.

"What have you done, Léa! You didn't, did you? Tell me you didn't, for God's sake!"

Astounded by his outburst, the uniform stepped in, moved him away from the stretcher and pushed him against the wall. Sam told him he would take over, seized Coste by the arm and led him out of the apartment. Ronan was busy relaying instructions to their control room.

"Emergency, emergency. Colleague in danger. All available cars to 5 rue de la Renaissance in Pré Saint-Gervais, the domicile of Lieutenant De Ritter. Colleague in danger. I repeat, this is an emergency . . ."

73

Ronan kept his foot down the whole four kilometres between Coste's apartment and Johanna's home. Siren, blue flashing light, traffic lights ignored, car horns and squealing tyres: the din outside the car was a perfect reflection of their inner turmoil. The radio crackled, and after the announcement that a colleague was in danger, even the operator's voice sounded anxious.

"Control room to Police Judiciaire. Rapid response team and two patrol cars will be with you within minutes. More back-up on its way. What is your exact position?"

None of them replied. On the back seat Sam was calling Johanna's number for the fourth time. Victor and Ronan were staring straight ahead, faces taut, minds haunted by whirling hatred and anguish.

Ronan mounted the pavement outside the house, drove on to the small front lawn and braked hard, embedding the tyres in the soft turf. All three of them leaped out, weapons trained ahead, ready to fire.

As he ran up the front path, Coste couldn't help calling out Johanna's name. Reaching the porch, he saw the door was ajar. He pushed it open with his foot and poked the barrel of his gun inside.

*

Alex had rung the bell. Johanna had opened the door, then stepped back when she saw the gun. She had glanced at her service pistol on the kitchen table, but it was too far away. So she obeyed the order and sat down. Without much hope, because she knew what was coming. In spite of this, she had managed to secretly push the warning button on Malo's tracker, still in the back pocket of her jeans. Maybe Sam and the others would get there in time . . .

Alex had stared at her impassively. She didn't launch into any tirade, or explain the how and why of her revenge. Johanna had made one last desperate appeal as the tears coursed down her cheeks.

"I have two children. Their names are Malo and Chloe."

And since Alex couldn't listen to any more, she put an end to everything.

Sam was slumped on the lawn, gun still in his hand, head between his knees. He hadn't been able to stay indoors more than a few seconds. Ronan staggered out, almost collapsed, and propped himself against the wall.

Inside, Coste was sitting down, hands spread on the living-room table. Facing him was Johanna, eyes closed, chin sunk on her chest, a scarlet hole in her heart and the lower part of her T-shirt soaked in blood. He sat staring at her.

Johanna, the lifebuoy for these three men, each of them in their own way drowning.

In the background, the sound of more and more police vehicles arriving and pulling up outside the house. Nobody dared step on the lawn, where the stupefied Sam and Ronan were stiff as statues. The sirens fell silent one by one, leaving only the whirling blue lights.

Johanna's mobile buzzed. Karl's name came up on the screen.

378

Coste reached for it but didn't have the strength to answer. He slipped it into his breast pocket. He searched inside himself for anger or sorrow, but could find neither, as if he had put all that to one side. He searched for appropriate human emotions, but could only find resignation and resolve. He knew that a sense of horror would return to him like a boomerang once this was all over. But it wasn't all over yet.

He stood up, went into the kitchen and picked up Johanna's pistol. He ejected the magazine to check it was full. As he came back past her lifeless body, he couldn't avoid giving her one last tender kiss.

When he emerged from the house, Sam and Ronan watched as he went down to the police gathered respectfully on the pavement, uncertain how to react. Coste addressed the nearest one.

"Call the Police Judiciaire headquarters and ask for Commandant Rivière or Capitaine Jevric. The victim's name is De Ritter. Johanna. She's one of ours."

The fifteen or so men stood aside to let Groupe Crime 1 through. Coste sat in the car with the front door open. Sam and Ronan stood next to him, crushed.

"When I get my hands on that bitch . . ." Ronan began. Then he remembered Karl and the children and wondered who was going to call them.

"She won't get far," said Sam. "She can't be thinking straight, she'll be picked up at the first police check point. She'll stay in Paris or Seine-Saint Denis, she'll make a mistake, and we'll be on to her."

Then reality hit him as well.

"Shit, what about the kids and Karl? Who's going to tell them?"

Still refusing to allow his emotions to get the better of him, Coste was guided entirely by a cold fury.

"Unless she follows the diamonds."

Sam and Ronan didn't understand, so Coste explained in an almost robotic manner.

"According to Rivière, the Mosconis used Le Bourget airport to smuggle out the jewellery from their hold-ups because there are almost no checks there. If I was her, that's where I would aim for."

Coste's theory offered them a way out of their nightmare. A mission, a course of action.

"If I were her," said Ronan as he got into the car, "I'd pull over onto the hard shoulder and put a bullet in my head."

The car doors slammed and Coste started up.

"Put the siren and the lights on, we're going to go fast."

"What do we do if we find her?" asked Sam.

"You know very well what we have to do, so if either of you want to bail out, do it now."

The engine roared and the tyres skidded as he made a rapid U-turn.

On the motorway Coste drove at breakneck speed, making it look as if all the other vehicles were standing still. Johanna's mobile buzzed again in his pocket. He gritted his teeth and accelerated even more.

74

Le Bourget private airport
Prime Flight Airlines

While they were driving, Sam had contacted the border police and been informed that of the eleven private airlines operating out of Le Bourget, only one had a flight to Corsica that day. More precisely, the aeroplane was due to take off in under an hour.

At the Prime Flight reception desk, Coste flashed his police I.D. and Sam opened his tablet to show a photograph of Alexandra Mosconi. The three policemen's hostile faces encouraged the receptionist to comply as quickly as she could.

"Yes indeed, she's in our lounge. She arrived about half an hour ago."

"How many other people are in the lounge with her?"

"We have three flights scheduled. The first to Corsica for one passenger. Two others for London with six passengers in total. So there are seven people waiting in the lounge."

"Can you broadcast an announcement?"

Since this was not really a question, the receptionist did as she was told.

Alexandra had got rid of the gun by slipping it under the seat of the taxi taking her to the airport. Now she was vulnerable, and the huge weight of stress she felt made her stomach clench, as if two powerful hands were crushing her insides. A physical, piercing pain. Stroking her belly, she apologised for everything she was putting her tiny guest through. Her words were drowned out by another voice floating through the lounge from the discreet loudspeakers on the wall.

"A technical issue means we have to delay our flights to London. Would passengers please come to reception for details of the new departure times."

A father grumbled as he picked up his two children's coats and stormed after them, picking his way past the armchairs and low tables. Three businessmen exchanged knowing, weary looks, then got to their feet and took out their diaries to see how this hindrance would affect their timetables. Alex was left on her own.

She had never seen Coste. Or Sam and Ronan. Yet she recognised them as soon as they burst into the V.I.P. lounge. Their eyes met from only a few metres' distance. Alex stood up, refusing to be arrested sitting down like a prisoner in the dock awaiting sentence.

Coste drew his gun and pointed it at her. She saw a fatalistic look in his eyes, as if he had reached breaking point, and realised he was not there as a police officer. They were so close now they could almost touch. His gun trained on her heart, Coste's finger slid to the trigger. But he didn't pull it.

Seeing him hesitate, Ronan drew his own gun.

"If you can't, I will."

Alex's stomach pains disappeared instantly. She felt free. She had achieved the impossible in springing her brother from prison; then, when everything had spiralled out of control, she had redressed the balance by shooting that policewoman.

They would be proud of her back in Corsica.

To their surprise, she raised a hand to the barrel of Coste's gun. When he didn't react, she lowered it until it was pointing at her slightly protruding belly.

"Shoot here. We'll go together."

Looking down, Coste saw the bump. This new piece of information only made the storm raging in his mind worse. His arm still extended, he cried out to give himself the courage to do it. For Léa. For Jo.

Sam came up to him. He had gone with the others precisely to be present at such a moment.

"Hey, you two, this isn't us. This isn't how we do things."

Alex held her breath.

"We would never forgive ourselves. It would be the end of us, and you know it."

Out on the tarmac behind Alex, a doe passed under an aeroplane wing. On the alert, the deer raised her eyes and sniffed the air as if she could sense danger. Coste blinked to make it disappear.

His gun weighed a ton. Slowly, his arm descended. He collapsed onto the nearest armchair, furious with himself for being so weak. Alex looked at the three of them, and it was only then she realised how similar they were to her. Just like her, they were overwhelmed by sorrow and hatred. Just like her, they lived only for revenge. But a sliver of conscience and the shred of humanity they still clung to had saved her life.

Ronan holstered his weapon and sat down beside Coste. Sam quickly handcuffed Alexandra before either of them could change their mind.

As they left the Prime Flight terminal and walked past one of the huge hangars, Ronan kept a firm hold on Alex Mosconi. Escorting her to their car on the far side of the fences surrounding the airport, he was thankful this case was being handled by Jevric. He wouldn't have had the stomach for questioning Johanna's murderer for forty-eight hours. Worse still, his initial instincts risked resurfacing.

"Do you know what her name was?" he asked, sickened at the injustice of seeing Alex Mosconi still breathing.

"Johanna," whispered Alex.

"You know she had two children?"

"That was the last thing she—"

A loud bang in the distance made birds fly up from one of the runways. At the same moment the right side of Alexandra's skull was blown apart, sending blood and splinters of bone spurting over Sam's face and sweatshirt. Her body collapsed with Ronan still clutching her arm, while a survival instinct made the other two reach for their weapons and sweep the area around them, searching for the gunman.

As he tried to work out where the shot had come from, Coste was in the crosshairs of Boyan's telescopic sights. Ignoring him, the Serb dismantled the rifle with three rapid movements and put the pieces back in his case. He had felt a certain affection for the feisty jewellery thief, and today's mission left a sour taste.

He returned to his car and dialled Monsieur Darcy's number to inform him his reputation and that of his businesses was intact.

75

Alexandra's hands were tightening still further round her neck . . . Léa woke with a start in her room in the police wing of the hospital, her throat still raw, but safe.

Seated on an armchair beside the bed, Coste was holding her hand to comfort her, even in her sleep.

Her mind still floating, Léa enjoyed a brief moment detached from reality before Coste's eyes could catch her and bring her down to earth, for everything to come flooding back to her. Without a word, she asked him the question, and Coste had only to lower his gaze to give the answer.

Fearing she would see reproach in his eyes, Léa turned her head away, tears welling. She recalled his violent, accusing face above her on the stretcher.

"What have you done, Léa?" he had shouted.

She defended herself out loud, her voice still sore and rasping.

"Was I supposed to wait and watch you die?"

Coste made no reply.

"I love you, Victor. I can't love anybody more than that. I chose you. Do you hold it against me? Do you hate me for it?"

He kissed the hand he was still holding.

"No, I'll never hold it against you. You saved my life."

This wasn't much consolation to Léa. She knew Coste didn't consider himself worthy of such a sacrifice.

"Karl? The children?"

"I didn't have the courage. They're away somewhere together, still having fun. Sam left a couple of hours ago to join them."

"Didn't you want to go with him?"

"I'm here where I should be."

Léa knew deep down inside it wouldn't be that simple. For a long time to come she would be the one who had brought misfortune knocking on their door. Perhaps forever.

"Will you ever forgive me?"

Coste stood up and wrapped his arms round her, nuzzling her and feeling the softness of her hair, breathing in her fragrance.

"You're not guilty of anything, and there's nothing I have to forgive you for, Johanna."

The slip of the tongue burned his lips. Johanna . . . Coste had just fired the name straight into Léa's heart. If she had been able to, she would have run away, but confined to this stupid bed all she could do was turn her head from him. The tears welled up once more. He would never forgive her.

"Please leave," she begged him.

It was too cold to swim, but the weather was good enough for them to stroll on the deserted beach. Malo and Chloe were wearing brightly coloured boots and carrying shrimping nets. Karl was recording the moment on his camera to send some memories to Johanna so that she would curse herself for missing it.

A photo with Malo sticking out his tongue. How original. Chloe with her piano-key smile, proudly holding up a tiny crab she's caught. Now the crab has rebelled and nipped her finger and she'srunning off as fast as she can.

A stone jetty stuck out into the sea from the promenade.

A man with his hands stuffed in his sweatshirt pockets drew nearer. Karl recognised his silhouette. He looked to see whether the rest of the team was with him. That would have been a pleasant surprise.

Sam didn't come any closer, but sat down on the jetty. Surprised at this reticence, it took Karl several seconds to comprehend. His heart began to race. He turned to the children.

"Malo, keep an eye on your little sister. I'll be right back."

76

Dorian was sitting on a terrace at the cliff top, protected by a guardrail that wouldn't take his weight if he slipped. Forty-five metres below lay the Mediterranean, as wild and calm as Alex had described it to him before his first visit to the island five years earlier.

Monsieur Mosconi walked down the steps from his villa to the gravel path that wound towards the terrace, where he joined Dorian. Up at the house, Rhinoceros and a servant were loading two suitcases into a car boot.

Tiretto had called the previous evening and told them everything.

Dorian had drunk far too much and pounded the bedroom walls with his fists. Monsieur Mosconi had retired to his room and had not reappeared. In the morning they had avoided each other. Until now.

"You left her on her own," the patriarch accused him, staring out at the horizon so as not to meet Dorian's gaze.

"She told me to. She said she wanted to make sure Nano's body was brought back."

"You left her on her own," Mosconi repeated. For him there was no acceptable excuse.

"Yes, monsieur."

"Turn round, please."

Dorian obeyed, and caught sight of Sofia, Alex's mother. She was standing outside the villa, gazing down at them.

"I wanted to throw you off here," Mosconi said calmly. "Over the cliff from the terrace, so I would be reminded of it every day. It was Sofia who dissuaded me. She says it's for Alex, because she loved you. Alex was always my favourite. I hope she knew that."

Dorian watched a wave crashing against the rocky wall. Alex's love had just saved his life.

"I want you to leave with your friend. Now. Stop at the Greek church in the village. A man will be waiting for you there. He'll give you money: change cars and follow him to the airport. I can recommend the Maghreb, it's the closest. But don't ever set foot on this island again."

Dorian did not dare thank him. He took one final mental snapshot of the view he knew Alex had loved at every stage of her life.

The sun was beating down relentlessly as their car sped along narrow dusty roads to the centre of Cargèse. Rhinoceros wanted to get everything clear.

"Excuse me, but shouldn't we be dead by now?"

"Speak for yourself. I don't exactly feel alive."

"I imagine you didn't fill him in about Alex. About your child, I mean."

"I didn't even realise you'd noticed."

"I may be a brute, but I keep my eye on my friends. So I reckon Mosconi knows nothing."

"That's the reason you're still breathing," Dorian said sombrely.

He slowed down at the entrance to the village and, following Monsieur Mosconi's instructions, parked outside the church, beyond a row of houses with closed blue shutters.

"Do we know what this guy looks like?" asked Rhinoceros.

"I didn't really ask for details. No doubt he'll recognise the Mosconis' car."

"We'll wait then . . ."

A black van with tinted windows appeared at the far end of the street. It came slowly towards them.

"Er . . . Dorian? Are you seeing this?"

"I can't see anything else."

Dorian tried to begin a U-turn, but three other vehicles fanned out behind them. They were blocked in on both sides. The van charged towards them, came to an abrupt halt, and its side doors slid open. Four men in black uniforms jumped out. They rammed their pump-action shotguns directly against the car windscreen, ready to blow it to smithereens at the first false move.

"Police!" shouted ten separate voices.

Rhino and Dorian laid their hands gently on the dashboard to avoid being blown to pieces by the Ajaccio police heavies.

Mosconi had asked his wife for permission to do away with Dorian and Rhinoceros. She had refused. So he had sworn that, as she wished, nothing would happen to them.

But Sofia had added that she wasn't *that* generous.

77

Three days later
Police Psychological Support Service

The shrink pushed the glass ashtray away from her. Although the blinds were three-quarters down, a shaft of sunlight penetrated the room, picking out the smoke curling upwards.

"Would you care to tell me how it all began?"

With a flick of his wrist, the man stubbed out his cigarette.

"It's a story that has several beginnings," he said.

The shrink was rolling a pen nervously between her fingers. It was plain she was intimidated by the man facing her.

"You do know why you're here, don't you?"

"Because I killed two people. Are you worried it'll become a habit?"

"You only killed one, and that was in self-defence. As for the second death . . ."

The man didn't let her finish. He snapped:

"A member of my team is dead. It was my responsibility. It amounts to the same thing."

Searching in his breast pocket, he took out a crumpled packet of cigarettes. The pen spun round in the shrink's fingers.

"Few people have experienced what you had to face. Nobody would dare judge you. I simply want us to go back to the beginning."

"From the murder or the prison escape?"

"A bit before that."

"So from the kidnapping of the boy?"

"That's a good place to start. And please, leave nothing out."

The man shrugged and lit another cigarette.

"I really don't see the point; I've already made my decision."

"I insist. Besides, as you know, in such circumstances this conversation of ours is obligatory."

He blew out a long mouthful of smoke, then reluctantly began:

"My name is Coste. Victor Coste. I'm a capitaine with Seine-Saint-Denis Police Judiciaire. Some days ago . . ."

He did a quick calculation and was himself surprised at all that had happened in such a short space of time.

". . . exactly twelve days ago, in fact, Groupe Crime 1 was put on the David Sebag case. A kidnapping with a ransom demand."

"Which meant, according to the dossier, that you investigated Yassine Chelli. He was arrested, jailed and then released. Do you feel responsible for that too?"

"I couldn't give a damn about him. I only think about his victim."

"And yet it seems likely he'll never face punishment. Isn't that what your job is about?"

"For a long while I thought as you do. But I realise now there will always be Yassine Chellis in this world. That it's endless. And whether he rots in a cell or not, there is never any atonement for murder."

"Nothing that justice could offer?"

"Justice is nothing more than a demand for revenge, and revenge has never comforted souls."

"What about a death sentence then? Would that be more just, in your view?"

392

Images telescoped in Victor's mind. Léa's tears. Johanna's blood-red heart. The barrel of his gun against Alex Mosconi's belly.

"I had the opportunity. I didn't take it."

"Do you know why?"

"I've already told you. There is no atonement. The harm is done."

The shrink leaned back in her chair.

"That's not a common attitude for a policeman pursuing criminals."

"Then you'll understand my decision."

78

Commissaire Divisionnaire Stévenin's secretary laid the documents to be signed on her boss's desk. As there was only a letter from the Interior Ministry, the list of those selected for an advanced driving course and a resignation form, she decided to wait, and stood politely in front of him.

Stévenin leafed through them, signed the letter, approved the course participants, then took out the third sheet and stowed it in one of his drawers.

"It's his decision, isn't it?"

The commissaire looked up, surprised at her unusual boldness.

"I know Coste better than he knows himself. He's a cop. Worse than that, he's a police dog. A hunter. That's all he knows how to do. He was trained for it. We can't do without officers like him. I've been sending him on the trickiest investigations in the region for fifteen years. Cases that would have scrambled anybody else's brain."

"That's what's happened to him, isn't it?"

"We wouldn't be helping him if we passed on his request. He just needs time. Wherever he may be and whatever he hopes to find there, he'll come back to his kennel. I'm merely leaving the door ajar."

EPILOGUE

Four days later
Pantin Cemetery

Sam kneeled on the impeccable lawn and straightened Milo's tie. In her father's arms, Chloe seemed focused on the avenues of trees and the flowers on the graves, as if she didn't really understand what was going on. Ronan accompanied Léa, hobbling on her stick. After the ceremony, they filed past Karl. Embarrassed at being there, Léa slowed up imperceptibly, and Karl spoke first.

"I'm glad you came."

"I don't know how you can forgive me," she whispered.

Chloe wriggled in Karl's arms, and Ronan carried her off to take a closer look at the tall lilac bush she was so interested in.

"I can't hold it against you, Léa. Probably because I would have done exactly the same thing. I would have chosen the person I love."

Then his face hardened.

"But I don't forgive you. I never will. You're here for Johanna and the children. Not for me."

Léa flinched at the unexpected blow. Karl strode away from her.

"Everything alright?"

She turned and saw Sam standing there, freed from Malo.

"Yes, thanks."

"Karl is going to stay with Johanna's parents. Best leave them to themselves, but Ronan and I are going to have a drink. Jo would want us to."

"Then we mustn't upset her. You go on, I'll follow."

Léa headed down the shady avenue and disappeared round the first bend. She took a few hesitant steps along the bumpy paving slabs and sat on a stone bench between two trees. Calling a number on her mobile, she let it ring all round the planet. Coste's steady voice calmed her.

"How was it?"

"Beautiful. And dignified. We missed you, especially the kids. They didn't understand."

"You mean Ronan and Sam?"

"Not funny."

"I know, I'm sorry."

"And you? How are you?"

Coste was wrapped up in an anorak. The cold pinched his nose and fingers. He pushed back his fur-lined hood and looked up. Above his head, the sky was covered with immense sheets of green. The Northern Lights.

"Multi-coloured," he said.

They let the silence hang in the air, as if Léa was watching this unique spectacle beside him.

"When are you coming back?" she asked.

Coste's breath came out in little white clouds as the Northern Lights changed from green to violet.

"You are coming back, Victor?"

TRANSLATOR'S NOTE

Administratively, France is divided into 96 *départements*, where the central government is represented by the *préfet* or prefect. The *départements* are numbered alphabetically: Ain is No. 1, Paris No. 75. In the 1960s, as Paris spread outwards into the *banlieues* (suburbs or outskirts), separated from the inner city by the *Périphérique* or ring road, three new départements were created: 92 Hauts-de-Seine, 93 Seine-Saint-Denis, 94 Val de Marne. The action of the novel takes place in Seine-Saint-Denis, formerly an area of heavy industry, but more recently one with a high proportion of tower blocks and a substantial immigrant population.

NOTE ON POLICE FORCES

S.D.P.J. 93 – Saint-Denis Police Judiciaire 93: the police force responsible for France's Département 93, led by **Commissaire Stévenin** and incorporating:

Groupes Crime – the crime squads. Led by **Commandant M.C. Damiani.** This unit breaks down into Groupe Crime 1, led by **Capitaine Coste**, and Groupe Crime 2, led by **Capitaine Lara Jevric**

Groupe Stups – the drug squad, led by **Capitaine Vincent Sylvan**

Groupe de répression du banditisme – the organised crime unit, led by **Commandant Rivière**

Brigade Anti-Gang – Paris anti-gang unit

Brigade Criminelle – central crime squad operating out of 36 Quai des Orfèvres

Brigade de protection des mineurs – child protection department operating from 2 quai de Gesvres

Brigade de répression du banditisme – organised crime squad

Brigade des moeurs – vice squad

Brigade de répression du proxénétisme de Paris – anti-prostitution squad

Inspection Général des Services (I.G.S.) – police inspectorate, led by Commissaire Dariush Abassian

OLIVIER NOREK served as a humanitarian aid worker in the former Yugoslavia before embarking on an eighteen-year career in the French police, rising to the rank of capitaine in the Seine-Saint-Denis Police Judiciaire. He has written six crime novels, which have sold a million copies in France and won a dozen literary prizes.

NICK CAISTOR is a British translator from French, Spanish and Portuguese. He has won the Valle-Inclán Prize for translation from the Spanish three times, most recently for *An Englishman in Madrid* by Eduardo Mendoza, published by MacLehose Press.